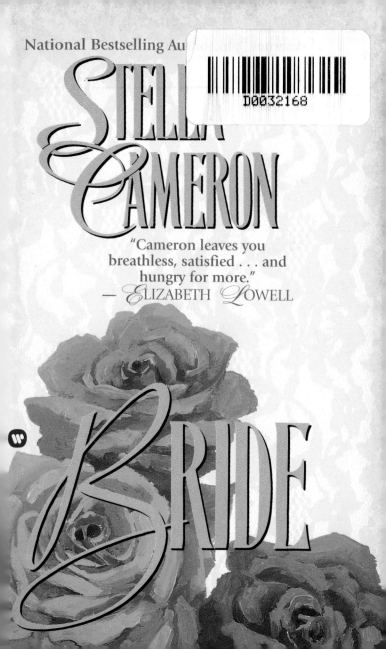

# STELLA CAMERON

"Cameron leaves you
breathless, satisfied . . . and
hungry for more."
— ELIZABETH LOWELL

# BRIDE

ISBN 0-446-60175-6

$6.50 US / $8.50 CAN.

# THE FIRST LESSON

Gradually, he lowered his face toward her and saw her eyes slowly close. Her lips, when he touched them with his own, were warm and sweet—and moist. Careful of the slightest movement, he made no attempt to part her lips farther. Instead he kissed her as he might have had it been his first kiss, and she a girl being kissed for the first time. He kissed her with his heart and soul and it was the sweetest thing, sweeter with all the years of his experience and the power of his restrained mastery, than any first kiss could be.

Pink flooded her cheeks. Candlelight picked out hints of red in the curls that had now entirely fallen from their coiffeur. She looked young, eager, quite kissed—and ready for far more.

"Justine?"

"Thank you," Justine said. "Thank you so much."

And Struan knew it was just a beginning.

The beginning of heaven?

The beginning of hell?

"The pleasure, I assure you, is entirely mine." And with this pleasure pain was almost certain to follow.

# BOOKS BY STELLA CAMERON

# STELLA CAMERON

# BRIDE

**WARNER BOOKS**

A Time Warner Company

WARNER BOOKS EDITION

Copyright © 1995 by Stella Cameron
All rights reserved.

Cover design by Diane Lugar and Elaine Groh
Cover art by Bob Maguire

Warner Books, Inc
1271 Avenue of the Americas
New York, NY 10020

Visit our Web site at
http://warnerbooks.com

A Time Warner Company

Printed in the United States of America
First Printing: December, 1995

10 9 8 7 6

For our daughter, Kirsten.
Loving, loyal, honest, and above all,
a faithful optimist.

# Chapter One

❦

**Scotland, 1824**

*I have lusted in my heart.*

For an instant, Lady Justine Girvin's heart stood quite still beneath the hard surface of the small Bible she clasped to her breast.

"I have," she murmured, closing her eyes. "And I do."

*And to do so is fruitless yet inescapable. I am blessed—and doomed—to love a man who would doubtless laugh with horror if he knew. But he will not know. I shall do everything in my power to remain close to him without his ever finding out my true feelings.*

She started at the sound of the salon door opening behind her.

"Oh, dearie me. It's a fact, then, m'lady," a girl's breathless voice announced. "Mr. Murray said ye were here and ye are. I can't think what happened t'your letter. The marquess and marchioness would never have left if they'd known ye were travelin' all the way from Cornwall t'Scotland t'see them."

No letter had been received because no letter had been sent. Justine slid the Bible inside her black velvet muff. She marshaled the courage she would need to continue on the dangerous course she'd begun, and turned to see a plump, pretty maid with round, anxious blue eyes.

"Och! Ye're so like your brother, m'lady. I'd heard tell it was so."

"No doubt. I'm frequently told I could be my brother's twin." Her brother, the Duke of Franchot, would doubtless have a great deal to say when he returned to Cornwall from London and learned of his "modest" sibling's escapade. Justine tried not to visualize Calum's outraged reaction to the news. She absolutely refused to consider her imperious grandmother's fury.

"There's none t'greet ye." The girl pushed straying wisps of fine brown hair away from her face. "And on your first visit t'Kirkcaldy, too. I'm Mairi. I'd not be here mesel' except the mistress wouldna hear o' me leavin' at a time like this."

Justine had expected to see Struan, Viscount Hunsingore . . . had longed to see him . . . and yet feared she might faint if she did see him. "A time like this?" she inquired politely. She could not risk showing her hand by asking where Struan and his two motherless children were—not immediately. "The castle seems quite deserted. There even appears to be a scarcity of servants. Is there some problem?"

"Och!" Awe clung around the single word that hovered between them.

Justine smiled and inclined her head questioningly.

"Ye've such a beautiful voice, m'lady," Mairi said, her words tumbling out. "Soft, like kelpie laughter. An' . . . Och, I'm doin' it, as usual. Forgive me. I'm such a blatherer. I say the first thing that comes into my head. Ye should hear my poor father speak o' it. Happiest day o' his life when her ladyship took me in. To tell you the truth . . ."

Two bright spots of color stamped the girl's cheeks and she clamped her lips tightly together. Justine decided she liked Mairi and her "blatherin'" very much. "Is something wrong at Castle Kirkcaldy?" she asked. "You mentioned certain, er, *times*?"

Mairi flapped a hand. "Think nothin' o' it. It's nothin'. But the marquess and the marchioness left for the Yorkshire estates weeks since. Wee Elizabeth's with them, o'course. And young Master Roger Cuthbert and his tutor. They've a mind t'spend a while there since his lordship's got some sort o' business t'attend to. Not that I'd understand anythin' about things o' that nature."

With a fire burning brightly at her back, Justine began to feel slightly warm inside the heavy travel garb she'd worn to shield her from bone-cold March winds. Trying not to favor her lame leg, she stepped to the center of the elegant rose and gilt room. "A person by the name of Shanks was instructing my coachman, Potts, to bring in my trunks. Mr. Murray must have been the dark-haired man whom I encountered upon my arrival. It was he who finally produced . . . He managed to find Mr. Shanks."

"Mr. Caleb Murray is estate commissioner at Kirkcaldy." Mairi's fingers made a crumpled disaster of her starched white apron. "Mr. McWallop—his lordship's steward—is in Yorkshire with the family. Mr. Shanks is the butler. Are ye truly plannin' t'stay at the castle, then, m'lady?"

Justine accomplished a surprised little chuckle. "I've traveled all the way from Cornwall, child. Naturally I'm going to stay. I shall simply wait until Arran and Grace return."

"But—as I've already told ye—the marquess and the marchioness'll no be returnin' anytime soon."

*I know! That's why I chose to come now!* In all her thirty-five years, Justine had never, ever set out to manipulate others

for the sake of achieving her own ends. The lie she had embarked upon would surely singe the edges of her soul, if it
didn't burn it up entirely.

Mairi smoothed the apron now. "Um. Forgive me, m'lady.
No doubt ye've a great deal on your mind, but Mrs. Moggach—she's the housekeeper—she tends t'take a wee break
from most o' her duties when the family's not in residence.
Truth t'tell, most o' the staff . . . Well, I'll be more than happy
t'direct your own maid until ye're rested enough t'go home."

*She would not be going home.* Not soon.

Perhaps not ever.

"I didn't bring my maid."

"Your companion, then, m'lady," Mairi said, bobbing a be-
lated curtsy. "I'll go an' see t'her. Will ye take tea?"

"There is no companion. I came alone."

Mairi's mouth dropped open and she whispered, "Ye're
funnin' me, m'lady. Ye'd never journey alone . . . all by
yoursel' . . . all the way from that foreign place?"

"From Cornwall," Justine said, her apprehension squelch-
ing any amusement she might have felt at the maid's amazement. "Hardly a foreign place. And I wasn't alone. Potts has
been with my family since I was a child. He looked after me
very well." *And complained and warned of impending dire
consequences at every opportunity.*

"But—"

"I am not a fearful chit, Mairi."

"But think o' the terrible things that might happen to a lady
travelin' alone. Why, ye might have been kidnapped. Or rav-
ished on the spot. Och!" The maid brought twined fingers to
her mouth. "The very thought o' it!"

"I am a mature woman, Mairi." A confirmed spinster. A
tabby . . . an ape leader . . . laid aside forever. "I have been
perfectly safe, I assure you."

"Well"—Mairi stepped backward—"well, then. If it'll
please ye, I'll care for ye until tomorrow. Pray the Lord

there'll be no trouble." The girl looked over her shoulder. "Not that he'll come when he'd likely be seen."

Justine set her muff carefully on the seat of a rose brocade chair and undid the satin frog at the neck of her cloak.

Mairi rushed to help. "Allow me, m'lady," she said, gathering the heavy black velvet garment.

"Who's not likely to come when he might be seen?" Justine asked, deliberately offhand.

"Um"— Mairi curtsied again—"would ye care for that tea?"

There was definitely something wrong here. "That might be nice. Perhaps you should bring enough for two just in case this person does decide to come."

"Och, no. The viscount never—" Mairi's pale skin flamed. "There, now. I've opened my silly mouth again. And I'm not supposed t'speak o' it t'anyone."

"The marquess's brother?" Justine said, feigning surprise while a thrill of excitement climbed her spine. "Struan's here? Viscount Hunsingore?" May she be forgiven for her deceit. She had been blameless until now.

"Aye. Viscount Hunsingore." Mairi wound the cloak around her forearms. "Poor, troubled man."

Justine grew still inside. "Why is the viscount troubled?"

"Dearie me." Mairi swayed and puffed at the hair that refused to be restrained. "I shouldna be speakin' o' such things. Not that I know the nature o' his trouble, except that he's here—or not exactly here—not at the castle. But he is about. And he's powerful angry at somethin'. Doesna speak. Hardly at all. Doesna even seem to see a body. Started a wee while after the marquess and marchioness left, it did.

"The marchioness wanted me t'stay because she feared he might be in need o' some sort o' help, but she didna know how it was likely t'be wi' him and I'll not send word t'worry the dear thing. Wild, Grumpy says he is. But Grumpy'd find a bad thing to say about anybody, and—"

Mairi bowed her head and appeared so miserable that Justine went to the girl and pressed her hand. "Don't worry about anything you say to me, Mairi. I count it a blessing to pass time with an honest soul. Who's Grumpy?"

"Dearie me. I was talkin' o' Mrs. Moggach. Disrespectful o' my betters, I know. It's only because I'm flustered—and worried. And I don't think young Miss Ella and Master Max are begat of the devil, either. Mr. Murray doesna either. He said people should watch their tongues. I think . . . Ye know the viscount's children, m'lady?"

Justine nodded. Anxiety built in equal portion with excitement. They were all here. Just as she'd planned. But she had not planned for Struan to be in some sort of trouble that might cause him to be branded "wild." "Is it Mrs. Moggach who says Ella and Max are—what you said?"

"Aye. On account o' the way Miss Ella spends all her days ridin' alone, dressed in boy's breeches and wi' her hair unbound, and wi'out a soul knowin' where t'find her unless she wants t'be found."

Justine swallowed. This information did not particularly surprise her. At least where the children were concerned her motives for being here sprang from genuine interest, and a determination to help. "And Max?" she asked, not at all certain she wanted to hear the answer.

A delighted grin transformed Mairi's worried expression. "Well, now, that one might try a body. If the body didn't understand the ways o' young laddies, that is. Never still, Max. Runnin' with the tenants' bairns. He's a shadow t'Mr. Murray whenever there's a chance. And he's made friends wi' the monk."

"The monk?" Religious leanings would certainly be a welcome development where young Max was concerned.

"Aye," Mairi said, smiling fondly. "I dinna know how the poor man stands all the questions, but he's good wi' all the tenants and their bairns and he's uncommon fond o' Max."

Justine's heart lifted. "These are good things, Mairi. Children need firm but kindly guidance."

Mairi still smiled. "That young Max's stories! Och, ye've never heard the like."

"Oh, but I believe I have," Justine said, remembering previous encounters with Max's outrageous imagination. "Surely the children are in the castle now, though." She glanced through thick, wavering windowpanes at a sky turned to shades of smoke-streaked pewter.

"No," Mairi said.

Justine regarded her seriously. "What does their nanny say to that?"

Mairi mumbled something unintelligible.

"Where is the nanny?"

"There's no nanny, m'lady. It's part o' the trouble."

Justine wasn't illuminated.

Mairi sighed a resigned sigh. "I'd as well tell ye everythin' I know. At least I'll tell it true and ye'll not be hearin' the lies o' others.

"The viscount came a few weeks before the marquess and marchioness left. We'd not known about Miss Ella and Master Max until then. But there was some sort of . . . Och, I don't know. There was anger. Then the marquess decided to leave and asked his brother t'take care of Kirkcaldy the while."

"Reasonable enough," Justine remarked.

"Seemed t'be," Mairi agreed. "Although the viscount dinna want t'stay at first. That's why I was t'remain behind—in case I could be o'use wi the children. Everythin' went well enough once the marquess left. Until the letters started coming."

"Letters?"

A fresh tide of scarlet washed Mairi's cheeks. "Now I really have forgot my place. I don't know anythin' more about those letters, but they started him off like . . . like a wild man, all right. Now he's livin' in the old marquess's huntin' lodge—his grandfather built it—and if anyone was to come askin', none o' us is t'let on he's there."

"I see," Justine said. She didn't.

Mairi trod determinedly to the door. "The children live at the lodge wi' him. Alone. There's no nanny. No servants at all. I think he rides here in the night t'check the vestibule for more o' the letters. They're t'be left there for him. And we're t'say not a word t'anyone on the matter. Not even to the master when he returns. There. I've told the truth—though I'd better have held my silence. Holdin' it all in and fearin' someone ought t'know was troublin' me. If I've done wrong in tellin' ye, I've done wrong. But I'll not say another word."

Justine held her breath before asking, "Are there any letters awaiting the viscount now?"

"One," Mairi said, letting herself out of the room. "And it's just like the others. Scented like holy incense and sealed with a bloody fingertip. I'll get the tea."

Later in the evening Mairi had settled Kirkcaldy's new visitor in comfortable apartments. Convincing the maid that her charge preferred to attend herself had taken more persuasive talent than Justine had known she possessed. The dear girl had finally left, still shaking her head, and making Justine promise to ring for assistance at any hour of the night.

Justine had waited until midnight passed before slipping out of her rooms. The gray stones of the ancient castle seemed to settle more tightly and deeply as they waited out the night. Moving toward her goal, Justine shivered, but not from cold. She could almost hear the rustle of dresses and the scuff of shoes from the many others, living and dead, who had passed this way before her.

For once her wretched leg had proved an advantage. Naturally no direct mention of Justine's limp had been made, but she had been discreetly and solicitously ushered into rooms only one flight of stairs from the ground floor and a fairly short distance from the great entrance to the castle. Having spent her life in homes as large and larger than Kirkcaldy, she was accustomed to finding her way among endless twisting corridors and hundreds of rooms.

But not in near darkness.

Still fully dressed in rustling black gros de Naples, she moved as swiftly and silently as she dared, holding the bannister with both hands as she descended the stairs to a dim corridor leading to the vestibule.

He wouldn't come. What would she say if he did? What would he say if he saw her?

She would simply say, "Hello, Struan." Yes, that would be perfectly appropriate.

The corridor opened into the vestibule where standing suits of armor gleamed dully on all sides. A massive battle relief, in white plaster and placed aloft above a great, bare fireplace, gave off an eerie glow. The wall sconces had been allowed to burn out and the candles never replenished—another evidence of servants slacking about their duties while their employers were not in residence.

Struan should . . . But Struan obviously had larger concerns than burned-out candles and slothful servants.

Justine reached the cold flagstone floor and crossed an expanse of carpet she remembered from her arrival as red Persian.

She stopped, pressed her fists into her stomach, aware of being cold but not caring.

He wouldn't come.

If she was seen here by a servant she'd be the one causing mean whispers belowstairs.

To the left of the huge double front doors, a black archway suggested a porter's nook. Justine approached cautiously and peered inside. As her eyes adjusted, she made out a wooden bench where some appropriate servant should have been ensconced and ready to perform his duties at all times.

She would rest on the bench—for a few moments—then return to her apartments and sleep. The journey from Cornwall had been long and tedious.

But she would rest here first. For a few moments.

She settled herself.

A clock ticked. Not loudly—but definitely. She could discern the instrument only as a corner shadow.

When she moved, the bench creaked.

The darkness seemed to have a substance, a thickness that settled around her, cool and oppressive—and alive.

Darkness was not alive; she was not a fanciful woman.

"Modest, circumspect, pious, and above reproach." How often had she been complimented on her virtues by Grandmama's friends?

*Virtues!* The devil take virtues. The time had come to make one last grab for happiness, and Justine was willing—no, glad to toss her virtues to anyone in need of them in exchange for freedom.

She could stay at Castle Kirkcaldy if she wanted to. No one would be rude enough to tell her she wasn't welcome.

Ooh, what a moonstruck widgeon she was. She stood up. Why had she thought Struan might be glad to see her? Why had she thought he'd welcome the proposition she'd decided to make him?

Footsteps sounded on stone outside the castle doors.

Justine plopped back down and held her breath.

An echoing grind meant the iron ring handles were being turned. A scrape, followed by a rush of icy air, told Justine someone had opened the doors.

*Why had she dared to come?*

She would hold very still, make not a sound, and return to

her rooms the instant she could do so without being seen—by anyone.

Heavy steps clanged on flagstones. Scrabbling sounded and light flared from a candle atop an ancient chest opposite Justine's hiding place. Before the chest, his back to her, stood a tall, cloaked figure.

She heard a drawer opening and the rustle of something being removed. Then she heard a low, angry oath and tried to grow at once smaller.

The man paced out of her sight, then back again, his boots cracking on stone, his cloak swinging away from his powerful shoulders. His voice came to her in a low, rumbling, unintelligible stream. It was Struan's voice.

Then he stopped pacing and stood, in profile, his sharply defined jaw outlined against the candle's light.

And this time Justine's heart did stop beating entirely.

Struan bore with him the very wind that streamed through the still-open doors. The cold air, snapping with scents of moor and mountain and crystal night, flowed about the folds of his cloak and settled in his ruffled black hair.

Struan, Viscount Hunsingore, appeared a man at one with the night. The flickering flame caught the glitter of eyes as black as his hair and his slanting brows. Shadows found the lean planes of his face, the slash of high cheekbone and straight, narrow-bridged nose. The same flame glimmered on white teeth between flaring, drawn-back lips.

Night became the man, even when rage made of his features a stark mask. Perhaps especially then.

She was not herself.

Without thinking, she walked into the archway to see the man she loved more clearly.

His head snapped toward her.

Justine took a backward step and stumbled. The cold had stiffened her leg.

His eyes narrowed, but then he moved. Swiftly. He strode toward her as she moved farther into the tiny porter's room.

"My God," he exclaimed, reaching for her.

She felt her lips part, but she couldn't form a word.

His strong hands clasped her waist, lifted her, swung her. Justine was a tall woman, but Struan was so very much taller.

She was sure he was angry with her. He'd found her spying on him in whatever this trouble was that turned his eyes the shade of devils' designs.

He swung her around and up into his arms. "Justine," was all he said, his voice breaking a little in its depths.

She still could not speak.

"I cannot believe this," he said, holding her against his wide chest.

Justine dared look no higher than his beautiful mouth. The scents of the untamed Scottish country prickled in her eyes and wrinkled her nose. His hair—longer than when she'd last seen him—curled at the high collar of his cloak.

At last she managed to say, "I did not mean to startle you."

"You almost fell," he said. "It's too cold for your leg here. You should be in your bed."

He didn't ask why she was here, why she'd come when she ought to know Arran and Grace weren't here.

"Oh, Justine," Struan said, and when she raised her eyes to his, she almost gasped at the intensity she saw there. He didn't smile. "Praise the Lord for letting me find you in this place on this hellish night, my lady."

Words deserted her once more.

He was about to speak again, but blinked and seemed to realize he held her in his arms and that such a thing was extraordinary—and inappropriate.

"Forgive me," he said, shaking his head. "I forgot myself." Very carefully, he carried her to the bench, set her gently down, and sat beside her.

Struan took her cold hands into his own and chafed them

with long, supple fingers. "I cannot believe my good fortune. You cannot know how I needed to set my eyes upon you."

Her mouth turned dry and she struggled to think why he should seem so delighted to find her here.

"Please tell me you'll spare just a little time for a man in need."

A little time? She'd spare him her entire life. "Of course," she told him. "Tell me, Struan. Tell me what you need." She had undoubtedly been wrong to employ falsehood to bring about this meeting, yet it appeared a nobler cause than her own might be served.

Struan simply looked at her. Holding both of her hands in one of his, he touched her cheek, rested a thumb on her lips.

Justine could not draw a breath. Surely he gazed at her with affection?

"I need very little, my dear one," he said at last. "All my soul requires is this chance to look upon a woman beyond reproach and above deceit."

# Chapter Two

❧

Struan bent forward, surrounding the woman who sat sideways before him on his horse, shielding her from the gale with his cloak and the heat of his body.

She had refused to allow him to leave the castle without her. "A mature female may choose to come and go as she pleases," she'd informed him tartly when he'd reminded her that her absence would be questioned. "I shall take a warm outer garment and write a message for the maid. Since none seemed particularly pleased at my arrival, none should be less pleased by my departure."

He smiled into the unkind night. From the moment he'd first met Lady Justine Girvin, he'd felt her quiet, patient strength, but he would never have wagered her stubborn.

They'd traveled some miles. The big black he'd appropriated from the castle stables several weeks since, followed the narrow trail north with unerring ease. Their destination lay beyond Castle Kirkcaldy's outermost fortifications, in the hilly area of the estate where Struan's grandfather had built his hunting lodge.

"Your leg?" Struan shouted against Justine's ear. "Are you too uncomfortable?"

She shook her head but made no attempt at a reply. There had been no question of alerting attention by going to the stables for a second mount.

Apart from her final pronouncement that she would go with him whether he approved or not, Justine hadn't spoken at all since he'd confessed how glad he was to see her. In fact, if he didn't know her to be a woman of few words by nature, he'd wonder if she'd had some recent and deeply disturbing experience. Perhaps his inappropriate exuberance at the castle had embarrassed her.

They climbed upward and entered a forest of sycamore and oak. By daylight budding leaves were visible. In the vague glimmering of the cloud-veiled moon, gnarled tree limbs laced overhead to fashion an arching canopy that swayed, snapped, and whined.

On the far side of the forest lay a slope where the trail wound downward in wide switchbacks to a slim valley, then uphill again to a pine-crowned knoll. The huge hunting lodge, his grandfather's only known act of fanciful extravagance, sprawled amid the shielding barrier of those pines.

Tossing his head and blowing clouds of vaporous breath, the black toiled a little on the final uphill pull. Justine sat rigidly before Struan, and he reached past her to lay a gentling hand on the animal's neck.

"Not much farther," he shouted.

She only nodded.

Cloud slipped across the moon, turning out the light over Kirkcaldy. The faintest touch of silver struggled to keep its hold beneath a lowering sky—then faded completely. Soon there would be rain in the wind. Struan could feel it.

He was glad Justine was here—puzzled, yet very, very glad. But he should not have allowed her to travel through such a night to the lodge. The act was selfish and unsuitable. Mature she might be, but some might find fault with a beautiful and unmarried woman riding alone with a man to whom she was unrelated.

There was no one in the area to know; none in a position to express disapproval.

And he needed Justine. He needed an honest friend, if only to be reunited for a short while with the sane world that he fled with the arrival of the first, damnable letter.

Struan tightened his arms around Justine and closed his eyes. The horse knew the way and this rider was unutterably tired. Justine smelled faintly of roses and her slight body felt strangely comforting pressed to his own.

*The letters.*

His wretched past contained a lapse in good judgment that had cost him what he had so dearly prized—his integrity and his belief in his own strength of character.

*The letters.*

Another rested in his waistcoat pocket. Even through the wind he would swear he could catch the scent of incense from its pages. Once that mysterious aroma had led him deep into himself, to a place where he was at one with God and with his own soul. Or had that merely been an illusion, the dramatic imagining of a fervent young man bent on finding the way to his own essential goodness?

Essential goodness? He almost laughed but made certain he held back the evil, hollow, hopeless sound such laughter would be in his gentle friend's ears.

Again the envelope bore the seal of the fingertip dipped in blood. Blood from where; from whom? And how did the unknown demon manage to deliver his foul messages without being seen? Struan shuddered. He must stop recalling the images of his past. How else could he heal himself and make a life again?

Justine slid a little sideways and instantly clutched at his hands on the reins. Struan surrounded her waist with one arm and held her tightly.

"You're all right," he called. "I won't let you fall." Fool that he was, for all he knew, she'd never mounted a horse since a childhood accident had left her leg so badly damaged.

After a moment, Justine settled one of her hands atop his at her waist.

She was a slender creature. Elegantly slender and tall and very, very feminine in her quiet, self-contained manner. When he'd first met her, barely a year earlier in Cornwall, he'd been instantly enchanted. Despite knowing that Justine was a year his senior he'd nevertheless entertained thoughts of courting her. Thank God he'd waited. The letters had proved how right he'd been in his reticence.

They quickly covered the needle-strewn path through the trees on the knoll. Before them rose the concoction of towers with castellated crowns, of spires, columns and statuary and, fantastically, a single pagoda joined to the main structure by an ornate covered bridge. The whole had been the result of Grandfather's travels to faraway places.

Now the place was Struan's haven, and his prison.

Urging the horse on, they clattered beneath the bridge into the stable yard. For the first time since he'd come here with Ella and Max, Struan regretted the absence of staff. He was forced to take Justine with him while he stabled his animal. She stood patiently by and he noticed how she seemed to want to wait close to the horse, and how she smiled and murmured and stroked its head until Struan had accomplished the essentials.

He considered lifting and carrying her again, but their eyes met and he knew she'd read his thoughts. Very firmly, she slipped a hand under his elbow and held on, limping badly enough to make him wince, but leaving him in no doubt that this was all the assistance she wanted.

"I can hardly wait to see Ella and Max," Justine said, raising her voice above the storm's gathering babble. "I expect they rise early enough."

He set his teeth. "Indeed. When did you arrive?"

"This afternoon. I find I am not at all tired, Struan. I think I shall sit by the fire and wait for the children."

He swallowed with difficulty. "The quickest way into the house from here is through the kitchens. Will you forgive the informality?" *Informality?* Good Lord, he was becoming accomplished in the art of understatement.

"Of course. What a delightful building, Struan. Calum mentioned a hunting lodge, but he never described it."

How could one describe the almost indescribable? "Is my old friend well?" Struan asked, desperate to find safe territory for discussion. "And his lady?"

"Remarkably well. Both of them. Philipa only grows more energetic. Everyone loves her." Justine stopped walking and arched her neck to gaze up a belfry banded with fanciful terracotta friezes. The blue and red tiled structure flanked the door to the kitchens.

"My grandmother was reluctant to add—er—*unusual* elements to the castle, so my grandfather simply put them all here—all the things he'd seen and wanted to be reminded of from his travels, that is. The Lords of Stonehaven had not formerly been known for fanciful excesses. I think this was his small—or should I say, rather extravagant—rebellion."

"I see."

"The belfry isn't entirely useless. The dairy's in its basement." Not that the dairy was used—or much else about the lodge.

"How delightfully resourceful."

And how delightfully kind and circumspect she was.

Struan led Justine into the totally dark and cold building.

He lit the candle he'd left ready near the door, and felt for Justine's hand. Her cool fingers wound around his—too tightly. She was frightened. He had scared her by bringing her here.

"I've felt a need for a simple existence," he said conversationally, praying he could reassure her. "That's why I decided to dispense with servants. There is one girl who comes from the castle on occasion to perform a few necessary tasks. I need no more." Already he was adding to his lies, doing so to the one woman he'd met whose goodness and truth shone from her every glance.

"How very sensible of you," she said in her unforgettable voice with its little break that suggested she might laugh at any moment. "I become so tired of the conventions, don't you?"

Surprise silenced Struan. Justine had always appeared entirely conventional, entirely above any form of eccentricity.

"In fact," she continued as they skirted the kitchen table and passed the shapes of idle utensils. "That is exactly what I hope we can talk about. Certain somewhat *unconventional* ideas close to my heart . . . When you are rested and feel like talking, that is. *If* you feel like talking at all, of course."

Unconventional ideas close to her heart? He hesitated in the act of leading her up stone steps toward the first floor of the wing he'd made into some sort of a home. "Naturally I feel like talking to you, Justine," he said. Perhaps he could manage to make her so engrossed in chatter that she failed to notice all was not exactly as she might have expected in these makeshift quarters.

They left the stairwell behind for a curving passageway where vivid and gruesome paintings of dead animal trophies lined the walls.

"Mairi—the nice little maid who appeared the only one available to assist me—" Justine said, her grip on Struan's fingers bone-grinding "—she said Ella . . . Ella is enjoying the freedom to improve her riding skills here in Scotland, I understand."

My God. Just what else had Justine been told? "Ella has a wanderer's soul, I'm afraid." He would do his damndest to keep lies to a minimum. "She's become very fond of an old chestnut I rode for years. She—"

"I applaud you for encouraging her," Justine broke in. Her voice was a little too high, a little too rushed. "A girl who is an accomplished rider is always looked upon favorably by gentlemen."

Struan frowned to himself, uncertain he followed this line of reasoning. "How so?" Drawing a deep breath, he threw open the door to the room where he'd assembled some of his favorite pieces from the entire lodge.

"Ella is sixteen—approaching an age when she must be brought out, Struan. Those qualities expected in the wife of a suitable husband must be encouraged. A fine seat on a horse is certainly noticed."

Struan glanced sideways at her, barely hearing what she said. Much more of interest was her reaction to the lodge's main hall. Generations ago men had gathered here after long days of hunting to eat and drink and brag about their marksmanship and the prizes they'd bagged.

To please Ella he'd removed the animal heads with their gaping jaws. A fortunate decision. He doubted Justine would have been more comfortable with the trophies than his young charge.

Drawing Justine with him, Struan made a circuit of stone walls, raising his candle to light others held in iron brackets every few feet. Gradually the colorful, curiously eclectic assortment he'd amassed emerged from shadow.

Justine said nothing at all.

"You must be utterly exhausted," he said rapidly. "And chilled into the bargain after I've dragged you through such a night. I'll make you comfortable and light the fire."

If he kept looking about him he'd start apologizing. In that direction lay danger, since he'd then have to explain himself. He could *not* explain his circumstances to Justine. *Never.*

An ancient Italian giltwood daybed upholstered in silk damask the color of old amber and emeralds pulled easily from its place beneath a high, heavily draped window. Struan situated the piece near the fireplace. He had found the daybed in a small salon off the ballroom and decided it might appeal to Ella.

"Rest here," he told Justine, guiding her to sit against the pillows and lifting her legs onto the elongated seat. "This will keep you warm." She still wore her cloak, but he took off his own to cover her and added an armful of jewel-toned silk shawls quickly snatched from their positions draped over a gold Chinese screen encrusted with mother-of-pearl figures.

The first clatter of rain sounded on windowpanes. Wind moaned between turrets and roared in the chimney.

Pushing aside velvet pillows—Max's favorite thinking spot—from their station before the hearth, Struan heaped up kindling and started small flames leaping in a fireplace tall enough for a man to all but stand upright.

He added larger pieces of wood and soon the blaze crackled. "There." Perhaps he could negotiate this difficult situation and send his friend forth without her truly noticing how extraordinary his circumstances were. "Now we shall soon be quite warm enough. Are you hungry?"

"No."

*Thank you, God.* He had absolutely no idea what food might or might not be in the kitchens. The maid Moggach had supplied, Buttercup Likely, or some such name, appeared infrequently enough to please him and said very little. When he'd told her he required no formal attention she'd seemed inordinately pleased and quite satisfied to spend her time primping a profusion of blond curls—and casting fluttering-lashed glances at him whenever the opportunity presented. Buttercup supposedly cleaned. She did not cook. Supplies were delivered from the castle regularly enough, he supposed, but he took little interest beyond asking Ella and Max if they'd eaten . . . when he saw them.

Struan pulled several of Max's vibrant pillows close to the daybed and lounged in what he hoped was a nonchalant attitude. "So," he said, smiling brightly. "Now there's a new Duchess to deal with Franchot Castle and you've decided to do a spot of traveling?"

The firelight turned Justine's large, heavily lashed eyes to a color that would rival the finest cognac. "I'm not particularly fond of traveling," she said, unsmiling.

Struan propped an elbow and rested his head on a hand. "On the way to another destination, are we?" he asked, aware of an odd, turning sensation in his belly. He should not care that Justine undoubtedly had a life of which he knew little. "I expect you must have any number of friends in Scotland." He did care.

"None I'd bother to visit, actually. Apart from Grace and Arran—and you."

"None . . ." Struan ran his tongue over his teeth. Surely she must have known Arran and Grace were in Yorkshire with their daughter Elizabeth and Arran's ward, Roger Cuthbert. Would she have come purely to see him? Madness was finally claiming him. He said, "I don't think I—"

"What's troubling you, Struan? The maid at the castle made mention of certain . . . She said you were hiding out here."

He sat up abruptly and rested a forearm on his knee. "I am not hiding out," he said sharply. "I am simply a man who prefers his privacy. There are those of us who do not care to spend their days and nights falling over flunkies at every turn."

"You told the flunkies not to let anyone know you were

here at the lodge. Anyone who might happen to come looking for you, that is."

"I—" He looked into her deep golden eyes and away. If she could see the darkness in his soul she'd run from him, and he couldn't bear that. "Very well, Justine. There is no point in trying to hide truth from you, even if I wanted to." It was imperative that she leave before she learned even more of his dreadful secrets than those she now sought.

Justine pushed aside the shawls but kept his cloak wrapped about her as she swung her feet to the floor. "Share your burden with me, Struan. Let me help you."

He almost laughed aloud. "I am in some small difficulty with someone who has decided they have a hold over me. Nothing more." *Nothing more*? The horror of it was almost more than he could bear to allow shape in his mind.

"Blackmail?" she whispered. "Is that it, Struan? You are being blackmailed?"

"No!" Or was it yes? He still didn't know exactly what the bounder wanted, dammit. "Nothing so dramatic. A simple case of someone pressing for favors I choose not to extend. Please—don't concern yourself further with this, dear lady."

Her dark brows drew together. "Earlier you told me you needed my help."

He studied her. The ride had dislodged the smooth coiffure and red-brown curls—so like her brother Calum's—tangled with the long, dark fur that lined the hood she'd pushed down.

A remote woman, some might say. Untouchable. How would it be to touch and be touched by Justine Girvin? How soft would her pale skin feel against his—beneath his?

She looked at him directly, unblinking, the faintest of smiles turning up the corners of her almost too wide mouth. In fact, Justine's mouth was a feature well worth a great deal of consideration. Naturally pink, the lower lip was full and the upper graced by definite points. Parted, those lips revealed the edges of small, straight, exceedingly white teeth. A man's tongue would pass easily along the moist skin that glistened just inside that mouth, would find pleasure in the sharp edges of those teeth, would thrust beyond with such exquisite enjoyment while other parts of him leaped in readiness to echo the small, sweet preludes to release.

"Struan? Are you angry with me for being direct?"

"Angry?" He shifted, conscious that his unruly brain had sent signals that must not be noted by this lady. "Absolutely not, my dear. You could not possibly make me angry." Damned uncomfortable, but never angry.

"Good." Her right hand went to her cheek and she smoothed back an errant strand of hair. "Is there . . . That is, have you perhaps met some lady who appeals to your higher senses?"

Struan stared at her, narrowed his eyes, and concentrated. "I beg your pardon?" His mind was truly suffering.

"A lady," she said. "Is there someone who has spoken to your heart, perhaps?"

Oh, good God. She assumed he had somehow managed to find a mate in the middle of the disaster that was his life. "No, Justine. No—no lady has spoken to my heart." *Other than you and I cannot have you.*

"Surely you must be considering the advisability of marrying again for the sake of your motherless children."

Naturally it was time for yet another of his damnable lies to surface—albeit a lie that began with the most honorable of intentions and which protected the children. "Actually, I had not been considering that particular matter."

"But you must," Justine said, moving forward in her earnestness. She set aside his cloak and undid her own. "You build a fine fire, Struan. I declare I grow exceeding warm. It is essential for Ella and Max to be schooled in those areas that will ready them for the life of a viscount's offspring."

Struan felt suddenly truculent—and trapped. "They do well enough as they are."

"You have a tutor for them?"

"No."

"A nanny?"

"No."

"A dancing instructor for Ella?"

"No."

"You take them to church yourself?"

He shuddered. "No."

Justine shrugged free of her cloak and leaned even closer. "Struan, Ella is sixteen?"

He began to feel particularly bloody. "When last I checked, yes, she was. Just."

"And Max must be eleven."

"Eleven follows ten. So you must be correct."

"*Sin's ears.* This is worse than I had imagined!" The neck of Justine's black gown was demure, but the faintest hint of her breasts, trembling with ire now, showed above pleated velvet trim. "Get the children from their beds."

"Get the . . ." His mouth remained open, but he couldn't recall the rest of what he'd intended to say.

Justine swept wide her arms to take in the gaudy room with its collection of outrageous furnishings from every country Struan's grandfather had ever visited. "I wish to see Ella and Max and assess the exact scope of the task that lies before me."

Struan glanced from her glittering eyes, to her moist and parted lips, to the rapid rise and fall of her breasts. Outrage did wonderful things for the cool Lady Justine. It made her absolutely irresistible—particularly to a man who hungered for emotion from a woman he admired. He truly admired Justine.

And he must send her back to Calum and Cornwall before the entire Franchot clan—together with his own egotistical, judgmental brother—descended like an army with sabers drawn. If he set a hand on this woman, they'd draw lots for the honor of running him through.

"Get them!"

"I can't . . . I mean, absolutely not, Justine. I would not consider disturbing their rest. Let that be the last I hear of such an irresponsible suggestion."

"Oh." She pressed her fingers to her mouth, and for an awful moment her eyes seemed to brim with tears. "Forgive me." She blinked rapidly, loading her lashes with moisture but blessedly saving the tears.

Struan ignored the battering of his own heart and patted the hand that rested on her knee. "You're tired, dear one. And a little overwrought, I shouldn't be surprised. You'll see the children soon enough."

"There are things I want," she said, sounding strangled and entirely unlike herself.

There were things *he* wanted—the devil take it. "You must rest, and then we'll see about getting you on your way wherever you're going."

"I'm going to write a treatise for young women."

Now he was puzzled.

She went on. "Do you realize that everything that has been written about women—about women and men *together*, that is—has been written *by* men?"

Oh, the hour grew very late. "That does not seem particularly surprising to me."

"No, no, of course it wouldn't. Well, that is to change, and I am the one to change it. I have already begun a volume intended to revolutionize the lot of young females faced with the terrifying prospect of marriage to creatures so entirely different from themselves, creatures about whom they know absolutely nothing."

"How . . . I mean *why* would you undertake such an unnecessary venture?"

Justine's fingers tightened around his on her knee. "Struan, because I know you are merely a product of what you have been taught by unfeeling men, I shall forgive you that question. I know you well enough to be certain that when I have explained my project to you, you will not be able to wait to assist me."

She would benefit from being taken in his arms and soothed—and kissed soundly. "Hmm. *Assist* you, Justine? I fear I—"

"It is too complicated to clarify entirely tonight. I simply hope that you will agree to help me explain certain elements of the male-female—um—experience, in such a way as to make the entire process sound pleasant to prospective brides. It is my intention that every young woman who reads my work will go to her marriage bed with alacrity! After reading the revelations I intend to set out, *my* girls will enter their bridal chambers triumphant in the knowledge that they are their new husbands' equals in the matters about to unfold."

Struan's head had gradually bowed while he watched her mouth form words. He shook himself slightly and said, "Unbelievable." Surely she could know almost nothing of what she spoke. And she wanted him to help her remedy that situation?

He must send her home. At once. "I'd help you if I could, Justine. You know that. Unfortunately, the matter of running Kirkcaldy is weighty. Perhaps at some other time. Meanwhile, I'll ensure that you are well rested before you continue your journey."

"Absolutely not," she said, straightening. "Do you think I would shirk my duty to a friend?"

Struan looked at the rising color in her face. "I fear I don't follow you."

"You are a man besieged."

He was tired. And she could not possibly know just how besieged. "Thank you for your concern, my friend. I cope well with my lot."

"You are too brave."

*I am a monster in retreat.* "I do what I must."

"And you no longer must at all."

"Justine?"

"It is decided." She smiled, but there was the faintest tremble about her mouth. "I shall take the children in hand and attend to their training."

*No, no, no.* "I could not possibly allow you to undertake such a burden."

"I will not listen to your selfless protests."

Dear God. "I will not listen to your selfless offer."

"Sin's ears, what posh!"

"Sin's . . . Does Calum approve of your colorful language, my dear?"

"I don't care a fig for Calum's approval. I simply decided to design my own means for venting irritation. Resourceful, I think. And satisfying. I plan to suggest the measure in my book."

Extraordinary. "Quite so" was the only response that came to mind. "You cannot give your valuable time to the training of my children."

She squared her shoulders. "My hitherto useless time will become meaningful while I coach and teach Ella and Max. And you will provide me with a sanctuary in which to write my instruction manual for young women. And—if you agree—you will instruct me in those matters so difficult to ascertain from the male viewpoint."

*Never.* "It will never do. Your reputation—"

"Because I will be spending time alone with you? My dear Struan. Your reputation as a gentleman and my age—I am thirty-five, a year older than you, remember—the facts will overcome any obstacle."

Her age did nothing to stop his increasingly pounding desire. Neither would her age stop her brother, or his own, from killing him if he did not treat Justine's reputation like a crystal egg. Then there was the question of his reputation. He'd laugh about that, if he didn't feel laughter might choke him.

"We shall speak no more of this, Justine," he said at last. "I'll return you to the castle."

"No."

"I beg your pardon?"

"I said no. I must be completely honest with you, just as you have always been completely honest with me. My main reason for coming here was to look after your motherless children. I *need* to be needed. There. I have told you the way of things."

Involuntarily, he touched her cheek. "You are needed." He stroked that soft skin and saw the tears spring again. This time they did not trouble him. "Your grandmother—"

"My grandmother, pah!" Justine said of the formidable Dowager Duchess of Franchot. Tears overflowed and coursed downward. The tip of her tongue darted out to catch one.

Struan watched her tongue and felt something close to a blow in his gut. "Yes, your grandmother needs you."

"That is not the kind of need I require." She turned her face away. In profile, the moisture on her cheek shone silver in the firelight. "I shall never have children of my own—a source of great disappointment I've been forced to accept. But in the short time I spent with them, I fell in love with Ella and Max. And they need a female's care, do they not?" She turned back and stared hard at him. "A gentle guiding hand in all things?"

"Well . . ."

"Do they not?"

"I suppose . . ."

"Of course they do. And I shall be the provider of that care until you marry again. We'll send for my things in the morning. I shall be living here with you."

# Chapter Three

❧

Slouched in a chair near her side, Struan watched Justine sleep.

With her legs once more stretched out on the daybed and her head turned so that her chin rested on her shoulder, she looked very young—and very vulnerable.

He got up from the deep leather wing chair he'd pulled close as soon as her eyes had shut, and piled more wood on the fire. Beyond the circle of its warmth, the big room was chilly. Outside the lodge, the storm raged.

Struan eased down into his chair, rested his elbows on its worn old arms, and steepled his fingers. The woman who slept on could not begin to guess the dilemma she'd presented him—or the battle she forced him to wage with his own selfish desires.

Her thick lashes rested, quite still, upon her cheeks. Although fatigue had made her pale, there was a bloom on her skin. In repose, her features were soft, the tumble of hair curly about her face. He'd already pulled his cloak up to her neck.

She'd said, finally too sleepy to be quite clear, that she would "wait exactly here until the children got up."

She deserved to know the truth. All of it. But if he told her, she'd flee and never want to set eyes upon him again. Perhaps, since there could never be anything deeper between them, at least that much—the truth—would be best.

But if he could only find a palatable way to reveal the small . . . no, the *huge* misconceptions she'd harbored about him since they'd met, there might be a chance . . . No, there was no chance.

Ella and Max were not his children. True, they were brother and sister—but they were not related to him. They were not his offspring by a very early marriage that ended with the death of an uncultured, anonymous young wife. There had been no early marriage—no children—no tragic death. Arran and Grace knew. A fiery disagreement with Arran had been the result of that discussion, and Arran continued to be enraged by the dilemma Struan could not decide how to resolve. Calum and Pippa also knew the real story. They had encouraged the original fabrication as a means to secure the children's acceptance at Franchot Castle. But the truth had been kept from Justine, who so abhorred dishonesty of any kind.

Oh, in Cornwall he'd intended to tell her exactly how he'd come by the orphans. Many times. But on every possible occasion something had intervened and, finally, he'd been forced to leave . . . No, not true. He hadn't been forced to leave Franchot Castle at the time of his good friend's marriage to Lady Philipa Chauncey. He'd left because although he could probably have explained the children to Justine, the rest was beyond him. Not even his own brother knew that story.

Justine thought him honorable!

She shifted, slipped a hand beneath her cheek, and nestled deeper. Her lovely mouth curved slightly upward at the corners as if some pleasant thought had found her in sleep.

Struan rubbed his brow slowly, repeatedly. *I cannot have you. If you truly knew me, you would not want to stay anywhere near me.*

The goblet of hock he'd poured stood on a brass-studded Indian table beside his chair. Struan took a long swallow and let his own eyes close as the liquor seared his throat. Liquor had seared his throat many times before, but there had been one night, one hateful night, when it burned, then boiled—then turned him to fire beyond his control. The wine had been the beginning.

In the pocket of his waistcoat rested the latest letter. Setting down the glass, he assured himself that Justine slept deeply, then removed the thin envelope with its dramatic seal.

The devil who had sent it, and all the others—by a messenger who was never seen—thought he could intimidate with cheap dramatics. Struan was not intimated. He was afraid for those he loved—which was why Ella and Max would not be rising to greet Justine in the morning. They were not here. He made certain they were never with him unless he was fully awake and on guard. True, by day they ran free on the estates among tenants and castle staff who also believed what Justine believed, that the two young ones were Struan's. But in those daylight hours he had loyal and keen eyes forever on watch. And the children were never left alone after dark.

Very lightly, without considering what he did, Struan tapped the envelope against his nose and grimaced. Once more his memory, the detested memory, stirred. The beginning of the other part of his past about which Justine knew nothing. He felt again the deep, deep cold in a small, windowless cell inside a venerable building where men dedicated themselves to God.

*Silence.*

There had been great silence but for the beating of his own heart and the thoughts that had dwelled deep within his being as he'd sought to examine his conscience and decide if he was ready for the next step toward taking his priestly vows. *"Forgive me, Father, for I have sinned."* Shortly he was to have sought out his confessor. Yet, at that moment, his soul had been valiant. A young soul that might, in time, have determined that its place was not in the halls of holy men—but still a soul searching and beginning to find its way.

As a mature man of thirty-four he was now certain he could never have belonged entirely to the church, yet he would have chosen to leave it in quite a different manner than the one that had been forced upon him.

Once more he pressed the envelope to his nose and breathed in slowly. He breathed the pungent aroma of old incense, of dust in dark crevices, of ancient chilled places where only carnal urges could create heat—desperate, destructive heat.

The aroma of incense seared his memory.

### *Moreton Abbey, Dorset, England September 1819*

"Father Struan?"

He did not answer, did not turn from the place where he knelt in prayer beside a rude cot.

"Father Struan?" a girl's light voice repeated. "The abbot sent me to you."

Hallucinations—such as enticing voices—might come to those who had fasted many days, prayed many days, held silence for many days while they looked inward to examine their hearts.

Beneath his knees, the stone flags of his cell floor struck cold upward through his locked thighs and into his belly. His back had long since grown too numb to ache. Tendons in his neck stretched with the weight of his head where it bowed forward. His fingers, wound together, rested like a stone sculpture on the brown blanket, the only covering on the cot.

"It has been four days," the voice said. "Only water. And nothing but the sounds of your own thoughts for company."

Struan squeezed his eyes more tightly shut and murmured senseless petitions. The testing sought to fuddle him. He must concentrate the harder.

The sound of something solid being set down.

The scent of a newly lighted candlewick to mingle with the incense.

The flicker of light through his closed eyelids.

The gentle resting of a hand on the back of his rigid neck.

"The Abbot told me to see to your comfort, Father Struan. He said you have prayed and fasted long enough"

He felt fingers softly threading through his hair. "You have such thick hair, Father. Thick and black and alive."

Please, he did not want this testing.

"Good," the voice said, and he felt the settling of lips where fingers had been. "So strong and good. I have brought you something to ease this time. This unnatural time. The abbot said I should."

The abbot was his friend. His confessor. His spiritual guide.

The touch left his neck. He heard the sound of liquid splashing into a vessel. "Here. Drink."

Struan shook his head and bent to rest his face on his hands.

"You've suffered too much. Let me help you now."

The creature knelt beside him and rubbed the length of his spine through the rough black tunic that was all he wore. Her hands were firm and sure, and after a while she wrapped her arms around his body and settled her warm, soft, woman's flesh against him.

Struan felt the fullness of her breasts and shuddered. The force of his instant quickening shocked him. He had not as much as touched a woman in longer than he remembered.

"Leave me, please," he whispered, hating himself for breaking the silence, yet desperate to be rid of this temptation.

"I will leave you soon enough. But not until I've done what I was sent to do, Father. I'd be in trouble if I went without that. You wouldn't want me to get into trouble."

Slowly, he rocked his head from side to side on his fists.

"Of course you wouldn't," she said. "Here, do what the abbot wants and take a little of this."

Her hand on his shoulder urged him to lift his head. Still he did not look at her.

"Come along, now," she said, her voice carrying the soft burr of the Dorset countryside. "It'll give you the strength to carry on."

Struan opened his eyes and squinted against the light from a single candle. Then he looked down into the face close to his shoulder.

Black eyes that stared unblinkingly into his. A small, up-tilted nose. Full red lips, moist and parted. A profusion of thick, black curly hair that fell, unbound, over white shoulders revealed inside a simple, dark-blue cotton dress. Cut exceedingly low at the neck, a band of paler blue lace rose and fell with each breath—rose and fell with the movement of large, perfect breasts so smooth he clenched his fingers the tighter to keep from touching them.

"A sip of this will do you good," the girl said, raising a pewter goblet to his lips and tipping. "There, there, then. Drink, Father."

With his eyes on her breasts, he forgot to protest. Wine, dark and sweet, ran into his mouth and his throat. Hot. Burning.

He gasped, and a little of the wine ran down his chin.

The girl laughed and stopped him from wiping it away. Instead, she held his hands and reached up to lick the drops into her own mouth.

The devil had sent a test.

He turned violently from her. The liquor's heat scalded its way into his belly and weakened the muscles in his legs.

But his rod leaped.

"I'm Glory," she said, the laughter still in her voice. "Did the wine taste good?"

With her cool, firm fingers, she eased his face toward her once more until he looked down into her smiling black eyes. First she sipped the wine herself, then raised the goblet to his mouth once again. With his gaze fixed on hers, unable to look away, he let her tip the vessel, let her pour its contents fast enough to force him to gulp. And all the while he felt drawn deeper and deeper into her fathomless stare.

"Good?" she pressed him.

After four days of fasting, the wine burst into his body with power that invigorated him and then drained his strength. Her face wavered before him. When he turned his head a little to focus, she tilted her head and ran her tongue over her lips.

Still on his knees, Struan swayed. "Go," he muttered. "Leave me now."

"I couldn't," Glory said. "You need me. You need me ever so much, Father."

His vows. He wanted to take his vows . . . didn't he?

Above her bodice, her white flesh shone in the candlelight as if oiled.

She lifted the wine to his lips again and this time he drank without restraint, drained the goblet, and rocked while she filled it again.

"Come on," she said. "Let me make you more comfortable. There are things you need. And then you must sleep. The abbot said so."

"You—must—go," he muttered, his mouth thick.

Her laughter filled the little cell. "I've been watching you, y'know, Father."

He blinked but could not see her features clearly.

"I never saw a gentleman quite the likes of you before. I've been thinking of you all day and all night."

"No."

"Oh, yes."

"I'm a priest."

"Mmm. And priests don't have women, do they? When was the last time you had a woman?"

Somehow he managed to get to his feet and point to the open door. "Out."

"How long ago?" She stood, the top of her head barely reaching his chin. "Surely you haven't forgotten. And don't tell me you've never had one, because a man like you starts his sowing early. Girls in the fields. Girls in barns. Girls who caught your eyes in taverns and came to you in warm dark rooms afterward. Come on. Tell Glory. How long ago?"

She rested her fingers on his mouth, then rose to her toes to kiss him. Struan's eyes closed. Her tongue passed his lips and wound to find his. She pushed a hand into his hair and held his face tightly to hers.

"How long?" she murmured.

"Too long," he said. "Too long."

"Unnatural," Glory told him. "A waste of a man the likes of you."

He had given himself to God. That's what he'd intended to tell her.

"I'm a girl who doesn't want just any man," she said. "But I want you. It's God's will that I want you and you want me."

Bright shapes parted before him and slowly came together again, and this time he sought her mouth, kissed her hungrily, covered the swelling mounds of her breasts above her bodice.

Glory moaned and panted, and said, "You poor thing. You're bursting with your need. I'm going to take all your need away."

The bodice laced. She pulled braided fastenings undone and let the dress fall about her ankles.

Naked. Naked she stood before him, a curving, narrow-waisted object of lust and longing that sent blood pounding into his temples and throbbing into his loins.

"I must not," he whispered, swallowing, taking a step backward. "I cannot."

"You must. You can."

"I am promised to the Church."

"The Church cannot give you what Glory can give you."

She moved so quickly, he could not stop her hand from closing on him through the loose tunic.

His knees all but buckled and he let his head fall back.

"Oh, yes," she whispered. "Oh, yes, my love. It will be fast. But then it will happen again and again. First, this."

Releasing him, she took one of his hands and guided it into the moist heat between her thighs. Mewling deep in her throat, she pressed his fingers to the swollen place at her center. She ground him into her, jerked her hips back and forth. Almost sobbing, Glory urged his head down to her breast and held her nipple to his mouth until he sucked it in, sucked and bit, mindless now—on fire in every vein.

For one instant she grew still, then she screamed and jerked and pushed against him so hard, his calves met the cot and he fell awkwardly onto the mattress.

Before he could catch a breath or say a word, she was upon him, pulling up the tunic, wrapping her strong legs around his hips, rolling until she lay beneath him.

Struan looked down into her flushed face, glanced from her parted red lips to her breasts, still wet from his mouth and tongue. And he felt the tip of his bursting rod against damp curls—and drove into her. He drove and drove again, all thought gone, all thought snuffed out by the searing sensation of her sheath drawing him in.

A third thrust and the pent-up male juices he'd sworn never again to spill burst into her.

Supported on his arms, he fought for breath while strength rushed away.

"You shouldn't have!"

Struan squeezed his eyes shut.

"I was a virgin. Who'll want me now?"

He saw tears coursing her cheeks. She clawed at him, pushing, writhing. Struan frowned, tried to capture her hands.

"Help me! Someone help me! I'm ruined."

Suddenly cold, Struan struggled to rise away from her. And then he heard another voice. "Dear Lord. Oh, my son, what have you done?"

Struan looked from the place where his body joined with the girl's, to the doorway, fully open now.

Framed in that doorway stood the man he admired most in the world. His confessor and friend. The Abbot of Moreton Abbey.

# Chapter Four

❦

"**S**truan?" He started, opened his eyes, and looked into Justine's worried face. "What is it? What's wrong?" she asked.

The envelope was still pressed to his nose. He withdrew it and stuffed it back into his waistcoat pocket.

"My dear friend," Justine said. She touched his cheek. "You were asleep and having a nightmare. You cried out."

A nightmare? He tried to smile "Did I? What did I say?"

She bent and wrapped her arms around him—and he could not deny himself the pleasure of that embrace. "You said: Forgive me for I have sinned."

Struan rested his brow on her shoulder. "Must have been something to do with you asking me if I took the children to church. My conscience making itself felt."

"Your conscience is above reproach," she said firmly. "You are tired and oppressed. Thank goodness I came. From now on you shall not deal with your burdens alone. If I had the smallest doubt about my decision to help you, it is completely gone now."

She caught his wrists and pulled until he rose from the chair. "Come," she said. "I have your cloak and you are cold. In the morning we shall see to putting this house in order. Obviously the bedchambers are such that you do not wish to show them to me. That will change. For now, we two friends shall warm each other. Put more wood on the fire. It is all but gone out."

The morning would not bring the domestic bliss she mentioned. Rather, it would bring sanity. He would thank her for her kindness, insist he needed no help, and make certain she was dispatched as quickly as possible. Struan piled fresh kindling and wood into the fireplace and used bellows to send flames leaping once more. The storm had quieted somewhat and he thought he saw the vaguest glimmering of dawn through a crack in the draperies.

"Now," Justine said. "Sit with me until you are warm and quiet again."

He stared at her a moment, then did as she asked, dropping down beside her and allowing himself to be covered with her cloak and his. She rested against him, her head on his shoulder, and within moments he heard her steady breathing as she must have fallen asleep again.

Struan dared not as much as close his eyes. To do so now might mean a return to that dreadful time and place and to the events that had followed his weakness.

He turned his head to stare into the fire. Justine was a slight, warm weight at his side. Why could it not have been that she should come to belong at his side permanently?

From somewhere in the lodge a thud sounded.

Struan stiffened. He glanced at Justine's sleeping face and tried to edge away.

The thud was followed by another and another. Struan made to leap up.

Too late.

The hard pounding of boots on stone heralded the arrival of a tall man with curling, dark red-brown hair. He burst into the hall and strode to the daybed.

Struan's tension fled instantly. He grinned up into the handsome face of his oldest friend, Calum, Duke of Franchot. "Welcome!" he said. "By God, this is a night to remember."

"It may be a night you never forget, *friend*," Calum said, white lines forming around his thinned lips. "If you have seduced my sister, this is the night you finally put your precious bachelorhood behind you."

Calum forced his fingers to uncurl. "I ought to call you out on the spot, damn you," he said through gritted teeth. "Better yet, I ought to beat the life out of you where you sit, you filthy—" He caught Justine's horrified eyes and managed to swallow the rest of what he had every right and every responsibility to say.

"Look here, old man," Struan said. "I know how this must look, but—"

*"But?"* Calum roared. "But, you son of the devil? You blackguard! You and my dear, innocent, virtuous sister lie together before my very eyes. I have only to look at her, at both of you, to see what has occurred here."

"Calum, please, you are wrong to speak—"

"Silence," he ordered Justine. Her heavy hair, usually brushed to shining, red-tinged brilliance—the profusion of curls smoothly restrained—lay in riotous confusion about her shoulders. Her cheeks were flushed, her brown eyes bright and, beneath the tumble of cloaks and vulgar silk shawls, her body and Struan's were pressed together, the bodice of her rumpled black gown stark against his disheveled white linen.

When Justine would have shifted away from him, Struan tightened his possessive hold on her shoulders. His hand curled over Justine's bare flesh.

"She had traveled far," Struan told Calum, his handsome

face set in the hard, flamboyant planes that stamped him a Rossmara—brother of Arran Rossmara, Marquess of Stonehaven. Struan said, "I confess I may have shown poor judgment in bringing her to the lodge so late at night, but evidently there was none at Kirkcaldy particularly interested in making her comfortable. And we had much to share. We are old friends, dammit, man!"

"Friends? Much to share?" Calum paced to the door and returned to stand over the evidence that "friends" hardly described the relationship between these two. What they had so recently shared didn't bear thinking about. "Our grandmother and I returned from London to Cornwall earlier than expected. But unfortunately not early enough. One day previous and I could have stopped this. Philipa tried to blame herself for having allowed you to leave, Justine."

"But she had nothing to do with my decision," Justine said, finally separating herself from Struan, if only slightly. "Pippa advised against my making the trip. Please do not in any way condemn her for my actions."

"Hah!" He raised his chin and filled his lungs with air that did nothing to calm him. "I do not condemn my beloved Pippa, I assure you. She is too good to have had any part in this debacle. There is only one who deserves to bear the stain here."

"And Potts," Justine continued as if Calum had said nothing. "Please do not castigate Potts. He was most unhappy at my decision. Most unhappy. Loyalty—and his position—forced him to comply."

"Potts," Calum said darkly. "I might have known you'd coerce Potts into helping with Struan's scheme."

"It was not Struan's—"

"Enough!" Rubbing his eyes, willing weariness from muscles that had ridden too far and too long without rest, Calum turned and bent to toss wood on the dying fire. "What in God's name has possessed you, Struan? And in this place of all places. To bring my gentle sister to this monstrosity and . . . and . . ." He could not bring himself to say the words. "I must think clearly. I must decide what is to be done."

"Perhaps it is not for you to decide," Struan said quietly. "You always were a righteous bastard—"

"I was always righteous?" Calum's black glare silenced the other man. "What are you doing in this place? Tell me that. Your grandfather's folly was always ignored. Look at it. A gaudy, moldering disaster, just as it has been since we were boys together here. Shanks—who ought to have been dismissed years ago—Shanks had the audacity to try to pretend he didn't know where you were. That silent estate commissioner of yours—Caleb Murray—he admitted to seeing Justine but couldn't bloody well say whether or not she'd disappeared. I'd be ignorant yet if that poor Mairi hadn't started babbling about Justine's trunks being at the castle even if she wasn't—and if some vapid creature called Buttercup hadn't piped up that the *lovely* viscount lived here. Good God!"

"The quality and nature of Kirkcaldy's staff is no affair of yours, Calum," Struan said with infuriating calm. He rubbed Justine's shoulder. "Shanks in particular was merely trying to do what he'd been told to do. I have had some slight inconvenience that has made it necessary for discretion in the area of my whereabouts."

"I have no further interest in your intrigues," Calum told him shortly. "Arran and I have spent far too many hours concerning ourselves with your petty mysteries. Keep them to yourself. But do not involve Justine."

"He did not involve me."

"Do you try to tell me that coming here was your own idea, my lady?"

Color left Justine's cheeks, but she sat up quite straight. "I do, indeed."

"Hah! He always had a way with women. He could always

make them do his will. Now he has the most honest woman I ever met lying for him."

Struan shot to his feet and advanced upon Calum. "That is enough. Brothers in all but blood we may be, but I'll not allow you to insult the sweetest lady ever to draw breath."

"Pretty words," Calum said softly, standing toe-to-toe with one of the two men who meant as much to him as his own life. "Tell me you did not wait until you knew I had to accompany my grandmother to London. Tell me you failed to calculate Arran and Grace's proposed absence from Kirkcaldy for some weeks, then managed—by what means I cannot imagine—to lure Justine to Scotland."

"He did not."

Calum ignored Justine. "What evil lies did you tell her? That you were ill and needed her cool hand upon your brow? You know well how softhearted she is. Or could it be that you used those two—"

"Hold your tongue," Struan snapped. "Leave my children out of this."

Calum paused when he realized that lie was yet in place. He glanced at Justine, who was attempting to smooth her skirts. The story that Ella and Max were Struan's children by a very early marriage ended by his wife's death, had been invented to cause Justine and others to accept them at Franchot Castle. Calum himself must bear some of the blame for the deceit. He and Pippa had concocted the tale together, never expecting Struan to embrace the falsehood about the two waifs he'd befriended so wholeheartedly as to eventually appear to believe it true.

"Very well." Calum made up his mind what had to be done. "At least be responsible in this, man. Come clean. What has occurred between you and my sister?"

"I . . ." Struan turned back to Justine, whose eyes had grown bright again, this time suspiciously so. "Oh, my dear one. Do not cry. You are blameless."

To Calum's amazement and ire, Struan dropped to one knee before Justine and began to straighten her hair with his fingers. All the while he murmured to her in soothing, unintelligible sounds. And she looked at him as if he were sent as a gift from God!

"Unhand her," Calum demanded.

Struan finished his smoothing of Justine's hair at his own pace, drawing it back to rest behind her neck. Then, as calmly as you please, he settled the neck of her gown more tidily. He plucked at the velvet pleated trim, set it to rights across the tops of her breasts!

And she still smiled at him.

"Give me strength," Calum said, to God and to himself. "I do not believe what I see."

"There, dear one," Struan said. "You are as close to your demure self as is possible at this moment." With a final, capable brushing at her skirts over her thighs, he stood and faced Calum again. "Perhaps we should go outside to continue this discussion," he said.

"You shall not," Justine said firmly. "If you leave this room, I go with you."

She was quite unlike herself. "Kindly remember that I am the head of the household," Calum told her. "In matters of your welfare, I must decide what is best."

"Piffle."

He gaped. "Has he fed you strong drink? Is that it? You are drunk, my lady?"

"*Sin's ears!* You, dear brother, are a turnip head."

"Good Lord. Obviously you are not yourself. Struan, I will have the truth now. Explain exactly what passed between yourself and my sister while you were alone."

"We comforted each other," Struan said quietly and Calum could not help but notice how weary his friend appeared. "I encountered Justine at Kirkcaldy and persuaded her to offer me solace. I needed someone I could trust. I trust Justine, Calum, just as I trust you."

Calum swallowed. He could not allow old loyalties to sway him from duty. "And what, pray, was the exact form of this comfort and solace?"

"Not what you think," Struan said, very low, inclining his head significantly in Justine's direction.

"So you say," Calum said, but the leaden ball of anger began to lift from his heart. "What proof do you offer?"

Suddenly Struan's old, wicked smile split wide over his white teeth. Dimples drove into his beard-stubbled cheeks. "What proof should you like me to offer?" he asked softly. "Might it not be a trifle difficult to offer any at all?"

Calum glowered but could not stop his lips from twitching. "You say, then, that you expect me to believe my sister's virtue is intact?"

One of Struan's dark brows rose. "I do indeed."

"Then I shall remove her at once, before more damage can be done to her reputation, and return her to her rightful place."

"You will do no such thing!"

At the sound of Justine's sharp announcement, both men swiveled toward her.

"You, Calum, may think what you will. I am here and shall remain. I intend to do as I wish."

"Justine, you forget yourself. You—"

"On the contrary. I have finally remembered myself. I have finally noted that if I am not exceedingly careful I shall end my days without ever having counted for a single matter of importance. Pah on that, I say. Piffle, I repeat."

"You are a woman of high moral character. Virtuous—"

"Virtuous be . . . Virtue be *discarded*. I am a new woman about to emerge from the foolishness of my past. I have things to do, brother. Things destined to change the future of other woman. And I choose to do them here."

Women. Calum looked at Justine as if to say he would never, ever, understand the creatures. "I managed to dissuade Grandmama from accompanying me by assuring her you would return with me."

"I do not belong to Grandmama. Let her find another servant."

Calum could not believe what he heard, but he rather liked parts of this newly confident Justine. "I shall be happy to help you establish a more satisfactory relationship with Grandmama, my dear. But we should leave at once."

"That will not be possible."

"Dearest Justine. Your virtue is—"

"I will say it again. I throw my virtue away. Virtue be gone. Virtue be tossed to any passing wind. Virtue, I want no part of your bonds from this day forth."

Calum looked to Struan. "Now I think I must truly question the *comfort* you sought in Justine," he said. "Did you? . . ."

Struan narrowed his eyes but did not respond.

To Justine Calum said, "Did he? . . ."

Justine frowned.

"Did you, Struan?" Calum pressed. He puffed up his cheeks and said, "Do it, did you?"

Struan made fists upon his hips. "I did not."

"You swear?"

Struan averted his face.

"Justine, I choose to believe Struan," Calum said. "Quickly. Gather your cloak. We will return to the castle to retrieve your trunks. I will think of some excuse for your absence."

Justine didn't move.

"Come," Calum urged. "There is no time to waste. Please make haste."

"No."

"You must."

"I cannot."

"My dear sister. Please do not persist in this foolishness."

Justine lifted her pointed chin. "This has nothing to do with foolishness, only necessity. I cannot come with you. I cannot leave."

Calum approached and offered her his hand. "Why would you say such a thing?"

She ignored his hand. "The fact is that he did."

"He did?"

"Struan did. And so did I."

"Justine," Struan said.

She ignored the plea in his voice.

Calum brought his face lower over hers. "You and Struan did what?"

"You know," she said airily. "You asked and I'm answering. We did *It*."

To Justine's dismay, Calum rounded on Struan, made fists, and drew back one powerful arm.

She pushed to her feet, threw herself between Calum and Struan—tripped, and found herself once more swept up into Struan's arms.

One more moment and Calum would have hit poor Struan.

"Put her down," Calum ground out. "I shall take Justine away from here this instant and pray no permanent damage has been done to anything other than her good sense."

"But we did *It*," Justine argued.

Calum held up a hand. "Never—not ever—do not say that to me again. I cannot bear to as much as consider such a possibility."

"Dash it," Struan said. "I begin to take offense at your tone, *and* your suggestions."

"Put my—" At the sound of approaching footsteps—an apparent herd of footsteps—Calum stopped speaking. Then he whispered, "*Down*, I tell you," urgently.

Too late.

Even had Justine not been holding Struan firmly about the neck, he could not have set her down before a whirlwind of young energy erupted through the open doorway.

"We've come!" Max announced, his overlong, shockingly red hair springing away in all directions from a slim, freckled face. A little blond girl clutched his loose shirttails. "Ella's in the kitchens with Mrs. Mercer and bubbly, bouncy Buttercup Likely. There's t'be porridge . . ." His green eyes settled on the spectacle of Struan with Justine in his arms.

"Hello, Max," Justine said, still clinging to Struan. "Who's this pretty child?"

He took several seconds to close his mouth and swallow. Glancing first at Calum he said, "Kirsty," very faintly. "Kirsty Mercer. She's got a terrible wee brother called Niall. He's two. Mrs. Mercer says two's the most terrible age on a wee one. He's in the kitchens, too. We've brought porridge on account o' Mr. and Mrs. Mercer worryin' about Papa not eatin' proper."

"My goodness," Justine murmured. "He speaks like a Scot, Struan. Only months since he sounded like—"

"A barrow boy," Max announced smugly. "Like a London barrow boy from a market. Grumpy told me so. Spawned o' the devil, she says I am. And—"

"Enough," Struan said and seemed to remember he still held Justine. "This is too much for you," he murmured, close to her face, and set her feet upon the floor with great care. He took her hand and threaded it beneath his elbow.

Justine studied Max and the ethereal blond child. "Were you not in your bed, Max? Have you just returned from . . . Have you just returned home?"

"Aye," he said.

"*Yes*," she corrected him automatically. "And Ella, too? Has she already been out this morning?"

"O'course," Max said as if he considered her lacking in simple understanding. "We've both been where we always are at night. Wait till Ella sees ye, Lady Justine. She'll be beside hersel' wi' happiness."

Justine's heart turned over. "What can he mean? Struan?"

She looked up at him. "Does he mean he and Ella are in the habit of sneaking from their beds without your knowledge?"

"I hardly think this is something you should concern yourself with, Justine," Calum said, but she noted the way his brows drew together. "I'm sure Struan can deal with his own affairs."

"And I'm sure he cannot. Which is exactly why he needs me. Max, you will speak to me with complete honesty. Why have you and Ella become wild things? What would possess you to leave your beds while you assume your father is sleeping? Where do you go? This really is insupportable."

"What does the lady mean, Max?" the little girl asked. "Is she one o' the ones ye told me about? Am I t'go find me da now?"

"Hush," Max said, his skin reddening.

"But ye told me to fetch me da if one o' them was t'come." A small-boned creature, the child's smooth brow puckered. "Is she one o' the ones wi' bloody murder in her heart? One o' the ones set on tearin' out your da's liver and lights?"

"*Max*," Justine, Calum, and Struan exclaimed in unison.

"This lady is a friend," Max said to Kirsty Mercer. "She's held in great favor wi' Papa. And wi' me. Away wi' ye. Go tell Ella there's someone here she'll want t'see. And tell your mam we'll come t'the kitchen for porridge shortly."

Justine shook her head. Things had come to a much worse pass than she could have imagined. Now Struan's English barbarian son had become a Scottish barbarian. She must start work very quickly.

As soon as Kirsty had scampered from sight, Max closed the door and approached the adults with a conspiratorial hunch to his shoulders. "Let me deal wi' this, Papa. Ye canna expect the duke and Lady Justine t'understand the way o' things here."

"Max," Struan said, his voice loaded with warning. "I think you had better leave us and join Ella."

"Not until I've explained about the wild bands in the hills."

Justine met Struan's eyes and he pinched the bridge of his nose.

"That's why we leave the lodge at night—Ella and me, that is. Bands of wild clansmen come down from the hills in the dark. They've great claymores and clubs and all manner o' fearsome weapons. The tenants are afraid o' them. Ella's afraid, too, but I let her come so's she'll feel useful. I have my ways of scarin' the wild ones away, y'see."

"Wild clansmen," Calum said. "The same type of people bent on securing Struan's—your father's *liver and lights* would that be?"

Max nodded sagely. "The very same."

"Nothing has changed, I see," Calum remarked. "I would suggest the boy spend long hours with a minister. Discussing the danger his deceit poses to his soul."

"He's eleven," Justine snapped.

"Quite," Calum responded. "Old enough to know better. Kindly leave us alone, young man. If there is time, Lady Justine will greet Ella—before we leave for Cornwall."

"But—"

"Go," Struan said in ominous tones. "We shall speak about your behavior later."

"But—"

"*Go.*"

Max backed up until he thudded against the door, then rapidly exited the room.

"He only does that when he's overset," Struan said apologetically. "That's when he tells the stories. The lad means no harm."

"He needs a woman's guidance," Justine said, already planning how she would read to Max from the Bible.

"He needs a good whipping," Calum retorted. "Now. This madness has progressed quite far enough. Justine, I will hear no more argument. As we travel, we shall discuss how best to explain your extraordinary behavior. We leave Scotland at . . ." His words trailed away. He stared toward the door.

Justine turned to see Arran, Marquess of Stonehaven, looming on the threshold.

Struan groaned, threw himself into a deep, scarlet, tapestry-covered chair, and buried his head in his hands. "A circus," he muttered. "Come one, come all. Don't miss the show."

"A show indeed," the marquess said, his massive, dark countenance moving into the room like an inevitable force. "I thank providence that I listened to Grace."

"Grace?" Struan moaned.

"My dear wife—as you well know—has always had other worldly powers. She felt the need for me to come here now. I tried to resist since I should not have left Yorkshire at such a time. But, of course, she was right."

"Preserve us all," Struan said, raising closed eyes toward the ornately carved, domed ceiling. "Here again is the man who once laughed at his bride's otherworldly talents."

"Indeed," Calum said. "Good to see you, Arran. Unfortunately we cannot dally to hear more on this fascinating topic. Justine and I are already running late on our travel schedule."

Arran's face, so like his younger brother Struan's, assumed an expression of distant confusion. "Travel? Surely the traveling has been done. Where Justine is concerned. Shanks and Caleb Murray—and Mairi—tell me our visitor arrived yesterday."

"I . . ." Justine looked to Struan, whose eyes remained closed. "That is so."

"She arrived yesterday and will leave today," Calum said, his mouth set in a firm line. "We will speak of this on another occasion, Arran."

"We will speak of it now," the marquess said serenely. "I understand Struan brought your dear sister here last night."

Calum snatched up Justine's cloak. "True. And now——"

"And," Arran continued, "my brother and your sister were alone here—no chaperon that I know of—alone for hours."

"Damn you, Arran," Calum said, flinging the cloak around Justine's shoulders. "Must you embarrass her further?"

"I am not embarrassed."

Her voice assured the attention of all three men.

"I am not embarrassed because I came here of my own will, Arran. I wished to spend the night with Struan."

"Nothing happened," Calum said hastily. "Nothing."

"It certainly did," Justine said. "*It* did." Whatever it was, and she'd better find out in case someone decided to quiz her more closely on the subject. From the response every mention of—of whatever *It* might be, the—whatever—must be quite fascinating. "It did happen," she repeated.

"Oh, my God," Struan whispered.

"You had better pray," Calum told him. "Pray there is no lasting harm here. I bid you good day, my friends."

"A good day indeed," Arran remarked. "We must make the best of it and start preparing immediately."

"We are already prepared," Calum said. "Justine came in a Franchot coach and the horses will be well rested by now."

"Horses won't be necessary." Arran draped a forearm on the mantel. "Struan and Justine will marry at Kirkcaldy."

# Chapter Five

"**M**arry at Kirkcaldy?" Justine said, with enough disdain to make Struan smart. "Marry Struan?"

"He does appear to be the man you spent last night with," Arran responded in a level voice Struan recognized as dangerous. "And everyone seems in agreement that the pair of you were alone here."

Struan splayed a hand over his jacket—on top of the letter. He had become a poison to those he cared for deeply. No more potential victims must be offered to his tormentor. "The situation has already been explained to Calum's satisfaction. Justine arrived late. We were pleased to see each other and wished to talk—as old friends. I may have shown poor judgment in bringing her here without a chaperon, but no harm has been done. Let us have no more of this foolish talk." This dangerous talk.

"Exactly," Justine said, her head held at a haughty angle. "Foolish talk, indeed. They will be waiting for us in the kitchens."

Arran drew himself up to his full and very impressive

height. "There are times when we are forced to accept the error of our ways and take the consequences."

"What the hell does that mean?" Calum snapped.

"Responsibility."

Calum's eyes glittered and he stood very close to Justine. "I repeat, Arran. Make yourself plain. And if you are calling my sister . . . If you are questioning my sister's character, I advise you to think hard before saying anything at all."

"Arran would never question Justine's character." A heavy ache pressed about Struan's eyes. This development must not divert his attention, his vigilance. "He sometimes forgets that I am past needing his guiding hand. I am not a child, y'know, brother. I'll attend to my own business."

"These decisions are frequently removed from our hands," Arran said. "I am merely insisting that for the sake of family reputation—our own and the Franchots—we must do what is right."

"We are doing what is right," Calum said, his color unusually high. "We are leaving at once."

"I think not," Arran remarked, almost offhandedly.

Calum placed an arm around Justine's shoulders and glared. "The devil you say. This is not your decision to—"

"It is not Arran's decision and neither is it yours," Struan interrupted. "I assure you that the two mature people involved in this are very capable of making their own decisions."

"Exactly," Justine announced emphatically. "And this mature person has decided to remain here to pursue her work and to help a friend."

Arguing openly with Justine would do nothing to further his cause. Struan addressed Calum, "We will deal with this, man to man."

"Indeed," Arran agreed. "We—"

"Calum and I are the men involved," Struan told his brother, tight-lipped.

"And I am the woman involved." Justine's serenity was

amazing. "Struan and I understand each other perfectly, don't we, Struan?"

How could he do other than nod agreement?

Her smile was jubilant. "Quite. Now I find I am hungry. Very hungry. If we keep those in the kitchens waiting longer, we shall truly run the risk of arousing gossip."

The world had gone mad. Even more mad than Struan had unwillingly accepted it to be in recent weeks.

Last night he had ridden to the castle alone, and expected to return to the lodge—alone. Instead he'd been confronted by Justine, who, at this moment, stood in the middle of this outrageously neglected kitchen like a slightly bedraggled princess misplaced in an abandoned dungeon.

And in their company were two men Struan had not thought to see for weeks, or perhaps months—and certainly not together, or here.

Gael Mercer, wife of Robert Mercer, lifelong tenants of Kirkcaldy and indispensable allies in Struan's recent trials, busily tended the fire in the great black stove. The occasional maid, Buttercup, stirred a large pot of porridge bubbling atop the stove. She stirred but kept her pink and white face firmly averted from the steam. Buttercup herself rather bubbled inside the uniform that didn't subdue her curves.

Ella, Struan's dark-haired, exotic "daughter," hovered near Justine, who regarded the girl with smiling joy.

"You are so beautiful," Justine said, not for the first time since she'd entered the kitchens. "Even more beautiful than when I last saw you in Cornwall—if that were possible."

"She's a wild one," Max announced, breaking into a boisterous jig that involved swinging his arms and hopping from heel to toe. "Ye should hear Grumpy talk about how wild our Ella is. Another one spawned o' the devil, she says."

Struan gave up trying to restrain the boy. "Gael," he said.

"You really don't have to do this, you know." He found himself repeatedly looking to the windows for signs of watching enemy eyes.

Slender, red-haired Gael kept her gaze lowered and took over stirring the pot. "Robert said I was t'feed ye," she said, her voice barely audible over Max's hummed accompaniment to his dance and the hollow banging made by a plump toddler thumping a large spoon on an upturned basin.

To Struan's amazement, Arran dropped to his haunches in front of the child and brushed fair curls away from his brow. "That's a fine drum you have there, Niall," he said, grinning indulgently. "May I have a turn?"

Struan scrubbed at his face. He sometimes forgot that Arran had helped bring little Niall into the world, but this was not the time or the place for glad reunions.

Max's dance grew wilder. Around and around the kitchen he cavorted, his shirttail flying, his muddy boots clattering a tattoo on the flagstones.

Arran covered young Niall's hand on the spoon handle and they beat out a rhythm to match the dance.

"Oh, how lovely," Justine said, pressing her hands to her cheeks.

Calum hoisted the thumb-sucking Kirsty into his arms and allowed her to anchor his face between tiny fists while she studied him very closely.

There were entirely too many people in this ghastly room. And everything had slipped from Struan's control—at the very time when it was essential that he maintain the tightest control ever. In daylight, with three formidable men present, he did not fear for those he intended to keep safe, no matter what the cost to himself. If he was forced to keep the children at the lodge tonight, he must mount a careful vigil.

Calum, still carrying Kirsty, came close to Struan. "Look at this place," he said. "Cobwebs and dust. Everywhere. I'll wager that stove hasn't been used in years before today. I was told the maid came here several times a week. What does she do?"

"Nothing, for all I know," Struan said. "It is of no concern to me."

"The floor is filthy. Everything's filthy."

Defiance destroyed Struan's caution. "The entire lodge is filthy. I have more important things on my mind."

"Do tell."

"I cannot. Not yet. Only trust me to take care of what I must."

"You haven't told Justine about Ella and Max?"

Struan thinned his lips and said, "Make no mention of that, please," in low tones. "I must break it to her in my own way and in my own time." A time he didn't wish to contemplate. He had rescued Ella from a London brothel where the owner planned to sell her to the pervert willing to pay the highest price for a beautiful young virgin. Ella had then beseeched Struan to find her brother, Max, then the property of a pick-pocket in Covent Garden. Struan shook his head. "Eventually I will find a way to explain it all to Justine." A truly revolting thought.

"Where do they go at night?"

"*Damn* your curiosity, Calum. They stay with the Mercers."

"Overly crowded in that little cottage, I should think." Calum's voice was even, as if he spoke of mundane matters.

"They are safe there, and I trust Robert and Gael. It's the best I can do for the present."

"It's amazing," Calum responded. He set Kirsty down and turned serious eyes—eyes so much like Justine's—upon Struan. "Something's badly awry. I knew it the instant I learned you had chosen to live here, and that you didn't want to be found by any chance caller. Tell me what's afoot, my friend."

"Not the time or place," Struan responded. The shame he

bore must remain his alone. Sharing his sordid past—with anyone—was unthinkable. And since he wasn't exactly certain what was in store for him, he could not truthfully answer his friend's call. He indicated the rest of the company. "Not the place at all. Don't worry. It's nothing I cannot take care of."

"You show me no evidence that I should believe you." Calum glanced at Justine. "She must come away with me. I cannot leave her here."

"I agree." Fate sneered at him yet again, this time in the tantalizing form of a woman who might be all he could ever desire yet could not have.

Heat rattled the pot on the stove. Gael Mercer began to ladle porridge into bowls. These Ella set upon the great square table that had been hastily relieved of its layer of dust by Buttercup.

To Struan's discomfort, Justine promptly sat on the end of a bench as if taking breakfast in a dirty kitchen was quite the thing.

Arran abandoned his musical efforts and sat beside Justine with Niall on his knee.

"Good God," Calum muttered. "Surely you do not intend to have your company sit in this mayhem and eat amid the filth."

"Gael came to feed me," Struan said simply. "She is a wonderful woman who has helped me greatly. I would not offend her and neither, I assure you, would Arran. He knows every one of his people—including their children—and regards them as his responsibility. He's particularly fond of the Mercers."

"But Justine has never—"

"Justine appears entirely comfortable," Struan remarked, smiling down into Kirsty's somber face. "This young lady looks hungry to me."

Calum shrugged and approached the table. "I give up. We shall get through this and remove to the castle where we can speak sanely."

Jugs of thick cream, a bowl of honey, and a pot of fragrant coffee graced the rude table. Gael placed cups before each diner and gathered her children to her side. "We'll be leavin' ye now." Her face was flushed from working over the stove, and from discomfort at her unfamiliar surroundings, no doubt. She bobbed a curtsy. From the sloping wooden board beside deep sinks she took a glass bowl crowded with snowdrops, purple sweet violets, and bright blue speedwell and set it in the middle of the table. "Robert and I will await your instructions, m'lord," she said to Struan. At Arran she directed the sweetest of smiles. "It's verra good t'see you, your lordship. Please tell her ladyship she's sorely missed at Kirkcaldy and we all look forward to her return."

"Your words will bring her great pleasure," Arran said.

Gael bobbed again. "Is wee Lady Elizabeth well?"

"Blooming," Arran said, grinning. "And a handful."

When the Mercers had left, Calum commented, "You always did have a way with the tenants, Arran. I do believe they love you. Not a usual situation between Scottish lairds and their people."

"A usual situation between the lords of Stonehaven and their people," Arran said. "But you already know that."

Justine ate her porridge with evident enjoyment. "Ella," she said, "your papa tells me you are a remarkable seat upon a horse."

"I ride well enough," Ella mumbled. Her black, waist-length hair hung in a tangled mass. Her thick lashes gleamed darkly about large, uptilted black eyes. At sixteen she was, indeed, a beauty.

Max squirmed on his bench. "I'm t'swim in the river wi' a bunch o' the laddies today," he said. "Can I go now?"

"No," Justine said, utterly serene. "It is far too cold and it is time for you to begin your instruction."

"Papa," Max said. "I want t'swim wi'—"

"You will not be swimming today," Struan said, avoiding both Arran and Calum's eyes. "I have need of you here."

"It is evident that I haven't arrived a moment too soon," Justine said. She waited until Struan turned toward her. "I'm glad you have agreed that I should take the children in hand and prepare them for their rightful place in society."

He put too large a spoonful of porridge in his mouth, burned his tongue, and coughed.

"Justine," Calum said. "This lodge is a disgrace. I mean no disrespect to Arran or Struan—in a way I still think of this estate as my own home. I did grow up here. But this lodge was all but abandoned many years since and it is unfit—entirely unfit—for habitation. Particularly by a gentle lady completely unaccustomed to discomfort."

Justine showed every sign of listening politely. When Calum had finished, she set down her spoon. "You misjudge me, brother. I am no milk-and-water miss. I am a mature woman who has passed from the spun-glass to the serviceable-plate phase of life. Do you intend to continue to live here, Struan?"

Whatever he said was bound to plunge him deeper into this new dilemma. "Yes," he told her. That, at least, was true.

"Why?" Arran asked.

The question stopped every spoon. Arran regarded Struan steadily. "What is this all about? A few weeks since I left you in charge of Kirkcaldy. I return to find the castle all but deserted and you living here in squalid conditions."

"Slightly unsuitable conditions," Justine said archly. "Squalid is such a nasty word."

"Slightly unsuitable conditions," Arran said dutifully.

Despite his tension, Struan hid a smile. Justine could quell the strongest of men.

"Answer my question," Arran insisted.

"I am not a child," Struan told him. "I confess I have certain concerns that have led me to seek distance from the castle. I can handle my own problems, Arran."

"You aren't handling your—"

"They are *my* problems."

"And you are *my* younger brother. And I am the head of this household. And you owe me your allegiance in matters concerning this family."

"You have my allegiance in all things. You do not have my permission to meddle in things that are my own affair."

An awful silence followed.

Justine cleared her throat. "Ella, will you kindly ride to Mrs. Mercer's cottage. Ask her if she can find some women who would be glad to augment their incomes by helping me here at the lodge. I'll need them at once. As many as can come."

Struan bowed his head. This only became worse.

"You, girl." Justine indicated the serenely oblivious maid. "What is your name?"

"Buttercup." The large blue eyes that turned on Justine held a hint of insolence. "I'm to do the viscount's bidding."

Calum breathed out loudly and Struan set his jaw.

"For the present you will do *my* bidding," Justine informed the girl. "Kindly begin by making yourself useful in the children's bedchambers."

Buttercup's blue eyes rolled ever so slightly before she flounced from the kitchens.

"And you, Max," Justine continued. "Go to the castle. Ask first to speak to Mr. Potts. He is my coachman. Tell him I require my trunks brought here. Then speak with the butler and ask if some of the castle staff might be spared. They did not appear particularly overworked yesterday."

Calum half rose. "Justine, we are—"

She cut him off. "Kindly leave at once, Max."

"Can I take the black?" the boy said, leaping up with enough force to rattle crockery and spill water from the flowers.

"You may not," Struan told him. "The little chestnut will do nicely." What was he saying? He'd have the place overrun and lose his precious isolation.

"Now," Arran said when Max—and Ella in her shabby brown breeches and frock coat—had left. "We have much to settle and probably not much time to do so."

"Quite," Calum agreed.

"Do not press me further," Struan said. "When I can explain myself—if that day ever comes—I shall do so. Until then I'll thank you to respect my privacy."

"They only ask because they care for you," Justine said gently. "But I know they will follow your wishes."

Calum coughed discreetly. "Whatever Struan wants. Just know you can come to me at any time, old chap. Come along, Justine."

"I'm not going anywhere," she told him. "Didn't you hear me ask Max to arrange for my trunks to be delivered?"

"You cannot be serious."

"I am perfectly serious."

Arran reached to cover her hand on the table. "You are an answer to my prayers."

She gave him a charming smile. "Why, thank you, Arran. How ever can that be?"

The corners of his eyes twitched slightly. "Naturally, this is all most unexpected, but it will be my pleasure—and Grace's—to welcome you into the family."

Struan made fists in his lap. "Arran, I think—"

Justine interrupted him. "Oh, you fun me, Arran." She tipped her head back and laughed.

The men didn't join her mirth.

She tapped Arran's wrist. "You know full well that I am long past an age where my reputation is an issue. And Struan's reputation is beyond reproach. There cannot be any question of silly talk about my being here."

"On the contrary," Arran said promptly. "You are a lovely,

refined woman and you are far from being old enough to be considered a tabby."

Justine stared at him, her lips parted.

She wasn't accustomed to compliments. Struan swallowed. If circumstances had been different, he would be delighted to put that omission to rights. Circumstances were not different, and for her own safety, Justine must not remain with him. He would say so.

"We must rely upon Calum to know what is best for Justine," Struan declared.

"No such thing," Justine said. "I know what is best for me. Please let us waste no more time on this issue. The subject is closed. You may return to Grace and give her my love, Arran. And you, Calum, may go back to Pippa. Tell Grandmama I'll write."

Struan could not help but laugh at gentle Justine's unexpectedly acid tongue.

While Justine managed to remain somber, Calum and Arran chuckled with Struan.

"Are you quite collected now?" Justine asked as the mirth subsided. "If so, I shall get to work. I will ensure that a room is prepared for myself and then set about putting the lodge to rights for Struan and for his dear children."

"Justine—"

"Hush, Calum. My mind is made up."

"You cannot stay, sister dear. There is not even a chaperon."

"Bit late for that, wouldn't you say?" Arran remarked, fiddling with his watch chain.

"Damn your nerve!" Calum grabbed Arran's neckcloth and hauled his face closer. "Take that back or I'll thank you to name your seconds."

"Would you not," Arran said reasonably, "admit that a chaperon is a trifle superfluous at this point?"

With a final tug on Arran's neckcloth, Calum released him and said, "I would not."

"Nor I," Struan added. He wanted this issue settled. Quickly. "I think it is essential that Justine withdraw from the lodge immediately and with as little fuss as possible." He wanted her departure to attract as little attention as possible.

"If the business of a chaperon is important at all, I'm sure that dear Mairi would be glad to come." Justine picked up her bowl. "Is Grace planning to return to Kirkcaldy soon?"

"Not for some weeks," Arran said.

"Then I'm sure you will be happy to spare Mairi," Justine said sweetly. "Kindly send her to me when you stop at the castle to prepare for your return to Yorkshire."

Arran ran a hand through his thick, curly hair which was restrained in an unfashionable but—according to the ladies—an irresistible queue. "This is not settled," he said. "I will send Mairi. And some of the castle staff to supervise things. I shall want to talk with you, Calum—in appropriate surroundings. And with you, Struan," he finished, glowering at his brother.

Justine carried bowls to the sinks as if she'd been a scullery maid in some previous life. "You should all go along and chat. I'm sure you have much to talk about. Many things to share. And I am anxious to put people to work here and get started on my book."

"Book?" Calum said.

"*Book?*" Arran echoed.

Struan tried, unsuccessfully, to smother a groan.

"Oh yes," she said. "My book for prospective brides. It will revolutionize the whole business."

"Good Lord," Arran muttered.

"You are addled." Calum sounded irritable. "Ladies do not write books. They certainly do not write books about matters such as the one you suggest."

"Piffle."

Calum planted his fists on his hips. "You have quite forgot yourself, Justine. That word has crossed your lips several times since I arrived. And the . . . Sin's ears, or whatever. You are not yourself."

"I am finally myself. My book will be highly instructional and highly sought after. Eventually men as well as women will clamor to read it."

Arran snorted.

"Men of inquiring intellect," Justine said, narrowing her lovely eyes. "Men with fine sensibilities. Men who seek to know more about the feelings of the women they plan to marry."

Calum shook his head. "You are an innocent, my dear. And your innocence shows, thank God. Men do not wish, or need, to know more about women's feelings in these matters. Men are perfectly capable of ensuring the outcome in such . . ." He reddened. "Men know how to deal with their wives, Justine."

She pointed a finger at him. "That is exactly the attitude I intend to combat. My book will detail events that transpire between men and women during courtship and after marriage. My mission is to remove the mystery from the entire process."

Struan watched Arran and Calum's faces and winced at their bemused horror.

"You know nothing," Calum said at last. "Absolutely nothing."

Arran patted her arm. "A noble ambition, I'm sure, my dear, but out of the question, of course. Leave the project to someone qualified for the work."

"A man, no doubt," she said sharply. "As has always been the case, only a man could possibly write about those things closest to a woman's heart. Am I correct?"

"Ah—" Arran's mouth remained open.

"Naturally," Calum said. "It is not for women to trouble

their pretty heads over these things. Now. Enough said. Don't give it another thought."

"I certainly shall. My plans are already under way."

Calum let out an exasperated breath. "Justine, kindly desist in this. Even if it were suitable, a single woman cannot instruct other women in matters outside her experience."

"They are not outside Struan's experience," she retorted.

Struan bowed his head and prayed for deliverance.

"And what," Arran said coldly, "does that have to do with this?"

"Why, it's simple," Justine announced cheerfully. "Struan is too polite to argue with Calum's foolishness. I am not too polite. Struan and I have come to an agreement. The terms are to our mutual satisfaction and no interference can possibly be tolerated. In return for my looking after his household and instructing his children, *he* will instruct *me* on every detail I require for my book!"

# Chapter Six

❦

The scent of steeping alkanet root, linseed oil, and rose pink drifted through the lodge. The mixture had already been vigorously applied to priceless but neglected wooden pieces to bring them to gleaming luster.

In the small billiard room where Justine had finally found Ella, green damask wallpaper had been carefully cleaned with lumps of old bread, and mahogany wainscots glowed from polishing.

Dressed in ill-fitting boy's clothes, as she had been on each of the four days since Justine arrived, Ella stood before the open casement. From outside came the sounds of sticks thwacking carpets hung in the fresh morning air for cleaning.

"Ella?"

The girl showed no sign of having heard Justine. With her booted feet braced apart and her hands clasped behind her back, she made a disquietingly defiant picture.

Justine went to her side and looked out onto a courtyard

where Mrs. Moggach, the housekeeper from the castle, over-saw several tenant women working on the carpets.

"They will be quite beautiful again soon," Justine re-marked.

Ella glanced at her blankly.

"The carpets," Justine told her. "Mrs. Moggach tells me there were few bad stains and they were easily enough re-moved. A little rubbing with hot loaves of bread will bring back their full color."

"How would you know about cleaning carpets? You've never cleaned anything."

Justine's smile slipped. "Is it necessary to be rude to me, Ella?" She instantly regretted her sharpness. "Mrs. Mercer ex-plained the process to me. Buttercup had one of the maids from the castle tell her."

"Someone would have to tell her," Ella said. "Mrs. Mercer doesn't have carpets of her own."

"You sound angry."

Ella returned her attention to the scene outside.

"I thought you would be glad to have me come," Justine said. "At first you were. But you seem less so with each day." And with each day Justine needed firmer resolve to continue with the bold plans she'd made in Cornwall.

Ella's throat moved sharply before she said, "I am glad you're here. And I don't mean to be rude. It's just that I'm not certain what's expected of me."

Neither was Justine certain what was expected of her—not anymore. Since that first strange breakfast she'd scarcely seen Struan, and spoken to him less. She leaned across the leather-cushioned window seat to get a clearer view of the courtyard. Mrs. Moggach, a large, gray-haired woman in a gray dress and voluminous white apron, stood with her arms crossed under an impressive bosom. Her florid face showed how little pleasure she took in her new responsibilities.

Ella touched Justine's sleeve. "I've made you unhappy."

"No." She shook her head. "Not you."

"But you are unhappy. I see that you are."

Nothing had progressed as she had planned—almost nothing. She would not be put out from Kirkcaldy as long as she chose to remain. In fact, Arran continued to comment at every opportunity that she was to become his sister-in-law. But Calum thundered and roared and threatened and demanded. She should go home with him at once, or . . . He was quite indistinct about what the "or" was likely to be.

And Struan? Struan's black eyes held the most disturbing of expressions. Anger? Confusion? *Pain?* Justine could not be sure, but she had never intended to cause him trouble. Knowing he already had trouble enough made her doubly horrified at the prospect of bringing him more.

Yet there was something else in Struan's eyes and she thought it was affection. Perhaps she was a hopeless dreamer, but even the slightest possibility that he enjoyed her presence meant that she must not leave without being certain of his wishes.

Today Ella's hair lay in a single thick braid down her back. She pulled it forward and played the end across her lips. "They're saying things about you and Papa," she murmured, her eyes lowered.

Blood rushed to Justine's face. "What sort of things? And who are *they*?"

"All sorts of people. They say Papa compromised you."

Justine held her throat. "You cannot possibly understand what is meant by such things, and neither should you."

"I understand. It has been explained to me."

Justine gave a small, involuntary cry. She could scarcely breathe.

"Is it true?"

"No! How could you imagine Struan capable of such a thing?"

"He likes you a great deal."

Justine's heart all but stopped beating.

"They say the marquess is insisting there be a marriage at once."

"How do these things get about so?" Justine said miserably. "Do not listen. Do you understand me? You are not to listen to such cruel lies. I am a year your father's senior and all but a cripple. Surely you cannot believe for a moment that he would be interested in . . . Oh, botheration, this is beyond all. We shall speak no more on the subject."

"You and Papa are almost the same age and you are not a cripple." Ella pushed back her frock coat and fiddled with the too-large waist of her breeches. Even in such unflattering attire her pretty body was impossible to disguise. "I for one would like it very well if the two of you found happiness together. Papa hasn't been happy of late. I try to be everything he needs, but I cannot, of course."

Justine quickly looked away. Her eyes prickled with the start of tears. "You are a sweet child. But you do not understand. *Liking* is not enough and liking is what your father has for me."

"How do you know?"

"I know." Justine drew in a long breath. "Let us forget we've spoken of this. Except that I shall remember your dear acceptance of me. I shall remain here with all of you and help you and Max with your educations. In time a tutor must be retained, especially for Max, but for now I can do a creditable job. In time I shall convince Calum to return to Cornwall and Arran will forget his foolish notions of marriage between Struan and me."

"I doubt it. Everyone's talking about—"

"Hush," Justine said urgently. "I do not wish to be cruel, but the chattering of the tenants will not decide what is to happen among the Lords of Rossmara. Now, on to more important things. Your time with us at Franchot served you well," Justine said, referring to Ella's speech. "You learned quickly there. Pippa will be gratified when I tell her how well you sound."

"Lady Philipa was kind. So were you. I don't want to be a disappointment."

"You are not a disappointment." A dilemma, perhaps, but nothing more. "Your papa means well. He is a good man, but you need a woman's guidance."

Ella's head jerked around. "Papa is wonderful. He is the best man in the entire world."

"Oh, yes," Justine said, unable to bridle her enthusiasm. "He *is* the best man in the world. And he wants the best for you. It's for that reason, as well as because of my fondness for you and Max, that I intend to help him do what must be done. Max must be taken in hand at once. He cannot continue to run like a hill goblin."

"He's happy as he is," Ella said.

Impulsively, Justine held the girl's shoulders and drew her closer. "Max is a viscount's son and you are a viscount's daughter. Max must be prepared for the life he was intended to lead and so must you. If your dear mama had lived I'm certain you would have been brought out this year. But we shall set about preparing for next year. Think about all the excitement that will mean, dearest."

"Brought out?" Ella sounded uninterested.

Risking the result, Justine hugged her new challenge tightly. "If I had had a daughter, I should have wished her to be exactly like you," she said. "Humor me, Ella. Let me fuss over you and enjoy doing for you what I would have done for a daughter of my own."

Ella's sudden, crushing return of her embrace shocked and thrilled Justine.

Then she felt the slight shaking of slender shoulders and grew very still. "What is it?" she asked softly. "Oh, my dear child, do tell me what's wrong."

Ella shook her head against Justine's neck.

"Are you not just a little intrigued at the prospect of pretty new dresses? And balls and routs and musicales and all manner of lovely times? When you ride in Town—in the Park with some handsome young beau, you will ride better than any other girl. And you will be the belle of any ball. I guarantee that you are destined to be an *originale,* my darling girl. Considered, justly, a diamond-of-the-first-water. A toast. We shall have to fight off the suitors."

"No!" Ella dropped her arms and pulled away. Moisture loaded her thick lashes. "Thank you, Justine, but no. My place is wherever Papa is. He needs me."

Justine's heart beat unusually fast. "Your papa will be in London for your Season, Ella. He will want to be and he will want you to find a marvelous husband."

"There is no marvelous husband for me." Color climbed Ella's smooth, tear-streaked cheeks. "There cannot be."

"Of course there is." Perhaps she should not have been so hasty in broaching a subject about which she, personally, knew so little—yet. "And there will be a fine home and, eventually, children of your own."

Ella wiped the backs of her hands across her face and sighed noisily. She walked past Justine and hauled herself up to sit in an ungainly attitude on the edge of the billiard table. "If all this is so desirable," she said. "Why are you not married with a brood of children of your own?"

"It's different—" This was to be expected. An intelligent girl like Ella would be bound to ask such questions. "I shall be blunt. You said I am not a cripple, but you cannot have failed to note my deformity."

"Deformity?" Ella's brow wrinkled. "You limp. That isn't a deformity."

"Ah, my dear, dear, child. How wonderfully kind you are. When I was a young girl I had an accident. I was caught between rocks on the beach not far from Franchot Castle. The tide rushed in and I might have drowned. Instead, the force of the water tore me free and tossed me on the beach—with a terribly injured hip and leg. The result, I assure you, is a deformity."

"Who decided it was? You?"

Justine bit her lip. "This conversation is not about me. It's about you. My life has passed the time when such things as husbands and children are to be considered. Your life is different."

"You are lovely and gracious, Justine. Many men must have paid suit to you. Why would you not have one of them?"

Justine ignored the question. "I don't believe we should shop in Edinburgh, although I'm sure there are fine establishments there. We shall go to London. To the marquess's Hanover Square house. And you shall visit the Franchot home in Pall Mall. There. London, Ella. Think of that."

"London," Ella echoed, lowering her black lashes over her eyes. "Think of that. Did you enjoy your Seasons?"

"I had one Season. It was dreadful." She hadn't intended to say that.

"Why?" Ella frowned at Justine.

Justine gestured helplessly. "My situation was different from yours. Please do not push me further in this."

"You're pushing me."

"You are a child and it's appropriate for you to allow yourself to be guided."

Ella's expression became wistful. "I used to dream of wearing lovely gowns and dancing the waltz."

Hope swelled within Justine. "Of course you did. And now it will become a reality."

"I love music. Yesterday I heard the marquess playing the piano. It was a waltz. Papa told me the marquess composed it himself and it's called 'Young Girls at the Ball.'"

Justine smiled. "Arran has extraordinary talent, but he is very private about it. Your papa plays a fine fiddle, but I'm sure you know that."

"He plays the fiddle for us sometimes," Ella said, a distant smile on her full lips. "The piano also. Papa makes me very happy. To him I am all I should be. He finds no fault with me."

The smile faded from Justine's face. "Of course he finds no fault with you. Who could?"

For a long time Ella was silent. Then she said, "Do you hear from Saber? How is he these days?" The questions were too lightly asked.

Saber Avenall, Justine and Calum's cousin, had made Ella's acquaintance at Franchot. The fact that he had been smitten with the girl was obvious to all. True, the difference in their ages might have seemed extreme at the time, but within a year or so it would have been of no account. Justine, always very fond of Saber and convinced the two would be well matched, had dared to hope they would eventually marry. But Saber had withdrawn his attentions to Ella abruptly and left Franchot shortly afterward. Justine had no idea why and there had been no one to ask.

"Saber has been in India," she said carefully. "He bought a commission last autumn and was eventually posted overseas with his regiment."

"India?" Ella's fingers played over her lips. "Are there battles in India presently?"

Justine drew up her shoulders. "I don't know a great deal about these things. There is talk about increased hostilities there, but I'm sure Saber is safe."

"I wish . . ." Ella averted her face and jumped down from the billiard table. "I hope he will be safe. He is a pleasant man."

"He is indeed. Perhaps he will return in time for your Season next year." Justine calculated how to proceed. Sometimes special conditions justified a small manipulation. "After all, he undoubtedly thinks of you like a sister. He would make a splendid ally in the matter of inquiring into the backgrounds of your suitors. If you decide to go to London after all."

"You think he might be in London when—if I go?"

"Oh, I . . . It's entirely possible."

"Mmm."

She would write to Saber. Why had she not thought of it before?

"I don't know how to dance," Ella said. Her eyes had lost focus. "And I've never even held a fan."

Struan should not have waited so long to take his children in hand. "We shall have you taught to dance. Max, too. It will save time."

"Max!" Ella laughed aloud. "Teach Max to dance? He would rather die."

"He will learn to dance," Justine said firmly. "Don't concern yourself with that. I shall deal with the rest of your training myself."

"Have you ever seen Saber dance?"

Before Justine stood a lovelorn young woman. Why hadn't she suspected the depth of Ella's feelings for Saber? "He dances well. I'm sure he will be happy to share some turns around the floor with you in London." Surely, once they were in Town Ella would meet so many charming and eligible men that she would be distracted from any infatuation with Justine's enigmatic cousin. Of course, if Saber were to put in an appearance and encounter Ella, it was always possible something might rekindle for him also.

"I shall think about it," Ella said. "Papa doesn't believe I should do things I really don't want to do."

Justine inclined her head. "He is a man advanced for his time." In some matters. "Of course, we shall defer to him in this as in all things."

"I promised Kirsty Mercer I'd show her my room here now that it's been made over. Will you excuse me?"

The sudden shift to impeccable politeness wasn't lost on Justine. "Of course."

Ella walked away but stopped at the door and turned back. "Do you think it would please Papa if I decided to be brought out?"

"I do indeed."

"Well, then"—Ella raised her chin—"I shall do it for him."

When the girl had left, her vibrant presence seemed to hover in her wake.

She would "do it for him."

The question was, which him?

And the probable answer disturbed Justine deeply.

"Call me out one more time and I'll accept the challenge," Struan announced, facing off with Calum across the raised lid of the piano Arran had been playing in the window of the gallery that was his music room. "I've taken about as much as I intend to take from you, *friend*."

"The situation here is intolerable," Calum responded, leaning over the exposed movement of the instrument to bring his face close to Struan's. "Four days ago my sister arrived in Scotland with an impeccable reputation. Rather than being made comfortable here at the castle, she was abducted to that damnable lodge by you. And today her name is on the lips of every peasant in the county. I have no doubt that before long all of Edinburgh will be agog at the news of her fall from grace."

"No doubt at all," Arran said pleasantly.

Struan glared at his brother. "She has not fallen from grace," he said. He was exhausted from too little sleep and no longer cared if he maintained cordial relations with Arran or Calum or any other man.

"Tell Justine you want her to leave," Calum demanded.

"Don't tell her any such thing, Struan," Arran said from his seat at the piano. "I forbid you to do so."

"Do as I ask," Calum said. "Word has arrived from Grand-mama. Evidently my poor Philipa crumbled under interrogation and the dowager demands that Justine be returned to her at once."

"Not the best part of the bargain you inherited," Arran remarked, his right hand flying repeatedly up a soaring scale.

"What does that mean?" Calum inquired, frowning deeply.

"Your dear grandmother. Quite a formidable creature, that one."

Calum brought his lips together and his nostrils flared, but he made no argument. Only a year before he had still been Calum Innes, foundling recipient of Rossmara charity since his abandonment in their stable yard as a young child sick unto death. His determined search for his past had led to Franchot Castle in Cornwall and the extraordinary truth that he was, in fact, Etienne Loring Girvin, Duke of Franchot. Stolen from his crib while his mother lay dying, another infant boy had been left in his place. The pretender's mother, the former duke's thwarted lover, planned to use her son to grab control of the Franchot fortune. The rightful heir was to have died, but the woman paid to kill him lost her nerve and eventually discarded him at Kirkcaldy.

Thanks to Calum's persistence, the entire plot failed.

He reclaimed his rightful title and inheritance and the shame the truth had brought the Dowager Duchess of Franchot had not, at first, endeared Calum to her, but she had adjusted to the new order of things remarkably quickly. Justine, so uncannily like him in spirit as well as appearance, had been overjoyed to claim him and be rid of her despicable fake brother.

"The dowager is admirable," Struan felt bound to comment. "No doubt her formidable will is responsible for her remarkable, er, presence." And her tyrannical attitude toward sensitive Justine.

"I have spoken to the minister," Arran said, adding his left hand to his right, experimenting, turning his ear toward the keys. "It's as well you're here, Calum. You can give the bride away and help dispel the rumors of dissension between us."

"They are *not* rumors. There *is* dissension between us."

Struan struggled to hold his temper. "No," he said through his teeth. "There is not dissension between us. And I wish you both to allow me to deal with this matter." He would speak carefully and kindly to Justine and persuade her of the wisdom of her returning to Cornwall.

"Remember how Moggach used to call you a wee upstarty laddie, Calum?" Arran said, smiling to himself and ignoring Struan. "She probably still does."

"I lose no sleep over your appalling staff," Calum said. "Will you do as I ask and inform my sister that you wish her to leave Kirkcaldy."

"No," Arran said. "Under no circumstances will I ever tell such a charming and respected creature—respected by me— that my home is not her home whenever and for as long as she chooses—"

"For *God's* sake," Calum sputtered. "You have become long-winded and totally bloody. If you respect our friendship, you will do as I ask."

"You came into Justine's life rather late, did you not?" Arran said.

"You know I did."

"Hardly surprising she isn't willing to bow before your will like a blade of grass assaulted by a low wind."

"By—" Calum stalked to the white marble fireplace and braced himself by both hands against the mantel. "A *low* wind. Your inference is not lost on me, my lord. The woman is not herself. She believes Struan has need of her with those . . . Give me patience. I speak no ill of the two young ones. They are delightful. But they are not Struan's children."

Arran stopped playing. "A fact that is of far more concern to me than to you," he said. "In time he will have children of his own seed and they, naturally, will be his line. The sooner this farce with the bastards is put to rights, the better."

"*Don't* call them that," Struan said. "And stop talking as if I'm not present. Stop deciding what I shall or shall not do with the rest of my life. Damn it all, you treat me like a child."

"You behave like one," Arran said. "Your charade with Ella and Max is out of hand. How long do you think you can keep people from asking questions? Why is Max an unschooled peasant? And why is Ella allowed to roam free?"

Struan crossed his arms. "I have all that in hand. They led a quiet life with their mother. I do not wish too much thrust upon them too soon. All in good time . . . That sort of thing."

"Poppycock," Arran said. "Then there is this latest development. Preposterous. You know Justine's reputation must be restored at once. There should be no question but that you marry her, and I cannot understand the delay."

"I will not have my sister made the fool," Calum shouted. "She approaches five and thirty. A confirmed spinster. There can be no question of some farcical marriage for the sake of propriety. But she will not listen to me."

"I've sent a letter to Grace," Arran said. "She cannot travel just now, but she will advise me on matters regarding the marriage. It is unfortunate that we cannot wait until she is no longer indisposed."

"Indisposed?" Calum turned to look over his shoulder at Arran. "Grace is ill? Why didn't you say so? How could you leave her at such a time?"

"What's wrong with Grace?" Struan felt sweat break on his brow. "You should have told us at once. We must go to her. What can you be thinking of?"

"Under the circumstances Grace is remarkably well." Arran raised his dark brows. "One does not speak of these things, but Grace and I anticipate the birth of our second child. As you know, she is a little thing, and I do not want her to take any risks. The doctor agreed that she should not travel for some weeks." His handsome face bore the stamp of proud pleasure.

"Congratulations!" Struan leaped to thump Arran on the back. "Another child! You and Grace make me very happy. *Another* child."

"Congratulations," Calum said. "Please tell Grace how delighted Philipa and I are for both of you—for all three of you. But first, please tell my sister she may not remain here."

Struan looked from Arran to Calum and felt an unaccustomed burst of the purest frustration and rage. "*Silence,*" he roared suddenly. "Not another word from either of you. What does or does not happen in the matter of Justine's presence as part of my life—"

"She is not part of your life."

"I warn you, Calum," Struan told him. "My patience wears thin."

"A book," Calum sputtered. "A book for *brides,* no less. A book detailing the intricacies of courtship and marriage! Written with the aid of your instruction. Saints preserve me. That notion paints some pretty pictures, don't y'know?"

"Justine is most sincere about her book," Struan said, despite his own misgivings on the subject.

"You," Calum said, leveling a finger, "will have no part in instructing my sister. Is that understood?"

"No."

"Then I will explain. Give Justine any demonstrations supposedly designed to enlighten her for literary reasons and you shall answer to me."

Arran resumed playing. "Once they're married, it will be up to Struan to decide what demonstrations he gives his bride." He chuckled. "All kinds of possibilities there, old chap."

"Name your seconds," Calum demanded of Arran.

"God help us all," Struan pleaded on his way toward the stairs leading down from the gallery. "We clearly are beyond helping ourselves."

# Chapter Seven

❧

***The Fiddler's Rest,***
***an inn in Dunkeld Village near Castle Kirkcaldy***

If hate had a smell, the air would reek of that odor. Hate, disgust, and the driving need for revenge. A deadly mixture.

Seated alone in a corner, all but hidden by shadow, he breathed in the fetid aroma of old ale, rancid food, and unwashed bodies—and waited for one whose appetite for vindication might even exceed his own.

A shadow passed across the table. "If we meet again, you will not know me," said the second man to arrive as he slid onto a bench. "Away with you," he snarled at a serving girl who approached.

The other rocked forward over his ale, one of too many he'd swallowed that evening. Rather than lift the measure, he clutched the edge of the table and sucked noisily at the rim of his pewter tankard. Less spilled that way. He wiped his mouth on the back of a sleeve and muttered, "I've not seen you, friend." Honest enough. The agreement had been that they would come and go to the appointed table, neither man looking upon the other. Not that his vision was what it had been when he'd entered this devil's hole.

Acrid smoke from the tavern fire curled about the drunken company. The hour was not late, yet raucous shouts and screams erupted in bursts. Disheveled wenches rolled from one pair of groping hands to another, giggling, and delving to retrieve coins pressed between their near-naked breasts.

"Let's be done with this." With each tankard, his tongue became thicker, as did his brain. Best come to a final agreement while he was still conscious—particularly since the newcomer had refused any drink. "What d'you want of me?"

"Listen," the second man ordered grimly. "You should know things have changed, become more urgent."

"How so?" His fingers threatened to slide away from the table's edge.

"He's got his claws into someone else. Another female."

"Who—"

"No matter who. If she remains, we'll use her to our own advantage. The more he has to lose, the better. He is already afraid. I have made certain of that."

He felt disoriented, sullen. "So, what d'you want of me?"

"Your word."

"On what?"

"I think you know. You will do as I have asked you to do. No questions. No changing your mind, regardless of what happens. You're my man to the end."

"Promised you as much already." He raised a wavering hand and stirred the brew in his tankard with one long finger. "That whore's s-son robbed me."

"He robbed us both. He's got to be made to pay."

"S'right." His head grew too heavy. "Tormented as we've been tormented. And I'm tired of waiting."

"The wait is all but over. The time for action is upon us. All you need do is listen a little longer for my word. Be vigilant. Be ready. Give me your hand on it and we'll never speak each other's names or meet again."

Their fingers touched, passed over palms, pressed briefly and withdrew.

If the eyes were the mirror of the soul, they were strangers in spirit. Strangers with a single wish—satisfaction—and the greater the cost to Struan, Viscount Hunsingore, the better.

By the time Struan rode into the stable yard at the lodge night had fallen. After leaving Arran and Calum to their bickering over what he should do with his life, he'd spent the afternoon going about the estates with Caleb Murray. Then he'd visited tenants, particularly Robert Mercer, whose help in recent weeks had been invaluable.

After the arrival of the first letter, and at Struan's request, Robert had recruited a band of loyal men to watch over Ella and Max while they wandered free during the daylight hours. Struan had needed only to say that he feared an old enemy. It had been Robert's idea that the children should spend their nights where none would think to look for them—in the tiny cottage he shared with Gael and their two little ones.

A boy Struan recognized from the castle stables ran out to catch the horse's bridle and hold the animal steady while Struan dismounted.

Deeply disturbed by the idea of so many knowing where he was living, he nodded to the boy and began drawing off his gloves as he approached the kitchens. Habit kept him entering by that route and he saw no reason to alter the routine. With luck his enemy might have no knowledge of the changes that had taken place here in the past few days.

Struan went into the kitchens—gleaming now in the light of freshly tended candle brackets. Pots and pans hung in resplendent brilliance before the great hearth where fresh venison had once turned upon the spit. The table and draining boards had been scrubbed white and the flagstones still smelled of the turpentine, soap, and pipe clay with which they'd been rendered to a pale shine.

All very appropriate. And all very dangerous.

In the wake of Justine's whirlwind efforts, Ella and Max were now permanently in residence. Not a comfortable thought. At least he'd been able to arrange, without difficulty, for a watch upon the lodge around the clock.

He entered the curving passageway leading up to the main floor of the building and took a flight of stairs two at a time. There had been no further letters since the one he'd received on the night of Justine's arrival.

That fact should bring him comfort.

It made his skin crawl.

Since they'd started arriving, never more than two days had passed between the letters—until now. The only reason for the interval that made sense was that the change in his circumstances was, indeed, known. Somewhere out there the faceless man might, at this very moment, be poised to strike.

Struan felt sweat on his brow and wiped at it angrily. Why didn't the swine ask for what he wanted? Why didn't he arrange a meeting? What kind of coward hid behind nameless threats?

All but the last question were mysteries.

The coward was potentially dangerous—potentially deathly.

The lodge was still. All the servants save Mairi had returned to their quarters at the castle, and the tenant helpers were long since back in their homes.

He would ensure Justine, Ella, and Max—and Mairi—were safe in bed, then station himself where he could watch their doors and listen for any sound of intruders. In the morning he'd return to Kirkcaldy and find a place to sleep undisturbed.

Caleb Murray, a man of few words but considerable efficiency, could be trusted to do what must be done with very little instruction from Struan. And after all, dear Arran—he who was head of the household—was in residence.

The lodge was barely recognizable. It *wasn't* recognizable. In his entire life the place had never looked as it did tonight. Despite fatigue and the daunting hours that lay ahead, he smiled. Lady Justine Girvin was a determined woman. Determined to put his present home and the rest of his life to rights. How damnably unfortunate there could be no question of his accepting her attention permanently.

A scowl replaced the smile. He couldn't have her, but neither would he allow either Calum or Arran to think they had the right to decide his future.

The chambers he sought were on the floor above the great hall. He climbed the stairs quickly and tapped on Ella's door. When he got no reply, he peeked inside and saw a dark braid snaking over white linen.

In the next room Max slept in his customary state—wound about by sheets, his arms and legs outflung.

Struan approached a larger room that had an adjoining sitting room. These were Justine's quarters—or so he'd been told.

The door stood open.

His night would be easier if he didn't have to see her, to talk to her—to hear her talk.

To avoid her completely was unthinkable.

"Justine," he called softly. "May I come in?"

A lamp glowed and he could see the bed had not been touched. She must be in her sitting room. Probably couldn't sleep. These times were difficult for her also. The rage he'd felt too often of late surfaced again. How dare any man or woman speak against one so pure?

He spoke louder. "Justine. It's Struan."

Only silence.

His belly clenched. What if the madman who had been stalking him had already struck?

Struan entered a bedchamber hung with dark-blue velvet and crossed a beautiful gold and blue Spanish carpet. A door to the left of the fireplace led to a sitting room—also blue; also empty.

Both rooms were cold. She hadn't been here for some time.

Hurrying, Struan retraced his steps and started for the end of the corridor and another staircase that led up to servant quarters where Mairi had been given a room.

He paused. If he awakened her and raised the alarm unnecessarily, there was a danger that more talk would spread among the castle staff. The children—whom he'd so far managed to convince that nothing was truly amiss—might hear that talk and become afraid.

Struan made a systematic search of every room on this floor, then went down to the great hall. Sparklingly clean but empty splendor met him there. He returned to the circular vestibule. Opposite the stairs that led to the bedrooms he'd just left, a second, spiraling flight of stone steps rose to his grandfather's prized covered bridge. Struan's apartments were in the pagoda on the opposite side of the bridge.

Justine would never go there uninvited.

There was no alternative but to rouse Mairi and get more help to probe every nook and cranny of the sprawling building.

Before he did so, he must be certain all the threatening letters were safely locked from sight. There must be no question of Arran or Calum happening upon them if they decided to search his rooms—exactly the first thing Calum might do unless Struan was much mistaken.

Struan's boots rang on the stone steps and on the yellow mosaic tile floor of the bridge. Through the row of narrow windows on either side he saw only blackness. There would be no moon tonight—to hinder or to help him.

An anteroom led to his own bedchamber. He was already marching past flanking glass-fronted cases where his grandfather's collection of European silver was displayed when he heard a sound. The unmistakable sound of scraping overhead.

Another flight of stairs led from the anteroom to what had once been a hideaway for the lodge's first owner.

Struan thought of Justine's leg. So much walking and climbing should be beyond her.

The scraping noise could have been made by someone far less welcome.

Armed with the small but deadly dagger he'd taken to keeping about him, he stealthily ascended the staircase.

*Humming.*

He stopped just short of the entrance to an odd room with tapestry-hung walls and a painted ceiling that looped to a soaring point beneath the dome of the pagoda.

Someone was humming, and he knew who that someone was.

If it didn't beat all. Spinster Lady Justine Girvin making free with a man's rooms!

He edged forward until he could see the entire room—and the woman who sat at an outrageous marble-topped Egyptian writing table. Legs fashioned from ebony into sinuous naked female forms with large, upthrust breasts supported the table. Struan winced. Undoubtedly—and fortunately—the lady had failed to notice such details.

Dressed in a high-necked, elegantly flowing poppy-colored silk robe, Justine propped her brow on the heel of one hand. And hummed. Struan recognized the strains of a Scottish song about a lassie waiting for her warrior husband to return from the battlefield. Justine hummed and swayed a little and wrote in a large, leather-bound journal.

Struan stepped into the doorway and leaned on the jamb, watching.

The song and whatever Justine wrote engrossed her beyond

noticing the approach of a mere man. He could not contain his smile. Ribbons of creamy satin closed the robe. Her hair was still drawn up to her crown, but swathes of curls had slipped free to lie against her neck and spill over a shoulder.

He rested a hand on his hip.

The ceiling above her head was painted in brilliant stripes, like the fabric of a Moorish tent. Everything else in the room was Egyptian. Golden serpents, their heads forming the ends of the arms, wound their way around mahogany chairs upholstered with scarlet damask. Between the chairs a circular leather-topped table dripped more gold serpents down its central pedestal. Struan steeled himself to look at the secretaire. Taller than himself, rows of figures decorated its doors and drawers, rows of figures encrusted with carnelian and lapis, with emeralds for eyes . . . and ivory penises . . . the men, that was. Rubies marked strategic spots on the women, and the whole formed an erotic depiction of a riotous orgy.

And Justine hummed.

And wrote.

Struan shifted his weight and leaned on the opposite doorjamb. Her cheek showed smooth, the bone high and touched by the crescent shadow of her thick lashes. Justine's mouth wasn't the mouth of a spinster lady. Too full. Too wide. Too made for laughter . . . and other things.

If she caught sight of him without warning she'd probably faint from shock.

With regret, he made a move backward.

"Oh!" Her head snapped up. "Oh, Struan, I did not expect you to return so soon."

"I've been standing here for some time." Watching her. Listening to her hum. Wanting to touch her. He swallowed and stood upright. "You should be in your bed."

Justine stared at him, her dark eyes troubled. "I've angered you? By coming here?"

"Surprised me."

"I'm sorry." She fiddled with the lid of the standish. "I'd been wandering. Looking for a place where I thought I could work well. I found this wonderful room. But I'd intended to return to my apartments long before you arrived home. I suppose I became too engrossed."

"This place is approached through the anteroom to my chambers, Justine."

"Is it?" She appeared stricken. "Oh, my, what must you think of me?"

He thought her lovely. Not beautiful or pretty. Not adorable as was the fashion in the young things paraded each year in the marriage mart they called the Season. Lovely. Justine had the quality of a piece of art that grew from the artist's pure joy in his work.

And her very purity and the inner perfection he felt in her made Struan burn to unravel the woman, to bring the female to writhing life like the jewel-studded creatures contorted on the secretaire.

Struan wanted to possess and mold Justine. Struan wanted to make her into a carnal thing who reveled in being a woman—with him.

"I lied," she murmured.

He looked at her lips. Where they remained slightly parted, the soft flesh was moist. "Did you?" he asked her.

"Yes. It isn't like me to lie. I hoped to see you tonight. I wore such inappropriate dress so that I could pretend I intended to be in my bed before you came back to the lodge."

Her gaze remained lowered. She passed her tongue over her mouth. Moist. Twined together on top of the book, her slim hands were pale. Her throat was pale.

Beneath the poppy-colored robe and whatever nightgown she wore, her breasts would be pale, the nipples pink—like her moist lips. Pink, and they, too, would be moist when he drew each one into his mouth.

"I have really angered you." She began to get up.

Struan drew in a sharp breath. "Sit," he said curtly. "Sit at once. You've already done far too much."

She was Justine, for God's sake. Untouched. Untouched Justine, his old friend's sister.

"I was wrong," she said, slipping back onto her chair. "I've never been able to lie and get away with it. I've always had to confess the lie and apologize. I do apologize."

Struan wrinkled his brow. "You hardly seem to have committed a great crime."

"I have been bold." She blushed delightfully. "I wanted you to find me here."

He inclined his head. "I see."

"And I wasn't actually wandering around looking for a place to write."

"I see."

"I already knew this was here."

"I see."

"Mmm. Yes, well—I also knew I would be coming through the anteroom to your chambers if I came here."

"I see."

Her smooth brow puckered. "And what do you think about that?"

"Nothing. Except I'd like to know why."

"To be certain we got the chance to speak alone and without interruption."

Oh, how very potentially unwise the lady was. "I see." What would she say if she could see inside his voluptuary's mind at this moment?

"Nothing has changed," she murmured.

He nodded while he tried to marshal his defenses against her allure. For her sake he could not give in to wanting her.

"I am here to help you, Struan. And in return, I hope you will help me."

"I see."

"Sin's ears! Can't you say anything but 'I see'?"

He arched his brows. "Why, Justine, I don't think I've ever heard you raise your voice before." But he had always known there was spirit here. "This 'sin's ears" business is definitely not refined."

"Pah! Neither is 'bloody hell' refined. You men say such words without a thought. As I have already intimated, I have simply invented my own note of exquisite ire, and it has great possibilities."

Confounded, Struan scrubbed his jaw and said, "I see."

"Sin's eyeballs. I have never before known you to be reduced to two silly little words. A change of subject before I am entirely separated from my patience. Are we agreed that in return for my overseeing your household and children you will help me with my book?"

"Your brother threatened me with bodily harm if I do so." The possibility of her own bodily harm had more power to frighten him.

She played with her pen before saying, "Leave my brother to me."

"He wishes to take you back to Cornwall."

"I do not wish to go."

Struan walked to stand before the writing table. "You don't feel you should obey his wishes—and your grandmother's?" How much fewer his problems would become if she did.

"At my age?" She laughed. "No, Struan. I have spent my life bending to the will of others. The time has come for me to please myself."

What would really please her?

And was he totally unbalanced? He should be trying, as carefully as possible, to urge her to leave. But he couldn't find the words. She looked at him with such hope, with such trust that he wanted her to stay as much as she obviously wanted it herself. And he did. But she couldn't.

Yes, he was unbalanced. The strain of the past weeks had

loosened his mind. And it had been too long since he spent himself with a woman—an annoyance that should be dealt with, and soon.

He could not upset her at such a late hour. "You should go to your bed now." In the morning he would do what must be done.

"Of course." She began to rise again.

"Sit down."

Justine bit into her soft bottom lip and did as he requested.

"Was there anything else you wished to discuss with me?" he asked.

"The matter of the suggestion that you and I should marry."

"I see . . . Aha. Yes."

"Do not give it another thought. Your brother is a very honorable man and acts accordingly."

Struan rested his thighs against the table. "And *I* am not an honorable man?"

"Oh, but of course you are!" Justine made to get up but quickly dropped down again. "The most honorable of men. That is why I am so drawn to you . . . I mean, that is why I admire you so very . . . Oh, dear, I am not good with words sometimes. I consider you very honorable."

"I see."

"I doubt if you see anything at all!"

He looked into her eyes. "I see you, my dear. I see you remarkably well." Even while his world fell in shreds about him he saw Justine with devastating clarity.

"Yes." She looked down at her book again. "I have begun my work."

"I . . . Yes, I rather thought that's what you were doing. You seemed very engrossed."

"I haven't progressed far."

"How will you organize the piece?"

Justine held her tongue between her teeth and frowned. "Why are you holding a knife?"

Struan started. He'd forgotten the damn thing. Sheathing it quickly in the narrow pouch at the small of his back, he shrugged his coat more comfortably on his shoulders. No lie at all was required of him. "I heard movement up here and feared an intruder. It is wise to be armed for such possibilities."

"And there was an intruder," Justine said, smiling. "Thank goodness you did not need the knife to deal with me."

"No, a knife is not what I should choose to employ with you." He must watch his mouth. "Tell me about your work. Perhaps I can give you some small assistance before I escort you back to your rooms."

She took a deep breath and Struan visualized again the rise of pale, entirely female flesh. He narrowed his eyes upon her face.

"I intend," she told him, "to organize my work into main sections, with small segments within those sections."

"And how have you begun?"

"With"—she coughed—"with the meeting when the suitor makes his very first overtures to the female."

Oh, God. "Are you pleased with your efforts?"

"Um . . . I haven't written them yet."

"You were writing when I came in."

"An explanation of my intentions for the book." She leaned earnestly forward. "This will be very useful for Ella, you know. Today I think I persuaded her to let me prepare her for the London Season next year."

"I see." The mire he'd made for himself only got deeper. How could Ella make a debut without the truth about her background—her lack of background—becoming public knowledge? He had kept so many secrets from so many different people, and now they all threatened to unravel at the worst possible time.

"Yes, well"—Justine was looking at him strangely—"I'm sure you'll appreciate what I mean about the book being helpful when the time comes. I thought I'd begin each segment with a scene. A sort of example of what to expect. That way the result should be to eliminate fear of the event."

"Innovative," Struan said, amazed he could still form words at all.

"Perhaps the first scene should be at a ball. The man has already seen the girl and finds a way to make his interest known to her."

"Reasonable place to begin."

"You think so?" Her smile was radiant. "Oh, good. Let me make a note of that." She wrote for several moments. "He dances with her and returns her to her chaperon. Then he dances with her again. Not too soon, of course. Not on the first occasion. At the next meeting, he openly monopolizes her dance card as much as possible."

"Sounds . . . reasonable."

"What does he do next?"

Struan rolled in his lips.

"After all the dancing? When he wants to make a suitable overture to the young lady? What does he do?"

"You never experienced this yourself?"

Justine bowed her head. "No."

"I see."

"Do you?" Her face came up and there was fire in her eyes now.

"Probably not," Struan said, shaking his head. "It's difficult for a man to understand how any lovely woman escapes even the simple niceties of courtship. The man would find a way to be alone with the girl, Justine."

She frowned and dunked her pen repeatedly in the standish. "So soon?"

"He could hardly make any sort of . . . He'd have to be alone with the girl to let her know what he felt."

Justine wiped the excess ink from her nib and jotted more notes.

"He might find a way to take her into a salon . . . or a study, perhaps. Somewhere he could close the door and be assured of privacy."

"Without her chaperon?"

"Without her chaperon. The girl would like the thrill of it all, don't you see? The danger. The fact that the man—who has been the soul of propriety to this point—is risking censure shows how desperately he wants her."

"Yes," she said slowly. "Yes, I suppose you're right."

"You should inform your readers that this is an excellent opportunity for the young lady to gauge the true character of the man."

Justine frowned again.

"By his restraint," Struan explained.

She continued to frown.

Gently, he took the pen from her fingers and set it down. "Observe," he told her. "Put your hands in mine."

He held out his own hands and, hesitantly, she rested her fingers on his palms. Struan bent to rest his mouth on the tender place between her thumb and forefinger.

He felt her shudder.

His eyes closed. He was an experienced man, yet his blood pumped because a woman shuddered when he kissed her hand.

Incredible.

Slowly, he brushed his lips over her knuckles. At the same time, he played his fingertips up and down the tendons on the soft undersides of her wrists.

And she shuddered, and shuddered. "And this . . . would be . . . appropriate?" she murmured. "Or should the young lady discourage such attention?"

"Not if she likes the man. Not if she likes what he's doing."

"Yes, of course that would be the case."

Releasing her took control. "You'd better make note of that," he told her, aware of a thickening in his voice.

Justine's breasts rose and fell. "Yes," she said, taking up the pen once more, a dazed expression on her face. "Yes. I shall make a note or two now and be more specific later. I mustn't press you for too much help all at once."

*Preserve him.* Someone, anyone, give him strength. "We could do a little more work tonight, if you like. Or are you too tired?"

"No! That is, no. I'd be very grateful for your insights."

Ah, yes, his insights. His insights were making him damnably uncomfortable. He sat on the edge of the table. "Imagine if you will that this is a study in a grand house where a large ball is in progress. You are a woman being courted by a man. He has alerted you to his interest. He has, perfectly appropriately, kissed your hands."

Justine's hands clenched. She put the pen down once more.

"The man would want to tell the woman something of his feelings," Struan pointed out. "If he were sincere, that is."

"Oh, he must be sincere. I shall emphasize that unless he says something appropriate, she should turn him aside at once."

"Quite." He lifted a heavy escaped curl behind her shoulder. "When I look at you I almost believe there is true goodness in the world."

Her lips parted and remained parted. Struan saw her pupils dilate.

"I am the suitor," he told her.

Justine nodded. "Oh. Oh, yes."

"The first time I saw you, my heart stopped beating. You stood there, tall and graceful and . . . *distinguished.* I had never before looked at a woman and thought her distinguished and utterly desirable at the same time."

"I see," she whispered.

"Since that moment I have dreamed of this moment. I didn't expect it to come, but I dreamed nevertheless. Is that . . . Do you mind that I thought of you that way?"

"I . . . No. I'm glad you did. I thought of you that way, too."

His heart did stand still—just for an instant. He must remember that this was playacting for her. "I have longed to do this." His hand shook a little when he touched her face. While she stared, wide-eyed, at him he rested his fingers on her jaw, gently slipped them over satin-smooth skin to sink into her hair. "I look at you and I see hope. I see what I thought for so long could never be mine."

"Such beautiful words," she breathed. "Such feeling."

Gradually, he lowered his face toward her and saw her eyes slowly close. Her lips, when he touched them with his own, were warm and sweet—and moist. Careful of the slightest movement, he made no attempt to part her lips farther. Instead he kissed her as he might have had it been his first kiss, and she a girl being kissed for the first time. He kissed her with his heart and soul and it was the sweetest thing, sweeter with the years of his experience and the power of his restrained mastery, than any first kiss could be.

Justine's breath caressed his face. He breathed her in, and gave himself back to her. In her innocence, she reached to mirror what he did, smoothing her cool hands along his jaw and winding her fingers into his hair. With her face turned trustingly up to his, she gave what she could not possibly know or understand.

He must stop. Now. Forcing a smile, he pulled away. "Shall you have difficulty putting that into words?"

Pink flooded her cheeks. Candlelight picked out hints of red in the curls that had now entirely fallen from their coiffure. She looked young, eager, quite kissed—and ready for far more.

"Justine?"

"I shall write it all down," she said, glancing away.

"Good."

"Thank you for taking my work seriously."

He had never taken any work more seriously. At this moment—with a more experienced woman—he would hesitate to stand unless he wanted her to know his shaft sprang hard with desire for her.

"Thank you," Justine repeated, closing her book and gathering it to her breast. "Thank you so much."

And Struan knew it was just a beginning.

The beginning of heaven?

The beginning of hell?

"The pleasure, I assure you, is entirely mine." And with this pleasure, pain was almost certain to follow.

# Chapter Eight

❦

Glory Willing returned the lascivious wink of the coachman who handed her down at the Fiddler's Rest. She was the only remaining passenger on the Edinburgh–to–Dunkeld Village run, but the customary blare of a bugle met their arrival nevertheless.

Shouting boys ran forward to divest the coach of its cargo of goods and mail from Edinburgh. The horses steamed and snorted in the lamplight and a pall of smoke from the inn chimneys hung over all.

At the stops the coach had made along the way, Glory had made certain her gaze lingered on the bulky coachman until sweat broke out on his brow and his thick tongue made urgent forays over his lips.

As he helped her to the roughly cobbled inn yard, he contrived to tip her close enough to brush her against his rotund body. He guffawed and spread a hand boldly over her breast.

"You overstep yourself a bit, sir," she said, taking her bearings. From what she could see in the near-darkness, the Fiddler's Rest exactly matched the description she'd been given. Glory covered the man's squeezing hand. "You come this way often, then?" she asked him.

"Often enough," he said, grinning broadly now. "I makes the run from Edinburgh to Dunkeld every week or so. Never remember carrying a female the likes o' you before, though."

She smiled up into his red face. "I'll not be staying in these parts long. I'm to move on a bit, see. I've been offered a place at a fine house. But I might have use for a man such as yourself." Under the cover of her cloak, she found his bulging rod. "If you know what I mean."

He groaned and leaned closer. "Why not now? We could find a place easy enough. Wait for the 'orses ter be changed and we'll leave the village a spell. The coach is comfort enough for what we 'ave in mind."

Glory ignored the snickers of passing post boys. "I fancy that, too," she said, and tucked his hand inside her straining bodice. His groping and panting quickened the need that never quite left her belly. "There isn't time. I'm expected here. Give me a way that I can get word to you. And when I do, be ready to take us away where we can be alone. All alone. I like more space than a coach. There are things I know that can keep a man very happy for as long as he can spare."

They held still while the team from the coach was led by. Too spent to do more than blow, their hoofs clopped wearily on the cobbles. Glory wrinkled her nose at the ripe scents in the yard. Her days amid the straw in stable lofts were past, and she didn't mourn them.

"I can't wait fer ye," the coachman said.

"You'll have to. How can I send for you in Edinburgh?"

Glory saw a shadow separate from a dim corner of the yard. A man, his right arm upraised. It was the sign.

"I have to go now," she told the coachman. "Give me an address. Quickly."

"The Running Footman," he said, pinching her nipple.

"Every man knows the place. Hard by the market in Old Town. 'Ave one of the lads 'ere bring me word and I'll come for ye in this yard four days after—of this time of a night—or as close in day and time as I can. It'd be a day later mayhap, but not a day before."

"And you are?" She rubbed the swollen handful inside his rough wool breeches.

"Len Bottwell. They all knows me."

With a theatrical sigh, Glory stepped away. "Until we make our rendezvous, then, Len Bottwell. Be sure you think of me."

"I won't stop thinkin' of ye. Who should I be expectin' to 'ear from?"

"A lady. You'll get a message from a lady and you'll know to come."

"Well . . . Fair enough, then, *lady*. I'll be waitin'."

Glory dimpled at him and sped lightly over the cobbles to the place where a boy stood beside her trunk. With a single backward glance at Len Bottwell—a possible boon in future plans—she waved for the boy to carry the trunk into the inn.

"Ye can go in by the front door," the lad said in the Scottish brogue Glory found irritating. "I'll tak' this to your accommodations direct."

"I'd like that," Glory told him, pressing a coin into his palm. "Tell the innkeeper it's Mrs. Smith who's arrived. Remind him that the best room in the house was reserved for me and my husband."

Ducking his head, mumbling thanks, the boy struggled into the building under the considerable weight of Glory's trunk. She pretended to fuss with her reticule, glancing to be certain the coachman no longer watched. He was in conversation with the farrier and the two walked toward the smithy's shop.

"Come closer."

The familiar voice had lost none of its power to thrill her. Glory stepped into the black shade close to the inn and a hand closed on her arm.

"There's a room," she said breathlessly. "I'll go and—"

"You'll do nothing until I tell you to do so. And you will call me by no name other than the one we have used on previous occasions. And you'll offer no opinions, Glory."

"But I—"

"Silence." His fingers dug into her arm—jerked her deeper into the shadows. He said, *"Whore,"* and thrust her against the rough wall.

"I didn't have to come," she whined.

"Didn't you?"

Fear, an old, never-to-be-forgotten fear, curled about Glory's heart. She tentatively said, "No. I came because I wanted to help you."

"Liar," he said, bringing his face close to hers. "You have no choice but to do as I tell you. You will never have any choice. *I* am your master. *I* own you. *I* can decide if you live or die."

Glory's blood pumped in her ears. Even as he uttered the words he'd used over and over through the years, words that meant he could be planning to prove his domination over her, the place at her center burned hot and wet with need.

"They're keeping a room—"

"I have no interest in a room here, you fool. I am known."

"Yes, but—"

"Dear God! I see I must teach you again who it is who makes decisions in this matter. There is no one in these parts who would not take note of seeing me in your company. The ends we desire would be lost forever."

Glory trembled. She touched his sleeve tentatively. "I'm very glad to see you . . . Mr. Smith. I've missed you."

He laughed, an awful, cold laugh. "Missed me so much you rutted with a foul, bloated coachman to help pass your journey?"

"No!" She tried to pull away. "No. I swear I didn't. There's no man for me but you. You know that."

At least his blow to her mouth was delivered with an open

hand—an open hand that smothered her scream and ground her head into the wattled wall.

"You rutted with him," he said. "Nod your head and confess it."

Stunned, tasting her own blood, Glory shook her head. She knew the rules. No matter how badly he hurt her, she must deny ever bedding another man.

"I saw you leaning on him. I heard him groan. Tell me you didn't have him by the cock. Tell me you weren't letting him touch you."

Again she shook her head.

"Filth," he hissed. "Filthy whore. I have no time for your lies. We have work to do. Come. You shall tell me what I want to know soon enough."

She knew better than to argue. She also knew a moment's wild panic. He sounded—*desperate*? That was new. Mr. Smith never lost control, never made a move he didn't intend to make, and never failed to be certain he would prevail.

He pulled her arm through his and told her, "Look down. Keep your face down and say nothing until I order you to do so."

Swelling thickened her lower lip. It wasn't like him to mark her face. While he hurried her between the main inn and an outbuilding, she kept her eyes on the shiny cobblestones.

The ground beneath her feet became more uneven, and she stumbled. A whip-tense arm shot around her waist and she was borne along at a great pace to a gig and pair tethered at the side of the deeply rutted lane.

"Mr. Smith?—"

"Get in."

He didn't attempt to help her scramble into the open carriage. "My trunk."

"Your trunk will be retrieved soon enough," he said, untying the pair and leaping up beside her. "You will have no need of it tonight."

Glory shivered, but she also smiled—and winced at the pulling apart of split skin on her lip. "We are about to come into our own," she said. "At last. I cannot tell you how I look forward to what lies ahead."

"I told you to be silent."

She knew better than to press him.

The small carriage swayed and rattled, its wheels grinding over rocky earth. The pair, both black, ran gamely. There was no moon, and with only one small lantern lighted, the cattle seemed to draw their burden into a cavern fashioned from trees that met overhead and dense hedgerows that all but touched the conveyance on either side.

Glory could not guess how much time passed while they traveled. She clung to the seat with both hands, fighting off the exhaustion of days on the road since she left Bath in response to a summons she could not ignore.

What felt like many miles of lanes gave way to a track that rose steadily into hilly country. The scents were of damp earth and furze. By day the heathland would be ablaze with yellow blossoms.

"Our destination," Mr. Smith said.

The sudden breaking of the silence jolted Glory fully awake. She looked around but could make out no dwelling. "Where?"

He chuckled softly. "Where I have made a place for my pleasure. Where I go when I am thought to be elsewhere."

The smoke-black sky pressed the hills' looming outlines. Glory peered, but saw nothing.

An abrupt downward drop threw her against the back of the seat. She screamed.

Her companion laughed loudly and fought to control the horses.

"Runaway!" Glory clutched at his arm.

He threw her off and worked the pair in another sharp turn,

this one to the left. "Whoa," he called, drawing back on the reins.

The horses clattered to a halt. Gasping, her heart still thundering, Glory clung to the side of the coach.

All of her questions were answered within minutes when she'd been pulled to the ground and beneath a rock ledge. "Nothing to be seen from the track above," Mr. Smith said shortly. "There's a cave here. Abandoned hideaway. Probably a battle refuge. Meant for someone of high rank, unless I miss my mark. Whoever used it last must have left in a hurry. We won't be uncomfortable. Neither will our future guests."

A gusty wind plucked at Glory's skirts. She saw where a black hole opened into the rock face under the cover of the overhanging ledge. "I don't like it here."

"You'll change your mind about that soon enough. We both know you will."

She tutted petulantly. "Does that mean you're going to be nice to me at last?"

"Very nice." He finished securing the horses, lifted a valise from the carriage, and unhooked the lantern. "We have work to do before the dawn—a great deal of work."

"Work?"

"Things have not progressed exactly as I expected. Unfortunate. All was perfect until a short while ago. There's been a complication. You're here to help me overcome that complication. But you must know every step to take. You'll do only what I tell you to do—when I tell you to do it. That will mean your close attention to every detail I tell you."

Glory yawned, and touched her lip carefully. "I thought all I had to do was go to his house and tell him what we want."

Mr. Smith held the lantern aloft. His face showed as a slanted, demoniacal mask. "Do you know what we want? Have you any idea how much we want?"

"Lots," she told him, and giggled.

"Get inside." He pushed her head down and thrust her into the black space. Once inside with her, he caught up a rope and dragged a bail of straw and branches into the entrance behind him. "Now there can be absolutely no danger of our being noticed."

Glory cast about. Shapes hung on all sides. "I don't like it here, I tell you."

"So you've already said." Carrying the lantern, he lighted several others balanced in niches high on the sloping walls.

Wide-eyed, Glory watched yellow light leap over heaps of wooden boxes, straw pallets covered with rich tartan cloth and sheepskins, a line of dusty green wine flagons in wicker skins. More sheepskins covered much of the floor of the cave. A flattopped sea chest surrounded by moth-eaten woolen pillows bore a weight of books and a supply of writing materials.

She glanced up at the roof. "I don't like it." They were under the hills. All that rock up there and all around them. "I don't want to stay here."

Mr. Smith hefted the valise onto one of the rude beds. He produced a slender bottle of dark fluid, several jars of salve, white cloths, and a pair of leather gloves. He closed away the rest of whatever the case contained.

Glory's uneasiness swelled until she clamped her hands over her ears. "Let me out of here," she demanded. "Let me out, I tell you."

Mr. Smith faced her. "Take off your clothes."

She giggled and hiccuped. "It's cold." Her breath came in shallow bursts.

He crossed his arms and came toward her. "You won't be cold for long."

Delaying would be pointless. Her gown was expensive and she didn't want it ruined by his careless tearing. Glory ran her tongue over her lips and drew off her cloak.

"Hurry. I've already told you we've got a lot to do."

He puzzled her, confused her, but that was part of what excited her about him—the mystery. "New things?" She turned for him to help her with her dress.

"Did you pack the gray gown I told you to bring?"

She pouted and stepped out of her favorite dark-purple carriage dress. "I wore this to please you. I thought you'd like it."

He spun her around, tossing the garment to the floor as he did so. "The gray? Is it in the trunk?"

"You'll ruin my—"

"The *gray?*" Another open-handed blow snapped her face away from him. He slapped her again and even as she cried out she tasted fresh blood. "The gray gown, Glory?"

"Yes! Stop it!"

"Soon enough. You'll soon understand why I must do this."

Her head throbbed. His fingernails had caught the corner of her left eye and she felt more blood oozing from a stinging scratch.

"I don't like this."

"For God's sake. Keep your mouth shut. The sooner I do what must be done, the sooner we will both be happy, my dove."

Glory dropped her hands to her sides. *My dove.* The words had always been a sign between them. They meant he wanted her in his special way—the way he liked best.

Glory liked being his dove.

"Drink this down." He uncorked the bottle. With one hand behind her neck, he tipped the dark liquid into her mouth. When she choked and pushed at him he forced her head farther back and kept pouring until the vial was empty. "You will be glad of it," he told her.

Still coughing, Glory wiped at her mouth and hunched over.

While she struggled to breathe, clever hands deftly stripped her.

"Stop," she muttered, batting at him. "I didn't like that."

He smiled, and while he smiled he pulled on the leather gloves. "You don't like a great deal tonight, Glory. I'll just have to find something you do like—later."

Her eye was swelling. She blinked to see more clearly. Why wasn't he touching her?

Glory supported her heavy breasts in her hands and swayed, inviting him . . .

"Nice," he said. "Later they'll be nice."

"Now," she said. She said the word but she didn't say it. The word echoed inside her head, but the sound that came from her mouth was a gurgle.

Heat flashed. Her jaw sagged. "Can't . . . Can't."

Mr. Smith's face changed shape. Eyes and mouth melted downward, and his nose. She blinked. Weakness slid along her muscles and she staggered. She was drugged.

His gloved fists, thumping into her shoulders, threw her to the ground.

Leather gloves. Rough leather gloves with heavily stitched seams that tore into delicate skin.

Melting. More melting. She was melting into the sheepskin, into the rock beneath, into the dark mass below.

Pain burst through her again and again. Where did it come from? This wasn't what he did when he called her *my dove*.

Her back and arms seemed to melt from suffering. Her buttocks felt beaten as if with a whip.

Rolling and more beating. And more. Then back on her face on the skins.

She couldn't move. There was a thudding in her flesh and agony in a body no longer her own.

Something was not right. Not . . . right.

# Chapter Nine

***T**he kiss.*
He had kissed her, Justine, she who had never been kissed before. And she had liked it. No. She had loved it more than anything that had ever happened to her in all her thirty-five years.

All those sensations!

The trembling in unmentionable places!

Places she couldn't mention because she didn't know what they were . . . But she would find out. Oh, there would be no holding back. She was becoming a woman of the world, and the price for enjoying that state was to ensure that all other women knew how to find and use it adequately.

Justine crossed her hands on her breast and stared up at the blue velvet bed canopy. Was this wrong? Potentially wrong? There was the possibility that the situation might progress into something wrong, yet wrongdoing only existed where it was perceived and, of course, she perceived nothing amiss in a purely academic enterprise.

Dawn's earliest silvery fingers plucked a way through cracks in the draperies.

Purely academic?

Surely, after so many blameless years, she could not be turning into a deceitful, pleasure-seeking doxy?

*Doxy?*

Justine shivered. The shiver was part horror, part anticipation. She welcomed the chance for more, for further experiences such as she had shared with Struan only hours earlier. Sleepless hours earlier.

This thing—these things—between men and women had been a shadowy mystery. She had watched courtships, watched the fluttering, blushing girls with their vaguely predatory courtiers change into complacent direct-eyed women married to possessive but somehow remote husbands.

To Calum she had confessed to doing *It* with Struan. Fortunately Calum seemed disposed to think her confused on the subject and therefore was not insisting on marriage. She would stay at Kirkcaldy regardless of Calum's wishes, but she'd been unwise to make such a confession in order to distract her brother from trying to take her home. Consequently Arran saw the matter in quite a different light, but no doubt Struan would have dealt with him by now.

Justine knew *It* must surely be the ultimate joining between man and woman—that which led to the husband's total possession of his wife. She had notions about *It*, but they seemed outrageous. Outrageous but not without merit—if a woman were with the right man.

Justine had seen animals mate. Her own maid had confirmed that this mating produced the animal offspring. She should absolutely not have glanced at that part of any gentleman's body.

Justine had glanced.

Justine had seen.

The process she envisioned must be entirely possible. The

question was how? And, since men clearly enjoyed the event, was it possible that women could, despite dark warnings to the contrary, also enjoy such activities? Surely, when a husband gained total possession of his wife, the wife gained total possession of her husband? That conclusion was absolutely logical. But there was still the how of *It*.

How infuriating it was to be ignorant of one's own body. One thing was wholly without doubt. This marital joining would require extreme closeness between the male and the female.

To be extremely close to Struan would be bliss.

Heat bathed Justine's body and she closed her eyes tightly. She felt again the foreign but wholly marvelous ache in those inside places.

If only there were someone to ask questions of, some woman who would answer without awkwardness or censure.

Struan would help. He'd already helped. Of course he was kind. The only reason he'd kissed her had been that she'd asked him to help with her book.

But Struan must think the project she'd undertaken contained merit. He absolutely would not have kissed her for any other reason. That fact was one she must call to mind whenever she was tempted to daydream otherwise.

She rolled onto her stomach and buried her face in pillows that smelled of soap. It was preposterous to consider Struan and herself and marriage in the same thought. How Justine wished it were not so. How she wished it were possible for Struan to look at her with love, to hold her with love, to look at her with possessiveness, and for her to know that he thought of her as his alone.

*Old. Plain. Deformed.* If she was destined to forever be a virtuous spinster not intended for anything but the service of others, why had the power to dream not been denied her also? Why had she been given this wretched, vivid imagination that made her feel, made her long for what could never be hers?

Justine turned her head to watch the early dawn's prodding at the drapes. She had always been reliable and sensible, and she would not change now. The decision to strike out and find satisfaction in the company of those she held most dear and most in need of her had been wise.

There. That at least was a beginning. Ella needed her, and Max—and Struan. Controlling silly, wholly unsuitable girlish fancies would be easy from this moment on. The mature woman would prevail.

But the mature woman would continue to seek enlightenment for the sake of other women. And that meant she would continue to need Struan's assistance.

Struan's closeness.

With the fresh rush of fire through her limbs, Justine threw back the bedcovers and swung her feet to the steps beside the bed. Early-morning cold sent a shiver of goose bumps over her skin.

The very first order of the day—now—at once—was to seek out Struan and speak, in a most straightforward manner, about last night. She had a terrible notion he might think that she thought . . . otherwise than the actual way of things between them. Or rather, he might think that she thought otherwise on her own behalf—not, of course, on his.

In her poppy-colored nightrobe, with her hair hastily brushed and wound into a single braid, Justine set off for the pagoda. He'd already seen her in her robe; silly conventions were no longer an issue.

She didn't allow herself to think anything in particular until she stood in the anteroom to Struan's apartments.

Then she thought.

Under other circumstances, if she were a young thing—if she were not lame and plain—this sort of approach would be absolutely beyond the realm of acceptable behavior. But she was not a young thing and she was lame and plain, and the sooner she made certain he understood her intentions completely, the better.

Some minutes later, hovering beside Struan's empty bed, Justine knew the flutter of early panic. He wasn't in his apartments.

Hurrying, she made her way down to the vestibule and paused, listening to the sounds of the sprawling building.

Struan wasn't in the great hall, or the billiard room, or the smoking room, or either of the libraries, or the study, or one of the salons. There was no sign of him anywhere, including the kitchens.

Dawn was still in its palest misty state, with more darkness than light stroking the woodlands and gardens she saw when she peeked outside.

*The letters.*

He must have gone to look for more of the letters.

What could possibly be in those communications that would send him forth in the middle of the night, or at least before the dawn, to search them out? What was in them that made him so desperately angry and so insistent on isolation?

Standing near the cold kitchen stove, Justine glanced toward the windows—and all but collapsed.

A face was shadowed there.

A hand shielded its eyes to give a clearer view of the gloomy interior.

She held still. With luck she was at an angle where whoever it was wouldn't notice her.

Her heart leaped and her stomach chased in its wake.

Then the face was gone.

Justine released the breath she'd held and blood rushed to her head. She felt faint, and sick—and angry—all at the same time. Alone, she was alone with a helpless maid and two helpless children, while some creature skulked around the lodge.

Struan had admitted he was oppressed, that someone was, as he put it, pressing for favors he didn't wish to extend. Was it possible that at this very moment the villain in question was prowling outside this building?

Stealthily, breathing through her mouth, struggling to control her trembling body and the weakness anxiety caused in her damaged leg, Justine removed a long-handled brass warming pan from its hook beside the fireplace.

With a burning throat, and hands that shook, she carefully found a place where she could see the area outside the kitchens without being visible to anyone looking back.

Nothing moved but a faint breeze through shrubs and bushes and the straggly kitchen garden plantings.

The house no longer seemed silent at all. Countless creaks and cracks and sighs pounded her straining ears. She made her way through the stillroom and pantries, into the cold rooms intended for the preparation of meat and fish, and down a short flight of steps to the dairy. No sign of life from any window.

She *had* seen a face. There was someone out there who should not be out there.

The warming pan's oak handle was cold and slippery between the linked fingers of her two hands. Adjusting her grip, she returned along the passageway to the kitchens.

In the entrance she halted. Her blood stood as still as her body.

Again a face pressed against a windowpane above the deep kitchen sinks.

She drew back into the passage. She was alone with three defenseless souls to protect. That creature could find a way into the lodge and murder them all in their beds!

Justine straightened her back. Not with Lady Justine Girvin alert and prepared to take action. No scurrilous intruder would be allowed to trifle with those she was bound to save.

Struan should hear about this debacle. He would discover

that she was no meek, milk-and-water miss. He would suffer the tongue-lashing he deserved for leaving his children alone—particularly when he'd as good as admitted there was reason for fear.

Anger made her brave. Anger pumped courage through her veins. On tiptoe, she retraced her steps along the passageway to the outside door in the dairy at the very base of the tiled tower.

If she were most unlucky, the crazed creature would confront her as she opened the door to the kitchen gardens outside. If the creature were unlucky, she would come upon him unawares.

Releasing one of her hands from its cramped grip on the warming pan, she turned the key on the inside of the door and, very slowly, pushed until cold air struck her face.

No leering criminal leaped upon her.

Quickly, she slipped outside and flattened herself to the wall. A boxwood hedge as high as her shoulders made its untidy way around the tower. Justine stood between the building and the hedge.

Doubled over, she hugged the boxwood and crept forward to the corner, turned, and continued along the perimeter of the tower.

Rock scrunched.

Justine all but went to her knees. Then her determination rushed back with a force that made her temples pulse.

Struan should most definitely hear a great deal about this. *If* she lived to tell him her opinions of his behavior.

Footsteps—measured, stealthily placed footsteps came from the direction of the kitchens. Searching for a way in, no doubt. Searching for an unlocked door.

The door to the dairy! She had left the door to the dairy not just unlocked, but wide open.

Casting about, she looked for a gap in the hedge but found none. The footsteps had passed her. The interloper would enter by the door she'd unlocked and murder Ella, Max, and Mairi before Justine could do anything!

With the handle of the warming pan resting on her shoulder, she scurried back the way she'd come. At least the earth was soft on this side of the hedge and her limping steps made no sound. She pressed her lips together to contain her rasping breaths.

Only yards from Justine, a man came into sight. He walked boldly through the break in the boxwood in front of the tower and made for the open door to the dairy.

A young man with straight blond hair and decidedly rough clothing.

*A murderer.*

The beast who had threatened Struan with nameless horrors that sent him riding off alone into the night, leaving his family unprotected!

Justine raised her weapon above her head and lunged. "You shall not harm them!"

As she shouted, the man turned. In the second before the brass pan met his skull, she saw his mouth stretch wide, and his eyes.

Face down, he fell at her feet.

He didn't move again.

"I say he should," Arran announced, dropping from his horse.

Dismounting his gray, Calum joined him. "And I say he should not. This delay is intolerable. With every day, the position becomes more outrageous."

"It has passed outrageous," Arran said. "There is no choice, and I intend to put an end to all this shilly-shallying."

Struan slid a blanket over his black's back and attended to the animal's feed. Yet another night had passed without the appearance of a letter. It had to mean that the change in his circumstances had been noted. He looked through the open stable door toward the lodge. Even with his trusty guards, there was always the possibility of a mistake, of someone finding a way inside.

Arran drew off his gloves. "We will confront Justine as soon as she arises and tell her to ready herself for the ceremony at once."

Struan started out of the stables, but not before saying, more calmly than Arran deserved, "If you think you can control me—or Justine—you are a fool, brother. I'll thank you to say nothing further on this subject." He'd tried to insist the two men return to Kirkcaldy, but they would have none of it.

"You will do nothing to bully my sister," Calum told Arran.

"I am not in the habit of bullying women. Ask Grace."

"Ah, yes." Calum made a snorting sound. "She whose otherworldly notions you now follow so slavishly. Let us not forget the days when she first came to this castle. Let us not forget the shameful way you bullied her when you insisted upon judging her without as much as giving her a chance to speak for herself."

Arran drew himself up to full and very impressive height. "History now," he said shortly. "Understandable misunderstanding. Grace is the center of my life. There is no woman to compare with her—except your Philipa, of course. Charming creature."

"Incredible creature," Calum said, his eyes flashing. "Most beautiful, intelligent woman I ever met."

"Certainly a great blessing to you," Arran said, slapping his gloves against a palm. "Do I recall a certain reluctance in you to admit that blessing?"

"Never . . ." Calum sniffed. "Certainly not once I understood her true nature—and my own where she was concerned."

"The minister is standing by," Arran said, all brusque business. "Let us have no more of this disagreement between us."

"We have no need of a minister," Struan said, visually

searching the area. "Send the man away." If only he could rid himself of the certainty that hostile eyes watched from invisible hiding places.

"And that raises an issue you have avoided." Calum pointed a long finger at Arran. "The wretch is a *Catholic*."

Arran struck a nonchalant pose. "If he were, it would make no difference. The fact is, for some fortuitous reason he did not choose to take his final vows. He was not *baptized* Catholic."

"There is so much about him that has been hidden from us." Calum's nostrils flared with suspicion. "I *feel* that secretiveness."

Struan set his jaw. "I, my friends, do not give a damn what either of you do or do not think. I suggest you retrieve your mounts and go back to the castle."

They dared to speak as if he had no part in this. As if Justine had no part. What, in God's name, had he done to that marvelous woman? Last night . . . He narrowed his eyes and strode across the stableyard. The sweet generosity—untouched generosity—he'd felt in her had disarmed him completely.

But he must insist she leave. Justine must be dispatched to Cornwall and a safe haven must be found for Ella and Max.

"Justine loves him."

Struan stood still. He did not trust himself to turn around.

"Poppycock," Calum sputtered.

"And if the bounder would admit to such folly, I think he loves her, too."

Very slowly, Struan rotated to face those who had decided to be his conscience, his brain . . . and his heart.

"Loves her," Calum said. "She's old enough to be his . . . Well, his sister, dammit?"

"Philipa's old enough to be your sister," Arran said, completely unruffled. "Grace is old enough to be mine."

The two men stood, glaring at each other.

"They're old enough to be our younger sisters," Calum retorted.

"And Justine is old enough to be Struan's wife," Arran said. "She is a mere year his senior, and she is exactly what he needs."

"And what," Struan said, his voice tight, "do I need? Exactly?"

"A steadying influence," Arran said promptly. "A woman to bring your life to some sort of order. Of course, you'll have to come clean about those—"

"Don't say that aloud. Ever."

"Well, you will," Arran said, undeterred. "You've had your share of running about the country doing God knows what."

"God did know," Struan reminded his brother. "God always knows."

Calum and Arran exchanged a knowing glance before Calum said, "I'll not have my sister made a sacrifice to civilizing Struan. She's not strong. The whole notion is absolutely not on. You will release her at once and insist she come away with me to safety."

"Safety?" Struan said. "Are you suggesting I have chosen to put Justine at risk?"

"You managed to get her here."

"I didn't *manage* to get her here."

Arran threaded one arm through Struan's right and the other through Calum's left and hauled them toward the building. "How Justine came to be here doesn't matter. She *is* here and that's that."

"She's not staying," Calum grumbled.

Arran marched on. "She *is* staying."

"Will you stop trying to organize my life? I . . ." Struan pulled to a halt. Arran and Calum stopped just as abruptly. "Oh, my *God!*"

Justine, dressed in the brilliant robe she'd worn when last he saw her, knelt on the earth beside a crumpled figure. On the ground lay a brass warming pan that had evidently broken free of the handle Justine still clutched.

Struan, Arran, and Calum ran forward.

"Justine," Calum shouted. "I'm coming. Don't worry, I'm coming."

Struan reached her first and went to one knee at her side. He wrapped an arm around her shoulders. "My dear one. Oh, my poor, dear one. What happened here?"

She looked up, directly into his face. "I *hit* him." Her mouth trembled and she held it tight over her teeth. "Is he dead?" Tears shimmered, but she blinked them back.

Her victim groaned.

"Not dead," Struan said soothingly. "Only stunned."

"Who is that bounder?" Calum asked. "By the devil, I knew I should have put a stop to this earlier."

Arran said, "Good Lord," very softly.

"You are insupportable," Justine announced, her voice climbing higher with each word. She shook off Struan's arm. "I am utterly outraged by your irresponsibility."

He flinched and attempted to help her up. The tears she'd suppressed suddenly overflowed.

"Look what you've done," Calum said. "I've never seen Justine cry. Justine does not cry."

"She's crying now," Arran murmured.

"Shut up!" Struan and Calum said in unison.

"You may all shut up," Justine announced. Without warning, she raised the handle above her head and wielded it at Struan.

He caught the wood easily enough with one hand and wrested it from her grasp.

"My gentle sister," Calum lamented. "Not herself. Not herself at all."

"Give that to me," she demanded of Struan, reaching for the handle. She shook violently. "Give it to me at once. I must remain armed at all times so that I may protect those poor, innocent children you abandon with such ease. You, sir, are a heartless villain. You, sir, are no better than this creature who would have killed those children in their beds."

For the first time Struan looked directly at the man on the ground, who had begun to stir.

"This is a pretty pickle," Arran said, bending over and carefully rolling the man to his back. "Something tells me this is another of your impossible-to-explain fiascoes, brother."

Robert Mercer, Gael's husband, pushed to sit up. Blood drizzled from a gash along his hairline.

"Restrain him!" Justine scrambled awkwardly to her feet and stood over Robert. "He was going into the lodge, I tell you. Struan, this must be the—"

"This is Robert Mercer," Struan said rapidly. Sometimes the best one could do was try to minimize damage. "Robert very kindly agreed to keep a watch on the lodge while I visited Calum and Arran."

"Robert Mercer?" Justine stared at Robert's pale face with abject horror. "Dear Gael's husband? Kirsty's father? Baby Niall's father?"

"I do believe you've identified the man adequately," Calum murmured. "Can you stand, Robert?" He offered a hand.

Robert accepted Calum's help and stood up, blinking and obviously unsteady.

"Into the kitchens with him," Arran said.

"Och, I'll do well enough," Robert argued. "I'll away home now. Gael'll be wonderin' if I'm a'right if I'm much longer."

"You're not all right," Arran said, putting an arm around the tenant's waist and all but lifting him from his feet. "You shall be properly patched up before you go another step. The stableboy from Kirkcaldy's on his way. He shall go and tell Gael you're with me. She won't worry then."

For a moment Robert seemed disposed to argue. Then he said, "Aye," and went silently into the building with Arran.

"Meeting with Arran and Calum before dawn?" Justine said. Her slender face had lost all color. "Are you certain you weren't—"

"It has been a habit of ours since we were boys here together," Struan said. If necessary he would beg Justine not to mention the letters in front of Arran and Calum. "I would not have left if I'd suspected you might arise early and become afraid."

Her chin arose. "I was not afraid. Not for myself. I only became disturbed when I saw that . . . when I saw Robert's face at the kitchen windows. Most disturbed."

"How did you know Struan wasn't in the lodge?" Calum asked offhandedly. Not offhandedly enough to fool Struan.

"He wasn't in his apartments," Justine said blithely.

"Do you mean you saw Robert outside, then went in search of Struan? Before coming outside to attend to matters yourself?"

Justine frowned and shook her head. "No. Struan had left his bed. Left the lodge. I knew that before . . ." Bright pink replaced pallor.

"Ah," Calum said.

"You don't understand," Justine said, her words tumbling together. "I went to Struan's bedchamber to see him. I mean . . ."

Calum turned dark, cold eyes on Struan. Coldly accusing eyes. "You damnable bounder," he said, not quite under his breath.

"You are wrong," Struan said, attempting a superior smile that didn't work at all. "None of this is as it seems."

"Oh, no," Justine agreed. "Absolutely not as it seems. You see, Struan helped me with the first phases of my book last night. He instructed me in—"

"Justine is quite serious about her project, Calum."

Arran reappeared. "Mairi's up and tending Robert. Quite a blow to his noggin, Justine. One wouldn't expect such strength from one so delicately made."

"I am not delicately made. Just because I'm a cripple—"

"You are not a cripple," Struan said heatedly. "You are a

lovely, exceedingly desirable woman who happens to limp a little. Do not let me hear you say such . . ."

Arran's black brows rose almost to his hair. Calum's brows pressed toward his eyes. Struan massaged his jaw.

"Justine was about to explain why she was in Struan's bed-chamber this morning," Calum announced. "And she was also going to reveal the interesting details of the instruction he gave her for the damnably foolish book she thinks she's going to write."

"I am going to write it," Justine said. "We dealt with the matter of the first meetings and the first kiss. And the first touches. These are not things a spinster is likely to know without instruction. Struan is very generous and supportive, and I for one consider him indispensable for the research I must conduct to complete my work. Without him I simply could not bring true veracity to the pages."

Arran smiled, damn him.

Calum looked like a man who wished a pistol would miraculously appear in his hand.

Justine's brow puckered with concentration. "The kiss is a most complex, most interesting subject. I do not believe it will ever have been discussed in the depth I intend to present. There are so many nuances and—"

"Justine—"

"Hush, Struan. I do not want to lose my thought."

*Lose the thought. Please, God, let her lose the thought.*

"I am certain that if young females were aware of the sensations such touches can evoke. The inner stirrings brought about by fingers placed softly on—"

"*Thank you,* Justine," Calum said. "I do believe we have the general picture."

Arran smirked. "Shall we continue this discussion inside? In the great hall Justine has made so habitable, perhaps?"

"That will probably be a fine idea," Calum said. "After we greet the latest arrival."

Preoccupation—and desperation—had caused Struan to ignore the sounds of approaching horses.

The gradual replacement of Justine's eager expression with something approaching disbelief—then despair—made him give his full attention to the newcomers.

"Oh, no," Justine breathed.

Calum, his feet braced apart, let out an exasperated sigh. "We should have expected this."

Drawn by two scruffy chestnut nags, a cart trundled into the stable yard. Perched inside, on a box, was a figure Struan would as well never have set eyes on again.

"Grandmama," Calum said, crossing his arms.

Justine clutched her robe about her. "Sitting on a box. In the back of a cart."

"Carriages don't make it along the track in its present condition," Struan remarked to no one in particular. "Neglected. Too narrow and rough. Needs attention."

The cart, driven by an exceedingly uncomfortable-looking Potts, drew to a halt. Potts climbed out and hurried to let down the backboard.

Calum cleared his throat and called, "Leave this to me, Potts," as if his grandparent were goods to be handled.

The tiny, rigidly straight-backed figure in the cart rose majestically to her feet, stepped around the box, and approached the back of the cart in time to be met by Calum.

"The cane," Justine moaned softly. "She's using her cane."

"Is that so terrible?" Struan asked, thinking a lady of extremely advanced years might be expected to need considerably more help than a cane.

"She only uses it when she's incredibly angry."

"Ah, yes." Struan remembered a certain event in Cornwall when the old lady had felt obliged to carry the cane to underscore her authority. "She can be magnificently angry, can't she?"

"Yes. But I shall not be moved this time."

Struan glanced sharply at Justine. Her features were set.

Damn, but she was finally resolved to shake free of this tyrant—to "help" him—and he couldn't allow it.

Puffing, his thin face purplish and sweating, Potts produced steps. Calum held out his arms to the Dowager Duchess of Franchot. Dressed in heavy, rustling black with a shiny black straw bonnet covering most of her white hair, she rested one tiny, black-gloved hand on the back of his wrist and descended, utterly calmly, to the stable yard.

"Grandmama," Justine said, abruptly rushing forward, her limp more pronounced than Struan had noted it to be since her arrival in Scotland. "My dear Grandmama. You should not have made such an arduous journey."

The dowager looked up into her much taller granddaughter's face. "It appears I have not come a moment too soon." She scowled at Justine's robe and sniffed at her all-but-loose hair. "Not a moment too soon at all. I shall sort out this little *contretemps* before it proceeds a second farther."

Justine wrung her hands. "But in a *cart,* Grandmama. A *cart.* Such discomfort, and for one who should be gently attended."

"Pah!" The dowager raised her cane and delivered a smart tap to Justine's arm. "What of it? I am a strong woman. I am in full possession of all my faculties. A little ride in a cart will do me no harm, my girl."

"But, Grandmama—"

"Don't Grandmama me, you ridiculous creature. It is you who are to be pitied. It is you who have behaved in a manner that might have caused my family's name—let alone their persons—discomfort. As for the cart—" She swept her pale, sharp eyes all the way to Justine's feet. "If it had been you making the journey we should have had cause for concern. I, at least, have two perfectly good legs."

# Chapter Ten

I f there were three more marvelously favored men in all the land, Justine doubted her heart could survive the sight of them—at one time.

Arran, the tallest by a small margin, stood between Calum and Struan in the great hall at the lodge. The marquess's long unruly hair, in its unfashionable but rakish tail, shone blue-black. His body exuded muscular strength. His aristocratically handsome face showed nothing of what he was thinking.

Calum's dark hair showed the same red lights to be found in Justine's. His almost-black eyes stared into the middle distance in the way Justine had come to associate with the approach of one of his rare rages.

And then there was Struan.

Justine glanced at him, met his brown eyes, and glanced away again. This was the most embarrassing moment of her life, but she would not bend before her grandmother. She would not beg forgiveness for wanting something for herself and for pursuing what she wanted.

She wanted to be free to write her book and she wanted to be with Struan.

Near Struan.

Simply to see him now and again . . .

He had looked steadily back at her and there had been no censure in his gaze. She raised her eyes to his again.

He smiled.

Justine's stomach dipped. Struan's heart was in his smile. His good, generous, kind heart. There could be no better man, no more charming man, no more beautiful man in body and in soul than Struan, Viscount Hunsingore. Every line of his lean face was precious to Justine. His lithe body, the powerful shoulders and arms, the legs any Corinthian would kill to possess . . . and any woman might kill to have brush her skirts.

Oh, my. If these were the thoughts of doxies or strumpets, or ladybirds, or whatever, then those females certainly did not live quite all of their lives in dejection over their lots.

Grandmama made repeated sweeps between the fireplace that soared higher than her head, and a round marquetry table on legs tipped with gold lions' feet. "A disaster," she said. "Philipa must be spoken to when we return, Calum."

"How so?" Calum asked.

"Refused to tell me what I asked to know," Grandmama said imperiously. "Collect that! Would not tell me exactly where this ninny had gone—where you had gone in such a hurry."

"Who did tell you?" Calum asked mildly.

The dowager checked her pacing an instant. "That is neither here nor there. There are still those at Franchot who know their duties, my boy." She moved on with short but measured strides.

Poor loyal Philipa, Justine thought. One could imagine the emotional torture she might have suffered at Grandmama's hands.

Mairi bobbed. Each time the dowager reached the fireplace and turned to retrace her steps, Mairi bobbed. The dowager duchess had ordered the bemused maid to the hall and instructed her to "stand quite still and say not a word until I am done with you."

Potts, summoned to receive appropriate chastisement for his part in the plot, clutched his hat before him by the brim and kept his head bowed. Buttercup, a late arrival, had slipped into place just inside the doors.

"Conspiracy," the duchess said. "Calculated outrage."

Mairi bobbed.

The dowager pointed at her with the cane. "What is the matter with that gel? And who is she?"

"My maid, Grandmama," Justine said from her place in front of the silk-draped Chinese screen. And that would be the last time her voice shook. "This is Mairi. When Grace is in residence Mairi waits upon her, but since Grace is—"

"I don't give a jot for whatever it is the creature does when she is not poppin' up and down before my eyes like one of those wretched James-in-a-box things."

"Jack-in-a-box, Your Grace," Potts muttered.

The tip of the cane moved to the coachman. "Out," the dowager demanded. "The duke will deal with you later."

Bowing, Potts backed away, but Justine saw him glance at Calum, who winked with the eye his grandmother's couldn't see.

The dowager turned her attention on Buttercup, who, with lips parted, concentrated on the three noblemen arrayed before her. "And you," Grandmama said. "Your name?"

The maid wetted her mouth. Her shapely breasts rose and fell noticeably.

"Name?" Grandmama demanded.

"She's Buttercup, Your Grace," Struan said, evenly enough. "Run along, Buttercup. I'm certain Lady Girvin has already assigned your duties for the day."

Nodding, and staring at her master with open adoration, Buttercup followed Potts.

"And you, gel," Grandmama said to Mairi. "Molly, or whatever foolish name you bear. From what I can gather from the totally impossible staff at the castle, you are little better than useless. I shall communicate with the marchioness and suggest she dismiss you forthwith. Out with you, too."

Arran reached the open door before Mairi could scurry away. "Please check on Robert in the kitchens," he said kindly. "Make sure the stable boy goes to Gael. Did I remember to give you the marchioness's regards? She asked me to compliment you on your attention to detail in the matter of her packing for Yorkshire. She will be glad of your help when she returns."

"Thank ye, m'lord," Mairi said, her fair skin flooded with color.

Arran closed the door and returned to stand, shoulder-to-shoulder, with Calum and Struan. The first rays of sun through sparkling windows shone on their impressively broad backs.

"Now," the dowager said. "We shall deal with this piece of nonsense in short order. What can you be thinking of, Justine? Paradin' about in your nightclothes? Lookin' like a strumpet? Hair all flowin' about. And such vulgar colors. Must be somethin' to do with your time of life. They say women faced with their latter years often suffer certain aberrant behavior."

Justine looked down at her poppy-colored watered-silk robe and bit her tongue.

"I find Justine's robe delightful," Struan said, so clearly that Justine jumped. "Women with vibrant coloring do well in strong shades, I believe."

The dowager narrowed her eyes. Paper-thin skin drew down in a web about her colorless mouth, like the crazed surface of old, white china. "She has no money of her own, y'know," she said, her pinched nostrils closing. "You've made a mistake, young man. But you're not the first younger son to think he could make a tidy sum by marryin' a cripple."

Justine saw Arran place a restraining hand on Struan's arm.

They felt protective of her, these three. For that she was grateful—and deeply moved.

Calum said, "*Grandmama*. What are you saying?"

The old lady raised her chin, stretching the ropes of skin that disappeared beneath the frill on her high lace collar. "It's of no matter. There were the odd fortune hunters who came asking for Justine's hand. Naturally I protected her from the fate of watching a faithless husband use her connections and otherwise ignore her."

Shocked, Justine turned away.

"Don't be a wet goose," Grandmama ordered. "It was all too long ago to matter. You were young, for goodness' sake. Which points out exactly how long ago it was. And not one of them was suitable or well-motivated. There. That's an end of it. You will have that incompetent creature dress you for travelin' and we'll leave at once."

"Your Grace," Arran said, "Justine is a guest on my estate. I hardly think that is grounds for your annoyance. I'm certain she intended you no inconvenience."

"Pah!" Grandmama thudded her cane on the floor. "She is not herself. That much I'll allow. But she considered neither my comfort, nor the matter of her family's honor. Runnin' away. Alone, mind you. Like some silly, moonstruck girl chasin' after a lover. A *lover,* mind you. Look at her. A *lover*—at her age!"

Justine wished the ground would suck her down. Her face must match her robe.

"Old *fool,*" Grandmama said. "Five and thirty and she suddenly tosses aside everything I've taught her in all those years to behave in a manner that'll make us the talk of the Polite World if I don't get her back to Cornwall quickly."

"I'm not going back to Cornwall."

Silence followed Justine's announcement.

"Madam," Struan said, his jaw tensed. "You must be exceeding tired. My brother and I insist that you rest at Kirkcaldy—"

"You, sir, will *insist* upon nothing." The cane rose once

more. "You, sir, will be grateful that I have arrived in time to save you from being made the buffoon by this—by this ungrateful relative of mine."

Struan stepped in front of the dowager and said, "There is no means by which Justine could make a fool of me, Your Grace. She is as generous and gracious as she is honorable."

"Honorable, indeed," Arran said, his chest expanding with an apparently thoughtful breath. "But there are, nevertheless, the facts."

Justine stared at him, uncomprehending.

He spread a hand. "The matter of Lady Justine having spent a night with my brother. *Alone.*"

The next silence rang in Justine's ears. She stepped backward, bumped the screen, and knocked a cascade of brilliant silk to the floor. Awkwardly, she stooped to pick up the shawls.

"Justine did *what*?" Grandmama asked. "No. Absolutely not. You will do well not to add falsehoods to an already unpleasant situation, young man."

"Nothing false about it," Arran said. "Struan and Justine spent a night alone in this very room. On that very chaise." He pointed to the daybed—now returned to its original place beneath the windows.

The dowager's mouth fell open and remained so. Her small, sharp eyes bulged.

Suddenly chilled, Justine draped a purple shawl about her shoulders.

"Tell the truth of it, Calum," Arran said. "After all, it was you who found the pair of them."

Calum coughed and frowned and approached Justine with question in his eyes. "Can't you do something?" He removed the rest of the shawls from her hands and tossed them onto the screen once more.

"Is it true?" the dowager duchess demanded.

Calum bowed his head and swung to face her. "It is, Madam. Absolutely true."

"That settles it, then." She wiped all traces of concern from her face. "We must move with all speed away from this place. If we do so, we shall get past this inconvenience."

"I doubt it," Arran remarked.

Grandmama made a most unpleasant sound. "Surely you don't truly think . . . You cannot think anyone would believe a man like the viscount would deflower a woman like—"

*"Grandmama."* Calum roared the word and went to take his grandparent's elbow.

"I believe," Struan said with a quiet control that clearly cost him dearly. "I believe it far more likely that no one would believe Lady Justine would want a man like me."

Tears—foolish, unwanted tears—rushed to Justine's eyes. "Oh, Struan. Do not feel you must defend me."

"I don't," he said, staring into her eyes. "You need no defense, my lady—from any man, or woman."

"That will do." Grandmama jerked her arm from Calum's hand. "I am taking the demented creature home."

"The event that occurred here is already the talk of the countryside," Arran said, fascinated by plaster stags on the ceiling now.

The dowager was unmoved. "Who takes notice of the opinions of peasants?"

"All of Scotland's inhabitants are not peasants. Edinburgh, I need hardly remind you, has a very active and influential Society."

"Edinburgh is hardly likely to hear of this."

"Really? It is my duty to inform you that Edinburgh has already heard of it. And naturally, the talk of Edinburgh becomes the talk of London in short order. Then . . ." He shrugged eloquently.

The dowager's eyes darted from Justine to Arran and back. "If you had been where you should have been, granddaughter, I should have had the pleasure of telling you that there has been a fresh offer for your hand."

Justine felt dizzy and slightly sick.

"Lord Belcher of Havershill has declared his very generous interest in taking you on, Justine."

*"Belcher?"* Calum said, his lips curling. "He has not spoken to me."

"You were not there," Grandmama said. "You had already left for Scotland. Lord Belcher spoke to me in your absence."

Justine's mind cleared. "Lord Belcher is ninety, if he's a day."

"Don't exaggerate," Grandmama said. "He isn't a day older than I, and I am certainly not ninety."

"Oooh," Justine muttered. "Ninety and constantly in his cups. And there isn't a young girl in the county who doesn't make certain to avoid his hands."

"Justine! Such talk. And who else do you think would be likely to marry a woman with a ruined reputation? And a lame leg—and who is already on the verge of becoming elderly?"

*"Madam,"* Struan said through his teeth.

Justine was beyond hurt. "Some man approaching his ninety-fifth birthday might also find me a boon."

A fine tremor jerked the corners of Grandmama's lips. "Disrespectful chit. And about the man who will save you from disaster."

"I am in no danger of disaster."

"None at all," Arran agreed. "Despite the additional questions raised by last night's events."

Calum motioned frantically for Arran's silence. "Why would you look favorably upon an alliance with Belcher?" he asked his grandparent.

"Justine isn't strong," Grandmama said promptly. "Belcher is past the stage of wanting a female for any shenanigans."

"Except to *pinch*," Justine said darkly.

The dowager was serene. "Belcher is a neighbor. It would be a simple matter for me to keep an eye on Justine. In fact, Lord Belcher has already agreed to her spending a good part of her time at Franchot Castle as long as she attends to those requirements he does have. The arrangement will be most agreeable."

"For you," Calum said.

Grandmama ignored him.

Struan regarded the old woman speculatively before saying, "Justine will not be going back to Cornwall—not unless she chooses to do so."

Justine wanted to thank him. She could do nothing but look at him . . . and love him for his defense of her.

The dowager leaned on her cane. "What do you mean by that, Viscount Hunsingore?"

"I mean that the time for simple solutions in this matter has passed," Struan told her. "We shall have to consider the next step with extreme care."

A tinge of color streaked white skin. "You think you have played your hand so well. You are no match for me, Viscount Hunsingore. And Justine may be a cabbage head, but she will understand your despicable game when I explain it to her. A widower and a younger son. A man dependent upon the kindness of his elder brother. You lured a light-brained old maid into your snare. She was to supply you with means of your own and take the onerous matter of dealing with your brood off your hands."

"No!" Justine clung to the ends of the purple shawl. "That is not at all what happened here. I intend to guide Ella and Max. I have promised them, and I shall take pleasure in the task."

"Marriage to a man such as the viscount is out of the question for you."

Justine stood as straight as her leg allowed. "No one has mentioned marriage here, Grandmama. I will remain and care for the children. That is all."

"Out of the question."

"On the contrary," Arran said, and pulled the cord beside the fireplace. "A marriage will take place between Struan and

Justine. I shall have you accompanied back to the castle, Your Grace. You must rest before we continue our preparations."

"I agree with Arran," Calum said. "Where your health is concerned. Your health and Justine's welfare are my concerns. You must submit to my wishes in these matters."

Grandmama's lips disappeared. She held herself erect and stared unseeingly ahead.

The rapid appearance of Shanks, the bald-headed butler from Kirkcaldy, surprised Justine. "Thought you might require my presence, my lord," he told Arran. "Just arrived."

"You will accompany me, Justine," Grandmama said.

Justine turned her back. "I shall go to my room here."

"Lord Belcher will have you—"

"Not now," Calum said. "I beg you, Grandmama, do not persist *now*."

Smoothly, Arran managed the amazing feat of having Grandmama leave the room without further comment.

Justine waited for footsteps to fade before rushing into the vestibule and pulling the door shut behind her.

She started toward the stairs, but paused. Calum's voice reached her through the heavy door to the great hall. "You're a bloody liar, Arran," he shouted. "They aren't talking about it in Edinburgh. There hasn't bloody well been time."

Justine crept back and placed her ear to a panel.

"Technicality," Arran said.

"Technicality, my bloody arse!"

Justine flinched.

"Technicality because the moment I decide to take the news to Edinburgh it will no longer be a technicality," Arran said. "Not that I would, of course. The point is that we've wasted days in discussion when a woman's reputation is at stake. Struan should marry her at once."

After a small pause Calum said, "I'm inclined to think you're right."

"Inclined?" Arran said, and laughed. "Then we are all but in agreement, my friend. The marriage must take place."

"Yes. But not with conspicuous haste. Let us remember that despite certain unfortunate, er, appearances, my sister is not compromised."

"*Au contraire*. You have not denied that she is indeed compromised. You found her in a most compromising position with Struan. And we heard her detailed account of last night's events."

"She is older than he is." Calum sounded deeply troubled.

"A mature wife is exactly what he needs."

"There is the matter of offspring."

"Certainly," Arran said. "That must be considered and we shall consider it. But after all, he is the younger son. Further issue is not essential."

"True," Calum said.

"That is all," Struan announced suddenly, his voice bearing an edge like fine steel. "All I will listen to from any of you. All I will tolerate in the way of interference."

Justine straightened and walked away. She mounted the stairs and slowly ascended.

"I will decide what is to be done here," Struan shouted, his temper clearly deserting him. "And when I decide, I will inform you."

She was not as much as consulted about her wishes.

"It may be," Struan continued, "that all will be accomplished before you know it. Regardless, you may keep your opinions to yourselves."

What if Struan did decide he should marry her? What would it mean to her?

Would it mean what Grandmama had suggested—a life of caring for someone who might respect her, but could never truly care for her?

Or would it mean a marriage in the real sense?

Could it mean . . . *It*?

# Chapter Eleven

❧

Ella wore a dark-green riding habit, complete with a demure little velvet bonnet perched upon smoothly coiled black braids.

Max, a spanking new beaver clamped to the breast of his immaculate blue jacket, planted polished boots in a perfect imitation of his papa.

"What's this?" Justine asked. She'd ignored their persistent knocking on her apartment door until Ella had called out, begging to come in. "You look . . . you look most unlike yourselves, children."

Even with the aid of enough pomade to turn his carrot hair dark red, Max's locks managed to pop up. He attempted to scrape the tufts down. "She doesna like it, Ella," he said. "I told ye we wouldna do."

"What will not do is the extraordinary manner of speech you've adopted," Justine said sharply. "We must work on it promptly. As for your appearance. Both of you. You look first rate and you make me very proud. I simply fail to understand what brought about the change."

"We're off to the castle," Ella said. She twitched cream lace at her wrists. "Max will not speak whilst we're there. Except for what we've practiced. He's promised."

Justine frowned. For the sake of these two she must put aside her own concerns—her own disappointments and embarrassment—but the morning's events had sapped her spirits.

Max scuffed his boots on the Spanish carpet that covered the floor in Justine's sitting room. "We heard it. The whole thing."

*"Max,"* Ella hissed. "I told you—"

"You heard what?" Justine interrupted.

"Hersel'," Max said, raising his pointed chin defiantly. "In the hall wi' Papa and Uncle Arran and the duke. We heard everythin' the old witch from Cornwall said."

This time Ella moaned, "Max!"

"I wanted t'carry her away t'the hill clans," Max said as if his sister were invisible. "They've a rare way o' changin' the minds o' thorny old witches, I can tell ye. Turn 'em into bags fer their pipes. Cut off their hair and—"

*"Max,* you promised you wouldn't go on. You *promised."*

He stretched his thin neck. "Aye, well, mayhap there's not enough o' her for a bag anyway. But we did hear everythin' she said. Worse than Grumpy. She wants t'take ye away and we'll not hear o' it. Ye've come and ye've said ye'll stay wi' us. We don't want ye t'go." He wrinkled his nose and pursed his lips. "We love ye. There. I've said it."

Perched on the window seat, Justine looked quickly outside and blinked back the tears she didn't want them to see. "I love you, too," she told them. "I don't want to go."

"And neither does Papa want you to go," Ella said. "You can marry him and stay here forever. It will be perfect. He needs you and you need him and we need you, and . . . We are going to greet the dowager duchess."

Justine looked at them aghast.

Ella raised both hands and her fine brows. "No, no, don't worry. Max will say nothing but . . . Go on, Max, *say* it."

His freckled face pinched with concentration. "Good day to you, Your Grace."

Ella, mouthing each word with her brother, had risen to her toes. "And?" she said, leaning earnestly forward.

Max frowned even more deeply. "Welcome to Kirkcaldy. We are delighted to see you again."

"Yes." Ella let out a huge breath. "That is all he will say. I shall ask after the duchess's health and tell her how glad we are that you've come to assist in our education at such a critical time in our lives. I shall remind her that we are motherless and that—in addition to practical considerations—we are in need of spiritual guidance. I shall not mention . . . I shall not mention M."

Justine screwed up her eyes. "M?"

"You know. *Marriage.* But once we get rid of the old bat, we can get on with the wedding at once."

Justine almost laughed. "Ella!"

Ella's expression became angelic. "Trust us, Lady Justine. We shall do nothing to shame you. We shall merely further the cause."

"I think this is a bad idea. Particularly after hearing Max's notions about the disposal of my grandmother."

"He will have his little jokes," Ella said, pulling on green leather gloves. "Don't give another thought to what he said. Come, Max. Let us visit Lady Justine's grandmama."

"I don't think—"

"Good day to you, Lady Justine," Max said, strutting behind his sister. "I expect the old bat will want us to take tea wi' here. If there's a jelly roll about, we'll probably gi' her the pleasure o' our company. I'll not drop crumbs on the carpet."

After they'd left, Justine remained where she could see through the leaded casement panes. Below the windows spread the swaying branches of a wych elm loaded with clusters of purple blossoms that heralded bright leaves to come.

The bursting forth of new things. New beginnings.

She had chosen a new beginning, also. Not the kind most single women dreamed of, but enough, certainly, for one who might have lived her life without any fulfillment. She spared a thought for the suitors Grandmama had evidently turned away but could summon nothing more than vague interest. Not one of them had been Struan. Grandmama had been wrong, but she had done Justine a favor. How empty life would be without at least knowing Struan shared some portion of it.

Then there were those two marvelous children and there was her book. The children would do very well. And her book would be a success—of that she was certain. The book was an event long overdue.

Dear Struan. He was a kind man who—once all the silliness about reputations had faded—would accept her presence in the capacity she'd suggested and give her pleasure simply by his occasional presence.

*It was not enough.*

She tipped back her head and closed her eyes. Why could she not tame this, this passionate part of her nature that had no right to exist?

"May I come in?"

Justine swiveled on the window seat. "Struan! I didn't hear you."

Standing with his hands behind his back, he regarded her intently. Today he wore a black coat and stock, stark against exceedingly white linen. Buff breeches fitted powerful thighs with never a wrinkle.

The same wind she'd watched in the trees had made a fine

tousle of his black hair, and . . . She was staring. Struan stared back. A faint smile played about his mouth.

"You surprised me," she said awkwardly.

"So it seems. I am in the habit of coming upon you unawares."

Justine wished to tell him she loved seeing him whenever he chose to appear. Instead, she nodded.

He strolled closer. "I saw Ella and Max. They look splendid, don't you think?"

"Absolutely splendid. You must be proud of them."

He chuckled. "I am proud of them. They told me of their mission."

Justine felt her color mount. "I suggested they reconsider, but—"

"But they are determined. I told them their motives are the best and wished them luck at the castle. Arran is fond of Max, y'know. The lad is quite musical and Arran has undertaken to give him some instruction."

"Oh." Justine smiled with genuine pleasure. "That is excellent news."

"Mairi has gone with the children."

"She has?" Puzzled, Justine frowned.

Struan came to stand beside her. "I suggested she should spend the afternoon there. One of her younger sisters works in the kitchens now. They'll enjoy the visit."

"How kind you are." Justine fiddled with the small buttons on the bodice of her rose-colored gown.

Struan cleared his throat. "Under the circumstances, it would seem appropriate for you and me to . . . to discuss certain things."

She could think of no response.

From behind his back, Struan produced a bouquet. "I brought you these," he said, grimacing. "Not exactly hothouse beauties, but lovely in their own way."

Justine's next breath lodged in her throat. The flowers were small, shades of blue and mauve and purple. "Thank you." The hand she extended shook. "What are they, please?"

"Mmm. Early orchid and dove's-foot. And bilberry. One of the benefits of countryside allowed its head. Wildflowers. They remind me of you."

She took the flowers and held them in her lap.

"They are delicately made but strong," Struan said. "Persistent. Perhaps a little deceitful in the faces they show to the world."

Justine looked questioningly at him.

"Oh, I mean what I say as a compliment, my dear. The beautiful wildflowers flourish despite odds. Like you, hmm?"

"I . . . I am not accustomed to responding to such words, Struan. I have brought you trouble, haven't I?"

He glanced away before saying, "The very best sort of trouble."

"How can trouble ever be good?"

His sudden move to rest a hand on her hair made Justine flinch. "Hush," he said, stroking. "Certainly I had not planned on these developments, but I cannot tell you I regret them. They merely require careful attention if we are to navigate certain . . . The potential for certain difficulties exists. I pray that we may make our way through those difficulties."

Justine brought the flowers, with their odd, untamed scents, to her face and inhaled deeply. Struan muddled her. "I would not make difficulties for you," she told him. "And I fear I have already done so. Perhaps I should do as my grandmother asks and return to Cornwall."

With his hand still on her hair, he took so long to respond that her heart seemed to stop. If he told her to go, then go she must. Why had she said such a foolish thing?

When he did finally speak, his voice held dark intensity. "God help me, I don't want you to go."

She closed her eyes. *That* was why she had said it—to hear him ask her to stay.

"You said there were things we should discuss. I expect you were referring to the children's welfare. I have already begun to give that a great amount of thought."

"Actually," Struan said. "What I thought we might do was continue with some work on your book—while we have some quiet hours ahead. Buttercup is not with us today and the lodge is blessedly empty."

"My book?" A faint but quite distinct buzzing sounded in her ears. "Now?"

"I thought so." He offered her his hand and waited until she took it. "You will probably want to continue your discussion on unmarried females dealing with balls. Did you find the ballroom here yet?"

Holding the flowers in her right hand, Justine gripped his fingers tightly and stood. "Yes," she said. "At least, I assumed that's what it was supposed to be."

"My grandfather thought to entice my grandmother into accepting this place. He decided that if he gave her the promise of intimate balls, with the wives of the men he invited here to hunt in attendance, she would look more favorably upon his creation."

"And did she?"

"I don't believe so. She never attended a ball in this building."

"How sad."

"Come there with me now."

He led her along corridors, up and down stairs and through numerous rooms to reach his destination. The ballroom, a small but perfectly proportioned ballroom atop a wing with a circular tower at each corner, had yet to be cleaned.

"Have I tired you?" Struan asked, studying her with concern in his eyes.

Justine inclined her head and smiled—and found a little flirtation came quite easily. "I am like the flowers," she reminded him. "Deceitful. All delicate disguise to hide a woman of iron."

He grinned, showing his fine, white teeth and making deep dimples beneath his cheekbones. "I shall remember that." The grin faded as rapidly as it had appeared. "I may need to test the iron."

Before Justine could question his meaning, he turned away and went to throw open heavy, dust-laden red damask draperies. The dust swirled in colored shafts of sunlight through stained-glass windows.

"Shall you be able to memorize what takes place here and write it down later?" he said, sweeping aside a cover from an elegant black piano and raising the lid. "I should have thought to have you bring your book."

"I never forget anything you . . . I shall remember."

Their eyes met, but Justine quickly looked away. She must not reveal what was truly in her heart. It might make him feel trapped—or bound by duty to marry her as Arran seemed so determined to arrange.

Oh, what bliss to be married to Struan and to have him want to be married to her.

Grandmama was correct. Justine was a simpleton.

"What are you thinking?"

His question startled her. "That I am foolish." Why must she so often speak without thought? "I mean, that I know I must appear foolish to you. My grandmother—"

"Forget what your grandmother said." He approached with determined steps. "Do you understand me? Forget every word that woman spoke to you."

He sounded angry. Justine swallowed and surveyed the room. The draped shapes of furniture ranged around a dance floor. Gilded mirrors lined red and gold-papered walls above gilt wainscoting. Ornate crystal chandeliers hung from a delicately carved plaster ceiling in a charming shade of deep pink. Dust coated everything, yet she could imagine how lovely the room could be.

"Did you hear what I said, Justine?"

She faced him. "Grandmama is old. She has come to rely upon me. But I have made a decision."

"And that is?"

Her palms were moist. "That I must live my life now or not at all. I can be useful to more than just one woman who already has all the pampering she can possibly need."

She heard his outward rush of breath. "I had intended to say something quite different," he said, and the bleak, troubled set of his features made her tremble. "But I must speak what's in my heart, Justine. You can be useful to me . . . to us. Everything seems . . . With you here everything seems different. Possible. Hopeful. There must be a way to navigate troubled waters without giving up the best that has ever come into our lives."

If she wasn't careful, she'd begin to imagine hidden meanings in his words. "I shall do my best for all of you," she told him quietly.

Struan's chest expanded. He seemed about to speak, then bowed his head before saying, "Yes, well . . . Let us continue our work."

"I had thought you considered the whole project silly," she told him in a rush. "Please, do not feel you have to pursue this. I think I rather made it sound like a condition of my working with the children and looking after the household. It is not, Struan."

"It is for me," he responded promptly. "A bargain is a bargain. You have a great deal of work to do with Ella and Max and I have a great deal of work to do with you . . . That is, with your project."

Justine set the wilting flowers carefully on a sheet-draped chaise. She pressed her hands together. Again they were alone. She glanced about. 'Where do they think you are?"

"Hmm?"

"Arran and Calum and the others? Where do they think you are?"

"About estate business," he replied promptly. "But I did not tell them I should be. So there is no deceit, Justine. Not really."

"No."

"Arran and Calum have gone into the village. Arran has business there and Calum wished to go along. There are many memories here for Calum."

"Of course." Sometimes she forgot that her brother had grown up at Kirkcaldy.

"Your grandmother is resting. Ella and Max will remain at the castle until she awakes. They are determined on their little charade."

"Yes."

"No. Yes. Of course. Why, Justine, I do believe you are afraid to be alone here with me."

"I'm not!" she told him fiercely. "Not at all. Why should I be?"

His flamboyantly drawn face held no softness now. "I don't believe I shall tell you that. No, not yet. Part of a much later section of your book, dear lady. Do you like to dance?"

"*Dance?*" For an instant she was furious with him. "You know I cannot dance."

He stared at her, then went to the piano and began to play. To her amazement, the instrument was in good tune.

"Arran ensures all instruments on the estate are well-tended," Struan said over the strains of a waltz she did not recognize. "Do you play?"

"Yes. But not like you. You are very good."

"You should hear Arran," he said. "I'll make sure you do."

"Tell me why your grandmother never came to this ballroom."

"Headstrong woman. All women are headstrong."

The music distracted her. It reminded her of balls held at Franchot Castle when men in military uniform whirled beautifully dressed women about the floor. Justine saw them now as if in shifting patterns, each pattern planned yet free.

"Did you hear what I said?" Struan asked over the music. "All women are headstrong."

She tossed her head. "You are right, sir. We have to be headstrong to keep our sanity while dealing with men. Men— for purposes God must consider important—are larger and stronger than women. For that reason, they consider themselves to be also of superior intelligence."

"Quite so."

"Hah! He admits it." She stood at his shoulder and watched his long, strong fingers fly over the keys. "And they consider their desires stronger and their appetites more fierce . . ."

Struan's fingers stilled.

Justine clamped her arms to her sides, appalled at what she had said.

A large hand pried her left wrist away from her body. "Look at me, Justine."

She would not.

"Look at me. This will be perfect for your book."

Reluctantly, she met his gaze.

"Stronger desires?"

She swallowed. "I meant that men think they want things more ardently than women."

"And do they?"

"I . . ." Academic. An academic exploration. "I believe women want things every bit as much as men do."

"Things?"

Surely he could not be trying to trap her into some indiscretion. "In relationship," she said boldly. "Yes, in relationship. They desire . . . intimacy. A oneness of heart. They long to share completely in those . . ."

"Those?"

"Sin's ears, you do persist so. Those passions. Yes, they desire to share the same passions men wish to enjoy."

"Why, Justine, you sound as if you need very little instruction in the business of passion and desire."

She would not look away. "I know nothing of passion and desire but my own imaginings. And my own . . . sensations. I do not set out to lie to you, Struan. I have often wondered if I may be an unnatural woman, but with maturity I have come to the conclusion that I am not at all unnatural. Most women simply fail to allow their . . . urges to develop. Or rather their urges develop but they deny them. To themselves. And to their husbands."

"I see."

"It is my mission to stop women from denying their urges."

"I . . . see."

"And I think a woman's appetite for fulfillment is equal to her husband's. In the matter of closeness, don't y'know?"

"No. No, I'm not sure I do. Closeness?"

She began to feel rather hot. "Perhaps we should concentrate on the ballroom? For now?"

Struan stood up. "I have the distinct feeling I shall become far more passionate on the subject of this closeness of yours."

"Oh, it's not mine, I assure you!" Whatever could he be suggesting? "No, no, not at all. I have merely constructed certain conclusions. Some of them . . . Well, anyway, I have no personal knowledge of these things and that is why I am so very grateful for all your unselfish assistance."

"I see."

"You do have an unfortunate habit of resorting to 'I see' when you don't see. Don't you?"

"Possibly."

Justine saw the need for clarification. "Because girls and young women are so sheltered from the truth. . . . The truth about life, that is. Well, because they are not told anything, it's very difficult not to be nervous and ignorant in these matters relating to what occurs between a husband and wife. After they marry. When they share time in the same bed." Her face glowed. "That sort of thing."

"Quite."

"I knew you'd understand." She smiled gratefully at him. "I've done some preliminary research."

"You have?"

"Oh, yes. We have a great many animals at Franchot. I observed certain activities——"

"Do you like to dance?"

Caught off guard by his swift change of topic, Justine blinked rapidly. "Why do you ask that again? You know I cannot possibly dance. I have never danced."

"I'll rephrase my question. Should you like to dance?"

"I . . ." He was honest with her. She would be equally honest with him. "I have always regretted that I cannot dance. I do love music. And I love to watch others dance."

"Do you feel wistful when you watch?"

He seemed to know her heart. "Sometimes." She sighed. "I've tried not to."

Struan put an arm around her waist and took her hand in his. "Then you shall no longer have any reason to feel wistful. You shall dance."

"No." She tried to wiggle free. "No, please."

"Yes, please. Can you still remember the tune I played?"

"Well . . . Yes, I can."

He began to hum. "Good. Listen to it in your mind and let me lead you."

Completely incapable of making her feet move, Justine stood quite still. "I cannot."

"Cannot? Or will not? For our purposes—on this first occasion—my legs will guide your legs. Allow the pressure of mine to show yours where to go."

"But——"

"But it's not appropriate for me to touch you so intimately? Come, my dear. This is for scientific purposes. We must sacrifice ourselves—our principles—for the good of others."

Justine stared fixedly at his black stock. "I am clumsy," she told him. "My leg may simply collapse under me."

"If it does, my legs will be your legs. What could be more simple?"

She felt weak and hot.

Struan took a step toward her and his thigh pressed her injured hip. "Backward," he said softly, and she tried and stumbled. "I've got you. Relax. This is new." His arm completely surrounded her waist and he contrived to make the step for both of them.

"A woman lets the man lead her," Struan said. This time it was his left thigh that met her body. "Yes. Yes, just like that."

Justine's breathing became shallow. She dared not look up into his face for fear he would see her—really see her—see how he undid her simply by his touch.

"There are times," he said, "when a man who is particularly fond of a woman wants to hold her near. If I held you in such a manner you would be able to report on the event for the book. And you might feel less afraid of falling."

Softly, Struan hummed more of the waltz, his breath shifting across her brow. Releasing her hand, he took her arms and placed them around his shoulders. "To steady you," he said. Then he spread his hands on her back and drew her against him. "And to assist you in writing your book."

Their bodies pressed together.

"This . . . this would not happen in the ballroom?" she said.

"It might if there were a particular reason for a man to hold a woman especially close."

"What reason could there possibly be?" Her voice sounded as if it belonged to a quite different woman.

Struan hummed on. His hands smoothed gently yet firmly over her back. He swayed, and she swayed with him.

All of her body touched his. And his touched hers—leaned into hers. He was big. Solid bone and muscle. Hard angles that, miraculously, accommodated her softer lines—her softer curves.

"The dress becomes you," he said. "Rose-colored. And there is rose bloom in your cheeks now."

"Thank you. You did not explain why a man would hold a woman thus."

"Because he wants to feel her." His tone lost its softness. "This is part of what you want your readers to know, Justine. A man wants to feel a woman. Feeling her quickens his blood—and other parts."

Her heart thumped. "I see."

He leaned away to look down at her. "Now it's your turn to see? Does that mean you're confused?"

She raised her chin. "When you say it—does it mean you're confused?"

The corners of his mouth jerked down. "I do believe you're learning to banter with me. Yes, dear Justine, it does sometimes mean I'm not sure what you intend or what I'm supposed to say."

"I see."

He laughed, but the laughter stopped abruptly. "We are in a pretty fix, y'know."

"I know."

"Everyone telling us what we ought to do."

"Or have to do," she told him.

He gazed into her eyes, then at her mouth—then downward.

Justine grew even hotter.

Struan spanned his big hands about her ribs. His thumbs came to rest against the sides of her breasts. "Your skin is lovely," he told her. "Rosy wherever I look."

He looked at the tops of her breasts where they rose and fell far too noticeably above the neck of her gown.

"A female becomes accustomed to a man paying her such compliments," he said. "You'll remember that, will you?"

The next breath she took made her breasts feel they would swell free of her bodice. "I'll remember," she whispered.

"I do believe you will." His thumbs smoothed flesh suddenly grown sensitive, grown raw to the touch.

"I don't think you should—"

"Absolutely, I should. This is natural, Justine. Don't you like the way it feels?"

His hips, braced against hers, distracted Justine. What she had so unsuitably observed on certain other gentlemen was happening to Struan. She could not contain her own small cry.

"What is it?" He frowned. A pale line formed around his compressed lips. "Have I hurt you?"

"No." Her own hips moved. She felt powerless to stop herself from thrusting against the solid length of the ridge within his breeches. "You surprised me. I feel what is happening to your body, Struan." Oh, she was cursed with a careless tongue.

"And it makes you cry out with horror?"

"It makes me cry out with . . . I feel . . . Struan, is it because you are touching me that this happens to you?"

"Yes." He covered her breasts, very carefully, keeping his gaze on her eyes as if he could see into her very soul. "If you wish me to stop, I will."

If she took her arms from his shoulders she would surely fall. "Do not stop," she said. "Please do not stop."

"Justine." He said her name the instant before his lips brushed hers. Slowly, his mouth caressed hers, moved over hers.

Her eyes closed tightly, only to fly open again.

Struan pushed one thigh between hers and drew her up the length of rigidly flexed muscle. Deep within her heat licked. She tried to push away, but he held her fast.

And he kept on kissing her. His clever lips made hers tingle. Then he did another extraordinary thing. With the very tip of his tongue, he sought the sensitive inside of her mouth and slid over moist skin until the heat at her center and the tingling in her mouth—and the swelling ache in her breasts—convulsed her in his arms.

"I want you," he murmured against her ear.

Justine heard but no longer understood.

With warm lips, Struan kissed her jaw, her neck, the hollow above her collarbone. And he kissed the tops of her breasts so softly that his mouth might have been a passing breeze, a breeze that did not cool but rather set her skin afire.

"This is the beginning of what you call closeness," he said, returning his attention to her neck. "Or so I believe."

"The beginning?" she asked him breathlessly. "Surely there cannot be much more."

He chuckled and nipped at her ear. "Much, much more, sweet lady. We have barely begun."

She should insist he set her from him this very instant.

She should protest his intimacy at once.

She should never, ever, allow him to touch her again as he touched her now.

"Barely begun?"

"Absolutely. There is so much more. And we shall ensure that you gather every possible detail. For your book, of course."

"Of course."

She would die if he never touched her this way again.

"When . . . when, exactly, would things such as this occur? In the courtship? Or whatever?"

Austere concentration settled on Struan's bold features. His dark brows drew lower over his eyes while he regarded her face. "These things happen when a man has decided he must have a woman—a particular woman—no matter what the cost."

She should not be all but riding his thigh.

"When a man reaches such a pass, there is usually little question but that . . . Passion is almost certain to follow. Ardor, Justine. The satisfaction of those urges you mentioned."

Filling her hands with his jacket, she attempted to slide from his leg—with disastrous results. Wonderfully disastrous results.

A burning dart speared through her very center. "Struan!" She clutched at him and pulled his stock loose.

"Yes, dear one," he said through his teeth. "Oh, yes."

"No!"

"Yes." Surrounding her with one arm, he slipped his other hand beneath her skirts and found the pulsing core that held the root of the marvelous pain.

He pushed a finger inside her.

"Oh!" Justine bucked. "You must not." She could not control her body.

His finger eased in and out. His thumb worked at the little place that swelled with a need she knew with her being but not with her mind.

"Let go," he told her. "It is time for this."

With parted lips, Justine drew in great gulps of air. All she saw were his eyes, his intensely dark eyes.

And a tide ripped through her, opened her, rendered her bare and helpless.

In the wake of the tide came searing ripples. Amazed, she struggled to collect herself. "Struan? What?"

"Passion, sweet. The fulfillment of urges. Closeness."

*It?*

No. "Not all, though, Struan? There is still more?"

His smile was cynical. "More indeed. There is the matter of my urges. Of my body."

Without thinking, she felt for the hardness between his legs.

Struan's smile died. His teeth came together. "My lady, I do not advise you to persist with that."

She drew her hand away. His flesh had sprung into her fingers.

"Very wise," he said. Muscles bunched in his jaw. Gradually, as if reluctant, he set her feet on the floor but drew her into a tight embrace. "This afternoon's work has not served to ease my dilemma," he said, his cheek resting against her temple.

Where she had been hot, Justine experienced the slipping in of unnatural cold. When he released her, there was in his expression a deeply troubled cast.

"You mean that the contact with me caused you to be left unfulfilled in some way?" Of course that's what he meant. "Naturally. It would be so with any female, wouldn't it?"

The pallor of his face, the tension, shocked her. "There are physical reactions that are inevitable," he said, narrowing his eyes. "What occurs elsewhere is a different matter."

Did he mean in the heart? *A lover? Old fool!* He'd told her to forget Grandmama's words. She never would. "You have certainly kept your end of the bargain. Now I shall have a great deal to write about." Even as she said the words she knew how absurd they sounded. "Max's accent must be attended to at once."

"To hell with Max's accent. Don't you understand—don't you feel my struggle?"

Already troubled, he was now the more troubled because of her. "I do understand. Truly, Struan, I shall go if it will be easier."

"It would be easier," he almost shouted. "I intended to come to you today and insist you leave. But I cannot! No, it's not possible. There has to be another way."

She put a hand over her eyes. "I'm sorry."

"Don't be. Do not ever be sorry. It is I who should apologize, and I do. But I am a match for whatever may come my way. We shall marry. There are grave considerations, but I will suffer them. I will control them."

Justine dropped her hand.

Struan strode away and sat at the piano once more. "We will proceed with the arrangements at once."

The music that flowed from beneath his hands was harsh. Harsh, angry music.

"Grave considerations, Struan?" she said. "I would not think of you dealing with grave considerations on my account."

"There is nothing more to discuss. There are certain provisions and precautions I must consider. Please allow me to think awhile."

The only reason he was saying this was that he and his brother—and her own brother now—had decided propriety and their damnable family honor demanded it.

Struan hated the idea of marriage to her, hated the prospect of the derision that would be heaped upon him by disbelieving friends and acquaintances. And why wouldn't he when he could have his pick of beautiful and suitable women?

But unlike many of those women, she was not simpering, blushing, or slavishly compliant. "I am not chattel," she said clearly.

A great clash of jangling notes came from the piano. Struan stared at her. "I beg your pardon?"

"I said, I am not chattel. This is demeaning. Who asked me what I want?"

He braced his arms against the piano. "That is hardly an issue here, is it?"

"Sin's ears!" Hair had slipped from her chignon. She pushed the locks angrily behind her shoulder. "It is an issue to me! I do not want a man who doesn't want me. I do not want a man to marry me because he feels forced to do so."

He shook his head. "You really don't have any idea, do you?"

"Oh, I think I have a great many ideas. Thanks to you. And they will be most useful as I proceed with my work."

"The hell with your work. It is not your work we're discussing here. It's the matter of our marriage. It's the matter of certain things I must consider and control after that marriage."

"Really?" Her dress was outrageously rumpled. "I do not regret what I have experienced with you. I will not lie. You mean a great deal to me, Struan, and I shall forever remember this afternoon. But although I am inexperienced, I believe we did rather more than was wise—for scientific purposes. We shall, if you agree, return to our original arrangement."

"Sin's . . . Agh, you almost have me using your frothy epithet! I do not agree, dammit. Your honor is my affair. And I refuse to have you surrendered into the clutches of some pinching old pervert. I have considered all aspects of the problem and decided I will have more peace if you are where I can control what happens to you at all times. You will be my wife, and that's an end of it."

Her head began to pound. "Thank you for your assistance in my project. Be assured I'll fulfill my promises to you and your children in return."

"Justine. I have decided—"

"What you have decided is immaterial."

"I don't believe this."

"Of course you don't." She swung away. "I'd appreciate your help in finding my way back to my apartments."

"I think we should go directly to Kirkcaldy and speak with the minister Arran—"

"You simply cannot accept fact, can you?" Justine looked at him over her shoulder. "I am not a box of cigars to be purchased and used or discarded, depending upon how well my taste pleases you. I am a woman, an intelligent woman who can make up her mind what she wants."

"In most things, yes," Struan said, as if she were a child and he a particularly patient parent. "But there are those areas where—"

"Where men behave like peacocks and consider themselves supreme?"

"Justine"—he came toward her—"forgive me. I forgot myself. Under other circumstances I should approach your father at such a time, but—"

"But I'm too old and my father is dead."

"I intended to say that you are mature enough to make most of your own decisions. Anyway, it is Calum to whom I must speak, of course."

"No," Justine told him archly. "No, you said it almost right. I am mature enough to make my own decisions. Not just most of them, but all of them."

"Well—"

"And I have decided that marriage to you is out of the question. Thank you, but I refuse your offer, Struan."

# Chapter Twelve

❦

"**W**omen are a damnable inconvenience," Struan said, slamming shut the door of his brother's study at Kirkcaldy. "Completely addlepated and incomprehensible. To be avoided at all costs. The audacity. The *audacity*, I tell you!"

Arran, his chair pushed back, sat with his booted feet propped on the desk. Calum occupied a leather chair to Arran's right.

Tall, silent Caleb Murray stood behind his master's chair with a large ledger open across his sinuous forearms.

"The less we have to do with them, the better," Struan continued when neither Arran nor Calum responded to his outburst. "Use them and ignore them. Only way to deal with the situation. And never—never *ever* allow them to think. Thinking is one of the greatest evils when it comes to women." He dropped into a chair that matched the one Calum was using and steepled his fingers.

"I think Struan's out of sorts," Arran said.

Calum puffed up his cheeks. "Would seem so. What d'you suppose may have brought about that situation?"

Arran frowned thoughtfully and motioned for dark-haired Murray to close the ledger. "Hard to say. Always been a diffi- cult fellow to read, Struan. Pulled the wool over everyone's eyes so many times in the past, we all tend to think he's still at it."

Caleb Murray bowed. "Is that all, your lordship?" The man's bearing suggested a certain reserved arrogance. Struan liked the man well enough but had found himself wishing he knew more about the estate commissioner's lineage.

Arran looked up at Murray intently. "The poaching matter? Any developments there?"

"We may never make ground there, your lordship." The slender lines of Murray's face showed little emotion, but he was a good-looking devil, Struan would give him that.

"As you say." Arran sighed. "That'll do for now, then."

"There was the matter Mrs. Moggach and—"

"Afraid settling the staff pudding issue will have to await the marchioness's return," Arran said, not unkindly.

"Very well," Murray said. His jacket and waistcoat were of good brown cloth and well cut. No expense had been spared on his linen or on his buff breeches and highly polished top boots. He continued, "Internal staff issues are no concern of mine, but Shanks is under the weather and asked me to bring the matter up. Evidently it was Mairi who used to come in and take care of the puddings, Moggach not being much of a hand in that department. Since Mairi became otherwise engaged there's really been no one to take—"

"*Puddings,*" Struan said when he could contain himself no longer. "Puddings? At a time like this? Grumpy should have been chucked out on her ear years ago. Old tyrant. You can tell her I said so, Caleb."

"Yes, my lord."

"I think I'd rather you didn't," Arran said mildly. "Why not go along and tell the staff their mistress will be home as soon as she can travel. They'll like to hear that."

"Aye." Caleb bowed his way to the door with every sign of wanting to be gone as quickly as possible. "Aye, I'll do that."

"I say, Struan," Calum said when the estate commissioner had left. "Having a struggle with things in general, are we?"

"Look here." Struan leaned forward. "This isn't a joke."

"Never said it was, old man," Calum said. "Certainly no joke to me, I can tell you. Quite a worry when I see the man who's going to marry my sister behaving like a maniac."

Struan pointed a warning finger at Calum. "Marry your sister? Have you lost your mind? What in God's name makes you think I'd marry that contrary, ranting female with her Sin's warts? Unreasonable creature. Ungrateful creature. Totally irrational creature."

"Ears," Calum remarked. "Mostly, anyway."

Struan clasped his knees. "What ears?"

"Sin's ears, old chap." Calum smiled cheerfully. "she usually says sin's ears, not warts."

"A pox on you, Calum, for the unfeeling rattle you are."

Arran uncrossed his feet and recrossed them in the opposite direction. "Sounds as if Struan's a bit disenchanted with your sister, old chap," he said to Calum. "Odd. Never would have said such unpleasant things about the lady meself. Seems a charming female. Charming and intelligent."

"Enough!" Struan shot from his chair to stride about the room. "You trifle with a man in a dangerous frame of mind, sir. A man already pressed beyond endurance."

"How so?"

Struan hesitated to glance directly at Calum. Damn his own careless tongue. "You know well enough. There is the matter of Ella and Max. Not a simple matter and one which I am far from sorting out in a satisfactory manner." Not for the first time, he wondered fleetingly if he should mention the letters and enlist help from these two. Just as rapidly the idea passed. A man had his pride, dammit.

"Seems simple enough to me," Calum said, his brow furrowed. "Why not revert to Philipa's original idea and say they are illegitimate. You don't have to shout about it, of course. Just state the fact without stating the fact exactly. They are illegitimate. No one has to know you aren't the father. Much simpler. No awkward questions in the event that there should be future legitimate offspring."

"Never. Philipa did not know what she said when she said it. She wouldn't have if she did."

"Riddles," Arran said. "All riddles. Pour me a drink, Struan, there's a good chap."

"Pour your own bloody drink, you bounder."

Arran clasped his hands behind his neck and looked wounded. "I can't imagine what leads you to abuse me in this way, brother. I who have never been other than your most staunch supporter."

"*Tripe.*"

"Nasty stuff," Calum commented.

"Not too bad with onions, so they tell me," Arran said.

Struan lost his temper entirely. "You two are driving me insane! I told Justine we must marry, and she refused. Do you understand? Justine told me she will not marry me!"

A lengthy quiet followed before Arran swung his feet to the floor with a thud and said, "The devil, she did."

"The devil, she did," Calum echoed.

"Will some higher force help me?" Struan intoned to the vaulted wood ceiling. "Will some generous being come to my aid in my time of trial?"

"Naturally," Arran told him. "Would Calum and I consider doing otherwise?"

Calum nodded. "We certainly will help. First, I'd like to know how you came to be asking my sister for her hand without speaking to me first—and exactly what foul insult you threw at her to bring about such an outcome?"

Blood pumped at Struan's temples. "All right." He raised his palms. "All right, you two. You've had a great deal of pleasure at my expense, but the fun is definitely over. I shall withdraw my offer from Justine forthwith, and from here on her welfare will mean less than nothing to me."

"I thought you said she'd already turned you down," Arran said mildly.

Calum got up and poured three large glasses of whiskey. "You did not answer my questions, however. How did you insult my sister?"

"I did not insult her. I paid her the ultimate compliment— by asking her to become my wife. I paid her many compliments, in fact."

"When?"

"Before I came here."

"Where?"

"At the lodge. In Grandfather's ballroom. I even played the piano for the woman, dammit. And she liked it. She liked everything I did, or I miss my mark."

Arran choked on the whiskey Calum had given him.

"Everything?" Calum said slowly, making no attempt to hand a glass to Struan. "What exactly would everything be?"

The rise of color in his face was an unfamiliar sensation. "Well"—he shrugged—"you know. A little of this and that. Very little."

Calum's voice became silky. "I sincerely hope I don't know in this instance. Didn't I see Ella and Max in the green salon?"

Struan snatched a glass from Calum and took a deep swallow. "They came to see the dowager duchess."

"But that maid is with Justine?"

Struan drank again and sputtered as the fiery liquid rushed down his throat.

"The maid—"

"She came with the children, damn your eyes."

"Is Justine alone at the lodge? Were you there with her? Alone perchance? Alone, again?"

Struan jutted his jaw. "Yes. What of it? She isn't a child and neither am I."

"Would that you were," Arran said, examining the fingernails of his left hand. "Clearly we'd better proceed with haste to make an honest woman of Justine."

"God have mercy!" Struan flung himself back into the chair near the fire and held the cool glass to his brow. "Do you not hear a word I tell you? I asked Justine to become my wife. No, actually, I begged her to become my wife. She says she will not have me."

"Come with me," Arran said. He marched from the room, still carrying his whiskey, and stopping from time to time to sip.

Struan quickly realized where they were heading and fought an urge to flee.

They entered the corridor leading from the vestibule to the impressive curving staircase and climbed rapidly upward. Their boots thudded over priceless red Turkish carpets toward the green salon that had been their parents' favorite room in the castle.

Struan sent up more prayers. With good fortune, the dowager would yet be indisposed and the worst he might encounter would be his two fake offspring on their best behavior.

"Oh, yes," Arran said, halting abruptly. "There is something else I should do, of course. Calum, go for Justine, would you?"

Calum appeared bemused. Then his face cleared and he handed Struan his glass. "Should have thought of it myself. I'll fetch her at once. You deal with the preliminaries, Arran. Give me a chance to talk some sense into Justine."

"Quite." Arran threw open the door to the drawing room and entered.

For one wistful moment, Struan watched Calum's retreating back. Running away really wasn't an option. He followed Arran.

"Hell's teeth," Arran muttered.

Struan glanced at him with surprise before looking around the beautiful room he'd known all his life. Ella, a beguiling vision in her green habit, sat primly on a brocade chair. Max's cheeks bulged with some delicacy that made his eyes appear unfocused with ecstasy. With a napkin tucked into his collar, he shared Ella's couch.

The Dowager Duchess of Franchot might have died and been propped, eyes wide open, in an ebony chair inset with gold ivy leaves. The woman don't move a muscle and showed no sign of breathing.

"I've had a great deal of experience in these matters, Your Grace," a fourth occupant of the room said. "I know what it's like to be unappreciated for one's sacrifices. I ought to. After my Ichabod died and I was left with nothing more substantial than one opinionated, untalented, clumsy, and completely ungrateful daughter to comfort me, I learned quickly the pain of dealing with disappointing offspring."

Struan took in Arran's hard glare and suppressed a grin.

"And now," the newcomer said with much wafting of a sequin-studded black feather fan, "and now I am forced by another unfortunate circumstance to throw myself upon that offspring's doubtful generosity yet again."

"Good afternoon, Uncle Stonehaven," Ella said to Arran. "Hello, Papa. We have been having a most interesting visit with Her Grace and Uncle Stonehaven's mother-in-law."

The sound Arran made resembled a toad's croak.

"There you are, Stonehaven," Blanche Wren Bastible said, as if suddenly realizing her son-in-law had entered the room.

"Perhaps you will explain why no coach was sent to greet me in Dunkeld."

Arran's face was devoid of either comprehension or expression.

"Had it not been for the kindness of this fine fellow"—Blanche waved toward Caleb Murray, who had been hovering awkwardly near the door—"Come, come, now, Mr. Murray. Don't be shy. Early this morning he rescued me from that wretched Fiddler's Rest place. So common."

Caleb yanked his waistcoat even straighter over a flat stomach. "I came to check on Mrs. Bastible, my lord. I see you are well-settled, Madam. I'll take my leave of you."

"I haven't thanked you properly," Blanche told him, a coquettish smile making dimples in her plump face. "I don't know what I'd have done without you. The wretched inn was filled with low women and cardplayers."

"Should have felt exceeding comfortable to you," Arran muttered, quietly enough that Struan knew he alone would hear. "We had no idea you were descending, Mother-in-law," he said more loudly.

Bedecked in voluminous flounces of black satin and lace, Blanche turned her round blue eyes dolefully upon Arran. "I shall have plenty to say to Grace when she dares to show her face, I can tell you. Imagine, my own daughter ensconced on holiday in Yorkshire and she didn't even bother to tell her tormented mother of the event."

"Your arrival wasn't announced," Arran said.

"I never like to make a fuss," Blanche said, her fan fluttering rapidly. A profusion of chestnut ringlets bobbled about round shoulders and jet beads at the low neckline of her gown pressed into impressively mounded white breasts. "I had Mr. Murray here bring in my trunks quietly. Fortunately my old room was bearable, if exceeding cold—even after some silly maid deigned to be roused to light the fire.

"When I arose this afternoon and heard the dowager

duchess was in residence, I came to pay my respects at once. Isn't that what I just told you I did, Mr. Murray?"

"Er . . . aye."

Blanche pointed her fan at Arran. "And don't you be cross with this dear man for not telling you I'd arrived. I told him I wanted to surprise you, didn't I, Mr. Murray?"

Behind his back, Caleb's hands curled into fists. "Aye, Mrs. Bastible."

Struan forgot his own problems long enough to be sorry for Kirkcaldy's quiet-mannered estate commissioner. "Did you talk to the landlord of the Rest about our problem, Caleb?" he asked. There was a likelihood that at least some of the poached Kirkcaldy game was being served at table in the Fiddler's Rest.

"I did mention—"

"I wondered what you were discussing so—spiritedly over your cards," Blanche said avidly. "I thought it was your fine winnings from that handsome monk that made the landlord shout so."

All eyes turned upon the woman, who showed no sign of discomfort. "I opened the wrong door, you see," she said. "I didn't realize that was the card room."

"We'll speak later," Arran told Caleb.

"Thank you, Mr. Murray," Blanche said. She lowered her lashes a fraction and peered through them at Caleb. "You may be certain I shall not forget that you alone have treated my arrival with kindness."

In his haste to escape the room Caleb all but tripped over Justine on her way in. Calum followed her. "I didn't have far to go," he said, appearing uncomfortable. "Justine was already on her way into the castle."

"Ah," Blanche said when the door closed again. "This must be the wayward granddaughter."

Moving for the first time since Struan had entered, the dowager duchess closed her eyes and kept them closed.

Max, steadily demolishing a plate of small cakes, spoke around a mouthful of ginger tart. "This is Lady Justine Girvin. The one we told ye about. She and our papa need t'be married on account o' they've been . . ."

"I think it's time for us to leave," Ella said. "We'll see you at the lodge, Papa."

Struan smiled gratefully at her.

"I've not finished m'tea," Max mumbled. "Compromised. That's the word."

Blanche Wren Bastible tutted and swayed and flapped her fan furiously.

"The duke found them on their own, y'see," Max said, waving a currant-filled biscuit in Calum's direction. "He's Lady Justine's brother. Anyway, Papa and Lady Justine'll have t'marry. Isn't it a good thing we're motherless at present?"

Utter stillness followed.

Struan saw Arran's mouth twitch. The traitor should suffer for that.

"I see I haven't arrived a moment too soon," Blanche announced. "Don't worry about a thing, Your Grace. I have considerable experience in the matter of marriages. Since you'll obviously want to accomplish this one with all haste, you may count me your faithful, knowledgeable, and absolutely circumspect helper."

"Who is this person?" Justine said.

"Grace's mother," Struan said. By God, she was beautiful, but she was also white-lipped with fury. "Obviously this is all badly timed, my dear. Are you tired?"

"I am not tired," she said without looking at him. "Did you think your little dancing lesson would tire me, Viscount Hunsingore?"

The dowager's eyes popped open. "Dancing lesson? What dancing lesson? You can't dance. You can scarcely walk. Why does the viscount find it necessary to have two drinks?"

He'd forgotten the whiskey glasses. Setting them down, he said, "Justine walks very well, Your Grace." He would not lose his temper. "She expressed an interest in the dance. I was teaching her to waltz."

"Among other things," Arran said, grabbing the complete attention of all. "Don't look at me like that, Struan. You are my brother and I only want the best for you. Under the circumstances, the best will be your marriage to Justine at the earliest possible moment."

"What things?" Blanche asked, her blue eyes glittering with interest. She deliberately sat farther back in her chair and concentrated on combing her nails through the feathers of her fan. "After all, the exact nature of what passes between people is important when considering exactly how much haste is necessary in such situations, isn't it?"

Struan moved closer to Justine. "I'm sorry," he said softly. "My fault. Entirely my fault."

"My fault," she said, still refusing to look at him. "You could not have known so much foolishness would follow a simple act of friendship."

"Yes, I could. I was selfish. I admire you and I wanted your company."

"And I wanted yours."

Struan covered her hands where they rested, tightly twined and too cold, at her waist. "We shall weather this, Justine."

"Not by my settling for an arrangement simply for the benefit of others," she said. "What happened in the ballroom was a mistake. Useful, but a mistake. In future I shall ensure that we are more careful."

Struan could not believe what she'd said. He swallowed air and coughed.

"Useful, hmm?" Calum said.

He was smiling, too, damn his soul. Struan said, "You are perfectly well aware of the book Justine is writing. I'm helping. She means our efforts in the ballroom were not entirely suitable for her work."

"This is pointless," Justine said. "I'd planned to visit Grandmama, but I find I'm very tired. If you'll excuse me, I'll return to the lodge. Potts shall take me in the cart."

"We'll ride along with you," Ella said promptly, and removed a wedge of fruitcake from Max's hand. As she passed Struan she rose to tiptoe and whispered, "All these noisy people are the problem. Lady Justine is gentle and very private and they confuse her. She loves you, truly she does."

He leaned over the girl and said quietly, "Have Mr. Murray accompany you back. Do not ask why. Just do it."

Ella met his eyes directly and gave a slight nod.

Overwhelmed with hopelessness, he watched the three of them go. He longed to follow Justine, to make her listen to him, to make her understand how much he wanted her.

"I trust you are well rested, Your Grace," Arran said to the dowager. When she didn't respond he said, "Good, good. You will need your strength in the days to come. Word of the situation between Justine and Struan is all over the country."

Struan drove the fingers of one hand into his hair.

Arran swirled the whiskey in his glass. "Devlin North— he's one of our neighbors—gets around a great deal. Young fellow. Fancies himself a bit of a Corinthian. Anyway, I ran into him in Dunkeld. Said he understood Struan was about to make a good match. Shocked me to silence, I can tell you."

"For the first time in your life," Struan said through his teeth.

"Devlin heard the news in London. Some gathering for an envoy of Wellington's."

"The Duke of Wellington?" Blanche said, shifting forward on her chair again. "I hear he's such a fine figure of a man."

Struan saw the dowager's knuckles whiten on her cane.

Calum clasped his hands beneath the tails of his coat. he also was observing his grandmother's reactions.

"Apparently the King was there," Arran said. "Showed a great deal of interest—according to Devlin. You'll remember His Royal Highness lent his personal blessings on the occasion of Calum and Philipa's wedding."

The dowager smote the carpet with her cane. "Gossip. How people love to spread gossip. Edinburgh to London in almost no time."

"In no time at all," Struan muttered, catching his brother's sharp green gaze.

"Understand Sir Walter Scott intends to send his congratulations," Arran said, smiling. "Probably write an ode or something, I should think."

"You will roast for this," Struan said.

The dowager duchess rose. "Very well. On her own head be it. I will not have my family's name besmirched from Edinburgh to London."

"And on to the Continent," Arran added.

Calum, Struan noted, no longer seemed to find much of amusement in the situation. His mouth was set in a grim line and he clearly had a great deal on his mind that he chose not to say—yet.

"There will be a marriage," the dowager said. "We shall have to find a minister prepared to—"

"Already done," Arran said.

Struan's brother wanted this marriage, was determined that it should take place.

"Let me see," the dowager said. "Three Sundays will take us—"

"Tomorrow and next Sunday will make the three," Arran put in. "The banns have already been called once."

Calum swung around. "Where?"

"Here in the castle chapel, of course."

"To a packed congregation, no doubt," Calum said under his breath.

Arran ignored him. "The license will be in order. The marriage can take place in little more than a week."

"We shall have to discuss a suitable settlement," the dowager said. "That foolish girl. Belcher would have paid us."

"The matter of Justine's dowry is my affair," Calum said. He switched his attention from his grandparent to Struan. "I shall expect my sister to be treated kindly at all times. As for finances, I will never allow her to want for anything."

Struan made fists, then forced himself to relax. "Contrary to your apparent assumptions, I am not a poor man. Justine will require no dowry and I shall be happy to add to the Franchots' endangered coffers if that will make you think more kindly of me."

The dowager swept to confront him. "The Franchot coffers are not endangered, young man. This is simply a matter of commerce. It has been by commerce—of an appropriately gentlemanly sort—that the Franchots have reached their enviable position in the Polite World. One can never be too cautious in the matter of fortune hunters."

"Grandmama," Calum said firmly. "We must attempt to reach a peaceable resolution between our families."

"The wedding must be quiet," the dowager said. "Only fitting under the circumstances."

"It should be quiet enough without a bride," Struan blurted before he could contain himself.

"Pish posh." With a wave of a clawlike hand, the dowager dismissed what Struan suggested. "The chit will do as she's told. Then she'll reap the miserable reward for her mistake, poor creature. And I shall show her no pity, no pity at all."

"Quite right," Blanche said.

Arran rounded on his mother-in-law and said, "Kindly hold your tongue, madam."

"Well, really." Settling her neck deeper into her shoulders, Blanche pouted.

The tip of the dowager duchess's cane rose and came to rest

on Struan's chest. "You, Viscount Hunsingore, shall regret thwarting my wishes. I do not pretend to understand your reasons, but I have no doubt they will become obvious."

He yearned to snatch the cane and toss it aside.

"Thanks to you and that ridiculous female, I am exhausted. I must rest. You will attend me tomorrow afternoon at two. Alone. In my apartments. There are concerns we must address."

"I shall count the hours," Struan told her, staring directly into her bright, hard eyes.

Calum shifted and said, "I shall be present, Grandmama."

"No, I—"

"Yes. Where Justine's future is concerned I insist upon being involved."

"And I must be certain my brother's interest's are protected," Arran said.

The dowager's face settled into its expressionless folds. "Why not? If we all understand the facts, so much the better."

"How jolly," Blanche said, smiling. "I shall come and stand in for Grace."

"No, you won't." The chorus that arose would probably, Struan thought, be the last moment of accord among most of those present in the room.

Fluffing out her skirts, Blanche rose. "You are being most unfriendly. I shall communicate with Grace at once and let her know I've decided to accept her offer of a home here."

In the act of raising his glass, Arran's hand hovered in midair. "Offer of a home? What can you be speaking of, Mother-in-law?"

She patted strands of jet beads threaded through her hair. "It was always understood that there would be a place for me with my daughter should the need arise. Now that I'm a widow again, the need has arisen. My dear Felix has passed on." Her sigh was abject. "Twice a widow, and at such a young age. Really, it seems so unfair. I would have written, but there was so much to do. Dealing with his wretched, grasping relatives. I'm sure you all know what I mean. They would have had me walk away without a single prize to show for my devotion. I made certain that didn't happen, I can assure you."

"The Reverend Bastible is dead?" Arran frowned. "My sympathies. When exactly did this occur?"

Blanche pursed her lips as if calculating. "Oh, two months ago at least."

"I cannot believe you didn't inform us earlier. What of your home—the home you shared with Reverend Bastible?"

"What of it?" Lace ruffles required primping. "That was part of the unpleasantness with his other relatives. Anyway, my place is with those who love me. I must put my troubles behind me and concentrate on my dear daughter and granddaughter now."

It was Struan's turn to suppress a grin. Arran was a man cast suddenly into despair. He regarded Blanche as if she were an invading army. "Grace isn't here," he said weakly.

"No matter. How fortunate that I am here to take her place. I've arrived just in time to help everyone, especially the dear dowager." She threaded her arm through one of the old lady's and moved her toward the door. "You and I have a great deal in common, Your Grace. We have both suffered at the hands of those for whom we've done the most. Fear not, I shall help you through your time of trouble."

As the high voice faded, Struan crossed his arms and prepared for Arran's outburst.

"Duck!" Calum shouted.

Struan ducked.

Arran's glass hit the wall beside the door and exploded into a thousand glittering shards.

# Chapter Thirteen

❧

"**W**hen shall we travel to Edinburgh?" Ella asked. Dressed in a night rail and robe, she stood behind Justine at her mirror.

Justine found she could scarcely concentrate on what the girl said. "I'm sorry, Ella?"

"For the dresses and things. For my Season."

Ella had not brought the subject up before. That she did so now pleased Justine. "Of course, dear. But London, not Edinburgh. I told you we should go to London."

"I've never been to Edinburgh," Ella said, carefully brushing Justine's loosed hair all the way to its thick curling ends. "Could we not visit there for a short while first? I think we should go soon."

It was natural for a young girl to be too swept away with the promise of such excitement to be concerned with the problems of an old maid. "I'll speak to your papa," Justine said. How would she bear to see him, to be near him after all that had passed between them? "You should be in your bed."

"I sent Mairi to hers so that I could help you," Ella said promptly. "I wanted an excuse to talk to you."

"We've already talked." And talked, and talked. All the way back from the castle Ella, with Max chattering his opinions, had lauded their papa's virtues—and the virtues Justine would add to his if they were to marry. "The subject you wish to pursue is closed, Ella. Do not distress yourself or me by raising it again."

Ella hung her head and replaced the silver-backed brush on its crystal tray. "Sometimes we have to learn to embrace what we cannot change," she said. "It will not be easy. I so wanted you and Papa . . . At least you will be here with us. I must be grateful for that much. Good night, Lady Justine."

Justine was surprised by the girl's ready acceptance of the inevitable. "Good night, Ella. We'll start making plans for our shopping—in Edinburgh to begin with if you'd prefer that."

She raised her cheek for Ella's kiss and watched her young charge leave.

After she and Struan had parted—before Calum came to take her to the castle—she had almost made up her mind to leave. But how could she when Ella and Max needed her so?

"How fortunate that they want you to stay, Justine," she told herself aloud. "They make a wonderful excuse for you to do what you want to do." She was despicable. Even with herself she found honesty uncomfortable.

At Kirkcaldy Struan had apologized to her for the fuss. He'd said it was his fault. He'd said they'd "weather this."

And she wanted to believe he truly felt something for her.

Pride. Yes, pride would stop her from as much as testing for the possibility that he might care for her other than as a friend.

Pride threatened to make her the most unhappy woman in the world.

She was already the most unhappy woman in the world.

Struan had wondered if she should have taken her notebook with her to the ballroom. He'd been afraid she might forget something. Her smile was bitter. She closed her eyes against a rush of tears. Never had she been moved to tears as easily as she was now.

The way he played the waltz.

The way he hummed the waltz.

The way he held her, moved her, moved with her.

His kisses.

She could still feel the pressure of his lips on hers. Her fingers stole to rest on her mouth.

And the *Other*. A shudder like lightning racked from deep within her all the way to her toes, all the way to the roots of her hair. Her skin tingled.

Her breasts ached.

Justine wrapped her arms about herself and rested her brow on the dressing table.

Was it possible that something more than a sense of duty had brought about his suggestion that they marry? Could he love her? Did men even know what love was? Some did. Arran loved Grace. Calum loved Pippa. But she, Justine, was not Grace or Pippa. She should no longer be thinking of such things as being loved by a man—in that way.

But she wanted love in that way. From Struan. With Struan, who had made the sensations she wanted to feel again, she wanted to discover the entire truth about *It* between humans.

This was all so important for her book. If only she could separate her mind from her body, the success of her project would be assured.

Tomorrow she would speak to Struan. She would set the stage for a tranquil existence at the lodge. Eventually he would want freedom to go about in places far from Kirkcaldy. She could give him the gift of that freedom, but first they must make peace over the present trying situation. Calum and Grandmama must go home and Arran must not press Struan further on the issue of marriage.

Going to Edinburgh with Ella might be exactly what was needed to clear the air. Yes, in the morning she would suggest to Struan that she take both children to the Stonehaven house in Edinburgh.

To Edinburgh to shop for a debutante's wardrobe. Justine looked down at her fine white lawn robe and night rail. The yellow daffodils embroidered at neck and hem had been her own work. When she'd still been young and foolish enough to dream of a marriage of her own, she'd worked the robe and gown thinking to save it for her trousseau.

Saving it had become pointless.

Some women would have snatched what Struan offered.

Some women would have told themselves that simply to count themselves his wife—even without true affection—would be a great boon.

It would be purgatory.

In that, at least, her grandmother had been right. To be married to a man whose natural appetites and desires would cause him to wander, to find solace elsewhere, would be an endless misery.

Ella had left Justine's hair unbraided. What did it matter? She had no reason to concern herself with being seen.

Favoring her weak leg, Justine blew out all but the candle she carried. She placed the candle beside the bed, removed her robe, and climbed the steps to the mattress. As she did every night, she reached into the pocket in the bed drapes where she kept her Bible. The small, black leather-bound volume had been her companion since early childhood.

The fire had burned low, and she pulled the covers over her shoulders.

What she held was not her Bible but another leather-bound book, this one brown. Justine frowned and turned back to the drapes. As she thought, she had returned her Bible to the wrong pocket. There it was, safely where she must have placed it the night before.

But how had this book gone unnoticed?

When she opened the front cover, yellowed parchment pages crackled. What she held was extremely old.

"Hannah," she murmured, reading the single name written inside the front cover. "1736."

Almost a hundred years ago.

*"Perhaps if I write down my feelings I shall forget to be angry. I am so very tired of being angry with Edward."*

Justine read on, turned a page, and read to the bottom again.

Hannah, she realized, had been Struan's grandmother, the woman he said had never been here, or at least had never been to the ballroom her husband built for her.

A sprig of dainty, pressed bilberry blossoms fell out. Justine marveled at the preservation of their delicate pink hue.

Bilberry. There had been bilberry in Struan's bouquet. She'd left it behind in the ballroom. Mairi had promised to retrieve and dispose of the flowers.

*"To be married because it is the expected thing is not at all acceptable. I know that had he had the choice of every woman in the world he would never have chosen me. But I do not care a fig for that. And I shall not be bought off with his extravagant gifts. What noble ladies does he think would accept an invitation to his precious monstrosity in the wilderness?"*

The ballroom, of course. That had been an extravagant gift. How odd that this book should have come into her hands tonight of all nights.

Justine turned another page and gasped. A carefully executed watercolor portrait had been slipped into the volume. Smiling impishly at her was a dark-haired young woman in Elizabethan costume. A tiny cap atop her head secured a long, transparent veil of the same creamy color as her embroidered, pearl-studded gown. At her neck a double ruff was visible and ropes of pearls rested against a stiff, elongated bodice.

The woman's eyes laughed. Green eyes. Like Arran's.

A beautiful creature. On the back of the portrait was the notation, *"Me, in the gown I shall not wear for him at the costume ball I shall not go to for him."*

So this was Hannah. How could she have thought any man would be less than delighted to call her his own?

The entries stopped quite suddenly. Justine was disappointed—until she went to close the book and discovered another entry, this one on the final pages.

*"I had forgotten this journal. Strange. Perhaps I found it because I needed to read what I had written. If I had ever had daughters, I should have told them about my mistakes and begged that they learn from them. Edward always loved me. Of that, I'm certain now. Perhaps my not believing him was a form of greedy vanity. Perhaps I needed to be told too often. Perhaps being told made me feel important.*

*"Most of all I regret never having given him the pleasure of seeing me enjoy the ballroom at his hunting lodge. The anger he showed when I failed to go to that costume ball was not feigned. I hurt him. Now his injuries from the accident keep him at the castle. He will never hunt again—probably never as much as see his beloved lodge again. He will definitely never attend a ball there with me at his side.*

*"What a foolish woman I was. To have recognized his love at last was a gift I did not deserve, but I mourn the lost years. I shall visit the lodge and spend time in the ballroom. Then I'll tell Edward and I think it will make him happy."*

Justine closed the book and found her cheeks wet. Poor woman. Poor man. If only they had been honest with each other. To think of so many wasted years was heartbreaking.

She would not sleep for hours.

Leaving her bed, she put her robe on once more. Hannah had gone to the ballroom with no memories of being there with the man she loved. For Justine the room would always bear reminders of a sun-filled afternoon and a lithe, dark-haired man who held her and danced for both of them.

With her single candle, Justine set off through the lodge, grateful for the sense of direction that rarely deserted her. The trek to the ballroom was long, and every step of the way she thought of Struan having been at her side when last she made the journey.

In the ballroom, her little light did no more than paint shadowy shapes on the walls. Struan had left the piano uncovered, and she sat on the seat. With one hand she picked out notes remembered from the waltz he'd played.

A sighing sound stilled her fingers.

Sighing and a current of air that reached her gently.

From the passageway, no doubt.

She set the candle on top of the piano and attempted the waltz again. Tomorrow she would ask Struan what it was. She might even ask him to play it for her again. The solution to the dilemma here was to banish awkwardness.

Hannah had misunderstood her Edward. She had mourned the loss of years when she might have enjoyed his love. If only they had spoken frankly to each other.

Another sigh raised the small hairs on her spine.

Justine looked past the candle, looked past the raised lid on the piano, and clung to the edges of her seat.

*A woman reclined on a chaise.*

A woman who sighed and then began to sob softly.

Justine couldn't make herself move.

The chaise was distant, close to the wall, but there was no mistaking the ethereal vision for other than that of a veiled woman.

Veiled and dressed in clothes from another era. Elizabethan. Creamy cloth studded with pearls that picked up the merest hint of shine from Justine's poor candlelight.

*Hannah.*

Hannah's ghost! Justine closed her eyes tightly. She was a sensible woman, definitely not given to fanciful imaginings. The journal and the late hour—together with her own disturbed thoughts—had made her fanciful and befuddled. She opened her eyes again.

The creature remained where she had been, and her soft sobbing held deep despair. "Oh, don't," Justine said. "Be at peace. All was well in the end."

More sobbing and sighing were the only responses.

Shaking, Justine rose, picked up her candle, and approached. Her heart climbed, thudding, into her throat. Perspiration broke out on her face and her body, perspiration that was instantly icy in the cold room.

A ghost.

Hannah had not found peace after all. Wasn't that what they said about ghosts? That they returned because they had not found the peace in this life that allowed them to completely let it go?

Justine knew so little about such things. She had never believed in them.

There was a ghost on a chaise in this ballroom.

Treading softly and slowly, Justine rounded the piano and approached the veiled creature.

And her candle blew out.

She dropped the holder, heard it smash, and uttered a shocked cry. A rush of air had hit her face and snuffed the candle.

The door slammed.

Justine stood quite still. In a dark room. No, a *black* room. Not a hint of light showed anywhere.

She shut her eyes once more, squeezed them tightly shut and held her breath.

To move would be to invite a disastrous fall.

To stay might mean she would die of pure terror.

*Wait for the dawn.*

Hours away.

Hours alone.

*With a ghost!*

* * *

"Papa! Papa!"

Still in his cloak and gloves, Struan caught the bundle of sharp bones that hurtled into his arms in the vestibule of the lodge. "Whoa, Max," he said. "What is it, old chap? Bad dreams?"

"Lady Justine's gone."

"Gone?" Struan said, aware of how foolish he sounded. "She came back with you and Ella."

"That was hours since. Wasn't it, Ella?"

Dressed for bed, Ella came forward. "I couldn't sleep." She lowered her eyes. "She seemed so unhappy. So a little while ago I went to see if she was resting. I wanted to comfort her."

"And she wasna in her bed," Max said. "Wolves. I heard them mysel'. And they sounded hungry—"

"Not now, Max," Struan said, striding past the pair and starting upstairs.

"She didna take any o' her things," Max called after him. "Snatched from her bed, I say. Wolves. Or mayhap the wild hill clans."

If anything had happened to Justine . . .

She wasn't in her apartments. Nothing appeared to have been removed. Her bed was turned back as if she'd decided to get up and take a stroll.

In the small hours of the morning, for God's sake?

"She is so very unhappy, Papa," Ella said from behind him.

He swung to face her. "How so? What makes you say she is unhappy?"

"I saw her hiding tears. And she could not concentrate on anything I said to her. She did speak to Mairi of flowers. Of having to get the flowers. I don't know what she meant. But that was all she seemed to care about. I—"

"Thank you, Ella," he said. "Please don't concern yourself further. Everything will be well. Justine is safe, I'm certain. You and Max—away to your beds, if you please."

"Aye," Max said with surprising meekness. "She'll not leave us, will she?"

"No," Struan said determinedly. "She will not leave you. She loves you and she is a woman of honor. Her promise to remain and assist with your upbringing is something you need never fear she'll break." If only he could be as certain of his own future with Justine. "To bed with you both. We'll speak in the morning."

"But—"

"No," he told Ella. "No buts, young lady. Off with you. If I need you, I'll come. I won't need you tonight."

Leaving them trailing back to their rooms, he dashed through the lodge, cursing his grandfather's wretched sprawling design every inch of the way.

Holding aloft the lantern he'd snatched in the vestibule, he wondered how easily Justine had negotiated the dark passageways.

He paused.

Surely he was right and she'd returned to the ballroom for the miserable wildflowers he'd gathered for her.

She should be on her way back by now, yet all about him was silence and—but for his own light—darkness.

He hurried on until he reached the double doors to the ballroom. Flinging them open, the first thing he saw was Justine.

She screamed.

"Oh, my God." He started forward and halted. "Justine, it's me. Struan."

At her feet lay the remnants of a china candleholder. Dressed in a softly flowing white nightrobe with her hair loose around her shoulders, she stood in the center of the ballroom floor with her arms tightly wrapped about her.

Her eyes shone huge.

"What is it, my love? What's happened here?"

One hand stole to her mouth.

"Justine, speak to me."

"I have been wrong. I should have been honest with you."

He didn't understand. Quickly, he set the lantern on the mantel and lighted a branch of candles beside the fireplace. Gas, he thought distractedly. Gas was becoming the thing, and they needed it here.

Justine stared straight ahead. He looked around but could see nothing that might hold her attention.

"Now," he said, forcing cheer into his voice. "I am here, and whatever has happened is over."

"She's gone."

Struan searched the room a second time. "Who's gone?"

Justine turned to him. She seemed to see him, really see him for the first time since he'd arrived.

"Someone was here with you?" he pressed gently.

Very gradually, color seeped back into her white cheeks. "I . . . No. The doors swung shut. The draft blew out my candle."

"I see."

"Honesty," she muttered.

Struan approached her carefully. "I should not care to be alone here in the dark," he said.

She gave a short laugh. "Why must you always be so kind?" Her thick, dark-brown hair curled about her shoulders. Fashioned of some cobweb-fine white stuff, the robe she wore accentuated her slender but enticing body. Struan could not help but glance at the thrust of her breasts, at the obvious evidence of crested nipples.

Words all but deserted him. He cleared his throat. "I am not particularly kind, Justine. Just plainspoken."

"I do not believe you would be so frightened by darkness that you would screech like a lunatic and stand in one spot, terrified lest you fall over something." She averted her face.

Struan raised a hand and held it, hovering, inches from her shoulder. "Was someone here?"

"No. I don't know why I said that."

"You've had a fright, that's why. Let me help you back to your room."

"I don't need help."

"No." He settled his hand on her shoulder. "But perhaps I should like to help you. Would that make a difference?"

As she turned her head her hair slipped over the soft white fabric of her robe—and over his hand. "When I said I had not been honest with you, that was true. I've lied from the moment I arrived at Kirkcaldy."

He watched her lips move, glanced into her serious eyes, edged her toward him a little—spread his fingers on her neck beneath her hair. "Justine, I cannot imagine you capable of lying. You are the most candid woman I've ever met." And he was a liar, a liar with another of the damnable, incense-laced letters burning him through the kerseymere of his coat. His enemy had finally made contact again—managed to come and go from the castle without being seen—yet again. Struan had taken the missive discreetly and had yet to open the envelope.

When Justine came closer of her own volition he inclined his head and met her steady stare.

"I knew Arran and Grace had gone to Yorkshire. Grace wrote to Philipa and told her. She told her she might be increasing again and that she did not expect to be able to return to Scotland soon."

He frowned—and played his fingertips over the soft skin at her nape. "You came although you knew Grace and Arran would not be here?"

Her chin came up. Softly, she settled a hand on his cheek. "I came because I knew they wouldn't be here. I planned to find you alone here—with Ella and Max, of course."

Struan shook his head. "You said . . ." What exactly had she said?

"I said I wished to care for Ella and Max and that I wanted your help with my book."

"Yes. That's exactly what you said." Her featherlike caresses over his cheek and jaw should not cause his gut to clench, or his manhood to quicken. "Exactly. And we did come to some sort of agreement, I believe." He wanted—no, *needed*—to spread his hands over her breasts and to kiss her until she willingly stretched beneath him. Naked. Her slender woman's body naked, as naked as his own—joined with his own, writhing with his own—eventually resting in mutual satisfaction with his own.

Justine's eyes went to his mouth. She put her arms around his neck, combed her fingers through his hair . . . And she rose to her toes to rest her mouth on his.

Breath rushed from Struan's lungs. His eyes closed and heat flashed along his veins. A second and he was weak. Another second and he was strong, so strong he could ward off any foe, even the nameless, faceless foe who threatened him and sealed the threat in blood.

Her kiss was chaste and he let it be so. A chaste kiss from Justine, delivered because she decided to deliver it, was more erotic than any he might have devised.

Slowly, their lips parted. He opened his eyes and found hers closed. Gradually, she sank from her toes but kept her hands in his hair.

"You are lovely, Justine," he told her. "I could never have hoped to hold one so lovely so close to my heart."

"I lied to you." Still she did not open her eyes. "When I came I intended to be alone with you. I planned it because I have thought of little else but you since the moment you first came to meet me at Franchot."

He was afraid to move, afraid to breathe, afraid to break the spell.

"All I have wanted since that day is to find a way to be with you. I plotted to do so. And then I came to Scotland, praying I might be able to stay where I could at least see you from time to time."

No woman had ever made herself vulnerable to him as this woman did now. "Yet you will not have me as your husband?"

"Please will you answer me honestly?"

"Yes. Oh, yes, Justine."

"Is it possible . . . That is"—she slowly raised her lashes and yearning shone in her eyes—"could you care for me? Enough to find me an acceptable helpmate?"

"Acceptable?"

"To share your life? All aspects of your life? Is it possible that you did not ask me to mary you entirely because it seemed the right thing to do?"

He took her by the shoulders and shook her gently. "I am going to show you the answer to that question, lovely lady. Containing myself until the appropriate moment will take great control on my part, but I shall manage."

"Is that your way of saying you do have some feelings for me?"

Struan gritted his teeth. He pulled her face against his chest and kissed the top of her head. Her hair streamed over his fingers and he tugged it lightly. "I have a great many feelings for you. All of them want me to do certain things right now."

"Then do them."

He laughed aloud, and as quickly sobered. With a knuckle, he raised her face until he could rain small, hard kisses over her brow, her nose, her cheekbones and jaw—the corners of her mouth. "I do believe I shall do some of them," he said when he paused for air. "But this ballroom is not at all comfortable. Do you think I could persuade you to come to my apartments for . . . for a little companionship before I return you to your own quarters?"

"Shall we . . . Struan, will I learn more of what happens between a man and a woman? In private? A man and a woman who wish for *It*?"

Sometimes she had the most peculiar turn of phrase. "I do believe you will. And I shall enjoy being your teacher." He must be very careful with her, not an easy task when he could not deny his own burgeoning lust.

Her brow pleated. "Well, in light of these developments, I think that would be a perfectly appropriate idea."

Struan pushed his chin forward and produced a jaunty grin. "Would you care to explain that statement to me?"

"I love you, Struan."

He stopped smiling.

"I will always love you," she whispered.

The slow revolution within him might be his stomach or his heart—or both.

"You said you thought we should marry. The rest of them agreed."

"I did," he managed to say. "And they did. And I still do."

Justine stepped away and put her hand in his. "I do, too."

# Chapter Fourteen

❧

"**W**ake up!"

Mr. Smith's voice came to Glory through a heavy mist of sleep. She groaned and coughed. Her mouth felt as dry as the earthen floor in the cave.

He shook her by the shoulder and stripped away the tartan he'd covered her with before he left. "It's almost time. We've got to make sure you know exactly what you're to do."

"Don't want to," she mumbled into a rancid-smelling sheepskin. "Sleep."

"You've slept enough. You've slept away many days, my girl. I need to check you."

She tried to turn over. "No!"

Mr. Smith pushed her back onto her face and shoved the thin gown she wore up to her waist.

Consciousness rushed back and she made fists beside her head. "Don't hurt me again."

"I'm not going to hurt you again, *my dove.*"

Glory lay quite still. He'd called her that several times

since she'd arrived in this terrible place. Each time, instead of the things she'd expected, he'd forced an opiate down her throat and beaten her. She still didn't know how badly or how often he'd beaten her. Steady doses of the opiate had assured that.

"A beautiful arse, m'dear." Something cold ran over her exposed bottom and between her legs. "This will make certain those nasty welts heal with as little marking as possible."

"You hit me, Mr. Smith. You've scarred me."

"No." He laughed. "Just created the knife to turn in Hunsingore's gut. I can imagine how that woman's heart of his will cringe at the sight of what he caused." The laugh rose higher.

"What am I supposed to do?" Glory asked. "Go to his doorstep and pull up my skirts?"

"You know what you're to do."

She sniffed into the nasty sheepskin. "I don't know why I should."

His slap on her slick, bruised skin slammed her teeth together and she choked on a scream.

The laughter became even higher. "That's right, *my dove.* You know what I like, don't you?"

At last he was going to let her have what she wanted. Glory's excitement rose. The pain where he'd slapped her only increased the thrill.

In one swift motion, he pushed the gown up to her shoulders. "Let's have a look up here. Pretty colors. Very effective. And how will you act, my dove?"

"Pitiful," she said, her breathing short. "And like I don't want to intrude."

"Very good." More of the cold liquid drizzled along her spine. Mr. Smith spread the herbal-smelling unguent from her neck to her knees. "And what will you keep on saying?"

His fingers touched the sides of her breasts and she wriggled.

"What?"

Glory wriggled some more. "Can't remember."

He smacked her rear again and Glory cried out again.

"What will you say?"

"Give me a little bit," she wheedled. "Go on, just a bit."

Rather than doing as she asked, Mr. Smith slid his hands beneath her breasts and squeezed, hard. "Say it."

She shook her head.

He twisted, then flipped her to her back.

Glory threw her hands over her head and licked her lips. "Come on, then." She deliberately taunted him. He liked her to taunt him.

From a pocket he produced one of his precious cundums.

"Ooh, been down the Strand again, have you?" she asked. He insisted on wearing the piece of dried sheep gut over his rod no matter what they did. "How many times do I have to tell you I'm clean?" Fastidious, was Mr. Smith.

With narrowed eyes, he stripped off his coat and threw it to the floor. He undid his breeches, pushed them down, and straddled her.

She sighed. "There can't be another one like you, luv. Oh, come to your darling, Glory." Desperate to urge him along, she undulated her body, thrust up her breasts, then her belly, almost bucking him forward.

An instant and he used a knee to pin each of her arms. With his cock so close she could almost reach it with her straining tongue, he slid on the thin bag and tied it in place.

"Let Glory have it, then," she said, smiling coyly. "All of it."

"Beg."

"I've been begging."

"Beg some more." Winding a lock of her hair around his fingers, he turned and turned until she yelped. "Tell me what you want?" he said.

"You know what I want."

Another turn of her hair tore at her scalp and she hissed out her pain. "Say it." The tone of his voice didn't change.

"I . . . want it . . . behind," she managed to tell him. "And in front."

"But what do you want first, my dove?"

Amazingly, the grip on her hair grew even tighter and she wailed. Between gasps she said, "I want to feel all of you, Mr. Smith. And I want you to do what makes you happiest."

"That's better." He lowered himself until his ballocks rested between her breasts, and took his fingers from her hair.

Glory gave a little shriek and wrestled to release her arms. To no avail.

"What are you going to say to Hunsingore, Glory?"

Tears seeped along her temples. "I'm sorry. I'm going to say I'm sorry."

"Very good." A slight shift of weight and the end of his rod pried her lips open. "And what will you say to the woman he's asked to marry him?"

She blinked. Mr. Smith pushed himself deep into her mouth, into her throat. Glory panted and sucked. *Woman?* He hadn't mentioned any woman.

Mr. Smith's hips moved rhythmically.

It always went this way. First what he liked best. Then what she wanted—after he got himself together again and emptied out his bloody cundum.

Glory concentrated, sealed her lips tightly around his shaft, and used her sharp little teeth to milk him to release.

And he never said a word—never did say a word when he came.

As usual, he drew in a long, shuddering breath and leaped from her as if she might get something he didn't want to give away.

With his shirt all but covering fine, strong hips and his breeches around his ankles, he braced himself against the wall and waited until his breathing grew slower and quieter.

"What woman?" she said.

"The one he's going to marry. The one you're going to use if Hunsingore gives us any trouble. Only not at first. I've got other plans at first. Tell me what you're going to do to Hunsingore."

"I'm going to make him sorry for me."

"Then what?"

"Then I'll get him to comfort me."

"What sort of comfort will that be?"

She smiled to herself. "I'm going to get him to take me into his bed—or somewhere else if that's what presents itself."

"And?"

Glory stroked her breasts and belly and pushed her fingers into the dark, slick hair between her thighs. "I'll make him want to give me what I need."

"What you always need," Mr. Smith said neutrally. "I do believe we understand each other well. Show me what he will do to satisfy you."

He needn't have asked. Already her hips writhed. The unguent mingled with her own juices and her strong fingers quickly gave her what she wanted.

Panting, she let her legs splay and spread her arms on the wool-covered pallet.

"Very nice," Mr. Smith said. "Too bad you can't service quite all your needs yourself, my dear."

Glory licked her lips. "I'm glad I can't, and so are you. So what's all these other things we're to do, then?"

"Tonight Hunsingore learned what it is I want."

"*We* want," she corrected him.

"He will be shocked. And he will become even more alert. It would not be surprising if he were to attempt to isolate himself and his brood entirely."

"So how will I get in?"

"The woman's name is Lady Justine Girvin. She's a cripple. Also very pious."

Glory raised herself on her elbows. "He's marrying a cripple?"

"So it seems. Tricked into it. You'll get at him through her. I'll tell you how to do that. Then you will help me force Hunsingore's hand."

Rolling her ample hips from side to side, Glory smiled up at him. "Why don't we have a little fun before you finish telling me all about this?"

"He'll marry her soon. Within days, unless I miss my mark. Once she's his wife he'll be looking for diversion. But he'd still try to turn you away. You'll approach the woman and explain how he always said you were to come to him if you were in trouble. Show her how much trouble you're in."

Glory turned onto her stomach. "Then she'll take me in? And I'll have a chance at Hunsingore? I shall like that very much."

"Not too much," Mr. Smith said, turning his cold face toward her. "Do not become distracted. Remember, I and only I can truly fulfill you, my dove."

"I'll remember," she said demurely, cupping her breasts. "So, is that it?"

"Only the beginning, I fear. He won't be easily frightened. That's where you will be so useful. You will keep me in the information I cannot get without living with the man. With your help we shall—if necessary—make sure he loses one or two things he cherishes more than his own life."

Glory's gaze flew to his face. "The woman?"

He shrugged. "That will depend upon whether he appears to care anything at all for her. And there are others who may be more easily disposed of."

"You make it sound like . . ." She'd better be careful what she said or he'd lose his temper again.

Smiling, he pushed away from the wall. With ease, he rotated her until her knees met the floor and her body folded across the pallet. "I believe this is what you were waiting for."

He forced his rod into her. Glory scrabbled at the twisted tartan and screamed afresh. "Go on! More!"

Mr. Smith's hips met her bottom and she almost fainted with pleasure. "So," he said. "What was it I made it sound like?"

She couldn't talk, not now.

He withdrew and lifted her to face him. "What?" The rutting began at once.

Sweat coursed between her breasts and down her back. Each thrust pushed her farther across the pallet until her head met the wall.

"What? I asked you a question, Glory."

"Don't stop!"

"I won't—if you answer my question."

"Oh—" This was why she could never leave him—even if she hadn't been afraid to try. "You talked like you were going to kill someone."

Just as she would have had it all, he pulled out of her. His grin chilled the protest on her lips. "Good. Very good. I'm glad you understand me so well."

# Chapter Fifteen

❦

Justine didn't waver until Struan began to lead her through the door to his bedchamber.

He looked deep into her eyes. "You don't trust me?"

"With my life," she told him.

"Then trust me not to do anything that will frighten you or make you unhappy. I'm tired, my love. Will you lie with me?"

"On your bed?"

"I thought that might be more comfortable."

"More comfortable than what?"

He sucked in the corners of his mouth before saying, "Oh, I don't know. The windowsill, perhaps, or my desk, or even the floor."

She smiled. "You do enjoy funning me, sir."

"I should enjoy lying on my bed with you in my arms even more."

The nameless place within her squeezed together. Such a thrilling squeeze. "I don't suppose this is appropriate," she said. "Really?"

"Really, it is." Struan settled her hand on his palm and smoothed her knuckles with his thumb.

Justine put her free hand on top of his. "I have quite tossed my virtuous reputation to the wind, haven't I?"

"Quite."

"Isn't that wonderful?" She sighed and traced the veins on the back of his hand. His cuff showed very white against a sprinkling of dark hair. "After all, we are to be married."

"We are indeed. You are my fiancée."

*Married.*

*Fiancée.*

*Bride?*

"You are suddenly very quiet, Justine."

"I am often quiet. I had never expected to be a bride, Struan—not since I became old enough to realize it couldn't happen."

"Old enough to be wrong, you mean? Lie in my arms, sweet."

"What if we fall asleep?" And she awoke to find this was as fictitious as Hannah's ghost.

"I shall not fall asleep. If you fall asleep, you may miss some of those things your curious mind spends so much time trying to imagine."

"Oh." She walked forward with him to his ebony bed with its golden tiger sentinel atop each post. "Your grandfather liked extraordinary things."

"Yes." The response was automatic.

Justine ran her fingers over a bedpost. "What was his name?"

"Edward. Why do you ask?"

"Curiosity. One must wonder about the man who gathered such a fascinating collection into one place. How did he die?"

Struan didn't answer until she looked at him when he said, "You are a curious creature. He was injured in a hunting accident. He lingered for several years but never regained his strength."

A chill slithered up Justine's spine. "How sad." What had been written in the book was accurate. But surely her imagination had conjured the apparition . . .

"Enough quizzing for now, dear one." Struan flung back the dark-green counterpane and turned to Justine. Without fuss—and without asking permission—he proceeded to undo the tiny buttons that closed her robe from neck to waist.

She stood quite still. And she found she could not breathe at all.

"Who would think of such infuriatingly small buttons?" he said, frowning.

"I would," Justine said. "I made them."

"I see."

"That means you don't."

"Not always." He completed his task and slipped off the robe in a businesslike fashion. After setting the garment over a chair he swept Justine into his arms and deposited her on the bed without ceremony. "There. I shall not bother with the fire. We shall keep each other warm."

Justine didn't need his physical touch to make her skin blaze.

"You do not appear comfortable." Studying her, he adjusted a pillow beneath her head, straightened her night rail, brushed her hair away from her face with his fingers. "Better?" He pulled up the covers.

Unable to make a move to assist him—or herself, Justine nodded.

"Wonderful," he said, too heartily. "This will be a fine opportunity to deal with several matters."

"What matters?" she asked through loudly chattering teeth.

Struan peered at her but made no mention of the clatter she'd made. "Just *matters*. You'd better be ready to make notes in your mind again."

He'd taken off his cloak. His coat and waistcoat followed. Sitting on top of them all, he worked off mud-spattered boots, then stood up again.

Now he was undoing his shirt!

"Um. What was the name of the waltz you played for me?" she asked in a rush.

Struan paused in the act of pulling his shirt free of his breeches. "Damned if—I mean, I'm not sure I remember the title." His shirt slid from his shoulders, down his arms to land on the floor. "No. I never knew it, did I?"

"D-didn't you?"

"I'll ask Arran." Hair on his chest, smooth and soft-looking, shone as black as the hair on his head. The dark pelt became a slim line over his muscular belly and disappeared beneath the waist of his breeches.

"You are quite differently made."

"Hmm?" His gaze settled intently on her face.

"Different. I said you are very differently made."

"Different from what?"

"Oh"—she shrugged beneath the covers—"from me, I suppose. I haven't seen a great many men without clothes."

"Well, well. You *do* surprise me."

"It's true, you know. This is quite an unusual event for me."

"I always do my utmost to provide my guests with entertainment."

"Oh, I *am* entertained. Most entertained. You do not need a great deal of padding and so forth, do you?"

Struan's lips parted—then he placed them precisely together.

"A lot of gentlemen do, you know?" Justine told him. "Require padding, I mean. In their jackets and so forth."

"The other gentlemen you've seen without their shirts, d'you mean?"

"Sin's ears, no! I mean, no. It's only that I've heard some gentlemen have their clothes made with certain enhancements because they wish to appear larger. You are quite large enough. Your shoulders are very large. And your chest is so . . . so . . . It's just *so*. And you certainly must be grateful to require no stays."

The crinkling of his eyes left her in no doubt that she knew more about the artifice some gentlemen used than he did. The idea amused her.

"Have I said something funny, Justine?"

She wrinkled her nose. "Not really. But you probably would laugh if I told you Calum explained to me that he'd seen gentlemen put on stays to make their waists seem smaller and their chests appear larger. What do you think of that?"

"I think Calum is less than circumspect to discuss such matters with you."

"I asked him. It was because of Lord Belcher. He struts and sometimes seems perilously close to missing the chair when he sits because his back is held so straight. Lord Belcher has a very red face and at least three chins. He wears diamond buckles on his shoes—in the morning. And his shoes have heels to make him taller. And he favors cochineal to color his cheeks and lips even more pink—and the backs of his hands."

"God! A *fop*."

Justine wrinkled her nose again.

"Forgive me," Struan said, and began unbuttoning his breeches. "I'm sure you don't appreciate blasphemy."

"Actually not. But you are right. Lord Belcher is a fop—an ancient fop. Are you going to take your breeches off?"

"Yes."

"I see."

"We both tend to see a great deal, don't we?"

"Sometimes more than on other occasions."

His sudden wide grin made it impossible for Justine to stifle a chuckle. As quickly as she'd laughed, she grew serious again. "Do you think you ought to take off your breeches?"

"Absolutely."

"I see."

Struan grinned again. "I'm glad you do. We must be certain that book of yours provides all the information it will advertise, mustn't we?"

"Mmm." There was always the book. My, she had gathered a veritable mountain of information in one single day. "Should you be offended if I pulled the bedsheet over my head?"

The sound Struan made resembled that of a strangling hawk.

"Are you all right?" she asked anxiously.

"Quite all right. But I should definitely be offended if the sight of me offended you so much that you hid your face."

"I see."

"You're going to, dear lady." Bending over, he stripped his breeches and stockings off in a single motion and straightened again. "What do you think? Horrifying? Passable? Intriguing, at least?"

Oh, my. Oh, sin's eyes . . . She thought . . . She thought she couldn't think of a single thing to say.

"Come along." He crossed his arms. "You could hurt a man's feelings greatly by refusing to give an opinion at a time like this."

"Can't," she muttered. "Speechless."

"That bad?"

Justine shook her head. Tiny muscles pulled in that soft place between her thighs—a soft place that began to feel less soft and a great deal more wet! Embarrassment brought blood rushing to her face. Why on earth should she grow wet? Thank goodness he didn't know.

"A flop, then," Struan said, shaking his head. "Not quite what I'd hoped for in the reaction department. Don't suppose you'd care to tell me the name of the man who puts me to shame?"

"Sin's ears!" She struggled to sit up and held the counterpane to her breasts. "No man! What can you be thinking? Other than in statuary I have never seen a man without clothes before. And if I had he certainly would not look like you."

"How do you know? If you've never seen one before?"

Her heart threatened to fly into pieces. "It wouldn't be possible. I had expected . . . I mean, I had not expected anything . . . anything even close to what you are, Struan. You are all muscles. Muscles on top of muscles. Your legs are . . . *magnificent.* Did you know some gentlemen wear sawdust in their—"

"Stockings? Yes, I had heard that."

"I see." Her reactions could not be normal. She should be overcome with shocked modesty—fainting away, in fact. "I do not find you fearsome, Struan. I find you—*beautiful.* I should like to put my hands on you. I should like to stroke you all over to see how each bit of you feels. Does that mean I am extremely abnormal?"

His throat moved sharply. "It means you are a marvelous woman," he said in a husky voice quite unlike his own. "It also means this night may prove more—taxing than even I had imagined."

"My age," she said, more to herself than to Struan. "It must be because of my maturity. Of course it would make a difference—to many things. I must make a note of that possible factor."

"Would you care to share that thought with me?" Struan asked.

"I think not. At the moment." She studied the thatch of dark hair that flared from a few inches below his navel—and that part of him she'd felt when he danced with her. It was even bigger than she'd thought, and it did not quite resemble the way she had imagined it to be. Statues were not exactly true to life.

"Justine." Struan chuckled. "Do you intend to record my dimensions, madam?"

Flustered, she glanced at his face. "Your breeches must be very heavy. I hadn't know men's breeches weighed so much."

He raised his brows. "They don't."

"But they must."

"They absolutely do not."

She waved a hand and her eyes returned to their previous points of interest. "It must be that you are accustomed to the heaviness. After all, Struan, one cannot deny science. Without a method of keeping . . . of holding . . . " Her hand drew an airy, generally downward motion, then sprang up again. "Well, you do see what I mean, don't you? I don't suppose it would do to go . . . unrestrained, as it were. Could be a frightful nuisance. Get in the way of all sorts of things."

He came closer. "What sorts of things?"

Justine frowned at the object of her fascination. "Tables, for one thing. Dining tables. When you were about to sit down. Might hurt, even, I should think. And doors." She shuddered. "Oh, horrors. Imagine a mishap with a closing door. That *would* hurt. Unless there is no feeling there, perhaps? Could that be the case?"

To her amazement, he turned his back.

"I have angered you? Said the wrong thing? Oh, I do think you should make allowances for a certain degree of unworldliness on my part."

"There is feeling," he said. "No part of a man's body feels more."

His spine was straight, the perfect foil to the flare of shoulder, the trimness of hip. And then there was his buttocks . . .

Justine closed her eyes and sent up a prayer. She prayed for forgiveness if, by her ecstasy at the sight of this man, she had committed any offense. And she prayed in thanksgiving that she had not gone to her grave without experiencing this bliss.

The mattress sank beside her.

Justine held the counterpane more firmly beneath her chin.

Struan stretched out against her entire length.

"Not even your heart?" she whispered. "Not even your heart feels more than that part?"

When he answered she knew his face was above hers. "A different kind of feeling, sweet." His breath crossed her brow. "Do you remember what you felt when we danced and I touched you?"

She squeezed her eyes more tightly shut.

"I see that you do. The feeling I am capable of experiencing in . . . Experiencing there. The two—your feeling and mine—they are similar, I'm sure."

"Aren't they wonderful?" She opened her eyes and looked directly into his. "Have you ever felt anything you wanted to feel again and again as much as you do that feeling? I was truly taken by surprise. I have never heard any mention of such a thing. And to think it was there all the time, why—"

One long finger descended upon her lips. "Hush. You are terrified of this moment and that's why you're chattering. I asked you to keep me company, and that is exactly what is happening."

She shook her head fiercely. "I'm not terrified."

"I think you are."

"I'm not."

"As you say."

She thought for a moment before telling him, "But I did not expect you to take off your clothes."

"Most people do when they go to bed."

"Not all of their clothes."

"I do."

"Always?"

"Absolutely."

"I see."

"You certainly do."

She would pursue this question at a later time—when she

could be more detached. "What causes you to have the special feeling?" Every woman should know these things. With each new experience she became more convinced of her responsibility to enlighten her own kind.

Struan lay on his side, his head propped on a hand. He said, "For both of our sakes, these are elements we should save for another discussion."

His scrutiny distracted her. With the very tips of his fingers, he traced her face, outlined her jaw to the point of her chin, and gently eased the bedcovers from her grip.

"Did you mean it?" he said, pulling the counterpane and bedlinens down to her waist. "That you think you love me?"

These were the moments when a woman who wasn't prepared might lose her head. Justine slipped an arm around his neck and brought his mouth to hers. "I should like the kind of kiss when you put your tongue inside my lips. It seems very intimate to me. It makes me feel joined to you."

He made a small, growling sound and did exactly as she asked. When he had explored the area mentioned very thoroughly in the manner requested, he finally raised his head again and they both struggled for breath.

"I don't think I love you," she told him. "I do love you."

"Justine—"

"No." She covered his mouth. "No, it's quite in order for you to say nothing at all."

"But—"

"Ah, ah. I am not a green girl, Struan. I am—well, we both know what I am. But I believe I shall give you value for your kindness to me. And I do not want you to concern yourself for a moment about the way I feel." A liar. She was a liar.

"I have deep feelings for you, sweet."

"Thank you. I could ask for nothing more." She could ask for a great deal more. She longed for a great deal more. "Now, I don't want to discuss that subject anymore. I like lying with you." She adored lying with him.

"Good."

Tentatively, she touched the hair on his chest. "Soft." Softness over solid muscle. The skin at his side was smooth—and upon his shoulder. The line of hair to his navel felt rougher over the ridged flesh beneath. She noted how each part of him recoiled a little at her touch and frowned up at him.

"I see you meant what you said."

Justine smiled questioningly.

"That you wanted to find out what each part of me feels like."

"I do."

"What a coincidence."

The bone at his hip did not protrude as hers did. "Why is it a coincidence?" Against the backs of her fingers his belly was at once rough and smooth—and very tense.

"Because I want to find out what each part of you feels like."

Her gaze flew to his face. "Would you rather I didn't do this?"

"I'd rather you didn't stop—ever."

She grew hot. "I could never be naked before you."

Struan covered her hand on his belly and held it still. "It's natural for a woman like you to feel modest. That will fade as you become accustomed to—"

"No!" His intense stare made it difficult to concentrate. She averted her face. "Anyway, before Pippa married she told me Grandmama said gentlemen don't require their wives to disrobe."

"Hah!"

His outburst made her forget her awkwardness. "What do you mean by that?"

"You tell me you want to dispel the myths of old women. Then, when it suits your purpose, you quote one of those myths."

Justine pursed her lips. "Well . . . " He had her there.

"I assure you, sweet, that *I* am a man who will want my

wife to disrobe—as you put it. It would bring me the greatest of pleasure to touch you as you have touched me."

Her long-sleeved night rail, also edged with daffodils, fitted loosely. Holding her breath, she slipped it from one shoulder, then from the other, and eased it down until it barely covered her breasts. "You may touch me, if you like."

"You do not have to do things that make you uncomfortable just to please me."

"I would do anything to please you."

"Because you believe I want a submissive woman?"

"You said you wished to touch me as I've touched you."

"That and more. A great deal more."

Her next, huge breath raised her breasts enough to tighten the gown across her nipples. "Then do a great deal more," she told him. "Now. I want you to do a great deal more, now." Quickly, she bared her breasts.

Struan's eyes became intent, hot and intent. With restrained gentleness, he stroked what she had revealed. "Funny girl," he said. "Funny, wonderful girl. So determined to be a pioneer."

Justine bit into her bottom lip.

The fondling stung in an intoxicating manner she could not describe even to herself. Struan circled each breast with his fingertips, then supported and pressed the aching flesh. Slowly, he bent over her.

"Struan!" She arched her spine and clapped her hands to the back of his head. "Oh, Struan!" Rather than pull him away, she urged him closer.

He had taken a nipple into his mouth. With his tongue he ran circles around the very rim. And then he sucked . . .

A blast seared Justine from breast to belly, to deep between her legs.

Mindlessly, she clasped him to her. Dimly she heard the tear of fabric. Her night rail would never be the same, and she didn't care a fig.

"Oh, my dear one," Struan murmured. He removed his lips

from her breast and drew her into his arms. His face rested in the curve of her neck and shoulder. "You are all I could ever hope for."

The hair on his chest grazed her nipples, and she moaned. So much exquisite sensation. Struan ran his hand over her back and her bottom. He caught at the night rail and began pulling it up her leg.

Justine grew still.

The flush receded, replaced by chill.

"Can we . . . Is it possible to do *It* without removing all of one's clothes?" she said rapidly. "I do believe it's growing cold, don't you?"

He grew still. "*It*?"

Justine withdrew her hands from his hair and attempted to wiggle the remnants of her night rail back into place. "The ultimate between a man and a woman. That which is necessary to the production of offspring."

"Good God!" He rolled to his back and rested the back of an arm over his eyes. "Forgive me. You are trying very hard, dearest, but we may have to deal with your many questions when we are not all but naked and on the verge, as it were."

"The verge?"

"Forget I said that. Time enough when we come to the next lesson. And that particular lesson should be saved for our wedding night. Yes, indeed, we shall have that to look forward to."

"Oh, no!" She had dealt with everything very badly. "I believe you were ready for those feelings, and I don't want to stop now."

"You don't want to stop, but you don't want to take any more of your clothes off."

He didn't understand. How could he if she didn't tell him? "If I take all of my clothes off you will not want me at all," she said quietly. "We must deal with this now—at once. I am deformed. You knew that, of course, but you had forgotten in the, er, *ardor* of the moment."

"You are not deformed."

"You have not seen my deformity."

"Show me."

She cringed into the pillows, rolled into a ball on her side. "My hip isn't properly made. I was young when I was injured. It did not grow as it should. And there are scars. And my leg is thinner than the other and also scarred. Ask Grandmama. She will tell you it is a frightful sight. She often reminds me, because she believes it is soul-building to confront one's defects."

Whatever he said next was totally incomprehensible to Justine. He pulled her roughly against his chest, tucked her head beneath his chin, and hauled the covers over both of them.

"You will never want to look at it, Struan. *I* shall never want you to look at it. Grandmama—"

"Damn your bloody grandmama to *hell*!"

"Oh."

"I shall make it the most important mission in my life to prove to you that you are not deformed."

"But—"

"You shall dance. You shall ride. You shall walk and climb and run. You shall enter London's ballrooms upon my arm and every man will wish me dead that he might have the chance to take my place. And, if God wishes it, you and I will produce children together. You will be a marvelous mother. There is nothing you wish to do that you shall not do. Do you understand?"

She held very still.

"Very well. Do not answer me. Listen, for once. In that beloved book of yours you will write about triumph over the expected—flaunting the expected—am I not correct?"

"Correct," she murmured.

"Quite so. And you, my dear one, are the perfect woman to write such a tome, because you have an added destructive expectation to foil. You asked for my help with this project, and you shall get it. I shall not rest until you stop thinking of yourself as less than whole."

"Perhaps we should go back to our original arrangement and forget this marriage."

"Hah!"

"Sin's ears, Struan." She struggled to release herself from his embrace but accomplished nothing. "Do not *hah* at me again. I find it tiresome."

"Your family has agreed that you shall marry me. My family has also agreed. And so have you. Tomorrow I am to meet with your wretched elder relative—to discuss financial arrangements, no doubt. Then we shall get the matter over with."

Like settling on the price of a horse . . . or a *cow.* "I shall go with you to Grandmama. At what time are we meeting?"

"You are not meeting. Struan, Calum, and I will do what must be done."

Justine planted her fists in the middle of his chest and shoved. "You will do no such thing. It was I, not you, who instigated this entire situation."

He was not to be budged from his hold upon her. "You are very bold about this thing. You may not go to the meeting."

"Bold indeed. Yes, indeed, I am bold and I will not have my future decided in my absence."

"But you have just said you designed your own future. *Fait accompli, ma chérie.* Whatever minor discussion takes place tomorrow is of no interest to you."

"I want—"

"No."

This was insupportable.

Infuriating.

And she was taking the completely wrong approach. She sighed. "You see? this is what happens when you allow yourself to be tricked into marriage by a conniving old ape leader.

You find yourself constantly henpecked. But you are right, Struan. I must allow you to guide me in these matters."

He was silent for far too long.

"Of course," Justine said, "there will be times when—after a suitable interval—you will come to see that I may be more insightful than you had at first thought."

"Perhaps." Arranging himself more comfortably, he turned her over and tucked her bottom neatly into his lap. "Perhaps."

Justine shivered deliciously. If simply being pressed to his naked skin made her pulse all the way to her toes, what would *It* do to her? She intended to find out—and enjoy every moment. She wiggled her bottom to get more comfortable.

"Don't do that," Struan muttered. "You will steal the joy from our wedding night, if you do."

Justine didn't understand, but said, "Yes, Struan," very meekly.

"Thank you."

"You are such a reasonable man. From the moment I met you, I knew you for the reasonable man you are."

Struan wrapped his arms around her and settled his knees beneath hers . . . and his hands over her breasts . . .

She tried, unsuccessfully, not to allow her breasts to swell. They did swell. Didn't they? Her nipples grew hard, and he must feel them.

These things were apparently beyond her control, and Struan made no mention of being disconcerted.

She moved to adjust herself even more closely to him. Really, it was no wonder gentlemen preferred to sleep naked. It must be such a relief not to have to *restrain* parts of oneself."

Justine liked the way he felt against her.

Actually, she cherished the way he felt against her.

Heat washed her skin and she tried desperately to stop what was happening to her again.

She was growing wet—very wet.

"Do you know what is happening, Struan?"

"Possibly."

"We're having our very first collapse of communication."

"Mmm."

He agreed. They really did have a most enviable way of arriving at a mutually acceptable conclusion. "Why don't we reflect on what it means when communication collapses?"

"Mmm."

"We'll just be very quiet for a few minutes. Reflection has always helped me with difficult decisions."

"Mmm."

Justine closed her eyes deliberately and tried to relax. If Struan's hands were not holding her breasts, his thumbs shifting slowly over her nipples, relaxing might be far easier.

His thumbs stopped moving.

She puffed up her cheeks. In truth, she wished he need never stop—stop anything.

But she would be quite quiet and give him time to reflect. When he was ready—and being the reasonable man he was—he could come to the correct conclusion and say as much.

His heart beat steadily against her back. Justine relished the strong rhythm of his life.

Soon, while he reflected, the answer to their dilemma would come to him.

Justine frowned. She opened her eyes, and, as discreetly as possible, pressed her bottom just a teensy bit harder against Struan.

How very odd. There was no doubt she could still feel that part of him, but it no longer jutted insistently against her. In fact, it appeared to have *shrunk*.

She was not certain why, but the thought didn't make her happy. It had shrunk and . . . *softened*. "Struan? Do you feel all right?"

When he didn't answer, she held her breath. Could this be something that caused a man embarrassment. If so, there was no question but that she must gather that information and commit it to paper at once. A woman should be able to assist her husband at such times.

For now she simply would not mention what she had noticed. Carefully, she rotated in his arms to face him. "Now," she said. "We have reflected and we are calm. You do see that it is only right for me to come to this gathering Grandmama has arranged, don't you?"

Struan didn't respond.

"*Don't* you?"

Justine pushed up to her elbow and peered into his face. "Struan?"

The next sound she heard was unmistakable. Faint but unmistakable. A slight snore.

He was asleep!

# *Chapter Sixteen*

❦

"**I** do not snore."

"You do snore."

"I can say with absolute certainty that I have never, ever snored."

"How would you know what you do when you're asleep?"

"No other . . . " *Damn* his mouth.

Justine slanted him a disapproving glance. With determined tweaks, she tied the satin ribbons on a dark-blue velvet spencer. Her India muslin morning gown, striped in paler shades of blue than the spencer, might have been chosen to complement her sitting room—which was where he'd finally found her after being disappointed and chagrined to awake and discover she had left him while he slept.

He would try a more pleasant approach—keep the mood light. "You arise early, my dear. I had thought to find you still getting your beauty rest."

"Because I need a great deal of that commodity, no doubt."

"Not at all! Quite the reverse. You are a lovely creature. A lovely, desirable creature, and I wanted to awake with you in my—"

"You and I have many things to discuss." She interrupted him quite deliberately. "I think you are keeping certain facts from me, and I shall insist that you and I have no secrets. You must be open with me about . . . conditions that affect you."

Struan grew cold. By God, he'd completely forgotten the letter. "I can't believe it. You waited until I was asleep and delved into my personal affairs?" She had the power to allow him to put aside that which had ruled his days and nights for weeks!

Justine regarded him narrowly. "Delved? What can you mean—delved? I could hardly fail to pay attention to the obvious."

He patted his coat and felt the envelope in the pocket where he'd placed it the night before. "Neatly returned," he said. He had raced from Kirkcaldy to read it where there could be no question of Arran or Calum coming upon him.

"I will not allow anyone to threaten your safety, Struan. Is that clear?"

He stared at her, then about the room without truly seeing anything. "This is unbelievable. I suppose that's chocolate," he said vaguely, noticing a tall, rose-garlanded Minton pot on a silver tray atop a small, Chinese chest. "I dislike chocolate in the morning." The letter would be like all its predecessors, filled with obscure threats.

"It's coffee," Justine told him shortly.

His spirits lifted a fraction. "Wonderful. I don't suppose— that is, would you mind if I had some? Coffee, that is?"

Rustling as she went, Justine poured coffee and faced him. She silently indicated a chair and waited for him to be seated.

He accepted the cup and drank gratefully.

Justine asked, "Did you breakfast?"

"Mmm? No. No time."

"The way you live will not do at all. There must be a full

staff here—on the premises. You should have a manservant. I intend to deal with that matter at once. You have neglected the niceties, Struan."

He set the saucer on his thigh and raised his eyes to hers. "You do not have to care for me as if I were a child." And he would not be overrun by more souls to confuse his task here.

"Oh, I am well aware that you are no child." Her delicate features could accomplish a dashed uncompromising set. "You are very much a man. And you are very much in trouble."

What had she read? He dreaded seeing the words and knowing she had read them before him. "You should not have interfered."

"I have not interfered. Yet. Who was the woman who made you drink against your will?"

He almost dropped the cup and saucer. "I beg your pardon?"

She turned, pushing the fullness of her skirts behind her. "The woman who made you drink? In the cold room? And the ones who want to take your life away now—all of your life that matters?"

Struan was presented with Justine's profile, her slightly tilted nose and soft mouth, her finely arched dark brows. With deep loathing, he eased the envelope from its pocket over his heavily beating heart. Evidently there were more specific remarks than previously.

"Who is it that you will protect at all costs?" Justine pressed him. "The one least able to protect herself?"

*Bloody hell.* "So," he said quietly. "He has finally begun to reveal his plan, has he?"

He turned the envelope over and frowned. Still sealed— with the customary accompanying bloody fingerprint unbroken.

Struan looked sharply at Justine. "You did not open it?"

"Open?" She glanced from his face to the letter. "Is that for me?"

She had not opened the letter. She had not as much as known of its existence. Tucking the envelope back into his pocket, he smiled engagingly. "My mistake," he said.

Justine did not smile. "That's another of those letters, isn't it?"

Lying would be pointless. "Yes."

"And you thought I had opened it?"

"From . . . I'm sorry. You mentioned certain . . . What made you ask those questions of me?"

"You do not only snore in your sleep."

"I don't—"

"You do. And you also talk in your sleep. Do you deny that something about a woman making you drink, and a cold room, and—"

"No! No, I do not deny it." Awful possibilities made themselves felt. "What else did I say?"

"Nothing. Only what I've told you. It was enough to make me fear for you. What you said in your sleep has something to do with the letters, doesn't it?"

She was no fool, and he would never treat her as one. "Yes. I ask you not to repeat a word of what you say I said in my sleep—nor mention the nature of the letters—to anyone."

She stood beside him, looking down. "I should hardly be likely to discuss what I heard you say in your sleep last night, should I?"

Struan took a fold of her skirt between finger and thumb and tugged lightly. "I suppose not."

"Are you going to open the letter?"

"In good time."

"Will it be threatening?"

He met her dark, troubled eyes. "Almost assuredly."

"Let me help you."

*Go back to Cornwall where you will be safe.* "You will help me by . . . by caring for me." He could not tell her to leave him and he had no right to mention again the love she had declared for him until he could feel safe in declaring his own for her—to the world. Surely he was right in thinking he might be best able to keep her safe if she was at his side.

"I am quite the hand with a warming pan, y'know," she said, the corners of her mouth tilting ever so slightly. "Ask poor Robert Mercer. Point out the enemy and I shall rattle sense into his brain."

"You broke the pan," Struan pointed out. Anxious to see what was inside the envelope, he set aside his empty coffee cup.

Justine, bending to plant one of her sweet kisses on his lips, swept away all thought but how desperately he wanted the world to leave them alone—together.

With very little effort, Struan landed the lady on his lap. "Got you. And I don't intend to let you go."

"Good," she said, laughing. "Because I need your whole attention while I ask my questions."

Questions were to be avoided at all costs. "I am concerned about the wedding trip," he said. "And the question of where we shall live."

"There will be no wedding trip," she said promptly. "I have far too much work to do here to take a wedding trip. As for where we shall live, Arran has already said he hopes we will make this place our home. The children are happy. The lodge delights me and I believe you have a fondness for the place. Why should we not remain here?"

That had not been quite the response he'd anticipated. "Arran should not have discussed our future living arrangements with you." Peeved, he concentrated on the fascinating fact that his hands could all but span her waist. He said, "We shall take our wedding trip when I decide the time is appropriate and possible."

"I'll look forward to discussing that with you. Did you manage to reflect at all?"

He regarded her without comprehension.

"On the subject we were discussing before you started snoring?"

"I do not—"

"Sin's ears, Struan! You do snore and that's an end of it. And you were supposed to be reflecting upon the obvious wisdom of my being present when you visit Grandmama this afternoon."

"Oh, that."

Her teeth came together with a distinct snap. "Yes, that. I am coming. I'm sure that's the decision your reflection produced."

All he recalled was the incredible pleasure of feeling her curled against his body. "Actually—"

A thunderous rap upon the door forced a blessed interruption. Struan was too busy thinking how blessed the interruption was to help Justine from his lap before Max burst into the room.

"It's one o' them!" he announced, his green eyes flashing. "From the wild hill clan. I'd know one o' them anywhere. He's a head o' shaggy hair and he's huge. A giant o' a man just like Caleb Murray says they all are."

With as much decorum as possible, Struan returned Justine to her feet. "Max, you are not to pester Caleb when he's about his duties. And you are not to rush into Lady Justine's rooms like this."

Max squinted at Struan, then at Justine. "She was sittin' on ye, Papa. Now ye'll be married soon. Then she'll be Mama an'—"

"That accent simply must be attended to," Justine said. "We shall have a lesson this very day, young man."

Max planted his thin legs apart. "Caleb says I sound like a Scot proper."

Struan held up a hand. "You will do as Lady Justine tells you and learn to speak like a gentleman. Now, kindly explain this rude visit."

"There's a man below wi' Ella. She'll not listen t'warnings. He's probably stolen her away by now. And dragged her off t'the hills where—"

"My God!" Struan dashed from the room and didn't stop running until he arrived in the vestibule. Wild hill clans, be damned, the wretch whose unopened letter he carried could have entered the lodge while Struan was too busy with other matters. He cast about, deciding where to go first.

Flinging wide his arms, Max leaped down the stairs. "They went into the great hall, but he'll have her on his horse and away b'now. Robert said they move awful fast. And the monk said all ye could do afterwards was pray."

With dread in his heart, Struan strode into the hall.

The man who gazed at Ella with avid interest was, indeed, large. He was also no member of any wild hill clan, and Struan knew the devil for the dangerous rakehell he was.

Relief made Struan use the back of the nearest chair for support. Ella, a vision in lavender, appeared every bit as enthralled by their visitor as he with her.

"North," Struan said sharply, more sharply than he'd intended.

Devlin North turned eyes the green of deep water upon Struan. "There you are, man. Damn, but it's good to see you."

Struan stopped himself from asking why. He nodded curtly. "What brings you to these parts? I thought Edinburgh was as close as you got to this uncivilized land of ours these days." And, in addition to Devlin being some years Struan's junior, there had never been a particular closeness between them.

"I clearly made a potentially costly mistake in remaining away from the countryside." While he made this pronouncement, Devlin returned his brilliant attention to Ella. "There has been a distinct improvement in the quality of the local flora."

Struan calculated Devlin's age to be perhaps seven and twenty. The man had deep pockets and a fine estate his shipowner father had willed to him. Nevertheless, Devlin was too old by far to be studying Ella as if she were highly desirable "flora" ready for picking.

"May I come in?"

Struan looked over his shoulder at Justine and smiled. "Of course, my dear. This is to be your home." He realized how much joy the words brought him. "Meet one of our neighbors. Devlin North. Devlin, this is my fiancée, Lady Justine Girvin."

Devlin approached Justine with the controlled grace for which he was famous with the ladies. "My lady," he said, bowing over her hand. "You are even more lovely than Saber led me to believe."

"Saber?" She inclined her head. "You refer to my cousin?"

Even Straun was forced to acknowledge the charm in Devlin's smile. "Your cousin, indeed. And a friend of mine for many years."

"And you are the gentleman who reported to Arran that the fame of my relationship with Struan had reached London?"

Devlin bowed his head once more and finally said, "I suppose that must have been me. I am occasionally forgetful of past conversations."

"You know Saber?" Ella spoke for the first time since Struan had entered the room, and he glanced to her anxiously. She had risen from her perch on the edge of the daybed and taken several steps forward.

"I do indeed." Beaming, Devlin turned back from Justine. "In fact, it is because of Saber that I am here today. Since Lady Justine is his cousin."

Ella lowered her great, exotic eyes. "Of course," she said. "How is he?"

So, Struan thought with a heaviness in his heart, the girl still bore a *tendre* for young Avenall. He'd thought the two well matched in their serious natures and affinity for the land—and in their gentle wit—but Avenall had turned from Ella for no reason that Struan could fathom.

Devlin North's disarming grin had deserted him. He cast Struan a significant stare. "A small mishap befell Saber in India. Have no fear. He is much improved, but in need of time to completely regain his previous vigor."

All color drained from Ella's face. "He has been wounded?" she whispered.

"A skirmish with some hill tribe," Devlin said.

"They're everywhere," Max announced, shaking his head and frowning. "We've the same problem here. Wild men—"

"That'll do," Struan told him.

"Sit with me," Justine said to Devlin. She led the way to a couch and he joined her—his gaze repeatedly returning to Ella, Struan noted. Justine continued, "Tell me about Saber. I am most fond of him. Have you spoken with my brother yet?"

"At the castle," Devlin said. "He and Arran sent me here. Calum thought you'd want to know Saber is at Northcliff Hall."

"With you?" Struan asked, amazed. "Now?"

Devlin regarded Ella yet again.

*Lecherous bounder.* Struan persisted. "You mean Lord Avenall is at Northcliff as we speak?"

Ella came closer. "That is where you live, Mr. North?"

"Devlin, please. Yes, that is my Scottish home." He laughed. "And, coincidentally, it is to the north."

"How long has Saber been there?" Justine asked.

Devlin puffed up his cheeks and spread his hands on massive thighs. "Oh, a while now. We were friends at Oxford and we kept up with each other through the years. Coincidence he should turn out to be related to Calum—but those things happen."

"I cannot imagine why he did not come to us direct," Justine said. "After all, we are his family." She sounded distressed.

"He'll come to you in good time."

There was something in what Devlin said—or perhaps in the way he did *not* say something—that troubled Struan deeply. "I remember Saber well," he said, all good humor. "Independent, unless I miss my mark. I imagine he wants to be his old self before he puts in an appearance. Am I right, Devlin?"

"Absolutely right." With hands the size of lions' paws, Devlin slapped his knees. "Anyway, I promised Saber I should drop in and give you news of him. Let you know he's recovering well."

"Does he know I'm here?"

All eyes turned to Ella, and she blushed so brilliantly that Struan had to stop himself from going to her.

Devlin's extraordinary eyes narrowed a fraction. "He knows."

The girl's smile had pathetic hope. "Should he like me to visit him? Did he say he'd like to see me?"

Evident discomfort powered Devlin's abrupt rise from the couch. "I'm sure he would have if he'd thought of it. He mentioned what an agreeable child he found you to be in Cornwall. I'll mention your kind offer to him."

Ella's heavy lashes lowered, but not before tears shone in her eyes.

"Duty dispensed, then," Devlin said heartily. "Shall I give Saber your good wishes?"

"That and more," Justine said, but she sounded strained and she did not take her gaze from Ella's face. "And tell him we are anxious to see him."

"I shall do that." Bowing deep, Devlin swung away and, with a last long stare in Ella's direction, left the room.

No one spoke until the ring of his boots receded.

"Well," Struan said, too loudly. "We must be grateful that Saber is on the mend."

"On the mend from what?" Justine said softly. "I do not like it. He is trying to ensure we do not go near him."

Struan shared her suspicion, but he said, "Nonsense. He had no way of knowing you and Calum would be in these parts now. I'm certain news of your presence surprised him and he is simply being polite. A man has a right to deal with ills as he chooses." A principle to which he subscribed but was having increasing difficulty clinging to.

"An agreeable child," Ella murmured. Her voice shook. "Once I thought he was my friend, the mirror of my own heart, but he calls me an *agreeable* child now."

"Hush," Struan said, going to her.

Ella would not allow him to hold her hands. "It is all for nothing. I am what I am and—"

"Please don't," he implored.

She looked directly at Justine. "No. No, Papa, do not concern yourself. I shall be very well as always. Best that I give up this coming-out nonsense. After all, we both know no man will want me. And I want only one man, so what point can there possibly be?"

Struan was helpless to do other than watch her sweep from the room, a truly beautiful creature wounded by early circumstances over which she'd had no power. "Go to her, Max," he murmured, but the boy was already hurrying after his sister.

"I feared it might be so," Struan said. "She did think she loved young Avenall."

"Men," Justine said, very low. "How do you avoid the truth of things. She *did* love him. And she *still* does."

Female wiles had their place in certain situations.

Justine watched from behind a drape in her sitting room as Struan rode away in the direction of the castle.

She was "resting"!

Her morning had been taxing, so Struan had informed her. She must take care of herself for his sake. Pretty words to guarantee he got what he wanted.

He had yet to take full measure of her determination.

"I'll have the cloak now, Mairi," she said. "And perhaps you'd tell Potts I'm ready for the cart."

"Och, m'lady," Mairi said. "Ye'll be the death o' me yet. The master'll have me liver and lights fer lettin' ye go when he's said ye're t'rest."

Justine decided not to explore the nature of Mairi's "liver and lights." "You are hardly able to stop a grown woman from deciding to take a ride if she chooses to do so. Please hurry, there's a good girl."

The black velvet cloak was the one she'd worn to travel from Cornwall and very heavy. Justine shrugged it more comfortably around her shoulders and shooed Mairi in front of her and out of the apartments.

"That was a bonnie gentleman who came t'visit this mornin'," the maid said over her shoulder. "He certainly sent Miss Ella into a swoon. Buttercup, too. She's still makin' moon eyes an' blatherin' on about him."

"I'm sure I can't speak for Buttercup's reactions to Mr. North, but I don't believe it was Devlin who sent Ella into a swoon, as you put it," Justine said. She liked Mairi. The girl was open and kind and to be trusted. "Ella is not happy. If you can find ways to cheer her, I should very much appreciate it. Without letting her know we have spoken, of course."

"Och, o'course!" Mairi glanced back frequently as they descended the stairs. "Ye leave it t'me, m'lady. Where does the green-eyed gentleman come from, then? I dinna remember seein' him before."

"He's a neighbor," Justine said. She recognized a case of infatuation-at-first-sight when she saw it. Mairi was as smitten with Devlin North as she reported Buttercup to be. "Apparently he does not spend much time in these parts. Too dull for him. He has quite the reputation. A man to be avoided at all costs, I should say."

"Dearie me," Mairi said, not with the horror Justine would have hoped for. "Is that a fact?"

Finally seated in the old cart with Potts driving, Justine swiveled on the makeshift seat to watch the fantastic shapes and colors of the lodge pass from sight behind trees. The place already felt like home.

She faced forward and felt proud of her lack of nervousness over what lay ahead. What could they say when she refused to leave their precious discussion about her future?

Bumping along the worn old track, Justine considered the odd visit from Mr. Devlin North and Ella's distress at learning Saber was so close yet had shown no interest in seeing her. And what could she have meant when she said, "I am what I am"?

Then there was Devlin's open admiration of the girl. Justine glowered at the hedgerows they passed. In the hands of such a man, her dear little Ella would be like a baby fed to a tiger. No such thing should happen if Justine had her way—and Justine *would* have her way.

But what of Saber? What could cause him to hide from his own family? He should be given time to come to them, but not too much time.

March had given way to early April and big, starlike white stichwort flowers showed off among the spring-fresh hedgerows. Wood anemones demurely drooped their pale-pink heads, awaiting warmer sunshine to raise their petals to the sky. A chaffinch with some morsel in its beak soared in for a landing. The jangling song of the bird's mate greeted the arrival of food.

Justine breathed deeply of Scotland's sharp moorland

scents. A wild and beautiful land. Struan's land. Her land, now, and she was glad of it.

Potts urged his nag onward until the castle came into view. Atop a flat mound surrounded at the bottom by a formidable wall, Kirkcaldy's massive bulk was not at odds with the craggy beauty of its setting. Dramatic, fronted by twin drum towers and with a many-turreted angle tower at each corner, the building flaunted an insolent grandeur.

At last the cart ground to a halt in a courtyard tucked into the lee of the L-shaped castle. A clock tower topped the castellated balcony over the double doors to the vestibule. On the previous day, as on the night of Justine's arrival here, she had been too preoccupied to take much note of her surroundings. She was preoccupied again now. She was also determined to be calm.

Shanks, his bald head glimmering in the pale sunlight, opened the doors to admit her. "Are you expected, my lady?" he asked, his manner hostile.

"No," Justine said, feeling contrary and more than a little tired of the Kirkcaldy servants. "And I require no assistance from you."

Unfortunately she was forced to ask for assistance anyway. "Where is the dowager, please?"

Shanks elevated his beaked nose. "In her boudoir."

Justine sensed more than saw a slight movement and swung about in time to see Mrs. Moggach's bulk creeping into the corridor leading to the main staircase. "Ah, Mrs. Moggach," she said to the housekeeper. "How nice to see you. I'd wanted to thank you for all your efforts at the lodge. On the way to the dowager's rooms, are you?"

The housekeeper stopped. "No one said ye were comin'," she said. "There's an important meetin'. They'd not want t'be disturbed."

"I'll be the judge of that," Justine informed the woman. "Is that where you're going now? To see if the dowager and her guests are ready for tea?"

"I am indeed." Moggach's florid face folded into a secretive and lumpy study in discontent. "I'll let Her Grace know ye're in the green salon. Mr. Shanks'll show ye there."

Moggach continued on and Shanks hovered.

With a withering glance of dismissal in Shanks's direction, Justine followed the housekeeper. Moggach clumped and puffed so with her own importance that she failed to check behind her until she'd ascended the stairs and arrived at a door. She knocked and awaited a faint "Come" from within.

Then Moggach saw Justine and scowled.

Justine favored the woman with blank serenity and let herself into the room. "Good afternoon, Grandmama," she said to her sartorially spectacular grandparent. "My, is that a new black silk? The jet looks quite splendid on the lace fichu—and in the cap. In fact, you look quite splendid altogether."

"She followed me," Moggach said. "I dinna know she was—"

"Out," Grandmama ordered, one rheumatic finger aimed at the door.

Moggach didn't argue. Moggach didn't say a word or make any sound at all. She scurried—if scurrying were possible in one so portly—she scurried from the lovely little boudoir and shut the door with a blurred thud.

"And out with you, too, missy," Grandmama ordered Justine. "This is no place for you, and I'm certain the viscount conveyed that fact to you with suitable force."

The old lady sat upon a gold-upholstered gilt chaise, her back so starched and her toes so firmly placed upon red and gold carpet that the considerable mound of tapestry cushions behind her were mere decoration.

Arran lounged with an elbow propped upon the ledge of a niche that held a white marble bust—probably of some former Stonehaven by the set of the nose. Calum stood behind Grandmama with his arms crossed.

Struan had paused in the act of pacing the carpet before the dowager and appeared both agitated and frustrated.

The door opened once more and Blanche Bastible entered. "Nothing's happened yet, has it?" she asked breathlessly, trotting forward in a froth of embroidered mauve crepe weighted down by row upon row of flounces.

*"Mauve?"* Grandmama said. "Widowed two months and already in mauve?"

Blanche tossed her abundant chestnut ringlets. "A year's mourning is an affectation. Felix always said one should get on with life. Never languish, he always said. Do not draw undue attention to yourself by wallowing in self-pity, he always said. I know, I heard him many times." She fluffed a flounce. "Anyway, he'll soon have been gone three months."

"Blanche has always made her own rules, Your Grace," Arran said.

"Well, she can make them elsewhere," the dowager pronounced. "This is a private discussion, Mrs. Bastible."

"Oh, I know," Blanche said, tripping to settle herself on the same chaise with Grandmama. "A family discussion. I know my Grace would want me here. And, after all, I have had experience in marrying off a difficult young woman."

"Bloody hell," Arran muttered.

Struan shocked Justine by turning on the Bastible woman and all but snarling, "Get out! We have more serious matters to deal with than your mindless babbling."

Blanche tossed her head and ignored him.

Calum rested his crossed arms on the back of the chaise and brought his face close to Blanche's ear. "Grace is a delight, Mrs. B. The puzzle is, why? Or should I say, how?"

Blanche cast a reproachful glance at Struan, then wiggled with evident satisfaction. "You see, Your Grace. Your grandson knows I am a veritable wonder with young women and their problems. You must allow me to help you with your granddaughter. I understand she is already compromised."

Deathly stillness descended.

"Of course, my daughter never stooped to anything like that, but, after all, as my Felix always said, there but for the grace of God go—"

"Lady Justine is not compromised," Struan said loudly.

Blanche smirked. "This is going to work very nicely, Your Grace. As long as the gentleman is a gentleman, there's never any problem. And you can be certain that I shall be the soul of discretion in the matter. Not a word of the truth shall pass my lips. Why, just this afternoon I told that lovely Mr. Murray that if he heard any rumors about Lady Justine and the viscount he should say they were forced to spend a night alone together because they were cut off by a storm. There."

Struan whipped open the door and said, "*There,* Mrs. Bastible. We wouldn't dream of taking up more of your time."

"But the dowager needs me."

"The dowager will not hear of your being taken advantage of," Arran said. Separating himself from his ancestor's niche, he placed a hand beneath his mother-in-law's elbow, drew her firmly to her feet, and propelled her from the room.

Her face jerked in all directions as if she searched for an ally, but she went quietly enough.

"Ghastly female," Grandmama said before the door had completely closed again. "One wonders about your wife, my lord."

"No, one doesn't," Arran said. "Grace is a miracle. Her mother is tolerated because she is her mother. No more need be said on the subject."

"True," Struan agreed, resuming his stalking back and forth across the carpet. "I'll ring for Shanks, Justine. He'll find you somewhere comfortable to wait. I'll have some tea brought—"

"No."

"Do as you are told," the dowager said, pressing her tiny

hands into the folds of the exquisite gown. "We are to discuss certain important issues relating to this sham of a marriage you've forced upon us. Obviously you do not belong here."

"What important issues?"

"Justine," Struan said gently. "You need have no fear that I shall do anything but what is best for you. Run along and think about some new gowns. Brides' head should be filled with such things at a time like this."

She could not trust herself to meet his eyes.

"Justine—"

"How dare you?" She trembled. Her face flamed and her blood thundered at her temples. "*Run along?* Think about gowns? You will do what's best for me. I am five and thirty. I chose you, Struan, Viscount Hunsingore. I chose you because I love you and I am not ashamed of the fact, or of stating the fact. We are to be married. That was not something I planned." It was not something she had dared to as much as consider.

"What do you mean by that?" Grandmama said. "You didn't plan on marriage? Do you mean you had some notion of carryin' on like some trollop with the man?"

Justine took a long, slow breath that did absolutely nothing to calm her down. "I mean that I had hoped only to be near Struan. To be his helpmate with the children. To keep his home if he needed that. To be a friend. And I hoped he would help with my book. I expected him to meet and marry someone else one day. Until then, I would have accepted whatever I could of him."

"Good Lord," Arran muttered.

Calum said, "You're a dashed lucky man, Struan. Don't you ever forget it."

"I should say not," Arran added.

Struan stood beside Justine and rested a hand at her waist. "I know how lucky I am," he told them all. "Luckier than I ever expected to be and certainly luckier than I ever deserved to be."

"Drivel," Grandmama pronounced. "Now get rid of her so that I may get this business over with."

Justine's leg ached. Her temper bothered her more. With gritted teeth, she limped to a chair near a fire in a small, Italian marble fireplace and sat down. "I will not leave and that's an end of it."

"You will do as—"

"She will stay," Calum said evenly, countermanding his grandparent. "We are discussing Justine's life, are we not? Of course we are. I shall make a handsome settlement upon her, Struan. As I have already told you, I expect my sister's every need and desire to be met."

Struan's jaw jutted. He took up position behind Justine and rested his fingers on her shoulders. "There is none better equipped to take care of her desires than I."

"It is your desires I intend to address, young man," Grandmama said. "Speaking of such matters in front of your future wife is highly unusual and unsuitable. Don't blame me for the consequences. We must deal with certain aspects of your natural appetites."

Justine found she had difficulty breathing at all—and in finding a spot to stare at.

Arran said, "I say," and his mouth remained slightly open.

"I assume you've actually seen the extent of Justine's deformity, Lord Hunsingore?"

Justine closed her eyes.

"Grandmama," Calum said. "I hardly think we need discuss such matters at all."

"We certainly must. Your sister suffered a childhood accident that rendered her a cripple. Her hip is not completely formed and her leg is a withered monstrosity. It is my duty to point out to her future husband that he cannot expect to receive other than damaged goods in this match."

Struan's fingers, digging into her flesh, became the focus Justine clung to. "If you were not my fiancée's grandmother, madam, I should refuse to converse with you further." His voice was barely audible.

"But I am her grandmother, and apparently I am the only one concerned enough about her health to ensure she comes to no harm. First I must ask if you have already had her. Don't hold back. What is said within these walls is of too much importance for it to be repeated elsewhere. Have you breached my granddaughter's maidenhead?"

Calum said, *"My God!"*

Struan brushed the side of Justine's neck and murmured, "It's all right, my sweet." To Grandmama he said, "No, I have not. And I will not until we are man and wife."

"Good. I am in time, then. You must understand that there is to be no . . . you must not risk entering her?"

Arran swiveled away and went to the windows.

Calum scrubbed at his face with both hands.

"What does that mean?" Justine whispered to Struan.

"The marriage will take place within a few days," Grandmama said. "It's imperative that I have your word before it does, Lord Hunsingore."

"Grandmama," Calum said. "Whatever are you talking about?"

"Justine could never give birth."

"How dare you speak like this in front of her," Struan said.

The dowager shrugged her frail shoulders. "I did my utmost to avoid her hearing any of this. I was overruled. Her deformities would turn the successful sowing of your seed within her into a potentially murderous act."

Justine slumped. She would faint. Surely she would faint. Why didn't she faint—or just die?

"Your word, sir," Grandmama demanded.

"I would never do anything to hurt Justine," Struan said. "But surely—"

"She would never bring a child into the world without killing herself and very possibly the child." Black silk rustled as if in emphasis. "Even if she were not severely damaged, her advanced years would make such an attempt ludicrous. She is elderly, frail, and deformed."

"And I shall not marry Struan," Justine said, her voice breaking with shame. "Kindly forget any of this occurred. All of you, forget it. I shall leave for Cornwall at once."

"Not with the Franchot name in ribbons, my girl," Grandmama told her. "You have made your bed and now you shall lie upon it. It must be a separate bed from your so-called husband's, that is all."

"No man should be shackled to a woman for reasons of propriety."

"He certainly should, and he will be. He has no one but himself to blame." The dowager stretched out her sinewy neck. "And he already has two perfectly dreadful children. Why should he want more?"

Struan stunned Justine by coming to kneel before her, gathering her into his arms and pressing her face against his shoulder. "We shall be happy, my love. I promise you that. This outrage will be forgotten."

"You will marry," the dowager duchess said. "On Monday morning next—the day after the final banns are called—you shall marry and I shall happily return to Cornwall."

"Praise the Lord," Struan muttered.

"Praise Him, indeed," Grandmama said. "And accept it as His will that you find your pleasures elsewhere than with your wife. If you make her truly your wife you may kill her. Not one of us would ever forgive or forget that. Once the ceremony is over and a respectable interval has passed—to still any nimble tongues—it might be as well for Justine to return to me in Cornwall."

# *Chapter Seventeen*

A dam and Eve.

There had been more than one lord of Stonehaven with an odd sense of humor.

The twin drum towers fronting Kirkcaldy were dubbed Adam and Eve. The tower Arran had made his own—which he now shared with Grace—was Revelation. Throughout the great castle, biblical names vied with those of Greek gods and Egyptian royalty.

Struan looked out from the Adam Tower at the view down the oak-lined Long Drive to the massive gatehouse with its castellated bridge spanning the carriageway. At the base of the castle's mound, beyond the walls, stretched low hills dotted with tenant crofts. The village of Kirkcaldy lay some ways distant and a river forked to surround the valley like the tongue of an elegant silver serpent.

From these windows, generations of Rossmaras—the family name of the lords of Stonehaven—had observed the land that was theirs.

Struan had come to the circular room at the very top of the tower to find solitude, solitude to consider how to deal with the dilemma that had been presented him by Justine's grandmother—and solitude to reread the sickening letter.

Justine had refused his company on her return to the lodge. And she'd refused with a tight-lipped, barely restrained agony that brooked no argument.

He made fists on the stone casement and rested his brow on leaded panes. He would allow her time for the private healing she would attempt. Then he would be the one to draw together the wounds a selfish old woman had wrought.

" . . . *successful sowing of your seed would be a potentially murderous act.*"

Why had he never considered that he could harm Justine simply by loving her—by taking her as his own?

"God!" He brought his fists together to pound his forehead. This was a burden he must carry alone, but carry it he would. "I love her." Aloud, the words brought a sudden burst of joy amid the pain. He did love her, dammit. Whatever it took to be with her, he would do it—bear it. And no man crazed with hate and a lust for vengeance would take her from him, either.

The only furnishing in the austere room was a single ancient leather chair, placed where a lone watcher might view sky and treetops—and sun and moon.

Soon there would be darkness.

Struan sat in the shiny, brass-studded chair and took out the letter. Once again he pulled out two folded sheets of paper. As ever, the elegance of the writing struck a discordant note with its mission—like a fine silver blade employed for a woodcutter's task.

*Love has no eyes, but you know that, my lord. Ah, yes, now you do indeed know that. You have found your own lady, your own love. At first I thought it to be a convenience. Other evidence has been brought to my attention which leads me to believe I was very wrong.*

*This match you intend to make is dear to you. You love
Lady Justine despite her infirmity, just as I love my lady despite the stain you spread upon her.*

*I love my lady but I cannot forget that you stole what was
rightfully mine. And now there is something that you want for
yourself and yourself alone. Perhaps it would only be appropriate for me to take from you what you took from me.*

*There is a price to be paid, my friend. You may have to pay
it more than once—or twice—or even more times to satisfy my
honor.*

Struan's palms sweated. He flexed his fingers, one hand at
a time, and glanced over the darkening landscape. Justine?
Ella? Even Max? Grace when she returned? Little Elizabeth?

He could leave this place.

The madman would punish him regardless; Struan knew it
was so. Somehow he must protect his own. They must never
be alone, never be far from his sight or the sight of someone
he could trust absolutely.

*Or*—the letter continued—*I may decide that I have no need
of human sacrifice.*

Human sacrifice? Mad! What sickening possibilities did
the creature contemplate? To rape them? To steal them away
never to be returned to him? To *kill* them?

*Yes, that is it. I want what you have, my lord. Riches and re-
spect. To look upon the land and know it is mine and that
every man I see will bow and every woman beg to be taken to
my bed.*

Struan's throat dried and he couldn't swallow. What would
appease this monster? What did he truly intend?

*It is time. Very soon it will begin. You will do exactly as I
order you to do, when I order you to do it. Be prepared to give
me whatever I ask for. If you offer no resistance you will be
allowed to remain where you are. If not, you will find it necessary to go elsewhere. And certain arrangements will have*

*been made to pass the ownership of a portion of Kirkcaldy—
including your present home—to me.*

*You will think me foolish. No portion of Kirkcaldy is yours
to give. It is, however, your brother's. When the time arrives—
not yet—you will take him and none other into your confidence. You will tell him that if he wishes to help you preserve
the safety of your loved ones, he will assist you in what must
be done. If that does not persuade him, remind him that he has
a succulent wife of his own and a charming baby daughter.
And I know where they are. I will not touch them unless you
and your brother leave me no alternative. I advise you both to
keep your own counsel.*

Why did he not simply ask for money? Why did he insist
upon drawing out this agony of waiting? Struan knew why—
to torture him. If he could only catch the creature out, surprise
and overpower him. The letter continued:

*There can be no hiding from me, Hunsingore.*

*Sending your lovely fiancée to Cornwall with dearest Ella
and Max, or trying to hide them anywhere else, would be a
waste of time. I shall find them.*

*And, no, you may inform Stonehaven that it will not be as
simple as disposing of me when I appear.*

Since opening the letter late that morning, Struan had regretted not drawing Arran into his confidence sooner. Now he
must decide whether to take the risk of defying the letter-
writer and doing so now.

*I shall not announce my arrival.*

*You will hear from me again very soon. I shall remain near,
as I have been near—so near you have looked into my eyes
and not known me.*

*If you attempt to force my hand you will discover what man-
ner of man I am—after the deed is done. If you force my hand
my decision will be difficult but far from devoid of pleasure.*

*Force my hand and I shall have to decide which of your
beloved ones to take from you first.*

# Chapter Eighteen

❦

"**W**ell," Blanche Bastible said, one pudgy hand spread upon the very exposed swell of her plump bosom, the other wafting a sugared confection in emphasis. "I must say that I'm disappointed. Far too small. Far too quiet. Not at all the kind of affair I should have expected."

Justine eyed the chocolate-dipped figs on her plate with distaste and reached for wine instead.

"As I remember, Mother-in-law," Arran said from his place at the beautifully decorated table in a dining room off the red salon. "As I remember, you chose not to be present at all for your own daughter's wedding."

Blanche pouted and raised a fan made of the same ivory satin as her fussy gown. "You seem to forget that I was about to be married myself at the time. This is quite a different matter. I can't see why we couldn't have waited for Grace to come from Yorkshire for this occasion, and for the Duchess of Franchot. And ever so many other people. Don't you agree, Mr. North?"

Devlin, who had arrived bearing Saber's apologies for not attending, made an unintelligible noise in response to Blanche.

"I should have thought the reason for simplicity obvious," the dowager said. She had already spoken her mind on the subject of Blanche's rapid and "amazing and utterly deplorable abandonment of mourning."

"Both of my weddings were simple," Blanche persisted. "But, I assure you, there was no hint of *haste* in either case."

"I hardly think this is the moment to discuss any wedding but the one that has just taken place," Struan said coldly, leaning aside to allow an under butler to pour champagne.

Justine smiled valiantly and was grateful for the warmth the wine brought. She had done everything within her power to avoid this marriage—and failed. Struan had simply refused to be dissuaded from the course he had chosen and, together with Arran, Calum, and Grandmama, had orchestrated the austere ceremony without her assistance.

Seated at her side, Struan said, "Are you comfortable, my dear?"

"Very," she lied.

He had eaten no more of the extraordinary wedding breakfast than Justine. His left hand touched hers on the snowy linen cloth scattered with wildflower petals. Justine felt nothing but that contact—his skin on hers—and wanted to feel nothing else.

Grateful for the shield provided by many-tiered golden epergnes spilling luscious fruits, and tall vases of flowers from she knew not where, Justine dared to regard her new husband. He returned her attention with steady intensity, as he had during the simple ceremony performed in the Kirkcaldy chapel.

The perfect elegance of his dark clothes and white linen served only to echo the forceful presence of the man who wore them.

"You look wonderful," he told her very softly. "The subtlety of ivory becomes you. The gown is a delight. I hope it pleases you, too."

"It is a marvel." She had been required only to submit to measurement and fittings. A modiste and four assistants who had miraculously appeared at the lodge had accomplished the seemingly impossible within three days. Of tulle over silk, the square-necked gown had been pleated, each pleat edged with a row of seed pearls and the same pearls used at the wrists of long, full sleeves.

Struan turned in his seat and framed her face. He behaved as if they were alone, or as if he did not care who saw them behaving as if they were alone. "My wife," he said. "I find I like the sound of those words very well."

Her eyes filled with silly tears. "Your burden," she told him. "If you allow such a travesty to occur." So far he had given no sign of responding to her insistence that she was perfectly fit, and capable of living life as a normal wife. "Do you understand what I tell you, Struan?"

His smile did nothing to halt the hardening of his eyes. "You must leave these matters to me. You must be led by me."

This was not the moment to assert her independence, but the moment *would* come.

With his thumbs, Struan wiped tears from her cheeks. He brought his brow to rest upon hers and whispered, "I love you."

Justine's heart turned and seemed to stop beating. She closed her eyes and pressed her hands over his against her face.

"There is nothing about you that does not please me," he told her. "I think I shall always want to see pearls in your hair as they are today. And flowers. You should be forever surrounded by beautiful things, and so you shall be."

"I intend to leave for Cornwall in the morning," the dowager announced suddenly. "Calum will accompany me."

Justine, intent upon staring into Struan's eyes, did not respond to the woman she could not see clearly for the screen of precious metal, fruits, and flowers.

"We will certainly be ready to receive you as soon as possible, Justine."

*Never, it would never be possible.*

"My wife will be otherwise occupied for some time," Struan said. He turned a strained face to the company and held Justine's hand tightly on the table. "Eventually we shall of course make the journey to Cornwall together."

Justine watched the figs removed. *My wife.* He regarded her as his. Finally, she was truly a bride. She smiled at him and he smiled in return. How long must they wait to be alone?

"Certain things to be taken care of," Calum said, his voice not quite hiding the emotion of the moment. "Pippa is beside herself that she could not reach Scotland in time for the wedding. But she sent a rider with a suggestion for what we might give Struan and Justine to mark this occasion. Naturally her suggestion is perfect."

How very much she loved this serious brother of hers, Justine thought.

Calum stood. "As you know, Cloudsmoor has been in Pippa's family for generations. The property borders ours in Cornwall, and we shall always require safe passage for our tin to the port that is part of that estate. But we have no need of the house. We wish you, Struan, and you, Justine, to make it your home whenever it pleases you. A parcel of land to the south—abutting the ocean—goes with the gift and we hope you and your children will enjoy it from now on. We shall certainly relish having you so close as often as you choose to come."

Justine found she could not swallow. She breathed through her mouth.

"Too much," Struan said.

"Never too much," Calum said. "Nothing is too much for my sister and the man who is as close as a brother to me."

"Then we thank you," Struan said.

Justine noted an edge to his voice that she didn't understand. His face revealed nothing but reserved pleasure.

"My turn," Devlin North said, standing as Calum resumed his seat. "I bring you Saber's gift to Justine. He is recuperating well, by the way, and hopes to feel like receiving company soon." He gave a velvet box to Shanks, who progressed at a stately pace around the table.

"For myself," Devlin continued. "Please accept the spices that will be delivered within the week. One of the benefits of attachment to shipping." As he spoke he looked steadily at Ella, who never raised her eyes from her lap.

Saber's gift was a necklace of diamonds and amethysts Justine recognized as having belonged to his mother. "He should have kept them for his own bride," she murmured. There was no note.

"That is a situation we must explore as soon as possible," Struan said softly, referring, she knew, to Saber's strange withdrawal from his family.

With self-conscious haste, Ella presented Justine with a length of lace she'd made herself. Max gave her a roughly carved footstool and said, "To rest your leg when it's tired. Robert found the wood for me."

Justine kissed the boy and managed not to smile when he turned as red as his hair.

"I grow tired," the dowager said. "From me you will receive your mother's Bible."

"Thank you, Grandmama."

"Don't thank me," the old lady said. "She died after giving birth to your brother. A worthy cause. Given the viscount's position, the cause served by your following her example would be virtually pointless. You would do well to consider her plight as you read the pages she turned to for solace."

Arran said, "Preserve us all," quite loud enough for everyone to hear. "Grace is also upset that she could not be here for this occasion. However, she'll return as soon as her doctors say it's safe enough for her to travel. Struan. Justine. This is for you."

Shanks made another trip around the table, this time to deliver a sheaf of papers into Struan's hands. He perused them and frowned.

Justine waited.

"Well," Arran said. "Can't you read, man?"

"The lodge?" Struan finally said. "You're deeding the lodge to me?"

"As of last Friday. And acreage surrounding the lodge. Also a house I have secured in Edinburgh. You will be our neighbors in Charlotte Square. I have no doubt the ladies in particular will enjoy that."

"Oh, Arran," Justine murmured. "You are too good to us."

"Too good by far." This time Struan's voice sounded decidedly odd. "We will be more than glad to be allowed to live in the lodge, Arran. This isn't necessary."

"It is done," Arran said, grinning. "And it gives us great pleasure."

"Thank you," Struan said.

He did not, Justine decided, seem grateful at all. His surly tone made her uncomfortable. "We all love the lodge," she said, gushing more than was her habit. "Thank you so much, Arran. You and Grace."

Caleb Murray entered the room, went to Struan's shoulder, and bent to whisper in his ear.

Struan leaned close to Justine and said, "Some of the tenants wish to give us a mark of their joy in this day."

"Then let them," Justine said, turning to Murray. "We shall be delighted to receive their gift."

Caleb nodded to a maid, who left the room.

It was Gael and Robert Mercer who timidly entered. Mairi followed holding the Mercer children's hands.

Red-faced, his fair hair tidily brushed, Robert came forward.

Justine got to her feet and Struan was instantly at her side. Gael wore a lovely lace collar over her simple brown dress and a gold cross on a fine old chain about her neck.

"We hope ye'll not think us forward," Robert said. He carried a bundle draped with white woolen cloth. "This is somethin' we've passed down in the Mercer family, and now we'd like t'give it t'ye because ye've allowed the Mercers their livin' and a good livin' it's been." He set his burden on the floor and removed the cloth covering.

An intricately carved oak cradle was revealed.

Justine took a step backward and came against Struan's hard, restraining arm.

"There's many who made the wee garments inside," Gael said anxiously. "And the coverings. I hope we've not offended ye."

"Never," Struan said. "And we thank you all. There are refreshments in the servants' hall for everyone who cares to come. Will you convey that message for me?"

"Aye," Robert said.

"Thank you," Justine managed to say. She could not look away from the cradle and its piles of tiny, carefully stitched garments. "Thank you."

She felt the Mercers retreat, heard the door close.

"Effrontery," Grandmama exclaimed. "Take the thing away. At once."

"Have it taken to the lodge," Justine said. "It's beautiful. It's their treasure and they've given it to us."

"They are special people," Arran told her. "The best."

Justine blinked several times and raised her face. "Thank you, everyone." If she held her back very straight and met no one's gaze, she would get through this. "If you'll excuse me, I'm a little tired. Please enjoy yourselves."

She left a silent room behind her and walked determinedly through the red salon to the gallery beyond.

Struan caught up with her there. Without a word, he surrounded her waist and accompanied her downstairs to the vestibule.

"The new little carriage was delivered," Caleb stated breathlessly, arriving behind them at a run. "I'll have it brought around. The track to the lodge is much improved."

"My black would be preferable," Struan said.

Caleb appeared confused. "Lady Justine will go alone in the carriage, my lord?"

"The viscountess will go with me, Caleb. On the black."

The estate commissioner hurried away and Struan tilted up Justine's chin. "I should like to carry my bride to our home just as I carried her there when she first saw it."

There were no words for what she felt.

"Soon I shall begin teaching you to ride yourself, Justine."

"Ride?" she asked him, amazed.

"Yes, ride. I've told you I intend for you to do everything you can do, and you can learn to ride, my love."

*Just as I can be a wife to you in the way God intended a woman to be a wife to her husband.* She must be patient. She must find a way to convince him that Grandmama had been wrong in her suggestions.

"I want to get away before the others come," she told Struan, glancing upward toward the gallery.

Mairi came into view and hurried downstairs.

"The rest will not come," Struan said. "Only Mairi because I told her to."

"Here, m'lady." Mairi draped a swansdown-trimmed ivory velvet cloak around Justine's shoulders. "All your needs have been attended to at the lodge." She curtsied deeply and hurried away toward the kitchens.

Struan led Justine from the castle in time to be met by a groom walking the great black into the courtyard. While the boy held the animal steady, Struan mounted, reached down, and lifted Justine to sit sideways in front of him.

Clear skies met the tender April landscape. Scant sun warmed the early afternoon, but the air held a crystal snap that soothed Justine's cheeks. She narrowed her eyes against the breeze as the horse trotted from the courtyard.

Going home.

Going home with her husband.

Justine looked up at his lean face, at his tossed black hair. She had lain with him once, but not as she wished to lay with him. He had said *It* must wait for this day. Now this day was here. Surely he would not turn from their joining because of Grandmama's terrible warnings.

"I'm sorry about the cradle," he said, his eyes trained on the path ahead.

She rested her face on his shoulder. "I'm not. It's a measure of how much the people of Kirkcaldy care for you and Arran. And it's very beautiful."

"It made you unhappy."

"Don't be silly." She forced a little laugh. "I was overcome by the thought of our baby, is all."

He took the reins in one hand and held her tightly with his free arm. He did not speak again on the way to the lodge.

This time they didn't enter by the kitchens. At the sound of the horse's hoofs, a man Justine had never seen before threw open the studded oak door leading from the front of the lodge into the center tower with its gilded crown of cavorting dragons. Behind the man filed a line of servants, male and female, to form a phalanx on the short flight of steps.

The tall, distinguished-looking man came toward them, but Struan had already dismounted and was lifting Justine to the ground. Her leg chose that moment to weaken, and she caught at Struan's arm.

"Welcome, my lord—your ladyship. I'm Nudge. Allow me to introduce—"

"Thank you," Struan said shortly, supporting Justine's weight. "We'll save the introductions for later, Nudge. This is our new butler, my dear. I understand he came with high praise from Northcliff Hall."

With that, and a brief nod to each servant they passed, he hurried Justine inside the lodge. She barely had time to smile at the little entourage, but she did hear murmured "oohs" from some of the maids and a whispered "what a bonnie gown."

He wanted them to be alone.

Anticipation of being with him—really with him—sent her blood thundering through her veins. The weakness she felt now had nothing to do with her capricious leg.

She checked her stride, uncertain what was expected of her now.

"You are tired," Struan said. "You should rest."

How could she be tired. "I do not need to rest."

"Your welfare is my responsibility. Come. Let us go to your apartments."

For the first time Justine realized she had no idea how they should manage their married life. Ella and Max were to remain at the castle for a few days. Suitable household arrangements must be established before they returned.

In her sitting room, Struan removed the soft cloak and set it aside. He turned her to face him and said, "I should like a painting of you in that dress. Would you allow me that pleasure?"

She nodded. Speech seemed determined to desert her frequently.

"We will . . . " He played with pearls at her wrist. "We will do well enough, Justine. We must be patient."

Her throat closed. It hurt.

"I told Mairi you would not need her assistance today. Was that all right?"

"Yes."

He raised his head. "Come. Let me help you."

At first she failed to understand him. When his meaning became clear, heat and cold crossed her skin by turns. She took his hand and went with him into her bedchamber.

Upon the counterpane rested a box. On the lid was the Princes Street, Edinburgh, address of the modiste who had made Justine's wedding gown. Struan removed the lid and drew forth a nightgown and robe of white silk broché, the satin figuring being in the form of lilies, each outline in thread of silver.

Justine gasped at the beauty of the garments.

Struan smiled, bringing back the devilish slant to his features. "I take it that means I chose well?"

"You chose?"

"Yes, I chose. Does it surprise you that I might be able to imagine what would please you?"

He had chosen her gown for their wedding night. "Nothing about you surprises me. I believe you can do anything."

His smile fixed. He glanced away, then at the nightgown and robe. "I wish that were true," he said. "I hope to God it *will* be true. Turn around. I will unfasten your gown."

An instant rush of heat suffused Justine, but she did as he asked and stood obediently still while he undid the small pearl fastenings on the back of her bodice.

What could he mean, *he hoped to God he could do anything*? Was he referring to fear over what was about to happen? Fear that Grandmama's dire projections might prove true?

Struan took the heavy gown over her head and stretched it out carefully on the long ottoman at the foot of the bed. Then he guided her before her glass and made her sit while he began the process of dismantling her elaborate coiffure.

Justine tried not to see herself, tried not to see how transparent her chemise was over her breasts and how her nipples showed plainly, and thrust against the tucked lawn.

At last the strands of pearls were removed, and the small

white rosebuds. Her hair came down heavily to curl against her back.

"I shall not brush it," Struan said, using his fingers instead. "It pleases me to see it tumbled so. This is who you are, my love. The wide-eyed girl for whom the whole world is fascinating. Not the serious, distant woman some would have you be."

"No." He was right, so right.

He studied her in the glass, his gaze drifting down to her breasts. "I am a fortunate man. I cannot imagine why I've been blessed with you."

"Struan—"

"Let me speak, my love. This is harder than you can imagine." He rested his hands on her shoulders and bent to kiss her hair. Slowly, he stroked her neck, and the soft rise at the tops of her breasts.

Justine caught her breath and leaned back against him.

"You will always be my only love. Do you believe that?"

"Yes," she told him. "And you shall be mine."

"I should like to see you without the chemise," he told her. "May I do that?"

Her gaze flew to his face in the glass. "It is still daylight."

"Just so," he agreed. "The better for me to see you."

She would not cover her breasts.

She would not hide from him . . . entirely. "I told you I could never be naked before you."

"Why?"

"You know the answer. I have a deformity. Grandmama told—"

"Do *not* mention that word—or that woman—to me again."

Justine shrank before his ferocious outburst. "I cannot," she whispered.

Struan crossed his wrists in front of her and grazed the tips of her peaked nipples with his palms. "You are perfect," he told her, making agonizingly slow circles on her aching flesh. His fingers folded over her breasts and he brought his lips to her bare shoulder. "And it is for me to make certain that you know how perfect you are."

She felt his hands tremble—and the answering shudder that blazed from those hands to the utmost depths of her body.

He helped her to her feet and led her to the bed where he had set the gown and robe. "Will you allow me to make you ready for rest?"

Rest? She shook so terribly that he must surely see. "You will turn away from me, Struan. I cannot bear to think of that."

"Will you allow me to make you ready?"

She closed her eyes and nodded.

He removed the last of her clothing slowly. Justine did nothing to accommodate him. She waited, her eyelids squeezed together, for his withdrawal from her.

Cold air smote her, but she was too hot with shame to shiver. He placed her hands upon his shoulders. She drew her lips back from her teeth. He must be kneeling before her, and she was entirely revealed but for her stockings and slippers.

One by one, Struan took off her slippers, then her garters and the stockings.

The first touch was from his lips, from his lips upon her belly.

Justine drove her fingertips into the fine stuff of his coat and the hard muscle beneath.

He held her waist.

His mouth slid, leaving a trail of warm kisses, to her damaged hip.

She waited.

Despite her best attempts to restrain them, tears escaped the corners of her eyes.

Struan spread wide his fingers to traverse her sides, to trace the contours of her thighs, and while he did so his kisses passed on to the sensitive, puckered scars upon her leg.

A choked sob escaped her throat.

"Hush," he said against her skin. "You are as I have told you. You are perfect and we shall share so much, you and I. Open your eyes."

She shook her head.

"Yes," he urged. "Do as I ask."

Unwillingly, she did so but trained her gaze upon the wall.

"How can you regard this as so terrible?" he asked, stroking her hip. "Look. *Do* you look at yourself?"

Justine shook her head again.

"Then do so now."

She would please him, even if only by obeying his wishes. Her tears flowed more freely but she did look, and shudder afresh. The scar on her hip curved like a crescent moon, the skin very pale and drawn tight after so many years. A single, shiny welt slashed from one groin to the outside of her knee. The rocks had left sunken hollows there.

"You see," Struan said. His strong, tanned fingers massaged the scars. "Not so terrible, hmm?"

She averted her eyes once more.

Struan rose to his feet. "A few scars, my love. And they will soften the more with loving. I love them because they are part of you and because the sea did nothing more than scratch you when it might have taken your life." He tilted her face up to his and kissed her with lingering passion. She made fists at her sides, fists that slowly rose to rest upon his chest beneath his coat.

This was one of the wonderful kisses that caressed the inside as well as the outside of her mouth. Justine ran her hands around Struan's neck and gave herself up to the kiss. He did not find her repulsive. Her heart sang the amazing news. Struan did not find her scars repulsive!

He muttered something she could not understand and lifted

his mouth from hers. Reaching behind her he took up the nightgown and slipped it over her head.

"Struan?" She felt him tense, grow subtly, amazingly *angry*? "You make me so happy," she told him, her heart beginning to drum the harder.

"I *will* make you happy." His eyes met hers. "I *will*. Only I must make certain . . . I must make certain of . . . of matters."

"Matters?"

With fierce haste, Struan dressed her in the gown and then swung her up into his arms. He tossed back the covers and deposited her upon the mattress.

Puzzled, Justine told him, "It will be all right for us," and smiled through the tears that still stung her eyes. "We must trust it will."

Abruptly, he thrust a hand into his hair and began to pace beside her.

She sat up and reached for him. "Come. Come to me, Struan."

He paused and stared at her. "I cannot," he said, very low. "Damn it to *hell,* I cannot. I must think my love. Decide how to proceed.

"Let me help you."

His snort of laughter wounded her.

"Is it what Grandmama said? Is that what keeps you from me?"

"Wrong," he muttered. "So much wrong. I thought it could be overcome."

"It *can.*"

"I will not have the loss of innocent lives upon my hands."

Ignoring her outstretched arms, he strode from the room.

# *Chapter Nineteen*

❦

usk inched over the day, spread a film of gossamer gray across the sky and the hills. Shadow painted the opposite bank of the river from where Struan's black lowered its head to drink.

Not as much as a breeze moved reeds at the water's edge.

The world seemed to wait.

Struan flipped the reins back and forth. He was waiting, waiting for inspiration—waiting for the unspeakable, praying for deliverance.

His wedding day.

Justine hadn't understood his behavior. How could she? How could she know that he was indeed afraid of harming her, but not only by making her with child? Almost more, he feared that she might be taken from him and exposed to abominable horrors.

At Struan's bidding, Robert had doubled the number of men hidden in the grounds surrounding the lodge. Now Struan could do nothing but continue this damnable waiting.

And hope that word of his hasty departure from his bride reached the enemy. If the creature thought Struan cared nothing for Justine, she would surely be safer.

That was a weak straw to clutch, but better than none at all.

At the sound of approaching hoofs he looked over his shoulder.

*Arran.*

Not now. How much more could a man endure on his wedding day? Surely he could be spared an inquisition by his brother, an inquisition bound to be only moments away.

"What in God's name are you doing, man?"

An inquisition already upon him. "Enjoying some solitude," he told Arran as he drew level. "Forgive me if I don't feel like companionship."

"I'll forgive you nothing. *Nothing.* Do you hear me?"

"I wish you joy in your ride, brother," Struan said. "Perhaps we shall speak tomorrow."

"We shall damn well speak *now,* you wastrel. I was suspicious when I found Caleb Murray wandering about the corridors of the west wing. He said you'd told him to keep a close eye on Ella and Max—"

"I am a protective father," Struan broke in while he silently berated himself for not swearing Caleb to silence.

Arran wheeled his mount around and roared, "You are not a father at all! Not unless there is truly something you have failed to tell me."

There truly was a great deal Struan had failed to tell Arran, and he didn't intend to begin revealing secrets now.

Arran maneuvered closer. "I didn't really intend to ride to the lodge. I still don't know what made me do so. Possibly I am developing some of Grace's otherworldly gifts. They do say a man and wife may—"

"Spare me," Struan said curtly. "Finish what you came to say, then leave me in peace. I have suffered enough." He averted his head. Those were words he'd had no intention of uttering.

"You have suffered? And how much is your bride of a few hours suffering? Is she glad to be so easily deserted by her husband and——"

"It was not easy!" Struan jutted his jaw toward his brother. "Nothing in my life is easy, damn you."

Arran watched him narrowly and said, "So you say. I believe you," very softly. "I encountered several male tenants skulking about the lodge. When I questioned their presence they each had some different so-called task to perform for you."

"There is a great deal to be done to tame the grounds around the lodge," Struan countered defensively.

"One does not engage tenants for such purposes. But that isn't what they're really doing anyway, is it?"

Deceiving Arran had always proved near impossible. "What else would they be doing?" Regardless, to reveal the truth now could spell disaster.

"You are afraid of something," Arran told him. "You are afraid of someone. I am no fool. Ella and Max are being guarded at the castle. Justine is being guarded at the lodge."

Struan returned his brother's stare. "Do not interfere with my affairs."

"Tell me what has happened."

"Nothing has happened." *Yet.*

"I don't believe you. Let me help."

Struan gripped the reins tightly. "There is nothing you can do." But he longed to bare his heart, to throw the truth to Arran and ask for his support.

"What are you afraid of?"

"I am not afraid." Beyond afraid.

"Then . . . Very well. We'll set the question of your guards aside for the moment. Why have you left your bride on your wedding day?"

"How did you know I wasn't with her?"

"Your horse was missing. The stable boy said you'd taken it. Coming here was obvious. In case you've forgotten, we've been coming here in times of trouble since we were boys."

He hadn't forgotten, merely failed to expect Arran to search for him. "There is no trouble," he muttered.

"I repeat. Why have you left Justine alone?"

"For . . ." Another rider crested the ridge. Struan lowered his chin to his chest. "Of course Calum is coming. Why not? No doubt you have both watched my every action and timed this meeting accordingly."

Rather than respond, Arran observed Calum's arrival in silence.

"What in God's name's afoot?" Calum called. "What has happened?"

This was the final insult to his already ruined composure. "Get away," Struan said, waving an arm. "Get away, both of you. Leave me alone!"

Eyes blazing, Calum bore down upon him. "You have left my poor sister alone, damn you. I intend to find out why or break your faithless back."

Shocked by the other's outrage, Struan subsided. "You have spoken to Justine?"

"She will not speak to me. Alone at such a time, and she will not as much as speak to her own brother. What have you done to her?"

"I have done nothing to her," Struan ground out. "Would that I had."

"The devil you say!" Calum retorted, his face tight with anger.

"I take it you have also developed otherworldly powers that caused you to go sneaking to my home."

"Murray is standing guard over Ella and Max and—"

"And—like dear Arran—you were moved to snoop about the lodge."

"I cannot speak for Arran"—Calum restrained his horse from nuzzling Struan's leg—"but this affair queers me. Is it because of my grandmother's? . . . *Is* it?"

Struan looked away, looked at the evening's thickening pall upon the land.

"Speak up, Struan," Arran demanded. "Have you taken that damnable— Excuse me, Calum. Have you taken the dowager's words to heart? You're a man of the world. There are ways to avoid . . . There are ways. If you believe there would be risks to Justine's health . . . If you believe . . . Well, precautions—"

"Enough!" Struan's head pounded. "It isn't seemly to discuss this, but I will tell you both once—only once. You do not know all that concerns me. Yes, it is true that there are certain difficulties that have taken me from Justine's side when I wish to be nowhere but with her. The question of harming her health does trouble me deeply. The measures you speak of are not for a gentlewoman's bed—not a gentlewoman such as Justine."

"But—"

"No," Struan interrupted Calum. "No, my friend. I will not approach my wife as if she were a whore."

"What, then?" Arran asked. "Surely you do not intend—"

"What I intend is my own affair."

Calum regarded the darkening sky. "I heard her crying."

He was a man tormented. There was no end to the torment. "You said she did not speak to you."

"I said she would not. She cried. And she told me to go away."

Arran cleared his throat and shifted in his saddle. "Struan, a woman's safety in childbirth is never a certainty. This terrifies no man more than it does me. But with expert care, and with prayer, surely Justine . . . " He gestured with one hand. "And it's entirely possible she may never conceive. With careful attention to certain womanly times, one could assist that eventuality."

"She cried," Struan said, no longer interested in the presence of the other two men. "My fault. I have ruined her life." He could even cost her her life—by more than one means.

"Justine loves you," Calum said, distress replacing anger now. "And I believe you love her."

"You cannot imagine how much."

"Then go to her, man," Arran pleaded. "Go and comfort her. Nothing more, if that's what you think best for now. She will not know that things should be otherwise between you. At least not until they are otherwise, so to speak."

Struan stared at his brother.

"We three can decide how best to proceed with the other— the rest," Arran continued blithely. "There are writings on the subject of avoiding conception, and we can go to London and consult with an expert. A physician. The man tending Grace seems more than capable. Possibly we should have Justine examined by him and—"

"Arran," Calum said.

Too engrossed in his brilliance for caution, Arran continued. "Yes, we shall go to London for a consultation and bring the physician back with us to examine Justine. He intended to return to see Grace shortly. The two tasks can be accomplished in the same journey. Yes—"

"Arran," Struan heard Calum say. "He isn't listening."

"I am your older brother, Struan. You will be guided by me."

Struan drove his heels into the black's flanks. "You, dear older brother, can go to hell. I have another place to go."

"But—"

The rest of Arran's argument was lost in the thunder of hoofbeats.

* * *

Justine detested displays of self-pity. Women who sank nose-deep in melancholy over slights—real or imagined—drove her to distraction.

Simpering, whimpering females were not to be tolerated.

But no other woman had experienced what she'd experienced in the hours since her wedding. If ever there could be reason for self-pity, Justine, Viscountess Hunsingore, had reason.

"*Viscountess Hunsingore.*" She sobbed her new name aloud. "A bride without a groom. A married woman without a husband. I am as good as widowed."

Her hands flew to her cheeks and she scrubbed at the tears. No, no, no. She was not widowed. What an unthinkable thought. Struan was alive, breathing, vibrant, strong, handsome, warm . . . His body felt so . . . so . . . When he'd tucked her into his naked lap and stroked her breasts . . . Oh, yes, Struan was so very alive.

And he was her husband.

Sin's ears, the knucklehead should suffer for this abandonment. Even if the sight of her old wounds, horrible as they might be, had turned his delicate stomach, he had no reason to behave like a girl with the vapors and rush away.

"I told you a husband does not require his wife to disrobe!"

The tears dried on her cheeks, leaving her eyes hot and stinging. Her throat hurt from the stupid crying over the stupid man who would discover she was no wilting bilberry blossom. He would discover she was not a woman to be trifled with. He would discover she would not be fobbed off with part of the succulent pie he'd wafted before her. She wanted it all.

"If you ever come back to me."

Barefooted, she tore open the door to her chamber and marched into the corridor. Darkness had fallen some hours since—not too long after poor Calum had come tapping at her door. She would apologize to him . . . *after* she made certain Struan understood the nature of the woman he'd married.

Here and there candles flickered in their sconces. Justine tramped to the Pavilion only to find it empty. He was not in the great hall or any other room she searched. And evidently the staff had taken Struan's dismissal on the front steps to mean that they were relieved of their duties until further notice. Not a sound punctured the oppressive hush.

Very well. So be it. She would sit on the steps to the Pavilion bridge until he came home. If he waited so long that she died of hunger—or cold—then he would regret his beastly treatment of her and she would be glad to watch him suffer.

She leaned against the heavy banisters. They hurt her shoulder. So much the better. There would be bruises and she would make certain he saw them. Then she would go into a decline and *die*. And he would be beside himself with grief. He would stand at her graveside and toss roses on top of her casket—and beat his breast and wail his agony. And he would be so handsome all in black—handsome and removed and inconsolable.

Justine ground her shoulder against the bannister.

Perhaps something had indeed happened to him. It must certainly be growing late, and he'd left her early in the afternoon. What if he was so beside himself with unhappiness at the marriage he considered a mockery that he'd cast himself into the river and drowned? What if he'd climbed to the top of the Adam Tower and tossed himself to the cruel ground below?

At this very moment his beautiful body might lie crumpled and broken . . . or pale, limp, and waterlogged . . .

A door slammed. Boots clipped on the flagstones.

She hid her eyes in her knees. Someone was coming to tell her the horrible news. She was a widow before she'd become a wife—in the true sense.

The footsteps stopped.

A cry escaped Justine, and she wrapped her arms over her head.

"Justine! My love. Oh, my love, don't cry."

Struan's voice came to her from below, then the sound of him running up the steps toward her. She didn't raise her head or lower her arms.

"You will die of the cold here, you silly goose," he said, reaching her.

Justine surged to her feet. Powered by consuming rage, she pummeled his shoulders. "And you will die of your own cabbage-headedness."

"My sweet, what—"

"Silence!" She shook so that her teeth clattered. "You might have drowned. Or been smashed to little pieces."

"I—"

"How dare you run such risks?" His surprised face infuriated her. "Damn you to hell, Struan."

"Madam!"

She shook a finger before his nose. "Don't you 'madam' me. From now on I shall say and do what pleases me. I told you . . . I warned you not to look upon my—scars. I said you would be disgusted and repulsed, but you would not listen. Then, when you could not continue the charade, you fled."

"You do not have the right of it, wife."

She rolled her eyes and sat with a thud. "Now you think to employ heavy-handed behavior such as you know I will not tolerate."

Struan drew himself up. In the candlelight his rakish features were sharp and pale—and taut. "I'll thank you to cease this ugly display where you may be overheard. Or do you want every one of those wretched people I didn't want to employ to hear you?" His gaze swept to her feet. "No shoes! On icy stone? In faith, Justine! I must take you to a fire."

When he made a move to lift her, she used a stiffened arm to ward him off. "Do not touch me." With her other hand she tugged her skirts down as far as possible. If her flesh offended him he should not so much as glimpse any of it.

"You must follow my instructions, madam. I will take you to your rooms."

"You will take me nowhere. I intend to have my say this night. In your rooms, my lord." Justine snapped her mouth shut and rose—albeit stiffly—to her feet. She turned majestically from him and swept over the bridge. Struan followed her all the way into his chamber and slammed the door behind him.

"There is no cause for losing one's temper," she told him. "Particularly when you are not the one wronged. I did not ask you to marry me."

"But you wanted me to do so."

She closed her eyes and turned her back. "Yes, I did. I will not lie. But in the past few days I gave you every opportunity to avoid the event."

"And I gave you no opportunity to avoid the event, because I did not wish to. I wanted you as my wife, and now I have you and I do not regret it."

Justine tried to draw a breath. Her lungs seemed to push out the air.

"I am not repulsed by your scars," Struan said from close behind her. "Your body could not please me more. You are my ideal, my dream. To touch you is heaven."

She flamed. The secret places within burned and clenched.

He gathered her hair into a fist and drew her head, gently but firmly, back against his shoulder. "Your face is the only face I shall ever long to see. To simply feel your presence can fill my emptiness. To spread my hand upon your breast . . . " He did so, finding a way beneath the robe and inside the gown. "To mold and entice your flesh incites me as nothing has ever incited me."

Justine leaned against him. Shifting, he slipped his arms beneath hers and loosened the front of her robe. The gown's shallow bodice slipped easily down, exposing her to the room's cool air—and Struan's warm, strong hands.

Her mind flew. The thoughts jumbled together, blurred by sensation, by need. Struan's lips were on her neck, her shoulder, her ear. His palms grazed her straining nipples and she rolled her head away.

Justine turned in his arms and slid her hands around his neck.

His tormented face shocked her. "What is it? Tell me."

For what felt like forever he looked into her eyes, then at her mouth—then her naked breasts. He uttered a deep groan. His own lips were parted before they met hers.

This was different from the kisses they'd shared. This kiss she received, absorbed, while Struan dealt its power upon her like a fascinating weapon. He cupped her head and swept their mouths and tongues together with urgent force. Arched into him, she felt his hardness again and her own body answered with the scorching tension she'd already come to cherish.

"Struan," she managed to whisper. "Struan, let us lie together."

He buried his face in her hair.

"Struan—"

"Hush. Hush. I cannot bear it."

Her heart beat fast and hard. "Tell me what—"

"No. God help me, no."

Framing her face, he stared into her eyes. His fingers hurt her scalp. "I must find a way through this for us, Justine. You must allow me to do that."

"Please—"

"What must be, must be. Trust me to do what is best. I cannot live with myself if I cause . . . " He shook his head.

Suddenly weak, she clung to him. "You are afraid of causing me harm. You are, aren't you?"

"Be led. That is all I ask."

"Be led to what?" His cloak had fallen to the floor. Justine wound shaky fingers about his jacket lapels. "Be led to loneliness and misery? To perpetual longing for fulfillment?"

"You do not understand," Struan told her, his teeth gritted. "I want you, but I cannot have you."

"Because you believe I am less than a woman," she said. Still holding his jacket with her left hand, with her right she stroked beneath his waist coat and over smooth linen where she felt the solid thud of his heart. Rising to her toes, she kissed his beard-rough jaw, slid her lips to the place where his collar met his neck. "I am not less than a woman, husband. I am whole. You have told me I am whole and I want you to help me prove that it is true."

Struan caught her wrists and held her hands against his chest. "You do not understand, my love. There are so many things you do not understand. I am going to return you to your rooms, and I want you to—"

"I will not go." To emphasize her resolve, she pressed her face to his chest, her bared breasts to the backs of his hands. "I will not."

His cheek came to rest atop her head, and Justine swallowed a sob. "Listen to me," Struan said. "There are matters we cannot speak of. Know that I love you. I have told you so and I do not trifle with such words. Remember them. Hold them in your heart. But do not press me—not now—perhaps never."

Emotion poured upon Justine as a warm wind bearing daggers of ice. Confusion. Joy and despondency. Hope and fear—desperation.

"You believe everything my grandmother said."

Struan caressed her shoulders, her back, her waist, with trembling hands.

"Don't you?" Confusion fled, leaving cold clarity in its wake. "Don't you, Struan?"

"I will not speak of it."

She raised her head and found his eyes tightly shut. "You will not speak of the truth? But I think you should. My misguided grandparent has persuaded you that should you become my husband in the only true sense, it may cost me my life. She——"

"I insist you do not speak further of this."

"And I insist that I do. And that you listen. Your concern is that you may hurt me."

When he opened his eyes they shone black in the shadow. "That and more," he admitted.

"Just as I thought." She drew a deep breath. A bold idea formed. "Especially you fear making me with child."

"No more, Justine. Do you understand?"

"Do you understand that you have nothing to fear?"

There was about him a glazed quality. "Come," he murmured. "To your rooms and I will ensure you are warm there."

"I shall be warm here. With you. Your body will keep me warm. You need not fear that I shall die from childbirth. It is clearly impossible."

He stared at her and his gaze gradually became acutely clear.

Justine pulled his neckcloth loose and removed it. She kept her eyes upon his and worked his jacket from his wide shoulders and down his arms until it fell away.

Struan frowned.

She undid his shirt, pulled it from his trousers, and sent it the way of his jacket.

"I find I prefer you without clothes, my lord." Once more she drew close, pressed her breasts to his rigid chest, and surrounded his waist with her arms. "Would you not feel more comfortable without the weight of your trousers?"

His response was the oddest sound.

The course she had embarked upon was reckless. 'If I were likely to bear a child I should undoubtedly already have done so."

Muscle grew solid beneath Justine's hands, and she closed her eyes. Whatever she did, she must not appear nervous.

Breathing slowly through her mouth, she smoothed his buttocks and let her touch rest there.

"What are you saying?" His voice held an edge of steel. "Be careful how you explain yourself."

Justine forced a laugh. "I only tell you to allay your foolish fears. You did not imagine Lord Belcher would offer for me out of simple generosity, did you?"

"I imagined nothing at all about Lord Belcher except that he was the fop you described. And that he was ninety."

With her eyes lowered, Justine shrugged out of her robe. His trousers were complicated, as complicated as they were unfamiliar in construction, but she accomplished their unfastening.

Struan gripped her shoulders and shook her. "Justine?"

The trousers slid past his hips easily enough. "Ah, I see you have reason to thank me for my efforts," she told him as his manhood sprang free and full. Her heart thundered now. Blood pounded in her ears and she feared she might faint away entirely.

"Explain yourself."

She would try. Within the bounds of her scant knowledge, she would attempt to convince him of a lie. "Lord Belcher is considerably younger than ninety. I do not like him, but neither do I entirely abhor him." Tugging Struan's trousers past his muscular thighs was a taxing task, and made the more difficult since her concentration threatened to fly away.

He stopped her at his knees and set her firmly away from him. In seconds he stood before her naked, his legs braced apart, his hands on his hips. "Satisfied, madam?"

Hot and cold by turns, Justine could not respond. Struan, Viscount Hunsingore, was a magnificent man. If she was indeed an unnatural woman for thrilling to the searing desire he aroused in her, then she wanted to be forever and increasingly unnatural.

Struan moved before she could react. He seized her by the

waist and swept her from the floor. A few strides and she was deposited atop the counterpane on his ebony bed.

All air rushed from her lungs. Some intense emotion haunted his eyes, the lines of his face, the set of his entire body.

Anger. No, not anger—fury. Struan pulsed with fury.

"I—"

"Enough, Justine," he said, his lips barely moving. "How many times?"

Quelling the urge to try to cover herself, she scooted to the far side of the mattress. "Come." She smoothed the space beside her. "Hold me."

"My God, I have been a fool. Tell me how often you've been with him."

The question seemed odd, but at least she could answer it honestly. "Many times. His visits to the area were not frequent when I was much younger. He was a boon companion of the Prince of Wales. Then he fell from the Prince's favor after the old King's first great illness—when the King recovered— something to do with having cast his political lot with the King and causing the Prince to give him the cut direct. Lord Belcher returned to Cornwall some time prior to the late King's death, and since then I have been in his company often."

"Often?" His tone faded to nothing. Slowly, he approached and climbed to sit, looking down at her. "Yet you pretended you detested the man and you allowed me to marry you thinking you an innocent—as you should be. You allowed me to play the fool with your damnable book. Did it amuse you to have me explain what you already knew?"

She had done what she set out to do. He believed she had done *It* with Lord Belcher. Justine suppressed a shudder of revulsion. If a woman were capable of bearing a child it would be as possible with one man as another. Therefore, had she been with Lord Belcher she would be as likely to increase as if she became wholly Struan's wife.

Justine smiled and felt muscles in her cheeks quiver. "I pretended nothing. You did not ask about such things. And I did—do need your help with certain aspects of my book. But that is not the issue here. Since I believe my grandmother is correct in saying you do not need more children, it seems to me the sooner we dispel your fears of my producing them, the sooner we can get on with the business of being husband and wife. Don't you agree?"

He did not answer.

She should withdraw the lie at once. Such falsehood was unfair to Lord Belcher, and she had accomplished nothing but evident disgust in Struan.

"Take off the gown."

Gooseflesh rose along her limbs. "No. I think it better not to—"

*"Take off the gown."*

"You are angry. I do not want you to be angry."

"Do as you are told."

His stillness turned her stomach. He was as some great, dark animal, its strength coiled, ready to leap upon her.

Struggling, Justine got to her knees. The room was chill but she did as he asked, pulled the gown entirely from her shoulders and pushed it down about her hips. "I have been wrong, rash and—"

"Say no more, I beg of you." Struan rose to his knees also. Wrapping an arm around her waist, he lifted her to strip away the gown, then set her down once more so that they knelt, thigh to thigh, his shaft an iron pressure against her belly, her breasts pressed to his chest.

Justine's hand went to her hip.

"How unfortunate your modesty is a false thing," Struan said. He bowed his head, but not before she saw the darkness of pain cross his features. He said, "What I have longed for does not exist—gentle honesty. I mourn its absence."

"It is not absent," she told him in a rush. "Not anymore. I have misled you."

"Indeed you have." His lips descended upon hers with little finesse, yet her eyelids drifted shut and she did with her tongue what he did with his.

He touched her everywhere, rubbing, pressing, probing her most sensitive places until she panted and felt herself grow slippery. Embarrassment mingled with anxiety, but if he as much as noticed she saw no sign of disgust.

He would not let her speak. Each time she opened her mouth, he filled it with his tongue. And he held her where she knelt, pushed her thighs apart and, amazingly, thrust *That* part of him between to rest against pulsing flesh.

Justine shuddered. And she felt an answering shudder in Struan. His skin grew heated and slick and his breath came in great drafts.

*It* must be almost over. A wonderful, terrible, intoxicating and shattering thing. If he did not allow her to admit her lie—and forgive her—at least she would have been with him once, and if she were very fortunate there might be a child.

"You are so very wet, Justine," he said against her ear. "Wet and hot, my dear. A passionate woman. How could one expect you to live the life of a nun?" His sudden burst of laughter was wild and near-crazed.

"Struan, please." She plucked at his hair, attempted to pull his head away, to remove his mouth from its fierce sucking at her breast. A sheet of fire burst from beneath his lips, seared downward, tightened her legs against his shaft.

"A nun," he sputtered. "That's rich. A nun and a . . ." Rather than finish, he made a simple chore of lowering her to her back, pushing her heels close to her body and burying his face in that "hot, wet" place.

Justine convulsed. She thrashed and pushed impotently at his shoulders. No words would form, only sounds with no meaning.

His tongue did *There* what it had done to her mouth, but with more devastating results. Those parts of her swelled, they swelled as her breasts seemed to swell and throbbed as her breasts throbbed. And another sheet of lightning heat burst beneath his mouth once more.

"*Struan!*"

Her hips jerked from the bed, but he did not stop.

She did not want him to stop.

The great building pressure exploded, shuddered until she cried out and was helpless to stop her legs from splaying wide.

Struan's mouth left her. Damp and throbbing, she struggled for breath and heard him extinguish the light.

"Now," he said, his voice the voice of a stranger. "Now you shall allow me what you allowed Belcher. I would make him pay for this, but such an action would make me a hypocrite, and that I will not be."

He had lost his mind. Nothing else could explain his senseless babbling. She managed to say. "You must banish Lord Belcher from—" Something . . . The end of his manhood pressed to the opening into her body! "Struan!"

His lips silenced her. He rocked over her, pushing *That* against the sensitive place, sensitive and still pulsating from the amazing act he had performed with his tongue.

Struan forced himself *inside* her body. Justine cried out, but she cried out into his mouth and the only noise was a moan trapped in her throat.

He was huge and hard—and heavy. She clutched at his shoulders and tried to pull away. Struan only rocked more urgently, drove deep into her until she felt he would tear her in half.

For an instant he paused, raised his face a fraction. She thought she heard him curse.

Justine shifted. Rather than curse, he shouted this time and delivered a fierce burst of fresh penetration. He thrust into her again and again, breathing as if he were in a desperate race and might fall before reaching safety.

Pain receded. Small frissons of sensation exploded like reflections of the wonder she had already felt. So this was *It*. Foolish tears welled and slid free. By deception she had caused him to join with her. By truth she must explain and then persuade him to accept that she would rather die with him than live without him.

Abruptly, he grew still.

Yet caught by the power that had grown within her, Justine stifled disappointment at its waning. She was not ready for his stillness.

Something had filled her. Something warm. Her eyes flew open in wonder. Part of Struan, from inside him, had entered her. She felt an inexplicable rush of ecstasy.

"Justine," Struan said. He pulled out of her and lay, one heavy arm and leg pinning her to the bed. "Oh, Justine. You lied to me."

"No. I didn't lie—not until tonight."

"But you lied tonight."

"Yes, I never—"

"You were never with a man before. And you didn't know enough to realize I would feel that you hadn't been."

"Feel?"

"*Feel.* Your sainted grandparent mentioned breaching your maidenhead, remember?"

She couldn't respond.

"I just breached your maidenhead, and if you had been with the odious Lord Belcher, that would already have happened."

Justine swallowed with difficulty. "I see."

"Do you?"

"I tried to take back the lie, but you wouldn't listen."

"You made certain I was beyond listening, my sweet. I am merely a man. And you are a very desirable woman."

"I liked *It*," she said in a small voice.

"I rather gathered you did, damn it all." He sat up in the darkness. "And if I am honest, I'll confess I doubted your wretched little story."

The loss of his embrace left her shivering. "Then why did you—"

"Why did I make love to you? Hah! Because I snatched the excuse you handed me. And now I must pay for it."

Justine reached for him.

At first he didn't move, then he gathered her into a crushing embrace. "Curse my own weakness. Pray to God I have not caused the unthinkable."

"You have not. No, Struan, it will be all right, I know it will."

"Nothing will be all right without a miracle. Without a storm of miracles."

"We shall do well. We shall be happy." Justine smiled against the smooth hair on his chest. "I am cold."

"And I am a heartless failure. I have failed at everything."

Struan left the bed and put Justine beneath the covers. She waited for him to join her. When he failed to do so she called, "Struan," very softly.

"Sleep."

"Not without you."

"I cannot lie with you, Justine."

"But—"

"As I have told you, I am merely a man, merely human. I do not trust myself."

She sat up and peered to see his silhouette against the window where a white moon demanded entrance. "This is our wedding night. Surely what has happened was as it should be."

"When did you last bleed?"

Humiliation stole thought and word.

"When? I must know."

"Sometime since," she whispered. "Why would you ask such a thing?"

"Because I must. When you bleed again, tell me at once."

She covered her face.

"Justine?"

"Very well." Later she would understand. He would explain everything when he became more accustomed to their new state.

"Listen to me carefully," Struan said. "And please do not ask for explanation. It will be easier for both of us. There are reasons why it would not do for others to think I bore any affection for you."

Justine's throat closed.

"Do you understand?"

She managed to say "No."

"It doesn't matter. Perhaps it may even be better if you don't understand. Merely accept that this will be the case. I have no desire to hurt you—the reverse. Shortly, when I have tended you and you are rested, I shall return you to your rooms. In company we shall maintain a distant relationship."

Justine's stomach ached with tension. "As you wish, Struan. I'm sure you will tell me the reason for this in time."

"Perhaps."

"As long as we are together in private I do not care for anything else."

The sound she heard was the thud of Struan's fists on the casement. Against the moonlight she saw that he bowed his head.

"Pray," he said. "Pray for our deliverance from evil. Pray for us all."

Justine's hand went to her throat. "Tell me about this evil."

"It's enough that you know of its existence. If you care for any of us, you will not press me further."

He frightened her. "Hold me, Struan. Come and keep me warm."

"Sleep," he ground out. "This night has been a mistake. The fault is as much mine as yours. Even more mine."

"No. Struan—"

"I shall remember what has passed between us. And I shall long for you with every breath I take. But we may never lie together as man and wife again."

# Chapter Twenty

❦

C old.
    Whipped by the wind, her hair bound her eyes. She heard his footsteps but could not see him. "Wait! Wait for me!"

The beating wind tore her words away, pressed her back, clawed at her bare, icy feet on wet and rotting leaves.

Her hair streamed behind her and she saw him, his cloak filled with the wind. He moved so rapidly—never looking back—that she would not catch him.

She could not stop trying.

Struan would take her with him if he knew she was there, if she could only make him see her. If he went from her sight he would go, never to return, and believe she had decided not to come this night, not to meet him as they had planned. How she had hurried, her breath ragged in her throat, desperately trying to meet him at the appointed time and place. But she had been late.

He had said that if she proved her love by coming to be at his side on the journey, all would be well. The past would be forgotten. They would be forever one in their love—but he would not wait.

Her feet had been too slow, and her leg too weak. She had tried, but the weight of slippery leaves covered her bare feet and dragged her down. And now Struan's tall figure grew smaller in the tunnel through the trees.

"Struan! Wait?"

"Wait. Wait. Wait."

Her own voice echoing?

Clutching her billowing nightrail to her body, she cast about. Not her voice, but another's. A crackling whisper that was neither male nor female.

Sweat broke upon her brow, upon her upper lip. It ran, stinging, into her eyes.

Darkness. Her lips parted. No breath entered. There had been light, hadn't there? Moonlight? Gone now. "Struan! Struan!"

"Struan. Struan."

Not an echo. A whisper like eddies in dry sand. Nearby. Whispering over her skin.

If she did not reach Struan she would lose him forever.

She ran, her feet sucking out of the leaves with each step. Rain hit her face, soaked her gown—slowed her toiling limbs. Each straining step pulled free as if from deep mud.

Exhausted, she paused, her heart pounding.

Other footfalls.

Behind her. Heavier. Faster.

"Struan!"

"Struan."

No one touched her, did they? She felt fingers on the back of her neck, sliding around to tighten on her throat.

The gown wrapped in a sodden rope about her body, lashed her legs together.

"He is gone. You will never catch him now. Gone. Gone. Gone. Gone . . . "

*The fine white bonds tripped her.*

*Slowly she fell, arms outstretched, to the slimy carpet beneath the wind- and rain-whipped trees. "Struan!"*

*"Struan. He is gone. I am here. I am here."*

*Brightness, brief and thin, rushed toward her from the tunnel. Struan was gone.*

*A shadow, its huge, long limbs spread wide like some giant bird, cast darkness over the light and descended, laughing, to cover her—to press her down.*

*It turned her until her face pointed upward to the rain. Rain like great flakes of snow, soft now, falling faster now, covering her face, burying her.*

*She clawed at the flakes and opened her eyes.*

*Not snow. Paper. Sheets of paper.*

*The other's laughter rose like the growing rumble of distant thunder.*

*Paper. Letters. There were words but she could not read them.*

*Laughter punishing her ears.*

*Evil letters from the evil ones who threatened Struan*

*"Let me help you," she cried. "Let me help you."*

*"He will not let you help him." Dry hands caressed her face, explored her body with a husband's intimacy. "He fears for you. Give up. Let go."*

*Large, crushing hands upon her breasts.*

Justine's eyes snapped open. Her breathing labored. Her nightgown stuck to her heated body. Strands of her hair clung to her damp brow.

No dark, hollow-eyed face hovered above her. No insolent hands fondled her breasts. It had been a terrible nightmare.

But Struan was afraid of something he refused to share with her. In the night he had washed her gently, not speaking, pressing a finger to her lips whenever she attempted to do so. Then he had brought her back here to her rooms and left without another word.

She felt about upon the covers, then grimaced. The dream had seemed so real, but her bed was not covered with letters that would reveal everything she needed to know if she was to help her husband.

Her husband. Yes, he was truly her husband now, and if he believed they would never lie together again then he must be a fool. Struan was not a fool. But he had not fully taken the measure of the woman who was his wife. She felt the faintest soreness where their bodies had joined, and she shivered at the memory. No, he had not taken her measure. She would have him beside her—and inside her—or die in the attempt.

How amazing an event their joining had been. Nothing, no imagining, could have prepared her for the wonder of feeling when Struan filled her. These were matters that must be recorded most judiciously. Her book would find a wide audience and might even prove quite controversial, but it must get into the hands of those who needed such a volume.

The next gust of air that crossed her face was a part of no nightmare.

Justine held still and lowered her eyes from the canopy to search the shadowy room. Perhaps a window was open.

A soft voice said, "I cannot rest."

Justine clutched the bedcovers to her neck.

"Men were always such foolish creatures."

She sank deeper into the bed. "Who . . . " Her throat clicked and she couldn't form another word.

A thin wail wafted through the shadows. "There is pain here, and sorrow. Who will ease the pain and sorrow?"

Justine saw her then. Hovering, swaying in the doorway to the dark sitting room, stood Hannah. Dressed exactly as she had been in the ballroom, her veil drifted over her face and about her shoulders.

"Only a woman may heal the division." Hannah's sigh reached Justine, a long, long sigh. "I waited until it was too late. I can never be free until I help another. Heed me, fair Justine, or we shall walk these halls together through eternity—weep together through eternity."

Justine muffled a cry.

"He loves you," the figure said, her voice high. "But something troubles him. Heal his troubles. Bind his heart to yours so firmly, it may only beat if yours beats at its side. If you fail . . . If you fail . . . "

Cautiously, Justine pushed herself up in the bed. Hannah's form began to recede, for all the world as if some unseen force drew her from sight.

"If I fail?" Justine said, throwing back the covers. "Don't go, Hannah. Talk to me."

*"Do not fail."*

Justine scrambled from the bed, lighted a candle, and hurried to the sitting room.

No woman in gorgeous satin and pearls remained. Justine scoured every corner but found nothing, not the smallest sign that anyone had been in the room since she left it the previous day.

In her bedchamber she threw open the heavy drapes at the casement and sat on the window seat with her legs drawn up beneath her gown. The dream had left her shaken. Hannah's appearance had left her more so.

But she didn't believe in ghosts!

Justine raised her chin and stared at dawn's first light banishing the night sky.

There were no ghosts, but if there were, Hannah's made some most sensible points. Men were obtuse. Arrogant. Too proud to accept the help of those they loved and who loved them in return—loved them to distraction.

Hannah was right. Struan bore a deep and destructive trouble, and he needed help. Justine remembered the cold sheets of phantom paper drifting down to bury her. She would not be buried by scurrilous letters—no matter what they contained.

The first order of business was to find a way to engage Struan's trust about whatever threatened his peace.

Movement below caught her attention. She knelt and pressed her nose to a pane. A man rolled into view from behind a large tree trunk. She did not recognize him, but he surveyed the lodge, then slid out of sight once more.

Justine sat again. She frowned and moved to a spot where she had a better view of the grounds to her right. another man, this one sitting cross-legged, bided his time amid her new rose bushes!

By moving from her own room to Ella's and on to Max's, she was able to count no fewer than five persons idling only feet from the lodge.

*Trouble.* Yes, trouble indeed. Did Struan believe she wouldn't notice his *army*? Unless they were surrounded by brigands, those men must be guarding the building—no doubt because Struan had, yet again, deserted his responsibilities. Too distressed to sleep after he'd returned her to her chamber, she'd heard a horse beneath her windows and seen her enigmatic husband riding away.

*And it would not do! None of it would do!*

How fortunate that she was a woman who had always preferred to attend herself when possible. Since Mairi remained at the castle and no member of the new staff seemed brave enough to approach, there was little danger of being interrupted.

With irritation building, driving her to move quickly, Justine dressed in a heavy rose silk dress with cream chiné stripe. She arranged her hair inside a French lace cap trimmed with ribbons to match the dress and sped from the room.

"This is for you and for me, Hannah," she murmured aloud, steadying herself as she descended the stairs. "You will be set free because I will *act*. I will not wait for disaster."

When she drew open the weighty front doors and walked out onto the steps, a scene of utter stillness greeted her. Day had broken but a chill still clung to the air and no sun had banished the early morning's dim light.

Justine set her lips firmly together and made her way down to the drive. Turning right, she strolled, deliberately studying plantings near the building. Much had already been accomplished in the grounds.

When she arrived at the spot she knew was immediately beneath her windows, she paused and listened—and set her mouth the more firmly when she heard a twig snap.

Onward she walked until she drew level with her new roses. With exaggerated nonchalance, she swung her skirts and approached the bushes. Buds had begun to form, and she bent to examine them closely—and looked through the branches into the blue eyes of Robert Mercer, who had hunched down as far as was possible.

Justine straightened. "Good morning, Robert Mercer."

He leaped to his feet and coughed loudly, once, twice, three times.

A signal, no doubt.

She turned about in time to see the man behind the tree double over and begin to retreat. "You there!" she commanded. "Remain exactly where you are, my good man. I shall wish to speak with you." The man did as she asked.

"Now, Robert," Justine said. "Kindly explain what you and your friends are doing here."

Robert—his brow still bearing evidence of their last encounter—whipped off his rough bonnet and rolled it between his hands.

Justine had little experience with the kind of annoyance she felt at this moment. "Speak up." She must be firm. "Answer me at once."

"Carryin' out orders, my lady."

"Whose orders?"

Robert frowned at the sky.

"Speak up!"

"Hmm. His lordship's."

"And what were those orders?"

This time Robert's boots claimed his attention.

Justine's patience threatened to desert her entirely. She must not forget that this was a very gentle man, a shy man if she was not mistaken. "Kindly explain the nature of the orders you were given."

His throat bobbled and he looked all about as if for inspiration. The sudden smile he bestowed upon her contained more hope than joy. "Cuckoo spit, my lady. I'm t'take the measure o' cuckoo spit."

"Cuckoo spit?"

"Aye." He grasped a rose stalk and didn't as much as flinch when a thorn raised a bead of blood on one of his fingers. "Y'see? it's the frothy white stuff in the crook there." He pointed and brought his eyes close as if to assess the exact number of bubbles in the substance.

"I have seen cuckoo spit, Robert, " Justine said carefully. "Pray tell me. Why exactly would the viscount request that you study *cuckoo spit*?"

"Angus!" Robert shouted suddenly. "Come and tell her ladyship about the cuckoo spit." Amazingly, he turned his back on her entirely and waited for the other man's reluctant approach.

Tall and thin, this Angus already held his bonnet in his big, white-knuckled hands. He stared steadily at Robert, who said, "I've been tellin' the viscountess about the cuckoo spit."

Angus's upper lip rose from his teeth and his nose wrinkled in confusion.

"Y'know," Robert said, his shoulders hunching. "*Cuckoo spit*. She wants to know why the viscount wants it looked at early in the morning."

Angus's eyes slid to Justine and back to Robert. "Aye, cuckoo spit."

"Looked at for what purpose?" Justine persisted. She

glanced over her shoulder in time to see another of the cuckoo spit experts slipping away.

*"Measurin',"* Angus said with the alacrity of a man possessed of sudden inspiration. "Is that not right, Robert?"

"Aye, measurin'," Robert agreed. His fair skin turned bright pink with misery. He squinted along the track leading to the pines that surrounded the lodge. "There's young Max." His relief at diversion was tinged with something else—concern, Justine decided.

Mounted on the little chestnut Struan preferred him to ride, the boy came at a gallop. He'd begun to head for the bridge and the stable yard when he caught sight of Robert's waving arms and turned toward them.

Spurring the chestnut, he rode to the rose garden and dropped from the saddle. After checking behind him, he turned a nervous face on the assembly. "I'm come t'get somethin'."

Robert said, "Er, I was just tellin' her ladyship how your papa has us come t'study the cuckoo spit early in the mornings sometimes."

Max opened his mouth, looked from face to face, and clamped his lips shut again.

"Aye," Angus said. "We're simple men, and explainin' these things doesna come easy."

Robert pointed to a delicate puff, no doubt a puff left by a mayfly or some similar insect. "You tell about it, Max. Why we *measure* it."

"Why ye measure it?"

"Aye, measure it."

Justine crossed her arms.

"When there's enough o' it, it's collected, y'see," Max said seriously. "It's important to have the absolute right o' this thing. T'get the very most out o' it, y'see."

"I don't see."

Max gave one of his most brilliant grins. "Och, forgive me. O'course ye wouldna understand. It's for herbs. There's nothin' like cuckoo spit for cultivatin' the very best herbs, and—"

"That will do," Justine said succinctly. "I think I've heard all I need to hear. You must be certain to let me know what you intend to study when your present fascinating project is complete."

Wait until his lordship deigned to return to his home—and his wife. He would not dare to deny that he feared some attack upon his home and family. And she would know the reason why. No knobby-brained excuse would suffice.

Max, whirling about, snapped her contemplation of what she would say to Struan.

A large, heavily muscled gray horse approached. Its rider was easily identified as Caleb Murray. Hatless and without as much as a jacket, he bore down upon the small group near the roses at a full gallop.

Max scrambled to mount his chestnut, but his foot missed the stirrup. By the time he'd pulled the horse around once more, Caleb brought his gray to a gravel-spewing halt. "This'll be the last time, lad," he said to Max. The man's face showed pale beneath his tan. "I'll put you back where you belong this once. The next time, I'll go to your father."

"I'm *tired* o' those stuffy rooms! I want t'run and swim with me friends."

In a single motion, Caleb swept Max before him on his horse and caught up the chestnut's reins. Without as much as a word to Justine, he wheeled about, leading the small horse behind him.

"I'll not go!" Max announced.

"You'll go and you'll do as you're told," Caleb said, sending his heels into the gray's sides. "Your papa made it plain."

Max squirmed and Caleb tightened his grip. "Be still, I tell you. It's for your own safety. You're to be watched closely."

"Why?"

Justine looked from Angus to Robert—who looked away.

"Someone wants you dead," Caleb said, his voice low and plain. "Someone wants you *all* dead."

Justine pressed her arms to her sides and watched man and boy ride toward the pines. Raising her chin, she brought a finger to rest atop a tightly furled rosebud. "Cuckoo spit, hmm?"

Buttercup had been pressed into service to wait upon Justine. Once it was known that the lady of the house would spend the day in her rooms, her meals were delivered on a silver tray borne by the brazen-eyed girl.

The last offering, afternoon tea and small cakes, remained on the tray. Justine sat close to her sitting room window watching, as she'd watched all day, for Struan's return.

A knock sounded at the door and Buttercup, her blond hair riotous and completely unsuitable to her station, tripped into the room with tiny, rapid steps. Her round hips swayed and her high bosom strained at the bodice buttons above her apron bib.

At the moment, Buttercup's eyes were more avid than brazen and her breath came in shallow gasps.

Justine turned back to her vigil. "I've finished with tea, thank you, Buttercup."

"Yes, m'lady."

"I shall not require anything further today."

"Yes, m'lady."

When there were no sounds of the girl gathering the tray, Justine glanced at her. Rubbing her apron between her hands, Buttercup jiggled from foot to foot.

Justine asked, "What is it?" and managed a smile.

"Mr. Nudge said she couldna come in, but she wouldna be turned away. She's outside. I thought I should tell ye on account o' some o' the others at the castle sayin' ye were kind and gentle."

Justine frowned and attempted to concentrate. "You must speak more plainly, Buttercup. Who is outside?"

"Her who came t'see ye. A sad sight, she is. And she says ye'll be wantin' to talk t'her."

Justine stood up and went closer. "Who is she? Do I know this person?"

"She says ye'd never turn her away. Mr. Nudge thinks she's a hussy . . . Excuse me, m'lady. He thinks she's not a nice person, and he won't let her in on account o' the master not bein' at home."

"I'm sure Nudge has experience with such matters."

Buttercup caught impulsively at Justine's hand. She lowered her voice. "I'd not take such a thing upon myself, but she's not well, m'lady. I could tell she ailed, so I waited my chance and followed her. She'd sat hersel' down against a wall, poor thing."

"She asked for me, you say? By name?"

"Aye. Ye and no one else but ye, she said. She wouldna give her name."

Justine was torn. She'd never turned aside from someone in need, but these were troublesome times, and although Struan had not confided as much in her, she knew he feared some unwelcome intrusion.

"I'm sorry, m'lady," Buttercup mumbled. She backed away and picked up the tray. "I'd no right t'bother ye with such matters."

What harm could an ailing woman do? "Leave the tray," Justine said. "Do not return to the kitchens. Get this woman by another route and bring her to me."

"Are ye sure?"

"Go quickly." Before her resolve failed.

While she waited for the visitor, Justine set about making chocolate in a small pot on the hearth. Chocolate, she had always believed, could be quite restorative—despite Struan's bias.

A method for dealing with her stubborn husband—at least a beginning—had begun to form. All day she had determinedly pushed thoughts of Hannah away, but, nevertheless, she silently renewed her promise to do as her imaginings had instructed her and ensure she and her husband went forward side by side.

In response to a light tap at the door Justine said, "Come in," and stood with her hands clasped before her.

Her face flushed, Buttercup entered first. Quickly, she urged her companion into the room and closed the door behind them both. "This is her, m'lady," she whispered hoarsely. "If Mr. Nudge finds out what I've done I'll lose m'place."

"He won't find out." Justine was already absorbed by the woman the maid had brought. "Go about your business."

"Oh, m'lady, I couldna leave ye—"

"You have no need to be concerned." The pathetic creature swayed where she stood. Dark curls escaped a simple gray bonnet that obscured her bowed face. "Run along. Return in half an hour for my directions," she added as a precaution.

"Will you sit by the fire?" Justine asked when she was alone with the stranger.

Without raising her face, the creature came slowly forward and sank into a chair. She wore a gray cloak of some thin woolen stuff over a plain gray dress.

"Will you have a little chocolate?"

The other nodded.

Justine busied herself filling a delicate blue Sevres cup. This she offered together with the plate of cakes from the tea tray.

The face that turned up to hers almost stopped Justine's heart. "Oh, my dear!" She set the cup and plate down and pulled up a chair for herself. "What has happened to you? You must tell me everything. The whole story. Are you a tenant here? What is your name?"

"Mrs. Smith," the woman said in a husky voice. "I've come a long way to see the viscount."

The answer startled Justine. Rather than address the last, she said, "How were you injured?" Bruises darkened the pale skin of a beautiful face. In one eyebrow there were signs of a healing wound. Another showed at the corner of an eye, and a narrow pink line suggested her lower lip had suffered some assault.

Mrs. Smith eyed the cakes and Justine hurried to hold the plate before her once more. The woman ate voraciously, devouring each delicacy in a single bite, one after another. She gulped down the chocolate and silently accepted a second cup.

"Can you talk now?" Justine asked.

Licking crumbs from her fingers, the woman took off her bonnet. "Forgive me," she said. "I haven't eaten in days. I came many miles—mostly on foot. I've no money, you see. But I had to get away." Her eyes, beautiful black eyes, settled anxiously on Justine's.

The woman's clothes should have distinguished her instantly from the tenant wives. Simple and far from new, they were nevertheless well cut and had once been quite fine. "Would you care to take off your cloak?"

At first Mrs. Smith's reaction was to clutch the cloak over her dress. Slowly, her fingers relaxed and she removed the garment. Still watching Justine, she reached back to loosen tapes at the back of her bodice. Wincing, she shrugged the garment from her shoulders until it rested at the tops of lush breasts. Then she stood and turned around.

Justine gasped and covered her mouth in horror.

"He did it," the woman said, her voice breaking. "My husband. He's going to kill me. I know he is."

She had been brutally beaten. Justine had never seen the results of such horrible violence. "You must be treated," she said. "We shall find you a bed and you shall sleep until you are strong enough to tell me your story. You are not to be concerned further. You are safe now."

Mrs. Smith eased her gown back over her shoulders. Justine hurried forward to retie the tapes.

"Where is your husband now?" An awful vision of the beast descending upon the lodge did nothing for Justine's composure.

"He was drunk when I left him," Mrs. Smith said, averting her eyes. "That was days since. I took nothing, so he'll expect me to go back. It'll take a long time for him to realize I've left, and then he'll have no idea where to look. I need a place to hide, my lady. To hide and think."

Justine squared her shoulders and paced to the windows. When she turned it was to find Mrs. Smith looking through the door into the bedchamber. Justine cleared her throat.

The other woman looked at her with no sign of embarrassment. "Such pretty rooms. You and the viscount must be very fond of blue."

"Yes," Justine said, uncomfortably aware that the chamber showed no evidence of a man's presence. Not that—according to Grandmama—it was less than usual for a husband and wife to have entirely separate sleeping arrangements for other than *It*.

"I shall ring for the maid. There are dozens of empty rooms in this lodge. You shall make one of them your home until we can decide how to proceed. May I ask you one question?"

Before Justine could react, Mrs. Smith threw her arms about her in a fierce embrace and said, "Thank you, my lady. Oh, thank you. I should have guessed his lady would be no less than the generous soul he is himself. Will you call me Glory, too?"

Justine patted Glory's arms. "I'm sure that will be agreeable. When you say 'he,' I assume you mean my husband? Viscount Hunsingore?"

"Oh, yes. We were friends once." She tilted her head to one side and smiled. Justine noted that the bruises did little to detract from the woman's beauty. "That was before Mr. Smith, of course. And before you."

"Of course."

"But he told me to come to him if ever I was in trouble, so here I am. I promise I'll be no trouble. You won't regret taking me in."

"I'm sure I won't," Justine agreed, no longer at all certain she hadn't acted too rashly.

"You won't even see me once the viscount returns."

"And why should that be—exactly?"

Glory Smith's face resumed its former serious expression. "Because I know he won't want you concerned with my troubles." She shook her head until her luxurious black curls swung. "No, not at all. He'll take care of Glory just the way he promised."

# Chapter Twenty-one

❧

From a knoll overlooking the castle, Struan surveyed the hills and valleys, the clusters of tenant crofts, Kirkcaldy Village, and the forking river that fed the estate's fertile fields.

Robert Mercer stood beside him. At Struan's request, the two had ridden out together. Now they were alone Struan couldn't decide what to say. The tenant would not speak until spoken to.

"I'm grateful for all you've done in recent months," Struan said at last. "All you've done for Ella and Max—and now at the lodge."

"It's no less than we should do."

"My wife is gentle. I do not want her worried."

Robert shuffled his boots. "Aye, she's gentle and fair—and kind. Did she speak of this morning?"

Struan looked sharply at Robert. "What about this morning?"

"Och, nothin', I suppose. She saw me and Angus, but we told her we were about some business for ye."

"And she believed you?"

Robert puffed up his cheeks. "Aye. Young Max happened along. He told one o' his fine stories and for once it was useful."

"Max?" Struan caught Robert's sleeve. "Max was at the lodge this morning?"

Robert grimaced. "Only long enough for Caleb Murray t'-catch him and bear him away wi' terrible threats and the like."

Struan relaxed a little. "But the viscountess suspected nothing?"

"Women . . . that is, the ladies' interests hop like crickets. A tale about somethin' they canna understand distracts them quickly enough."

Struan nodded and fell into a pleasant moment of shared understanding with Robert before telling him, "I should like you to know why all this has been necessary. I'll explain the way of things as soon as it's safe to do so." Robert would expect no such confidence, but Struan felt a kinship with the tenant.

"Ye'll be the judge o'that, my lord," Robert said. "Was there somethin' special—somethin' else ye wanted to speak of?"

Keeping Arran and Calum completely ignorant of his position had become impossible—and possibly unwise. He might be forced to ask for their help, and today he'd take them partially into his confidence. How unfortunate that they'd been less willing than Robert to accept that he could not reveal everything yet. Arran had stormed and shouted and demanded the entire truth. Calum, pale with concern and divested of all patience by the dowager's inexplicable refusal to leave Kirk-caldy, had all but threatened to retain a private regiment to protect his sister.

Struan dropped to his haunches and picked up a stick. His horse cropped the grasses nearby. Robert's shaggy mount kept a respectful distance from the Thoroughbred.

"Your people have been on Stonehaven lands a long time, Robert."

"Aye. Generations."

"We're glad you're here. I was speaking with Arran earlier. He told me I'd chosen well when I'd asked for your help with Ella and Max. Calum agreed."

"Aye. The marquess is a fine man. He's been good t'me and mine. My Gael thinks him the best ever t'draw breath, and the wee ones love the very sight o'him."

"He can be generous." When he wasn't ranting. "I expect you're wondering why I asked you to come up here with me."

Robert turned candid blue eyes upon Struan. "Ye're troubled, my lord."

"More troubled then you know."

"If it'll help, we can keep a watch day and night."

"You have your own affairs to attend to."

Robert shrugged. "We're good at helping each other. We'll manage."

"For the next few days I'm going to leave Ella and Max at the castle with Caleb."

Robert picked a handful of grasses and let them drift through his fingers.

"They'll be safe enough there," Struan said.

"Ye canna keep young ones locked indoors forever," Robert said. "It's easy t'tell ye've a terrible affliction. And ye can only wait for it t'come t'ye. If it was otherwise, ye'd not be barring your family away. Can ye not ask guidance from another?"

Struan snapped the stick in two and tossed away the pieces. With the arrival of afternoon a weak sun had escaped the clouds, but there was little warmth in the day. He bounced to his feet. "I'll be honest, Robert. If I thought there was someone who could help—and whom I could trust with the lives I must protect—then I'd be happy to meet that man."

"Brother John," Robert said.

Struan paused in the act of reaching for his mount's bridle.

"The monk," Robert continued. "Did ye ever meet him?"

"Ah, the monk Max speaks of. No, our paths have never crossed, but I understand he's not averse to an evening of cards in Dunkeld." He had yet to mention his disapproval of such unsuitable encounters to Caleb.

Robert hid a smile. "Aye. At the Fiddlers' Rest. And he wins. And then he shares his winnings with those in need. He's a simple enough man, my lord. And a man of God. But human, if ye know what I mean. There's little t'spare t'pay him for his help—but he's always the first t'offer that help."

"Why have I never met this paragon?"

"Ye were away from these parts when he came. Wanderin' he was. Searchin' for a place where he'd feel the Lord in every day, so he said. And he stayed here."

Struan looked toward the village again. "A man with fine taste." Unfortunately Struan had begun to wonder if the Lord had temporarily forgotten at least one of his errant children.

"Will ye meet Brother John?"

"I'll consider the prospect." Struan mounted the black. "If it seems like a good idea I'll ask you to arrange it. We'd best get back."

Robert climbed onto his horse and the animal immediately ambled downhill.

"I don't think there's any need for you and the others to spend your days at the lodge," Struan said, catching up with ease. "But I'll thank you to stand ready to be there at night when necessary."

"Aye."

Robert pulled his nag to a halt and pointed.

Struab followed the direction of the other man's finger. At first he saw nothing of note. Then a movement attracted his attention. From behind a thicket a donkey plodded into sight, a cowled figure astride its broad back.

"I dinna believe it!" Robert looked to Struan. "Brother John himself. Will ye not speak wi' him? Just t'get his measure?"

Struan was of a mind to refuse. He hesitated.

The brown-clad figure continued on his swaying way.

"All right," Struan agreed abruptly. "Let's meet this holy man of yours." The time for avoiding men of the cloth must pass, just as the events of long ago must pass—assisted by force, if necessary.

Robert grinned and urged his horse on. "Brother John!" he cried. "Halloo, Brother John!"

Rather than overtake, Struan hung back and followed at a leisurely pace in the other man's wake. Robert was almost upon the monk before the cowled head rose from apparent deep contemplation and the donkey slowed to a stop.

Gesturing at Struan, Robert gained the monk's side and clapped him on the back with unexpected familiarity.

"A saint for the simple folk," Struan murmured, and instantly chided himself for his own mean spirit. Perhaps he still, somewhere deep inside, mourned the loss of what had once been his own deep spirituality.

"I'm tellin' Brother John about ye," Robert announced cheerfully as Struan reached him. "The marquess has given him a livin' place in the old mill, but they've not met."

"We must remedy that, Brother," Struan said.

The cowled head was averted. A low voice said, "Blessings, my lord. Forgive me if I take my leave of you. There are pressing—"

"Brother?" Struan said, interrupting. His heart beat fast and hard. "Can you not spare me a little of your time?"

Slowly, the man turned his face and looked up at Struan.

For a moment it was as if he'd received a blow. The air left the day—and the light went away. He opened his mouth but could not speak.

"Hello, my son," the holy man said. "I have awaited this meeting. I have longed to see you—and I have dreaded seeing you. But there must be only honesty between us. It was with the hope that I should encounter you that I came to Scotland. But I find my courage has deserted me."

Struan took the hand the man extended. He wound their fingers together and hung on. And he stared into eyes he had never thought to see again. When last he'd spoken to Abbot John Grably it had been on the steps of Moreton Abbey in Dorset. The abbot's face had borne deep sorrow. Struan had begged forgiveness for ruining an innocent maid.

"Justine? It's Struan. May I come in?" He tapped on her chamber door for the third time, then pressed an ear to a panel. No sound came from the room.

Carefully, he turned the handle, pushed open the door, and peered inside. Her bed was untouched, but a stroke of light showed around the edges of the door to her sitting room.

Lighter of heart than he'd felt in many a month, he crossed to knock the second door. "Justine?"

"Come," she said, sounding preoccupied.

He followed her instruction and found her seated behind a small leather-topped desk with her famous notebook open before her.

She did not look up.

Smiling, Struan advanced. "Busy, I see."

"Indeed, my lord."

So that was the way of it. Not that he could expect a more enthusiastic greeting under the circumstances. "I've come to apologize."

"For being a shatter-brained ass?"

Startled, Struan halted. "Surely I've misheard you."

"I doubt it. We frequently pretend not to hear those things

which hold too painful a thread of truth. It must be exceeding uncomfortable to know one is a cocklehead."

"A *cocklehead?*" This woman would undoubtedly never shed her ability to amaze him.

"A suitable term for a man who by turns ignores and supposedly adores his wife of only hours."

"You are harsh, my lady."

"I am honest, my lord."

His own sudden smile surprised Struan. "Ah, but your spirit is irresistible, Justine."

She raised one fine brow. "I'm glad I entertain you. Currently I am recording what passed between us last night."

"The devil you are?" He felt an unaccustomed heat beneath his collar.

"I find accuracy more easily obtained if one doesn't allow too much time to pass following the event one wishes to record."

The thought of Justine attempting to write down the details of their lovemaking temporarily dulled Struan's happiness at being reunited with his old friend and mentor. The abbot had been quick to reveal that he'd come to Scotland as much to seek forgiveness as to offer the same to Struan. He'd alluded to his own search for humility and understanding, and assured Struan he should not continue to blame himself for the fiasco with the girl at the abbey. Struan had alluded to his predicament, and the abbot readily promised to lend his considerable intelligence to solving the dilemma.

"How do your herbs grow, husband?"

Struan wasn't sure he'd heard Justine correctly. "I beg your pardon, my dear?"

"Your herbs? I trust they flourish."

"That would be a question for the gardeners, I should think." Really, females could be damned puzzling. "I hadn't realized you had an interest in such things."

"I am interested in anything and everything that concerns you, Struan." For the first time her eyes met his. "How late it is. You must have had a great deal of business to attend to today."

He knew the discomfort of guilt. His neglect of his new bride was all but unforgivable. "You know I have been beset," he told her. "I thought it appropriate to spend some hours considering how we should proceed."

"How very sensible of you. I shall look forward to hearing how you have decided to arrange my life."

"And I shall tell you," he said cheerfully. "I met an old friend. A man of the cloth. He is most wise and has made me take a more optimistic view of things. We have made a pledge to spend considerable time in exploring these matters."

"Does that mean you will abandon your study of cuckoo spit?"

Struan could think of no response.

Justine laughed, and her serious face was transformed. Dimples appeared beside her lovely mouth and her brown eyes sparkled with humor. "Give no more thought to my foolishness. I am a trifle giddy today. No doubt my changed state is responsible."

"No doubt." What a fetching creature she was. How delightful she looked in a satin pelisse robe of mint green—how fresh and appealing.

"I am anxious for Ella and Max's return. We have much to accomplish. And I am not certain Caleb Murray should use threats of death to discourage Max from seeking freedom. He did so this morning, you know."

So Justine had not been oblivious to the morning's intrusions. "I'm certain Caleb simply sought to make the boy more easily controlled." He must warn Caleb to say not a word to anyone but himself in future.

Justine's brow puckered. "Perhaps you are right. Even more important, I am determined that Ella should be ready for her Season by next year. She is a beautiful creature, Struan, and I would prefer that she not be too long available."

More of his lightheartedness slipped. "I'm not certain I understand."

"Men." With an eloquent sigh, Justine rose and walked around to lean on the front of her desk. "Will you sit while I explain?"

"I should rather stand close to you," he said, never intending to say such a thing.

Still smiling, she continued to regard him. The robe opened from a high collar to a point where the shadow between her breasts was visible. The gown she wore beneath was of layers of sprigged green muslin. Struan found himself more interested in the suggestion of her skin that showed through the muslin than in its decoration.

He swallowed and raised his eyes to hers. She no longer smiled. "You were going to explain why we should be in a hurry to marry off Ella. She is, after all, but sixteen."

"Sixteen. Seventeen when she comes out. And the most exotic young female I have ever seen. Exotic and irresistible. I assure you that Mr. Devlin North finds her so."

Struan frowned. "He has met her once—or perhaps twice."

"Today I was told by one of the maids that Mr. North has become a frequent visitor at the castle in recent days. Does he come to see you?"

"Of course not."

"Arran, then?"

"Not that I've heard."

"No, because it is not for you and Arran that he brings expensive gifts."

"North does that?"

"He does indeed. All for Ella. I understand there is a puppy obtained in China. And a fan of white jade. Also a gold chain and bell for her ankle. The bell is rung by a suspended diamond. What do you say to all that?"

"Outrageous. The bounder's old enough to be her father!"

Justine smoothed the pelisse over her waist. "Hardly her father, but certainly a more than mature husband. Mrs. Bastible was heard to remark that the two would make a most handsome pair."

"Husband!" Struan exploded. "Damn Blanche Bastible's eyes. I'll order North to stay off this property, dammit! The gifts shall be returned. I'll—"

"You'll make certain that I have an opportunity to speak with Ella at length and to guide her in dealing with such matters. And very soon we shall start shopping for her gowns and so on. Naturally we shall all go to London in the spring."

Struan found himself little mollified. "I should probably call the lecher out."

Justine laughed. She tipped back her head, displaying the length of her white throat, and laughed heartily.

"I'm glad you find my discomfort humorous," Struan told her, more than a little chagrined.

Once more she was serious. "Your discomfort is the last thing that would ever amuse me. I desire your comfort and your company. I desire to be your helpmate . . . and your mate in all other things."

He grew still.

"Should you care to hear what I've written about our wedding night?"

Struan swallowed with difficulty. "If my opinion would be of use to you."

She reached back for her book. "Of great use. You can inform me of any inaccuracies." With a frown in his direction, she added, "I do believe my book will be the talk of Society. There will be those of narrow-minded persuasion who will seek to stop its publication. But I know that—with your help—those bigots can be silenced. Or, at least, disregarded."

Apprehension moistened Struan's palms. He brought a

chair close to the desk and sat down with a most pleasing view of his wife's serious face—and her enticing body.

This course he'd chosen would not be easy. To be close and not to touch could only become more challenging.

"The Wedding Night," Justine began. "I am continuing with my plan to divide the volume into titled sections, you see. Later I intend to add information gleaned from Ella's experiences in London as a companion volume. This work will become a veritable treasure to women."

"Hmm." Her waist was so narrow. The fastenings on the pelisse robe allowed the garment to flow away, revealing the curves of her breasts above a narrow band of satin—and the suggestion of softly rounded hips.

"Do you dislike my gown?"

His eyes rose at once. "I think your gown delightful. I was merely preparing to concentrate on your writings, my dear."

"The Wedding Night," she repeated. "The wedding day is inevitably a time of strain and anticipation. Strain because one is observed by others and one's behavior assessed for its suitability to the occasion. Anticipation because the bride knows she is about to become different in a most exciting, but also a potentially frightening way. She is about to be revealed to her husband in a totally intimate manner, just as her husband is about to show himself as he really is."

Struan cleared his throat.

"I thought that a tasteful explanation," Justine said. "Do you not agree?"

"Absolutely."

"Good. Here I digress a little to events leading up to the husband and wife being alone together. So, the wedding breakfast. The wedding breakfast is a trying meal. Guests expect fanciful treats and good humor. New husbands think only of what is to come once they are alone with their brides. And brides—without the benefit of this book—are likely to suffer pangs of abject fear."

Struan squirmed.

"Do you consider that a fair interpretation?"

"Hmm. Quite possibly."

"Good. My advice to brides is that they are charming to their guests, that they deal graciously with speeches and gifts, but that they find a means to hasten departure to the chamber where they are about to become wholly women—through an extraordinary and marvelous encounter." She glanced up at Struan. "Still acceptable?"

"Absolutely." To this point he'd barely considered her book as more than an amusing diversion. But her "amusing diversion" began to make him dashed uncomfortable, and he feared she had every intention of trying to publish the thing. He'd never live it down . . . But then, he'd have to make certain the volume didn't see the light of day.

Justine watched him so carefully, he felt forced to look away. "There are myths to be dealt with," she continued. "Such as the matter of a husband preferring his wife's absolute submission."

He pressed a fist to his chin.

"It is important for the bride to let her groom know that she desires him as much as he desires her." She paused before saying, "This is the part where I must be very cautious not to become too meek in my approach to the topic. I have written: Once closeted together with the man to whom one has given one's allegiance, obedience, honor—and body—the time for celebration has arrived."

Struan found himself silently praying that each sentence be the last.

"During courtship, the female—despite the convention of pretending innocence of such things—despite this, she is perfectly aware that her courtier gazes upon her body with anticipation."

"A little strong, don't you think?" Struan said before he could stop himself.

"Is it true?"

He opened his mouth, closed it, and nodded.

"Quite so. A piece of flimmery-flammery foolishness about hearts and roses will do my readers absolutely no good. Listen. Our gowns are designed to encourage the interest of males. I do not suggest that such gentlemen do not consider our minds important, only that they may not be particularly interested in our minds until their interest has been engaged by rather shallower virtues—virtues of fleshly appearance."

"Oh, my God," Struan said under his breath.

"Hah!"

He observed a wholly satisfied glitter in Justine's dark eyes and frowned.

"Your discomfort means I am unveiling masculine secrets, Struan. Be strong, dear one. I intend to make certain your assistance with this book receives the public recognition it deserves."

What had he done to deserve such added horrors?

"The female breast is of particular interest to—"

"Justine!"

"Of particular interest to the male—and do not shrink from this truth. Try not to react too strongly to any not-very-cleverly disguised and wholly longing assessment of this part of your body. Also, of course, do not behave in a brazen manner by excessive display. It has been my observation that male interest is raised to a higher pitch by the exercise of his imagination, than by his being presented with so much bare womanly flesh that nothing at all remains for that imagination."

Struan slipped lower in the chair.

"Am I wrong?"

He tipped his face up to the ceiling.

"Am I wrong, Struan? Or do men dwell excessively on thoughts of what lies beneath a female's gown? That which they cannot entirely see?"

"I would not have called it *excessive* dwelling."

"Hah!"

"I find I do not especially like your 'hahs,' my sweet."

"Concentrate. On the wedding night, your husband will see your breasts. This—"

"This is impossible," Struan said, straightening. "You cannot seriously consider looking for publication of such writings?"

"I can and I will. How can I be denied a forum for the truth?" She set the notebook aside and removed her pelisse robe. "I find the evening warm."

"Not as warm as I find it, I'll wager," Struan muttered.

Justine retrieved the book and continued, "You, dear readers, will find unspeakable pleasure in your husbands' ministrations upon your breasts. Some actions will render you speechless. For instance, when he touches their tips with his tongue and draws them into his mouth."

"Justine." His breeches began to be far from comfortable. "I beg of you to reconsider this."

"Your breasts will feel as if they are swelling—a wholly delightful sensation. Sharp tightenings will form inside you and you will wish for this wonder to continue. Cast aside the foolish tales that suggest a husband will not wish his wife to disrobe at such a time. A husband longs for his wife's naked skin to be pressed to his own."

Struan leaned forward and buried his face in his hands, as much to conceal the burgeoning evidence of his arousal as for any other reason.

"Revel in these wonders, sisters. They are but the beginning."

"Preserve me."

"Oh, I shall. I have no intention of not enjoying these things I write of again and again—with you."

He lifted his face.

Justine smiled. She pulled a stool near his feet and sat. "One of the most amazing revelations," she read, "is the discovery that one's husband's body is as enticing to you as yours is to him. But do not forget that he is as bound by foolish stories and conventions as we have been."

Her knees were between his calves. She arranged her skirts, rested the book more comfortably, and rubbed the fingers of one hand steadily back and forth at the side of his thigh. "You will possibly be surprised to discover hair on your husband's chest."

If he didn't know better, he'd think this intoxicating witch of a woman sought to seduce him. But such an event wasn't possible.

"I find that hair stimulating. Particularly when I feel it against my bared breasts—"

"*Stop!*"

Her head jerked up. "What? What is it?"

Struan gritted his teeth. "A lady cannot write such things as these."

"Why?"

Her eyes flashed, and before he could grasp what she intended, she set the book aside and undid a row of small satin frogs between her breasts. Her bodice opened. He flinched at the leap of his manhood and made fists on the chair while she stood over him and worked deftly to reveal his chest.

Kneeling between his legs, she wrapped her arms around his waist and dragged her nipples slowly back and forth on his flesh.

Struan gulped a breath. His chest was not the only part of him exposed to a tantalizing massage.

He heard her small moan and reached for her shoulders.

Justine promptly sat back on the stool. Her breasts rose and fell rapidly—a sight guaranteed to demolish any man. "My point is made, I believe," she said. "I can write these things because they are true."

Did she intend to sit before him half dressed?

"Let us continue."

And he had his answer. With her lovely breasts open to his view, she proceeded with her reading. "There are places we have never been allowed to mention, much less explore."

Her nipples were pale pink and uptilted. Struan tried, but found he could not avert his gaze.

"When tended by the man with whom you wish to enjoy such intimacies, these places are capable of causing exquisite sensations. But I implore you to learn those skills which will enable you to increase your ecstasy—and his. Your husband will enjoy *your* touches. He goes through life with a certain part of him restrained by clothing. This is a great trial, and you have it within your power to relieve the condition—for considerable periods of time if you so choose.

"To do so it is at first necessary for one's beloved to divest himself of his trousers, breeches, or whatever. Help him to feel comfortable about this development whenever you are alone. Possibly a dressing robe might be employed to assist in maintaining some degree of modesty in the event of intrusion."

"Unbelievable," Struan said, hearing the huskiness of his own tone. "You are truly amazing, my lady."

"Only because you have allowed me to learn so much. Tell me if you think the following will be of assistance to husbands." Her free hand came unerringly to rest upon his throbbing shaft.

"That, my beloved wife," he said, barely able to form the words, "that is guaranteed to entirely *undo* a man."

She frowned but kept her eyes on her book—and her hand on his rod. And Struan could not bring himself to deprive himself of the pleasure she brought him.

"I'm not certain how I shall incorporate that comment," Justine said. "Perhaps a mere aside that a man's enjoyment of being held so approaches that of a woman astride a man's thigh."

Struan groaned.

"There is something women do not learn until far too late,"

Justine went on. "The part of a man responsible for *It*—an aside, ladies—I now know that *It* used in a certain way is nothing more than a euphemism for the joining of a man and wife via the insertion of his manly protuberance into her womanly passage."

"I'm dying," Struan heard himself say, as if strangling. "I am strangling, damn it."

"You most certainly are not strangling." No pity there. Here, let us dispense with this foolishness. You feel you are strangling because all your energy—probably all your breath and blood, too—are engaged in trying to uphold the flag of masculinity against crushing obstacles."

"Justine!"

"You say that entirely too often. Off with these breeches at once."

He gave up. Sweat coated his brow, his back, and chest. He helped her with his boots and splayed in the chair while she unfastened his breeches and allowed him blessed, explosive release from confinement.

"There, there," she murmured softly, massaging that which needed no further encouragement. "This really is a shocking abuse and explains the generally unpredictable nature of so many gentlemen. No wonder they are given to duels and rudeness and the like. Tell me, Struan. On the first occasion when we slept together you fell asleep, and this"— she stroked him from tip to base, a sweetly affectionate expression upon her face—"this became quite soft and, I should suppose, quite comfortable to you. Was that normal? Or would that, in fact, cause you some embarrassment were others to know of it?"

"Normal," he managed to grind out.

She expelled a relieved sigh. "Thank goodness. My next question is whether you experience any relief from this condition when we do *It.*"

"Absolute relief."

"Wonderful! Then we shall do it often. No, more than often. We shall do it *all the time.* Your comfort is my mission in life, dear one."

He attempted to rally. "I could not contemplate such a thing."

"Piffle! Rest assured that the prospect is not at all without appeal to me. In fact, I shall make the sacrifice with alacrity. Struan, I hesitate to ask you this, but there is a certain urge I'm experiencing as I sit here . . . holding you."

He rolled his head to one side. "Name it." Could a man die of pleasure—and frustration excruciating enough to bring him near to madness?"

"Oh, no. You will think me most odd."

*"Name* it. Now!"

"I shall not name it. I shall simply do it. If you consider it unsuitable, you will let me know. If not, I shall have saved myself the embarrassment of risking ridicule for my words."

He felt her warm breath the instant before she slipped her moist lips over the head of his penis and began to draw him into her mouth.

"Oh—my—God!" Struan sank his fingers into her hair. "Oh, yes. Yes. *Yes!*"

He did not stop her to ask how she knew that what she did would shortly bring the relief she so desperately wished to afford him.

Justine's head moved over his lap. He looked down at her red-tinged dark hair spilling over his belly, mingling with the hair at his own crotch.

In the last instant, he attempted to draw back. Too late. His release came. Panting, he fell back, dimly awaiting her cries of horror. Instead, he found himself covered by the weight of her soft body, her breasts pressed to his chest, her face buried beneath his chin.

"Justine," he breathed. "How . . . What made you do that?"

"You liked it, didn't you?"

"Oh, I liked it marvelously."

"Well, today I considered the kisses when you put your tongue inside my mouth. They are a symbol of *It*, aren't they?"

Fog clung to the edges of his mind. Concentration didn't come easily. "Yes," he said at last. "Yes, I suppose so."

"Well, I decided there might be other ways in which pleasurable suggestions of the—the ultimate might be created. And I was right! You ... That is, with the letting go of your ... essence, shall we say, you are relieved of that painful swelling!"

Struan's eyes snapped open. *"Painful swelling?"*

"Well—"

"You, dearest wife, promise to keep this simple husband forever entertained. There is much you have learned and much you have divined. And there is much you simply do not know."

"But—"

"No. Now I will give you something new to write about."

Leaving his breeches where they were, he changed places with his bright-brained darling. Depositing her upon the chair, he knelt where she had knelt—between her legs. He lifted her skirts, brushing away plucking hands that would have held cover over the scarred leg he'd already come to adore.

Without preamble, he bent to dart his tongue into already moist curls at the apex of her thighs.

"Struan! Struan, you will stop at once. You will ... Aah!"

He smiled, breathing in the musky, utterly feminine scent of her. Holding apart plump little folds, he showed her another form of "symbolic" lovemaking.

Justine's hips writhed, and he grinned—and tightened his belly against his own renewed arousal.

When she sought to clutch him with begging fingers, he concentrated his attention on the swollen nub that would release her need. Within seconds she threw herself forward over his back and he knew her nails would leave evidence of this adventure on his buttocks.

She made no complaint when he carried her—still tossed over his shoulder—to her chamber. With what remained of their clothing flung aside, he joined her in the blue-canopied bed. She snuggled beside him—replete, as he was replete.

"Have we given you more to write about, sweetness?" he asked gently.

"Oh, yes. Much more."

"You enjoyed—"

"I *loved* what we did. How fortunate I am. Now I know there is more than one way to reach the ultimate with one's husband."

"Oh, yes." Indeed. And this way would not cause him to live in fear for her life. He knew more than a small spear of guilt at what he contemplated. "Rest, my love. You must be tired, and I know I am."

"Mmm. Very tired."

"Sleep, then." His problems were far from solved, but at least his encounter with the abbot had given him hope, and for now he would allow himself to enjoy this woman whom he loved. "Sleep very well."

"Struan!" She sat so abruptly, he jumped. "My goodness, I became so engrossed I forgot."

He stroked her back indulgently. "We will deal with Ella and Max's education. And I will take Devlin North aside and tell him the way of things."

"No, no. Not that. A woman came today. Looking for you."

Exhaustion threatened to take him. "A woman?"

"Yes. She said you promised she could come to you at any time if she needed help. She is not of genteel birth, but is certainly a most pleasant soul. And she is in need, poor creature."

He opened his eyes in the darkness. "What are you talking about?"

"Oh, she said it has been a long time since you last met. She has since married—to her dire regret, I'm certain. I know you will wish to fulfill your promise to her."

Struan was awake now, and growing cold. "Where is this woman?"

"We put her in one of the freshly made-over rooms in the Grecian wing. Her gratitude was pathetic. I promised her that you would speak with her as soon as you returned. Then I forgot. Oh, dear."

Struan rose to an elbow. "Did she give her name?"

"Of course. She is Mrs. Smith. And her husband is clearly a beastly person. Why, Struan, he has been beating her. She has bruises and old wounds."

His clenching stomach unwound slightly. "She must have come to the wrong address. I know no Mrs. Smith."

"Oh, but that is her married name. And she definitely knows you. Do you remember a lovely dark-haired woman called Glory?"

# Chapter Twenty-two

❦

"**D**inna do it, Ellie. *Please.*" This Max was quite unlike himself. His freckles showed dark on his pale face and his green eyes shone with worry. "Caleb said there's them as has a mind to kill us all."

Ella fixed her new green velvet bonnet more firmly atop her smoothly coiled hair. Tonight she must appear composed and mature. Tonight she would take steps guaranteed to shape the rest of her life.

"Say you won't go!"

She turned sharply on the stool before her glass. "Hush, Max. You'll have Caleb hammering upon the door, or sending Mairi to check on us."

He pursed his lips and set down the tiny sand-colored puppy Devlin North had brought. "I'm goin' t'shout. I'm goin' t'give ye away for the mad one ye are."

Ella crooked a long forefinger, signalling for Max to come near. When he stood before her in the oppressively paneled room, she got up and looked directly into his eyes. "There are things you do not know, Max. Dangerous things that threaten us. The longer we remain here and do nothing, the greater the danger becomes."

His mouth fell open.

"Why do you think Papa has arranged for us to be here in the castle guarded like two criminals?"

Max shook his head.

"Why do you think these particular rooms were chosen—rooms with no windows, and doors so heavy an army couldn't breach them?"

"Nasty rooms wi' weapons on the walls," Max said, although those weapons were confined to the so-called sitting room. "A dungeon wi' furniture in it."

"A fine description. And we're here because we are in danger. There is someone who wants to kill us."

"No," Max whispered. "That was just a story t'make me do what Caleb wanted."

"You are wrong." Ella brought her nose close to his. "You have been so busy with your stories that you have failed to see how we are in the middle of a great intrigue. We were allowed to sleep at the Mercers' because no one would think to look for us there. And our every move has been watched by people loyal to Papa just to ensure our safety."

"Ye weren't watched when ye rode around like a wild boy!" Max announced explosively. "Ye said as much. Ye spoke of doin' as ye pleased all day. And I wasna watched either."

"You were. You simply didn't know it. And I lied. There, now you have the truth of it. I lied because I was unhappy and needed to pretend to myself that I was free. There was always someone watching over me."

"Well . . . Well, then. Why? You tell me that, Ellie. Why would anyone want t'hurt two such as us who amount t'nothin' between us? We're no one and ye know it."

Ella looked away. Abruptly, she sat upon the stool again. He was right, they were nothing, but she couldn't bear to hear her own brother speak of himself in such a way. "Of course we are something. You are a very special person, a person with a brilliant future. You have a fine mind and it will be cultivated. And we have been fortunate. Papa loves us."

"He's not our papa. We dinna even know who our papa was."

"I don't care," Ella said vehemently. "The viscount told us we were his children in all the ways that matter. And Lady Justine loves us, too. She told us as much."

"Aye. D'you suppose Papa's told her we're not his bairns yet?"

"Ooh, Max, that mode of speech will not do if you are to move in Papa's society."

"I'm not to move in it," Max said, but his lower lip trembled. "He's not told her, has he? And when he does, she won't love us anymore. Rough bairns brought up wi' travelin' players. And me a pickpocket in London. And you—"

"Stop! Stop it, Max. That's all in the past." And she would not allow herself to think of it.

"She'll not love us, I tell ye."

"She will," Ella said fiercely, taking her brother's hands in hers. "You listen to me, Max. Good people are good people, and Lady Justine is good. She would not know how to stop loving someone."

"She'll stop soon enough," Max argued. "She will."

"No, she won't. She loves Papa and he loves us. She loved us before they were wed. Now we will be even more important to her."

"And what if they have bairns o' their own?"

The question had circled Ella's mind a thousand times in recent weeks. "I still say we'll never be turned aside. Learn to trust. And don't stop me from doing what I intend to do. Listen carefully and do as I say."

"But where are ye goin'?" Max implored. "It's almost night, Ellie. I'm scairt fer ye."

Impulsively, she drew him into her arms and hugged him. "Thank you. But don't be. We've been through a great deal, you and I. Tonight I'm going to do something to help us both, but, most of all, to help Papa. Max, I believe Papa is in terrible trouble."

He moved only far enough away to see her face. "How d'ye know?"

"It's obvious. *Think.* There's not a soul who would want to do anything to us. They must want to do something to him, and he's afraid we'll be hurt as well. Mayhap by kidnapping. I heard Mairi talking to Caleb, and they were whispering about the lodge being guarded to keep Lady Justine safe."

"Did they say why?" Max sounded desperate.

Ella sighed and ruffled his hair. "No. I don't think anyone but Papa knows. They were saying they would do anything to help Papa, and they wished they knew what they were guarding against. Mairi thinks Lady Justine's lovely, and she's worried because she thinks someone should tell her she's in danger."

Max clutched her hands. "Don't go, Ellie. Don't leave me."

"I have to." The thought of his being alone and frightened drowned her in guilt, but she couldn't continue to do nothing. "I'm going to lock my chamber door on this side. It may be quite a long time before anyone tries to come in. With fortune, I'll have returned before they do. But, if not, you tell them I've asked to be left in peace. Say I'm feeling contemplative."

"Con . . . Contem . . ."

"Say I need time alone to think. The most important thing is for you to attract as little attention as possible."

"But ye *are* leavin' the castle this night?"

"I am."

"And ye've a journey ahead o' ye?"

"I have." And she wished her stomach didn't curl with fear at the thought.

"Can I come?"

"No."

He heaved a huge sigh and retrieved the puppy. "Verra well. I'll do as ye ask."

"Good. Without your help this couldn't work. I have to rely upon you. I must go now."

Max frowned. "How can I tell them ye're thinkin' and wantin' t'be alone if I'm in here?"

"You won't be. You'll be in your own chamber. Or in our sitting room."

"But ye said your door would be locked on the inside."

Ella stood up, flung a heavy cape over the shoulders of her green riding habit, and picked up her gloves. "Off with you." She opened the door and waited for him to go into the sitting room.

He passed her and said, "But ye told me it'd be locked—"

"On the inside? It will be."

She felt him leave her.

After she'd explained about Mrs. Smith he'd grown quiet and distant. Then he'd pretended to sleep. She'd known he was only pretending, but she did likewise and when her breathing was slow and deep he'd slipped from the bed and begun gathering his clothes.

An awful premonition had come to her.

She was already certain Robert Mercer and his friends had been watching over the lodge to keep her safe. Caleb Murray was watching over Max and Ella to keep them safe. His threats to Max of dire danger had been real threats.

Something was dreadfully wrong.

Something dreadful threatened Struan, and he feared it might touch those he loved.

He was waiting for whatever it was to come to him.

Could she have let the danger in? Was Mrs. Smith part of that danger?"

"Struan!"

His shadowy form stopped. "Go back to sleep."

"What are you doing?"

"I'm restless."

"Come back to bed and let me help you."

The silhouette of his raised jaw showed sharply against moonlight through the windows. "Oh, how tempting you are. There is a matter I must attend first. Sleep, my sweet, and I'll return to you soon."

He went without another word.

To the castle. He would go to the castle to look for more of those letters—and to ensure his children were safe, of course.

She settled back onto the pillows and closed her eyes.

There were noises. Shuffling, scraping—cracks. The night had so many sounds, and she was entirely too sensitive to every one of them.

A current of air passed over her face, and her eyes snapped open. *"Hannah!"* With a thundering heart, she pushed up to her elbows.

The door to her chamber stood wide open.

*"Hannah.* Are you there?"

Gradually the door began to swing shut.

Outside, light flickered, casting the wavering shadow of a figure.

For an instant, Justine saw the glitter of candlelight on staring eyes. Then the light went out.

There was always a vague hope that some other woman might have the first name of Glory. Whatever. He must be alone to decide how to proceed if this should prove to be the same creature who had all but ruined his life.

With his shirt flying behind him and his jacket over his arm, Struan ran up the steps to the Pavilion bridge and strode across. In the Grecian wing there was someone who said he'd promised to help her if she was desperate. That did not have to be the Glory Willing of his cursed past. Logic assured him it was indeed that person.

Earlier he'd tried to persuade the abbot to come to the lodge with him. If the identity of the visitor proved to be as feared, Struan would go in search of Abbot John and beg him to come here.

He entered the anteroom to his chamber and halted.

Dressed in demure gray, Glory Willing—or Mrs. Smith—sat in one of his grandfather's serpent-laden Egyptian chairs. Her back was straight, her hands, like her feet, placed precisely together. She wore a thin cloak and a gray bonnet. Only her eyes, her great black eyes, moved. They sought his, and what he saw there belied the modest picture she made.

He threw his jacket on a chest and began buttoning his shirt. "What do you want here?" he asked shortly. "Let's have it quickly and be done with it."

"I'm sorry," she said.

He paused in the act of pushing his shirt inside his breeches. "Sorry because you made a weakened man drunk and proceeded to seduce him?"

"Sorry," she murmured. "I regret having to cause you inconvenience."

"A little late, wouldn't you say? Wouldn't you say it was already late when you screamed that I had ruined you and then set about extorting money from me for years?"

"You paid willingly enough. You knew you bore blame."

"But I no longer bore blame once your livelihood became assured."

"Assured?"

"By your marriage."

She pursed her lips.

"But you and your *husband* decided you would find a way to keep getting money out of me, didn't you?"

"Taking your money wasn't my idea," she murmured. "It was his. I didn't want any part of it."

Struan circled her slowly. "Is that a fact? Well, well. When I saw you in Bath—when was that, more than a year since? You did not appear threadbare and regretful then. But, of course, you were still receiving the money I sent, weren't you?"

Her expression became startled. "I did not see you in Bath."

"But *I* saw *you.* You were getting into a carriage. Your finery caught the eye of many a man and woman. I noted your wedding ring then and your laughter—with your companion."

"What companion?" she asked sharply.

"I could not see him—only hear him. But I assume he was either your husband or your lover."

Her shoulders became straighter. "How dare you suggest it could have been a lover. I was a married woman. I *am* a married woman."

"Commendable," Struan said. "Was it your husband or your lover who hit you?" The marks on her face turned his stomach, but he must not weaken with this creature.

"I told you I'm married," she said. "It was my husband who hit me."

"A charming fellow, but what has this to do with me?"

She stood and untied her bonnet. This she set on the seat of the chair before sweeping into his bedchamber.

He followed her. "This is inappropriate—and given your history, very possibly dangerous. Kindly remove yourself. You may use the refuge of the room my wife so kindly provided you for the night. I shall not expect to see you in the morning."

"I'm sorry to be a nuisance."

While she was being so sorry, she toured his room, running her hands over the bedposts and across the counterpane, ex-

amining twin gilt tigers that flanked the black marble fireplace.

"Were you not given a room?"

"I was."

"And taken there?"

"Oh, yes."

"Then why are you not there now?"

"I'm lonely."

Struan set his teeth.

"And I'm frightened. You said as how Glory could come to
you if she needed anything. You said it after you'd ruined
me."

Struan looked behind him, half expecting to find someone
listening to their conversation.

"Afraid your *wife* will hear?"

He didn't respond.

"Just come from her, have you?"

This must be part of what the *thing* who had written the letters intended. "Who sent you here?"

"I did. I came because I need help."

"I don't believe you."

"You will. I'm ever so sorry I've got to ask, but there's no
one else I can turn to." She faced him with her head shyly
bowed. "And anyway, I know a gentleman in your position
wouldn't want his business talked about to others."

Blackmail. Further blackmail? Or the beginning of what
was to come from the letter-writer?

"What is your husband's name?"

Her chin rose sharply. "I said I was giving you a chance by
coming here. A chance to make sure what we know is kept between ourselves."

"And I asked your husband's name." Weakness—even a
hint of weakness—could be disastrous with such a baggage as
this.

She said, "Mr. Smith. What else would it be?"

"And where would I find this Mr. Smith?"

She smiled secretively. "Maybe I don't know."

"But you do know, don't you? Just as you know all about the letters he's been writing—just as you've been sent here as part of whatever foolish scheme the two of you hope to bring to pass."

"I don't know anything about letters," she said, raising her face.

Struan remained in the open doorway. "Of course not. You simply happened to arrive on my doorstep at a time when your husband—I assume this is your husband, since he claims to be so in his scurrilous missives—has been annoying me with his insolent approaches for weeks."

In the years since she'd come to him in his cell at the abbey she'd grown more maturely seductive, if in a coarse manner. The gray dress enhanced rather than disguised her voluptuous body—no doubt by deliberate design. With a nonchalance he doubted was real, she took off the cloak and spread it on his bed. "You have no proof that I know anything about any letters."

"I wish you to leave my house—*now.*"

"That won't be possible, m'lord." She began untying the tapes on her gown. "I'll be comfortable enough here—with you to keep me safe."

Rough treatment of females wasn't within Struan's experience. He flexed his hands and sought for what course he should take to rid himself of this venomous nuisance.

The dress descended over her shoulders and breasts and fell in a heap at her feet. She stepped out, swept up the garment, and deposited it atop her cloak. The chemise she wore was little better than no covering at all. Her nipples showed big and dark, their centers poking at the thin fabric. The triangle of black hair between her thighs was obscenely revealed.

"I see you haven't lost interest in what Glory's got," she said, raising a hand high up a bedpost and swaying a little.

She played with a nipple through the bodice of the chemise and passed her tongue over her lips. "Your new wife's a cripple, then. And very much the cool lady. Not at all the kind of woman for a man like you—a man of hot tastes."

"Hold your tongue—"

"You hold my tongue. With yours, darlin'. I remember how you felt. Never could forget that. Come on. We've already wasted too much time. We shouldn't waste any more." She drew the chemise up about her hips, revealing the silvery gray stockings she wore beneath. Garters of red satin were tied above each knee. The rest was naked enticement. "Come on, then. Come on. That cold one can't give you what Glory can. Close her eyes, does she? Press her legs together to keep you out?" Glory splayed her legs and propped her elbows upon the bed.

Struan slammed the door and planted his fists on his hips. "Do not mention my wife. I do not wish to hear her name upon your lips."

"Ooh, we mustn't mention the fine, crippled lady."

He alternately clenched and flexed his hands. "My wife is—" Words would be wasted on this whore. "Dress and get out."

Her face crumpled theatrically. "You said—"

"Get *out.*"

"I do know about the letters."

Muscles in his shoulders lowered a fraction. "Do you, now? And what is it you know about them?"

Keeping her eyes on his, Glory Willing Smith ripped apart the front of her chemise and stripped off the tattered remnants.

"What in God's name are you doing, woman?"

Her breasts were ripe white globes, tipped dark and traversed with pale-blue veins. Her waist was still narrow and her hips lush. Once more she propped herself against the mattress and raised one silver-silk-clad knee. She rocked the leg back and forth, displaying herself with evident relish.

In a single motion, Struan retrieved the remains of the chemise and her dress. "You will be leaving. Will you put these on yourself, or shall I summon a maid to assist you and one of the male servants to eject you?"

"I know about the seal on the letters." Holding the tip of her tongue between her teeth, she revolved and leaned forward, presenting her buttocks, laying her torso, arms outstretched, upon the counterpain.

He felt his color drain. "Lord." No other words would come.

"Like it, do you?"

"He did this to you? Your husband?"

"He had to get the blood for the finger spot from somewhere, didn't he?"

"Oh, my God." Struan drove the fingers of both hands into his hair. "Why?"

"He did it more than once, y'know. It looks better now since I ran away from him. He'd strip me naked and thrash me with those big, heavy gloves on his hands. Then he'd write his precious letters while I screamed, and take my blood to make a seal. Said it was symbolic."

A shudder passed the length of Struan's spine. "Cover yourself, please."

"Squeamish, are we?"

"It isn't seemly for you to be naked before me."

"It was seemly enough when you took me in that cell. If you hadn't done that, Mr. Smith wouldn't have used me so."

Struan turned away and fought for control. He must not forget the falsehood that had probably been invented to involve him with this female in the first place. "How did your husband learn of what had happened to you . . . earlier?"

"With you, you mean? When we rutted?"

He bit back a curse. "Yes."

"Told him, didn't I. Had to when the money stopped coming. He thought it was by way of being some settlement from an old aunt of mine. When the money stopped, he was angry. Then he found out there'd never been an aunt and he beat me till I told about you. No man's pride will take that. He said you should have to pay for the rest of your life for picking what he should have picked."

"Odd he didn't notice the bare tree earlier," Struan said wryly.

"That's as may be—or not. It doesn't matter now, does it? He's decided to make you pay anyhow."

"And you are here to help him, of course?"

She stood up and flew at him, both fists raised. "How could you! You don't know what I've suffered."

He caught her wrists and held on while she wriggled and fought, her fine breasts swinging where he could not fail to watch them with fascination.

Panting, she grew still. "He's going to make you pay more than you've ever paid. I didn't have to tell you that, but I wanted to."

"To tell me what I already know from the letters? Thank you."

"Let me stay!" She struggled afresh. "Please let me stay. He'll kill me if I go back, I know he will."

"You cannot remain here."

"But I can be useful to you." She became limp, and Struan released her wrists. Promptly, she threw her arms about his neck and layered her body to his. Her heat struck through his clothes. "Use me, my lord. Use me in any way that brings you pleasure or usefulness—"

"Stop."

"No. I won't stop. I can't. I'll warm your bed when you can't abide the cold one anymore. I'll—"

"You'll get away from here." He managed to drag her

hands from his neck, only to all but buckle when she thrust inside his breeches to squeeze his shaft.

"Damn you, woman!"

He leaned over her back and surrounded her waist. The instant her feet left the floor she kicked him—kicked him and sank her teeth into the flesh at his side.

Struan gasped and staggered, crashing into a writing table. They fell together, smashing the delicate piece to splinters that gouged wherever they found skin. Struan grabbed for the woman, but she squirmed away. He would not hit her, he would not. The welts and bruises on her back and buttocks sickened him. No man would take pleasure in wounding a creature so much weaker.

"Glory! Be still."

Her response was to surge over him, rending his shirt as she went, flattening her breasts to his naked chest. Her teeth were bared. "I can't go. I can't and I won't. I'll be good. I'll be so good. And I can help you, I tell you, if you'll only listen."

She'd succeeded in tearing open his breeches and sitting astride his hips. "I'll tell Mr. Smith I'm here to help him. I swear to God I will. I'll write and say I'll be his eyes inside your home. Don't you see what he'll think about that?"

"He'll think you've made an excellent job of what he sent you to do."

"No!" she screamed. "No. My life depends on this, my lord. Send me away and he'll find me and kill me. He intends to get everything that's yours, I tell you. And he'll kill anyone you care about to make you do what he wants. You won't believe that, but it's true."

Struan grew still. "I'm listening."

"I'll not tell you everything, because then you'll have no reason to let me stay." She began to cry, great heaving sobs that displayed her flesh to advantage. "What I've said is the right of it. If I say I decided to come here and help him, he'll have to hope I've not given him away. I'll tell him I'm doing it to make sure he shares everything with me. He'll believe me, I know he will. And I'll tell you everything he intends to do before it happens. That way you'll be prepared."

What choice did he have? If he sent her away, he might never know if he'd missed the best chance he had to get the better of her husband. "You'll write to him?"

She wiped away tears and pushed back the riot of black hair that had fallen loose. "I know he intended to come this way shortly. I know a way of getting a message to him."

"How?"

"I won't say another word until I'm sure you'll keep your end of the bargain."

"Get up," he ordered her. "I am a man who keeps his word. I do not like the set of this, but I'll test you, Glory. One false step and you'll be glad to return to your monster husband."

Grasping her shoulders proved a mistaken strategy. Crooning, she fastened her clever fingers on his rod and all but managed to push him inside her.

With a violent shove, he tossed her to the floor beside him and stood, pulling his breeches to rights.

"You want me," she whined.

"There are some things over which a man's mind has little control. A bodily reaction is all you accomplished, my dear— all you could ever accomplish again."

"Is that why you sleep so far from your beloved wife? Because it's only your mind that needs anything from her?"

"Push me, madam, and I shall have to rethink our bargain. How are your husband's letters delivered? Who brings them?"

She scrambled to her feet and said, "I don't know."

"Come now, you must know."

"I'd tell you if I did."

Struan did not believe her. He longed to look upon Justine again, to behold her gentle, intelligent face and feel her tenderly sensual touch. "I'll leave you now," he told Glory. "I suggest you find your way to the room you were given and stay there until morning. After that we shall decide how best to proceed."

He took a fresh shirt and set his clothes to rights. While he did so, Glory made a haphazard job of putting her own garments together. At least she covered her nakedness, more or less.

Struan didn't wait to usher her from his rooms. Rather, he strode through the anteroom and crossed the bridge, desperate to return to his wife. From now on they would share the same rooms. The difficulties to be overcome there could be discussed. He would explain them to Justine and she would help him make appropriate decisions. A woman with such a fine mind should be included in decisions about how her life might be lived. She had told him as much and she was right.

And the next step would be to tell her about the children—and even, perhaps, about his early conviction that he should embrace the priesthood and swear his oath to celibate abstinence.

He hit the steps at a run, his boots clattering downward on stone.

"Struan!" Justine met him in the vestibule. "Oh, Struan, I saw someone. I was too afraid to come, so I waited. Then I was too afraid not to come in case—"

"Hush," he said, framing her face. "Slowly, my love. Tell me slowly—once we have returned to your chamber."

Her tension flowed away before his eyes. "Yes. Yes, of course you are right. I am overset. You will think me foolish, but I thought I saw someone looking into my room after you left. Then, while I waited there, I decided whoever it was might have been looking for you and might then have gone to do you harm."

"You feared for no reason," he told her.

Justine's smile faded. She looked past him and all color ebbed from her cheeks.

Struan turned to see Glory, her dress undone and sagging, the tatters of her chemise trailing from her bodice, slowly descending the steps from the Pavilion.

Justine covered her mouth.

"I'll go to my room now, then, my lord," Glory said. "Just like you told me to." Her hair still flowed about her shoulders and she dragged her cloak behind her. The bonnet hung from her fingers by a single ribbon. She accomplished a demeanor of complete confusion. A dazed, foully used woman . . .

"Justine, this is not as it appears."

Tears filled her eyes, and she drew away from Struan as if he were a fiend.

"Thank you, then, my lord," Glory said vaguely, walking between her host and hostess as if in her sleep. "I'm glad I can do your bidding. I'll be in my room when you need me."

# Chapter Twenty-three

❦

Ella rode north and prayed her excellent sense of direction wouldn't fail her tonight.

What she intended could end in disaster—or it could help Papa and take away the ache that hadn't left her throat since Devlin North's first visit to Kirkcaldy.

Saber wouldn't refuse her request—not the Saber who had become her friend in Cornwall. She remembered the evening when he'd searched her out because he'd failed to see her at the Franchot Fair. She blinked back tears. Even now she knew the scent of him, clean, masculine—and the feel of him, strong yet gentle and so very protective.

From the first moment they met, she'd felt the drawing together of their two spirits. Saber had been a little drunk! The memory warmed her and she grinned. He flirted openly with her—something he would never do sober—and Papa and Justine had been indulgently amused. They had encouraged Saber to court her. Papa knew she was not Saber's social equal, but he considered her worthy of him and thought Saber would be good for her. Justine, who had said Ella brought out the best in Saber, had clearly hoped they would eventually become more than friends.

But Saber had left. With polite but distant farewells, he'd simply said he must leave and had evaded her questions about any future meetings.

Ella pressed her lips together and raised her face to the night sky. Saber would not turn her away now. He would help her.

Hoping its absence wouldn't be quickly noted, she had taken a piebald filly intended for the marquess's daughter, Elizabeth, when she was old enough to ride. The horse was small but game, and Ella was certain they were making good time. She had nothing to guide her but the few comments she'd heard about the location of Devlin's home. The Kirkcaldy estates had a common boundary with acreage surrounding Northcliff Hall.

Unfortunately, Ella had only the vaguest notion of the distance to the farthest northerly reaches of Kirkcaldy, and she knew nothing of the actual placement of Northcliff Hall on its grounds.

The moon, high and white, aided her on her way. The night was warm and still. With fear as her greatest enemy, she followed a well-beaten track used by tenants from far-flung reaches to bring produce to market in Kirkcaldy Village.

She had no idea how long she'd been riding when she heard the "hoo—hoo—hoo—hooo," of a Tawny owl. The filly broke stride and skittered sideways. Ella quieted her, and worked to calm her own beating heart. She looked up. The owl's graceful shape flew silently across the moon's glow and abruptly swooped.

Ella listened to the hum and snip of insects and the faint rustle of larger creatures going on their way.

A whinny ... She clutched the reins. For a second she thought she heard a horse nicker and a muffled sound of hoofs.

Her stomach seemed to echo the beat of her heart.

*Alone.*

She looked behind her and then along the trail again. No horse and rider traveled her way this night—except in her fear-filled imagination.

To go back might take as long—or longer—than to go on. And if she went back she would have given up on her only hope for help . . . and peace.

At a fork in the track, she chose the left way and prayed she'd chosen well. Breaking from a copse, she arrived at the top of a knoll. She looked down upon a wall that showed pale in the moonlight and stretched as far as she could see in either direction. The bulk of an impressive house stood only a short distance inside the nearest stretch of the wall.

The little filly had tired. Ella rested her awhile and ordered her own thoughts. Devlin North had made his interest in her quite plain, and even though she had given him no encouragement, he could doubtless complicate what she had come here to do.

She would plead a private family matter involving Saber and hope Devlin would not press her further.

The approach was to the back of the house; nevertheless, a handsome stone stag topped an archway over the entrance to a well-kept drive. Ella chose to take her horse onto the smooth grassland where the sound of hooves would be dulled. The less attention she excited, the better.

Northcliff Hall lay where sloping, tree-dotted parkland swept down on all sides. Devlin had spoken of the place with barely concealed pride, and Ella understood why. Devlin had also hinted—while gazing at her—that the place needed a mistress. Ella sighed in the gloom. Poor man. He was charming, handsome, and very kind, but probably wanted a connection to a titled family. He would not gain such a connection through the likes of one who did not even know her family name.

She discarded the notion that she might seek entrance through the rear of the house and rode around to the main doors. Light showed in a number of windows, but an air of slumber hung over the grand building.

Ella dismounted, tethered the filly to a stone bench, and climbed the fan of semicircular steps to the door. Taking a giant breath, she pulled the bell and stepped back, wincing at the echoing ring that gradually faded.

Seconds passed before the door opened the merest crack and not one, but three faces—one above the other—peered out at her. The crack became a few inches wider.

"A gir-rel," the middle, round-faced man said. His red hair stood on end.

"Lost," the uppermost, bald man announced.

Beneath these two hunched an ancient with creased white skin almost as pale as his hair. "Ye barley-brains!" Spittle flew with each word. "What would a girl the likes o' her be doin' lost at this time o' night?"

"Good evening," Ella said with extreme politeness. "I am—I am Ella. I live at Kirkcaldy and I am acquainted with both Mr. Devlin North and with Saber, Earl of Avenall."

"She's acquainted with the master," the bald man said.

The red-haired servant announced, "Called away on business," with evident relish. "Left suddenly. For foreign parts."

Ella was afraid they would slam the door. "Mr. North isn't here?"

"Let the lassie in." Straightening with enough bony force to knock his companions backward, the old man opened the door fully and beckoned her inside a vestibule lined with green Italian marble. A circle of columns of the same marble rose to the perimeter of a domed ceiling. Green and white marble tiles completed an austere and cold welcome to Northcliff Hall.

"Thank you, Mr.—?"

"Nudge," the three chorused. They wore identical garb that suggested they were butlers.

She puckered her brow. "I do believe there's a Nudge—"

"Newly installed butler at Lord Hunsingore's establishment," the oldest Nudge announced. "Nephew. Family tradition."

"I see." Ella smiled uncertainly. "Well . . . in fact, I came to see Lord Avenall. He—"

"Doesna see anyone," the bald servant pronounced.

"He is my . . . my stepmother's cousin," she said around a lump in her throat. "There is a family matter of some urgency, and I have come to make certain Lord Avenall is informed."

The three men looked at each other, then back at Ella.

She checked her habit and brushed at her skirts. "This is of the utmost importance, I assure you."

"Hmmph." The oldest member of the committee was stooped but still taller than the other two. "Away wi' ye," he told his cohorts. "I'll see t'this."

Without another word, the men did as he bade them.

"Ella, y'said?"

"Yes."

"And his lordship'll know ye?"

Ella's hands were so cold. "He'll know me."

"How should I announce ye?"

"As Ella. Nothing more."

He turned away. "Follow me if ye please." They started up a beautiful, curving staircase—marble, naturally. "The master keeps worryin' I'm too old. Y'said ye know Mr. North?"

"I do. A fine gentleman."

"Fine indeed. There's not many in his station as would consider an old man's bones. It's only that he worries about me bein' put out by the likes o' this visit o' yours and so on. He brought in my son. The smarmy one wi' red hair. Supposed t'help me. Then the master thought mayhap my grandson— him wi' no a hair on his daft head—thought he might be of service t'us both. Hah! Useless, t'pair o' them."

Ella smothered a laugh and the desire to ask just how old her guide was.

"The earl's a quiet one. But I expect ye know that."

"Yes," Ella said, thinking of the times when Saber had been full of spirit and anything but quiet.

"O'course, wi' his trouble he's not fond o' visitors. But, since you're family, I expect . . ."

Knowing she was supposed to offer reassurance, Ella said, "Oh, yes. He'll be quite agreeable to seeing me, I assure you. We're old friends."

Their ponderous progress took them to double doors at the end of an easterly wing. The butler knocked discreetly, entered without being told to do so, and closed Ella outside.

Within moments the door opened again and the butler emerged, his face expressionless. "Follow me, please, miss," he said, heading back in the direction from which they'd come.

*He'd refused to see her.* "But—"

"Lord Avenall isn't able t'have visitors. I'll show ye out."

Ella looked from the butler's back to the door he hadn't quite closed, and stepped quickly into the room. She searched desperately about a library of elegant proportion. At any moment the servant would return and insist she leave with him.

Books lined the walls from floor to ceiling. Drapes the color of fine Burgundy and tied with gold satin ropes looped back from a bow casement.

The light in the room was so dim, Ella could make out nothing that moved or breathed.

"Saber?" she whispered.

Dark-green leather wingback chairs flanked the hearth. A meager fire burned.

In front of the window stood a majestic rosewood desk, but the chair behind it was empty.

"You should not have come."

She jumped and spun toward the voice. "Saber?"

Then she saw a hand on the arm of one green leather chair. A long, elegant hand and a full white sleeve.

Ella crept forward. "Oh, Saber, It *is* you." He stared into the fire's embers, his dramatic profile somber. His dark hair curled past his collar. "It's me—Ella. May I sit down and talk with you?"

"No."

She felt ill. Finally she managed to say, "I had to come."

"Why?"

"Because I need help. You once told me that if ever I needed help you would be as a brother to me."

"I cannot help you."

Ella glanced nervously at the door but heard no sound of returning footsteps. "Lady Justine and Papa are married now."

He pinched the bridge of his nose.

"It is because you and Lady Justine are cousins that I come to you for help." And because she thought he had shared some measure of the feelings she had for him.

"Viscount Hunsingore is *not* my cousin. And he is not your father. Did you think I would forget that?"

Her stomach twisted. "No. No, I did not think that. But when I told you I was a . . . when I told you, you said it did not matter."

"When you told me you were a bastard I said it did not matter. It doesn't. It also doesn't matter that you were in a brothel, or that the viscount bought you at auction or some such monstrousness."

Ella crammed a fist against her mouth.

"Is my cousin well?"

She could not speak.

"*Is* she?"

"Yes."

"The viscount treats her well?"

"Yes."

"Thank you for coming to tell me as much."

Blinking back tears, Ella made herself ask what she'd truly come to ask. "All is not well with . . . with the viscount. I believe his life may be in danger."

Saber rested his head against the back of the chair and regarded a palm. "What is that to me?"

Stunned, Ella took a step forward.

"Come no closer," Saber said, motioning her away. "I do not wish to look upon you."

*"Why?"* She did as he asked, retreating again. "What have I done to make you hate me so?"

"I do not hate you."

"Why will you not help me, then?"

"What do you think of Devlin?"

"He is a nice man." Saber did hate her. "You have not told him about me, have you?"

"No. You will tell him yourself when the time is right. I think he would make you a fine husband. He is certainly very taken with you."

"But"—Ella's chin sank to her chest—"I am not a good catch, am I, Saber? I am nothing. Nobody."

"You are incomparable, my dear. Forgive me if I distress you. I have not been well."

"Let me tend you. Let me—"

*"No."* He cut her off sharply. "And I cannot do anything to help Viscount Hunsingore. I can urge you to encourage Devlin's suit."

*I do not love Devlin.* "You cannot help?"

"I cannot."

"And you want me to leave?"

He averted his head so that she saw only the back of his overlong hair. "God bless you always, Ella. Good-bye, little one."

She wrapped her arms across her middle. "Could I . . . Can I give you just one hug? As sister to brother?" To feel him, just to feel him once more. Little enough to ask for a lifetime.

"Good-bye, Ella. Neither the viscount nor my cousin would approve of this jaunt. I hope you have a coachman who will not reveal that you have taken such an unwise outing."

Coachman? She was about to ride back through the darkness without as much as a word of hope of affection from the one man who held the power to make her the most happy creature in the world.

"One of the Nudges will see you safely to your carriage. They greeted you when you came."

With her lips pressed together, Ella swung away and ran across the room. "It did matter," she said, her throat aching. "And it does. All of it. Everything about my hateful past. I disgust you."

As she pulled open the door, she glanced back in time to see Saber leaning from the shadows of his chair to watch her. Instantly he averted his face.

Ella didn't stop running until she'd let herself out of the icy cool vestibule. No servant appeared to help or hinder her. Her heart pounded. Pulsing thudded at her temples and she let tears pour, unchecked, down her scorching cheeks.

She stopped, casting this way and that. The filly wasn't where she'd left her. The animal must have tugged her reins loose.

"Here, girl," Ella whispered hoarsely. She could not face the Nudge trio now—or anyone else.

A nicker from somewhere nearby brought a great leap of relief. Ella lifted her skirts and rushed in the direction of the noise. "Come on. Here, girl. Here. Oh, there you are, *silly.*"

The piebald horse cropped the grass close to a large Grecian urn mounted on a short, thick base. Desperate to be gone, Ella grabbed the bridle and brought the horse around.

A length of something rough—swung over her head from behind—jammed her teeth apart.

Ella had no chance to scream.


The old mill stood beside an overgrown tributary of the river some distance from the castle. In disuse since Struan's father's time, what had been the mill house now amounted to little more than a shell with holes in the roof. The rotting mill wheel creaked in the morning wind and there was no sign of life.

"Perhaps your holy man has spread his golden wings and flown away," Arran said grimly.

Calum clapped Struan's back. "We don't need him, friend. Let's turn back and make this female tell us where to find the man who threatens you."

"You cannot begin to understand what manner of woman this is. I cannot risk inciting danger to my family—or yours."

Arran reined in his horse. "If only you'd come to me direct. I could have stopped this foolishness before it ever began."

Struan laughed without mirth. "Come to you and told you I believed I'd as good as raped an innocent maid when I was supposedly making up my mind to take my final vows as a priest? And knowing how you felt about the entire affair?"

"You only went in that direction to spite me. You—"

"We'll not waste time on that now," Calum broke in. "It is in the past. Are you set upon speaking with this abbot?"

"I've told you as much," Struan said, dismounting. "He's got a wisdom few men can hope to have. And he told me he came here hoping to be of some help to me. I want him to know what's happened."

Calum swung down to join him. He walked his horse toward the ramshackle building. Arran remained astride his mount but rode beside his brother and his friend. "Struan," he said when they were close enough to see through the gap where the front door should have been. "Whatever happens, you know you have my support."

"Mine, too," Calum said promptly. "I shall speak with Justine and explain the way of things."

"No," Struan said quickly. "I thank you both for supporting me, but I will win my wife's trust in my own way—through making her believe in me again."

Calum grasped Struan's arm and put a finger to his lips. He pointed toward the river.

"I'm damned," Arran muttered. "He is here, then. Someone should have told me the condition of this place. I'd have made certain he was better housed."

Kneeling on the riverbank, Abbot John Grably, his brow pressed to his entwined fingers, bowed in an attitude of deep prayer.

Struan halted and turned away.

"What is it?" Arran asked. "You wanted the monk. There he is."

"He's at prayer," Struan said.

"You, there!"

At Arran's shout, Struan closed his eyes, remembering how it had once been to sink deeply into himself and to feel the separation from all worldly matters.

Calum's arm descended firmly over Struan's shoulders. "Take heart. You are no longer alone in this horror. If you weren't such a stubborn devil, you need never have been alone with it."

Struan looked over his shoulder and saw that the abbot had risen to his feet and now hurried toward them, the skirts of his brown habit flapping about bare ankles.

"Good morning to you, my lord," he said to Arran. "I know you from Robert Mercer's description of you. Bless you for your goodness to your tenants."

Arran's response held derision. "I doubt you would thank me for my goodness to you, Brother." He indicated the mill house. "This is not a way I come. Had someone told me the condition of this hovel, I would have found something more suitable."

Grably pushed back his graying hair. "I am comfortable enough. I have many friends who make certain I want for nothing."

"They tell me it is you who share what little you have," Struan said, advancing on the abbot. "But we have other things to discuss this morning. I need you. We three will speak together, and then I would ask you to come to my home. I believe you can be of great service to me and the question of a suitable lodging for you will be solved."

Grably frowned.

"We know what happened to Struan at the abbey," Calum announced. "The woman. Glory Willing."

The abbot tilted his face to the sky, and Struan heard his slowly expelled breath. "I was wrong to allow the viscount to leave under such circumstances." The man leveled an intense stare at Struan. "I was not certain you would ever take your final vows. I never doubted your sincerity—only the wisdom of encouraging you to leave behind your family, your music, your keen interest in this estate, and the others the Rossmaras command."

"You considered me wedded to earthly things?" Struan knew he should be beyond feeling judged unworthy of a state to which he no longer aspired.

"I considered that you could be of more use here. There are plenty of men available to pray and read scholarly books. You can do these things *and* be useful to your brother and the people of Kirkcaldy." Grably smiled, sending deep lines into his lean cheeks. "And now Robert tells me you are married to a wonderful lady. Allow me to congratulate you."

"Thank you." Struan could not bring himself to smile in return.

"All is not harmony in my brother's house." Arran, ever blunt, delivered the news without finesse. "His new wife has expressed a desire never to lay eyes upon him again. She believes he is a debauched fiend."

Grably frowned deeply. "Surely you jest."

"My brother has no sense of humor," Struan put in, glowering at Arran. "Neither does he believe in tact. The unspeakable has happened. In my absence yesterday a visitor arrived and contrived to get herself installed at the lodge. None other

than Glory Willing, or Glory Smith as she now says her name
is."

All color fled Grably's face and he whispered, "No."

"Yes. Later she managed to make it appear that I had rav-
ished her."

"To your wife?"

"Who else? The plan is to force a way into my life where
she can help her husband in some damnable scheme to part
Arran and myself from a goodly portion of the Rossmara fortune."

"That is preposterous."

"Do you believe I raped her at the abbey?"

Grably shook his head slowly. "My son, I know what I saw,
but I do not believe you instigated the act. I assure you I could
not possibly believe it."

"Help me deal with her," Struan begged. "Come with us
now and . . . why do you say you could not possibly believe I
instigated the act?"

Grably studied the sky again. "No matter. I hope what I
have said helps you find peace. Thank you for offering me a
place in your home, but I cannot accept."

"I need you," Struan told him. "I need your wisdom. And
with you present and clearly my boon friend, Glory will be
shaken. Surely she will leave at the very sight of you."

"My shame knows no bounds."

Struan looked sharply at the other man.

"It was not merely a desire for a less structured life that
made me leave the abbey, my son. I had to leave."

Calum shifted impatiently at Struan's side but subsided
when Struan shook his head slightly.

"My brother has made a plea for you to lend him your support," Arran said. "Is there any good reason for your refusal?"

"I will come with you," Grably told Struan quietly. "She is
an evil creature and must be banished from your doorstep

with all haste. Before she poisons everything you hope to build in this new marriage of yours."

Struan drew in a great, grateful breath. "Thank you. You shall not regret your decision. Justine and I will make you a place for as long as it pleases you to remain. Perhaps you will consider becoming instructor to my son"—he met Arran's narrowed eyes and immediately returned his gaze to Grably's—"Max is a fine boy, but sadly lacking in formal lessons."

Grably inclined his head. "I know Max. A fine boy indeed. But you will not wish me to become his teacher, my lord."

"Yes—"

"No. It's only appropriate that you know why I will come with you—even though I doubt I can be of assistance with the woman. You see, she in unlikely to listen to any threats I might issue."

Struan spread his hands. "It cannot hurt to try. Such a creature is almost certain to be shaken by your authority."

Grably laughed without mirth. "The authority of another man she toppled from his virtuous throne? A man she contrived to ruin with her beautiful, sinful body? I was forced to flee the abbey and roam—a man of God with no right to approach that God, a man sentenced to forever search out ways to make amends for his wrongs."

Arran and Struan appeared as uncomprehending as Struan felt. "To look upon a woman with . . . You always told me such lapses were to be expected and that with prayer one might be forgiven."

Grably pulled up his hood and threaded his hands into his loose sleeves. "For looking, yes. But I, too, was seduced by Glory Willing."

# Chapter Twenty-four

**M**airi fussed around Justine. "Ye look like an angel, my lady. The viscount's right t'want ye with him when he's entertainin' a visitor."

Justine stood mutinously still, suffering Mairi's primping and poking with stoic indifference—at least on the outside. Struan had sent for her!

She bit the inside of her cheeks to stop her lips from trembling. "I don't believe I feel well enough to join my husband," she said.

Mairi finished fastening Saber's amethyst-and-diamond necklace above the bodice of a dress the same color as the pink-lavender stones. Next she pulled a small stool close and stood on it to place a diamond-studded comb into Justine's simply coiled hair.

"Have you misunderstood me, Mairi?"

"It's such a pleasure t'be back wi' ye," Mairi responded. "Miss Ella's a love, but it's so much more excitin' t'be here.

Mr. North visited a number o' times, but I'm not certain Miss Ella's taken a likin' t'him, if ye know what I mean."

"I know you are avoiding my question."

"What d'ye think o' Mr. North?"

"He is too old for Ella. But he is charming."

"Have ye taken the measure o' his eyes, my lady?"

Irritation and apprehension grew in equal parts. "I cannot say that I have made particular note of Mr. North's eyes." Struan's were quite another matter. Struan's eyes held the depth of the man, the passion . . . Justine could not stand this. Loving him and wanting him, being furious with him and determined to avoid him. All at the same time.

Mairi touched her shoulder lightly. "Are ye feelin' ill?"

"No! Would you kindly help me remove this gown? I wish to rest."

Mairi clapped her hands. "Oh, my lady. Are ye increasin' already?"

Justine pursed her lips and turned her burning face away from Mairi. "I fail to see how you would make such a connection, and—"

"A newly wed lady," Mairi said, all coy. "Too indisposed to be at her husband's side when he's receiving company. Well, y'know what everyone'll think. Is it so?"

"That will do, Mairi."

"Yes, my lady." The maid was instantly demure. "Mr. North has the greenest eyes I've ever seen. And he's built like a great tree. A girl could die of delight just lookin'—"

"Do not look at Mr. North," Justine ordered. "He has a . . . a reputation. Dear me, there is so much work for me to do with my writing, so many desperately urgent topics to address for the good of all women."

"Ye're distressed." Mairi clasped her hands before her. "Ye need t'calm yourself. Mayhap I should explain t'the master."

"Oh, really!" Justine walked away, leaving the maid on her stool. "I shall go down for a very short while. Kindly be ready to attend me when I return. This wretched gown is impossible to shed on one's own."

She didn't wait for Mairi's next response, but made her way to the freshly refurbished suit to which Struan had summoned her. In the same wing as the ballroom, the apartment consisted of three rooms: bedchamber, small study, and sitting room. Justine arrived to find the sitting room door open. Inside she could see a tall, distinguished-looking man standing with his hands clasped behind his back. He wore a brown monk's habit and sandals.

What new trick of Struan's was this?

Justine entered the sitting room and discovered Struan stretched out upon a Chinese divan. At the sight of her, he leaped to his feet and advanced. "My dear. I want you to meet a very old and treasured friend."

With a hard stare, she willed him not to touch her and he dropped the hand he'd extended toward her arm. She turned to the newcomer and said, "Welcome. Kindly tell me how I should address you?"

"This is Abbot John Grably," Struan said, his eagerness cutting into the pathetically fragile shield she'd hastily erected against him.

"I was an abbot," the man said. "I have chosen to leave my order and take to the highways and byways of our beautiful countryside. I should be honored if you called me Brother John.

"Brother John," she murmured.

"Struan has told me he met you in Cornwall."

"My home is in Cornwall."

"It was in Cornwall," Struan corrected her. "Brother John is to stay with us, dearest. I am hopeful we may persuade him to undertake Max's education."

Justine looked at the monk with fresh interest. "You have taught before?"

The man was handsome in a hawkish manner. Thick hair, more gray than black, swept back from a high brow. His deep-set eyes appeared almost the color of pewter. "Teaching has been my life," he told her. "But I am not certain we should make very definite plans as yet."

"Why?" Justine asked, even as she saw Struan about to argue the point himself.

"Because I may not be able to stay very long," Brother John said. "I do think it admirable that you and Struan have undertaken to care for two children who are not your own."

"I love Ella and Max," she said promptly.

"Such generous hearts. How fortunate for Struan that his wife is as willing to accept those orphaned waifs as he was."

Justine frowned.

"Abbot—Brother John"—Struan enclosed her wrist in a bruising grip—"this is not something that should be discussed now. I will explain why later."

"Explain now," Justine said through barely parted lips.

The monk shrugged eloquently. "I merely wished to commend you both for your dedication to two children who are related to neither of you. A most unusual and unselfish act."

"Not related . . . to you?" Justine said to Struan. "What can he mean?"

Struan's mouth worked soundlessly.

"Oh, my goodness." The monk appeared stricken. "Oh, dear. Struan, my good man, I had no idea. Since you've chosen to tell me, I assumed . . ."

"The children are not mine," Struan said, his features hardening. "The story that they were mine by an early marriage was concocted to ease their way when I took them with me to Franchot Castle."

"You lied to me."

"I failed to tell you the truth—exactly."

"This is terrible." Brother John's voice trembled with emotion. "My dear people, how can I make amends?"

"I should have told you the truth, but my thoughts were for the children's comfort. Please believe that, Justine."

"Believe?" How could she believe anything he told her?

"Of course she believes you," the monk said with a forced laugh. "I understand your courtship and marriage has been something of an unexpected event even to yourselves. It is little wonder some minor points have yet to be addressed."

"Minor?" Justine stared at him in furious amazement. "It is minor that the children I took as my stepchildren are not related to my husband? A husband who supposedly prized honesty so highly. How, pray, did you come by Ella and Max? *Who* are they related to?"

"They—"

"Hush, now." The visitor took Justine's hand and led her to the divan Struan had vacated. "Sit down and be calm. Such things as these will only strengthen your union in the end. I may never have enjoyed the married state, but I have observed it in a scholarly manner. Adversity draws husbands and wives together."

She could scarcely concentrate on his words.

"After all, surely you didn't accept the same unlikely story as the staff and tenants of Kirkcaldy."

Justine shook her head slowly.

"Brother John," Struan said urgently. "I think my wife and I need time alone."

The other man smiled wryly and stepped away from Justine. "Of course. I cannot express the depth of my distress over any dissent I may have caused. But, after all, you cannot have thought clearly, my lady. Had he been married and a father, a man of Struan's honor would not have come within hours of taking his final priestly vows."

Short of using force, stopping Justine from locking herself in her rooms—and locking him out—had been beyond Struan's power. He'd then been compelled to all but beg Brother John to remain at the lodge. The man was, even now, overcome with grieving self-recrimination and lay prostrate in his bedchamber. That he would not insist upon leaving once he'd rested was far from certain.

There was a tap at the door to the library where he'd closeted himself. Struan ignored the intrusion, but the door opened anyway and Buttercup trotted in. "Mr. Nudge sent me, m'lord. Says I'm t'warn ye."

Sunk deep in a chair, Struan did not answer.

"Company comin'. Now. The old duchess and that Mrs. Bastible."

Struan massaged his temples.

"Her ladyship sent Mairi away hours ago. Said she wouldna' see any o' us. No one dares go near. Mr. Nudge thinks ye'll want t'be ready for the duchess."

"Ready?" Struan thundered, leaping from his chair and striding about the room. "And how exactly should I be ready for the duchess in any way other than the expected? Have Nudge show her in here. And that damn . . . and Mrs. Bastible. Bring tea. Bring cakes. Bring anything you bloody well please."

"Yes, m'lord." The girl ducked her head and curtsied. "I'll tell Mr. Nudge."

"You do that," Struan said to the door as it closed behind the maid. "Come one, come all. My wife thinks me a damnable liar—which I am. And a lecher—which I am not, although I might at least be diverted if I were. The man I most admire in the world is collapsed because I failed to warn him that I *am* a liar who has told his wife barely two words of truth since she came into my care. The whore who brought me to this low point is ensconced beneath my roof, and it can only be a matter of time before my brother and best friend decide to abandon me.

"Oh, and my wife will probably die rather than converse with me again!"

He minced with tiny, exaggerated steps toward the center

of the room and executed a flourishing bow. "Welcome, Duchess. I am so glad you could join me for tea."

"Don't you toy with me, my boy."

Struan raised his face to be confronted by the Dowager Duchess of Franchot with cane brandished. If it were possible, her shrunken figure appeared even more so. Blanche Bastible, on the other hand, positively bloomed inside her canary-yellow gown and matching plumed bonnet.

"Tea, did you say?" Blanche inquired. "Thank goodness. I am quite peckish. Are you also peckish, dear Duchess?"

Max suddenly appeared from behind Blanche's voluminous skirts and plodded past Struan as if he were invisible. The boy went to the fire, where he held out his skinny hands.

Struan collected himself and said, "I can tell you are troubled, Your Grace."

"Troubled?"

Borne by three maids and presided over by dour-faced Nudge, the dratted tea arrived and was set upon two tables before an Aubusson-upholstered couch.

The duchess, Blanche, and Struan observed in silence. Max did not as much as turn to look. Struan could not decide if he should pray to be spared from madness, or hope to be entirely claimed and released by that condition.

Brother John Grably entered as the serving entourage departed. He appeared surprised to find the room so filled with visitors. "Excuse me," he said. "I wanted to let you know I have attempted to—make contact with our *acquaintance.* I was not successful. I'll leave you to your company, Struan. We'll speak later."

"Absolutely not," Blanche Bastible caroled, avidly perusing Brother John's considerable length. "We should never forgive ourselves for causing a man of the cloth to be turned away, should we, Duchess?"

The dowager concentrated only upon Struan.

"Why," Blanche exclaimed, "you appear near-starved, Reverend . . ."

"Brother John."

"We are *soo* pleased you're here." Rapidly dispensing small sandwiches onto a plate and surrounding them with miniature cakes, Blanche swayed and pirouetted, and linked an arm with Brother John's. "We shall sit together and enjoy this bounty, Brother John. My late husband was a man of the cloth, you know. The Reverend Felix Bastible. A dear, fine man taken from this life in his prime. But Felix never complained—even when he was desperately ill. He bore his pain with such bravery. I miss him so."

Struan took up a mince tart and thrust it at Max, who ate the delicacy in a single bite and returned to warming his hands. If only all these people would go away and leave a man to find peace with his wife. Given time he could do that; he knew he could.

Brother John listened in silence to Blanche's prattling. His gray eyes held no expression. He allowed her to stroll with him to the couch and pull him down beside her.

The duchess's cane, connecting with the floor, made a tableau of the room and its occupants.

Max burst suddenly and astoundingly into choking sobs.

"A disaster," the duchess proclaimed. "I should have allowed myself the luxury of admitting a premonition. From the first moment I set foot in this dreadful lodge I knew no good lay ahead."

"Pray, calm yourself, Your Grace," Brother John said, clearly concerned at such a display of agitation in one so elderly and frail. "Allow me to counsel you."

"Twaddle." The duchess's bright eyes glittered. "Find someone in need of counsel."

"Isn't she *wonderful?*" Blanche, popping a sugared almond into the amazed monk's mouth, reduced him to spasms of coughing. She promptly thumped his back.

"I avoid shows of emotion," the duchess told Struan. "All that outpouring and such. Demeaning. But I will tell you that I am concerned for my granddaughter. She is your wife and that cannot be changed. I also cannot deny my feelings—or my fears. And I cannot bring myself to leave this place without knowing she is safe."

"She *is* safe," Struan said vehemently. "I would give my life for hers."

"So you say."

Max's sobs rose to a wail before he fell to huddle in a ball on the rug.

"Silence, boy," the duchess said. "Leave these things to those better able to deal with them. And stop that noise, I tell you."

Struan dropped to a knee and drew the pointed muddle of arms and legs against his chest. "Hush, Max. It's all right."

"S'not."

The cane hit the floor again. "I will get to the bottom of what's afoot here. It might occasionally appear that I am a less than gentle woman. That appearance is entirely erroneous, I assure you.

"My granddaughter is dear to me. If she were not, I would be less distraught at losing her under such circumstances. And because she is so dear, the disappearance of the girl has all but undone me. There is great danger here, I'm certain of it."

Struan looked up to see Brother John's alarmed expression. "Explain yourself, Your Grace," Struan demanded, getting to his feet.

"The foolish creature has simply *gone*. Not a trace, I understand."

Max positively shrieked.

"Stop that!" The dowager pressed a finger to each ear. "What are you going to do about this, Viscount Hunsingore? Be quick, young man, or I shall take matters into my own hands."

Brother John got up with Blanche still wrapped around his arm. "Struan—"

"Gone. Did she go of her own ... Do you mean she was abducted?"

"Her room was secured from the inside," the duchess responded. "I had the lock forced. No sign of her."

Casting wildly about, Struan strode to the door. "I heard Justine lock that door myself. If she's not there . . ."

Blanche flapped a hand. "Not Lady Justine. Your daughter. *Ella.* Gone from a locked room and without a trace."

# Chapter Twenty-five

Justine pulled the covers up to Max's chin and sat still beside him, listening to his even breathing. Finally, on the second night since Ella's disappearance, he slept.

The memory of Struan's anguished voice begging her to help him from the other side of her door still rang in Justine's mind. Nothing could have stopped her from answering that cry. Bringing Max, they'd come together to the castle and searched.

Careful not to wake the boy, she got up and looked down on his pale face. Blue shadows underscored his closed eyes. "Found in a pickpocket's den in Covent Garden," Struan had said. Not "I rescued him."

Struan never boasted, never spoke of his accomplishments at all.

She crossed her arms tightly. He'd lied to her and she'd felt betrayed. Vast, incredible lies. He'd never been married, never had children, never been widowed.

Ella—that beautiful, gentle girl—removed from a house of ill repute. "Removed." Not "Saved." Not "I saved her."

They were all out there now, the men—Arran leading one search party, Calum another, while Struan, Caleb, and the servants scoured every inch of this immense building for the third time.

The monk had gone with the Mercers and a band of other tenants to walk the riverbanks. *Black hair floating amid the reeds* . . . Justine covered her mouth. She let herself quietly into the sitting room between Max's room and the one that had been . . . the one that was Ella's.

A dreadful, dreary sitting room. Windowless, just as the children's bedchambers were windowless.

A small fortress.

She set her lips in a firm line. The time for falsehoods was past. Struan must tell her exactly what had been in those letters and what had led up to this desperate pass.

*Kidnapped.*

Pacing, Justine battled a swell of sickness. Struan had as good as admitted he was being blackmailed. And she'd as good as proved he had men standing watch over her in his absence. The children had been kept here under guard. Caleb Murray's wild words to Max when he'd caught up with him at the lodge had been more than an empty threat. The man's job had been to keep Ella and Max safe from . . . from whomever.

And Justine would know who that person was, and why he had a hold over Struan.

She had been less than truthful. The circumstances of her being here at all were entirely a fiction. Struan had eventually been trapped into marriage by her lies!

But she'd admitted the truth before that marriage.

He hadn't asked her to come and interfere in his life.

But he'd been glad to see her—he'd said as much.

He'd defended her again and again against Grandmama's sharp tongue. And he'd almost made her believe she *could* do the things other women did.

And he'd told her he loved her.

And she'd believed him.

She still believed him.

The door flew open with enough force to slam it against the wall, and Struan scuffed into the room.

"Hush!" Justine whispered urgently. "Max is finally asleep."

Struan's dark eyes passed over her and away. Fatigue stretched the flesh of his lean face more tightly across flaring bone.

Justine closed the door softly behind him. "That child was exhausted, yet he would not sleep lest Ella returned and he wasn't awake to greet her."

"Why her?" Struan said through his teeth. "Why punish an innocent? The argument is with *me.*" He turned away, rested his fists on darkly paneled walls, and bowed his head.

"Tell me who has done this? And why. I want to help, Struan."

He flung himself to face her. "Don't pry, woman. You have made your feelings toward me plain."

His words stung. "And you have made yours plain toward me, sir. You have not trusted me as an equal. Equals share their problems."

"Leave me be."

"A *priest.* You were once ready to take your final vows, yet you did not think to mention the fact to me."

"I . . ." He dropped into a chair and stretched out his long legs. "You cannot know what it meant to me. What I suffered then. I should have told you, but I didn't. I cannot change it."

Did he want her acceptance, her consolation—her affection? Would he rebuff her if they were offered?

Could she offer him solace?

"My God!" Struan buried his face. "She has done nothing, yet she may be dead. Dead of who knows what horrors."

If her eyes were not too dry, she would cry. "There is something we're missing. No one can take a girl from a room locked on the inside and leave it locked."

"Can't they? She is not there, is she?"

Not bothering to reply, Justine entered Ella's room. She already knew every nook and cranny. The bed draped in somber brown. Oppressive tapestries covering the walls. The dressing table with stool pushed back as Ella must have left it. A writing table with unused paper and a standish. A romantical novel on the table beside the bed. Everything just as the last time Justine checked.

"We cannot stay here and do *nothing!*" she shouted, and clapped her hands over her mouth. She never shouted.

Struan appeared in the doorway. "What do you suggest we do?"

"Anything," she implored. "Please let us do something."

He stared at her. "You care about her—about both of them."

"Of course I care. I came to love Ella and Max for themselves. I cannot stop loving them."

"You are unusual."

She shook her head and laughed harshly. "Not as unusual as you, my lord."

"I am a fool."

Justine was incredulous. "For being a champion to oppressed children?"

"Not for that." His intent eyes revealed nothing of what he felt—or everything. "For other things, but never for that."

"How much longer must we wait?" To break the tension she lifted the bedskirts and peered beneath. Of course, there was no sign of Ella. There was no sign of her anywhere in the room.

"I cannot bear this." Justine trailed to a corner and beat her fists against a faded gray-green tapestry.

She paused, hands in midair. "Did you hear that? Struan, did you hear that noise?"

"No."

"Well, I did." Struggling with the weighty hanging, she

lifted it aside to reveal more of the ghastly paneling used in the sitting room. *"Look!* Sin's ears, Struan, come here at once!"

He came to her shoulder and propped up the hanging.

"A door. Oh, Struan, there's a door. Of course, there had to be. How else could she be gone from a locked room?"

"I searched for one," he said, reaching past Justine to push the row of four square panels wide open. "Evidently I lacked your touch. Pray, Justine. Pray with me that this may lead us to Ella—and that she is safe."

"I haven't stopped praying," she told him. "I'll get a lantern. We must see where this leads."

Struan was already striding away. In seconds he came back with a lantern from the hall outside the apartments. "If I do not return in reasonable time, go for Caleb."

"I'm coming with you."

"You are *not* coming with me." He held up a palm. "Please. Do not waste time in argument. I shall be faster without you."

Justine glanced away. He would be faster because of her wretched leg.

"I need you here," he said softly. "To ensure I am not trapped and to go for help if necessary."

She nodded. "Yes, yes. Go. I will be here."

He hesitated, and for a moment she thought he might kiss her. But then he turned away and she heard his boots descending stairs.

If he'd tried to kiss her, she would have accepted that kiss. She would have returned it. And if that meant she was weak and foolish, so be it. He was her husband because she had loved him from the moment she first saw him. She still loved him—would always love him.

Time passed. Justine didn't know how much time, only that it was very long. Perhaps only minutes, but the longest minutes of her life. Now and again she leaned through the hidden door. Light from the room revealed stone steps winding downward and out of sight.

How long should she wait before going in search of Caleb? The castle felt heavy and unfriendly. Announcing she would come out when the "nonsense" was all over, Grandmama had closeted herself in her rooms. For much of the day Blanche Wren had insisted upon sitting with Justine. The woman was annoying but surprisingly sympathetic. Justine had eventually insisted Blanche go to her bed.

At first the sounds that arose from the secret stairway brought Justine to her toes in anticipation. A thud. Then another thud. And another. Slow.

Her heels sank to the floor.

Struan—she hoped it was Struan—was dragging something heavy up the steps.

She must not call out.

The thumps grew closer. A hard surface hitting the stones.

Justine craned her neck into the opening again. At last she saw his broad shoulders. Struan struggled awkwardly backward up the stairs, and she soon saw that his burden was a large wooden trunk.

When he arrived in the doorway, she moved aside, drawing back the tapestry.

Grunting, Struan hauled the trunk into the bedchamber. He raised a sweat-soaked face and his eyes bored into Justine's. "The steps lead all the way to a little chamber with a rotting hatch. It opens into a stable building that hasn't been used for years. The hatch has been opened recently."

"But Ella isn't—"

"Waiting for me to find her outside the hatch? No, Ella's not there."

Struan looked at the trunk. "This was in the chamber. It's locked."

Justine swallowed. "Probably been there for years."

He swept a finger over the curved lid. "No dust. But it's heavy."

"Is it?" Breaths were hard to come by.

"I'm going to break the lock."

Justine wiped cold, sweating palms on her skirts. "You think . . . Struan, Ella could be in there, couldn't she?"

"Go and wait in the other room."

This time she would not allow him his way. "Open it."

Resignation stilled his next protest. Using a sturdy silver buttonhook from the dressing table, he worked at the lock. Several sharp twists broke it free of the hasp.

Struan rested his hands atop the trunk and closed his eyes.

Using his shoulder for support and praying aloud, Justine knelt beside him.

They lifted the lid together.

# Chapter Twenty-six

They lifted the lid together and held hands tightly while they looked down into the chest.

"Clothes." Struan pulled out piles of heavy, jewel-encrusted satins, fragile silks and lace, embroidered headpieces and exquisite fans, buckled shoes and finely embroidered gloves. "Look at these. They're old. And these . . ." He held up several long strands of pearls—and a small, brown leather-bound journal.

Beneath the journal lay a gown of creamy, pearl-studded satin, its bodice stiffened. And a veil attached to a tiny cap.

Justine clapped a hand over her mouth. She tried but could not trap the laughter that bubbled forth.

Struan glared at her. "I fail to see humor here."

"Han—Hannah's masquerade gown," she sputtered, pointing. "Your grandmother's c-costume."

He frowned even more deeply. "How did you know my grandmother's name was Hannah?"

"I w-worked it out." Justine hugged her middle and laughed until tears fell. "That's her journal."

Struan opened the book. "You've seen this before?"

"Hm-hmm. Hannah's g-ghost l-left it for me."

"Collect yourself. You are overwrought."

He was right, but at least one mystery was a mystery no more. "These," Justine said, reaching into the chest and withdrawing a set of brass and leather bellows. "What would a ghost want with them?"

"What ghost? What—"

"I used the bellows."

Startled, they turned their attention to the doorway where Max hovered, a pathetic figure in a loose nightshort with his legs and feet bare. He held Ella's small, flat-nosed puppy in his arms.

"Go back to bed," Justine told the lad kindly. "Everything's going to be all right, you'll see."

"No it's not. We're bein' punished. Probably the spirits took Ella because we played tricks on 'em." He sat on his haunches and looked upward. "That's where they've got her. I'll be next. We only wanted you two t'be together and happy. We just helped a wee bit. Ella was Hannah and I was the wind. She dressed up and pretended, and I used the bellows to blow out the candle in the ballroom and such. We meant no harm."

Justine and Struan eyed each other, both struggling to be serious. "You didn't tell me," Struan said, and coughed.

"I almost did. But I obviously wasn't going to be believed, and quite right, too."

"She said she was going."

Justine snapped her gaze to Max. "Ella?"

"Aye. She wouldna listen t'me. I told her no good would come o'it, but she wouldna listen."

Struan was on his feet and striding to help the boy up. He took him to a chair, set him down with the dog, and pulled a second chair near. When he was seated himself, he leaned over Max. "Ella said she was going to leave?"

Max nodded. "Aye. She got ready in that fancy green habit with the silly wee bonnet. But she said she'd be back before anyone noticed. Only, she wasna back a'tall." He sniffed. "She still isna back, and I'm scairt."

Justine went to the boy's side. "Where did she go, Max?"

"I don't know." He shook his head miserably from side to side. "She wouldna tell me. All she said was that she had t'help Papa. She said he was in trouble, only nobody knew exactly why. She thought she could do somethin' about it."

Struan ground the heels of his hands into his eyes and muttered a muffled curse.

"Don't," Justine placed a hand tentatively on his shoulder. "We don't have time for looking back—except at whoever it is who probably took Ella. That's what you think, isn't it? That she's been kidnapped?"

If he intended to answer, Buttercup's arrival stopped him. She carried an envelope on a silver salver. "There's none but us maids t'do anythin'," she said. "The rest is searchin'. I found this in the vestibule."

Struan took the envelope. When the girl didn't immediately leave, he stood up. "Take Max back to his bed, if you please."

"Is it about Ella?" Max asked, crushing the puppy so hard it squeaked.

"To your bed. If there's news, I'll come to you."

With a yearning stare at the finery piled upon the floor and spilling from the trunk, Buttercup took the boy and the dog and closed the bedchamber door behind her.

Slipping the envelope into a pocket, Struan offered Justine his arm. "I'll see you to your bed, my dear. This has been far too much for you."

Justine sat in the chair Max had left.

"There is no point in your waiting here," Struan said.

"Read the letter. *Now.*"

He swung away. "I hardly think it appropriate for you to give me orders, madam."

She got up once more and touched the back of his neck. "You cannot expect me to sleep when you may just have received some word of Ella."

For a moment he looked at her. He produced the envelope and passed a finger beneath the flap in one motion. Withdrawing a single sheet of heavy paper, he flattened and read it quickly.

Confusion and pain crossed his features by turn.

"What does it say?" Justine asked in a whisper. "Is it about Ella?"

He nodded and thrust the paper at her. "I cannot believe it. You will not believe it."

Justine sat down again and read the elegant hand aloud:

*"Hunsingore, Ella is in my care. You are the lowest of men and deserve death. Had you not"*—she bit her lip and fought for breath—*"Had you not pretended paternal affection in order to defile this girl, as you defiled the other creature in the abbey all those years ago,"*—goose bumps shot out on her clammy skin and she could not look at Struan—*"then this business would not be necessary. You must atone for your sins. I had intended to take your home and then reveal your sins to the world, but matters have not evolved as I planned. Instead you will place two hundred thousand golden guineas in bags and leave them beside the northerly track from Kirkcaldy. As soon as darkness falls tomorrow evening, place the bags near the five-mile marker and leave. Later I shall send word of Ella's whereabouts."*

*"Avenall"*

Her heart hurt. "Saber?"

"Yes, *Saber*. Your beloved cousin. How he must have laughed at us from his hiding place on our very doorstep. No doubt our marriage was an unwelcome complication to him—possibly it was what stopped him from trying to commandeer portions of Rossmara lands. He might also hesitate to brand his cousin's husband a criminal lecher."

"Did you tell him about your past?"

"I told no one."

"Then how would he know about the abbey?"

"Diligence will produce whatever information a man wants to learn. He was taken with Ella. Then he turned his back on her. She must have told him about her early life and he decided my reasons for taking her under my protection were not pure."

A logical argument, but Saber had always been gentle. Deceit and vengeance would be beyond him. "I know Saber. He would not do this, Struan."

"He has underestimated me. And overestimated me. I have no means of putting my hands on the sum he mentions. And I also have no intention of waiting until tomorrow to retrieve Ella. Defiled under the guise of paternal affection? The man is a foul aberration."

She would not argue now. "What do you intend to do?"

"Ride to Northcliff at once. I'll take him by the throat and show him who is to suffer for this."

"Wait," Justine implored. "Something is very badly awry here. It is an attempt to divert your attention."

"Because no relative of yours could possibly be a scurrilous bounder?"

"Because Saber could not do this. And he could not frighten Ella. Also, he is a very intelligent man. He would know this cannot succeed."

Struan took back the letter and read again. "You may have a point there. But Ella is gone and this is a ransom note. Explain that, if you please."

"Is it in the same hand as the other letters?"

He frowned. "I cannot be sure." He glanced at the back of the envelope and sniffed the paper. "No particular scent and no seal made by . . . Possibly not."

"There, then!" Triumph brought blood to her face. "If Saber had been . . ."

His smile was as much sad as cynical. "If Saber had written the other letters, this should be the same? How true. And, since it is not, it is perfectly sensible to assume the earlier letters were the work of another while this is, indeed, Saber's hand."

*"No."*

"It is also the first mention I've had of my committing some crime against Ella."

"But not against . . . You have been accused of wrongdoing with a female at an abbey?"

Struan's face became expressionless. "That was suggested in the previous letters."

"And for that you were threatened with bodily harm."

"And worse."

"Such as retribution against your family?"

"Yes."

She drew a slow, shaky breath. "Was Glory Smith the person at the abbey?"

"Yes." He averted his face.

"The abbey where you were to have taken your final vows?"

*"Yes.* But it is not as you imagine. She made me drunk and I had not eaten for days. I was wrong, but it was . . . I now know what manner of woman she was, and is."

"You did not touch her on the night when I saw her coming from your apartments?"

He ripped his neckcloth undone and tore it off. "If you must ask, then you have decided upon the answer."

A light tap at the door brought his sharp "Come."

This time it was Mairi who trod reluctantly into the room. "I've a message from Mrs. Moggach, my lord. She says t'tell ye Robert Mercer's at the kitchen doors. The tenants and

Brother John have taken their search all the way t'Northcliff Hall and back."

Justine held her hand toward Mairi. "Did they see any sign of Ella?"

"In a way."

"In a way?" Struan roared. "Be plain and be exceeding quick, my girl."

"Struan."

He waved Justine to silence.

"It was the little filly the marquess bought for Miss Elizabeth. The one for when she's big enough—"

The last of Struan's patience snapped before Justine's eyes. "What of the filly?" he demanded. "The purpose for which she was bought is of no import here."

"No, my lord," Mairi agreed. "Well, the filly was found in the grounds of Northcliff Hall. And Miss Ella's new riding bonnet was tied t'the bridle."

Potts didn't grumble in earnest until Justine told him to drive on. Struan had been given enough of a start toward Northcliff not to hear carriage wheels behind him.

The coach would be slower than the stallion Struan rode, but if he even suspected Justine was following him he'd make her return to Kirkcaldy.

She had pleaded with him to wait for Arran and Calum and seek their counsel. Struan had refused to listen to her. Struan had refused to speak to her.

The Franchot town coach in which Justine had traveled from Cornwall covered the rough roadway toward Northcliff Hall with remarkable ease. Fine springs cushioned each jolt.

Justine peered anxiously from the windows until, at last, a sharp rise gave way to a downhill sweep and a stone wall bordering a large estate. Not far from the wall stood a massive house.

Potts brought the carriage to a stop beneath the statue of a stag atop an archway through the wall. Justine lurched to open the trap and shout, "Onward, Potts. As fast as you can now."

"I don't like the looks of things, my lady."

"Please go on."

"I don't like the feel of it, my lady."

"Potts."

"Your grandmother would never forgive me if anything happened to you. Your husband would never forgive me. My duty to you and your family comes first. It isn't right. We should—"

"Drive on, Potts!" Justine slammed the trap.

Leather creaked. Wheels ground on gravel. The carriage shot forward, throwing Justine against the squabs. She held on to a strap while Potts contrived to hit every dip in the driveway. He shot around the building and came to a halt before the front door of Northcliff Hall.

Grim-faced and breathing heavily, Potts appeared to open the door and place the steps. He handed Justine down. "You'll rue this night," he told her. "You mark my words. Not a light showing in the place."

"Don't exaggerate. There aren't many lights." She hurried toward the house, passing Struan's grazing black horse on the way. "No need to accompany me, Potts. Wait by the carriage. I don't anticipate being here long."

That was when she noticed the front door was open and that a rumble of masculine voices came from inside.

Justine pushed the door wider and stepped gingerly into a cold marble foyer. The voices she'd heard belonged to Struan and an aged, stooped butler.

Struan was the first to notice her. "Justine!" He covered the space between them entirely too quickly. "How dare you disobey me!"

"How dare I disobey you? *Sin's ears!* One would think we were still in the eighteenth century! I did not disobey you. I merely did what I considered essential. I came to ensure you were safe—and that you didn't make a *fool* of yourself."

His mouth remained open while Justine swept past him. "I am Lord Avenall's cousin," she told the butler. "I understand he is a guest here."

"I only do as I'm told," the man said. "That's all. What I'm told t'do is what I do." He peered around the green and white museumlike space as if looking for approval—or an audience. "Nudge. I'm one of the Nudges. Butlers all, we are. Always have been."

"The man's incompetent," Struan said. "And he seems to be the only servant around. I've asked him to take me to Saber."

Shuffling, arching his head on its bent neck to squint up at them, Nudge pushed the front door shut.

"Is Mr. North in residence?" Struan said.

Nudge fumbled with his untidy neckcloth. "Gone t'the Continent."

Justine smiled reassuringly. "We're sorry not to see him, but we came to visit Lord Avenall. He's my cousin."

"Ye already said as much. Back t'his regiment, he said. Orders came, he said."

Justine looked as Struan, who narrowed his eyes "Lord Avenall was recalled to his regiment?"

"Aye. He's left. Went in the night."

Suddenly weak, Justine sat on the lowest step of the staircase. "Only the servants are in residence at this time?"

"Aye."

Struan began to pace, his boots echoing in the domed space. "Which night? On which night did Lord Avenall leave? Tonight? Yes, of course, he must have left earlier tonight."

"He left the night the gir-rel came."

Struan stopped pacing. He spun toward Justine. She got to her feet and took hold of the old man's arm. "The girl? Was she dark-haired? Wearing green?"

"Came from Kirkcaldy," Nudge said, his head on one side

as if he'd been cuffed. "Wanted to see Lord Avenall. Old friend, so she said. Ella."

"That's right!" She accepted Struan's steadying hand beneath her elbow with gratitude. "Ella. Did she see Saber?"

"Wasna supposed to," Nudge muttered. "She was supposed to follow me back here, but she didna come. I was too tired to climb up after her again. She let herself out."

Justine expelled the breath she'd held. "You saw Ella leave again?"

He blinked slowly. "Aye. Ran out, she did. Wasn't long afterward when Lord Avenall asked for a carriage himself."

"We're wasting time here," Struan said. "Come. We'll return to Kirkcaldy. This only becomes more impossible."

When they emerged into the cool night, Potts had already tethered the black to Justine's carriage and resumed his place atop the box.

"Back to the castle, man," Struan shouted, helping Justine into the coach. "There's no time to waste."

Potts made off with one of his bone-jarring bursts of speed, jostling Struan and Justine together. They flew from the Northcliff drive to the straight road home.

"You should not have followed me," Struan muttered, staring into the mirror-black glass of the windows. "I'd have been faster on my horse."

"You are a stubborn man, Struan. You are my husband and your concerns are my concerns. I told you from the beginning that it is my mission to help women find equal footing with their husbands."

"Not *now.*"

Justine turned her back and moved as far from him as possible. Argument would accomplish nothing, and they were both deeply fearful for Ella.

An abrupt turn tossed Justine against Struan.

"What the . . . ?" He wrapped an arm around her waist and held her while the vehicle gathered speed. "Damn it all! *Damn* the man I say. Has he taken leave of his senses?"

Justine clung to Struan's arm while they were jounced wildly. "This isn't the way," she gasped.

"Don't concern yourself. These coachmen have a nose for short routes."

"Potts has a nose for nothing but the expected. We have left the road to Kirkcaldy, I tell you."

Struan reached across the carriage and hammered a fist on the trap.

Another sharp turn sent him sprawling on top of Justine.

"My God!" He tried to brace her safely in a corner, only to slip to the floor when Potts drew the team to a complete halt.

Justine slid down beside him. "Something's wrong."

Fury strained Struan's features. "Obviously." He deposited her back on the seat, opened a door, and promptly drew back.

A hunched figure flung itself through the door and the carriage rushed forward before they were completely closed inside again.

The crackle of Pott's whip split across the rushing air, and the crazed protests of abused horses.

Swathed in a hooded black cape, the newcomer knelt on the opposite seat and opened the trap.

"What is happening?" Justine asked, expecting no reply.

Struan squeezed her hands reassuringly.

"Through the trees ahead, Len," came the interloper's cry.

Justine shifted forward on the seat. *A woman.* "Len? Potts's name is William, not *Len.*"

"This *is* your coach?" Struan asked.

"It's her coach," the woman shouted without turning around. "I preferred my own coachman, is all. Now, Len, my lover! Yes, *here!* Stop here."

Once more the carriage slowed down amid the screech of wheel blocks and a deafening chorus from the team.

Another figure in black leaped aboard, this time closing the door tightly.

The woman sat and pushed down her hood.

Glory Smith stared at Justine with unconcealed hatred.

The latest arrival left his cowl draped about his stark face. "A job well done," he complimented Glory. To Struan he said, "I could not have hoped for more willing cooperation, Viscount Hunsingore. You have followed the trail I prepared to perfection. In fact, you even did what I hardly dared to hope for. And your lady was deliciously predictable. You alone might have been enough. The two of you are a prize beyond compare."

Justine saw the pistol the instant Struan made to rise from his seat. "He will kill you!" She hung on his arm. "He has a weapon."

"And you are right, my lady. I will kill him. I'll kill both of you. But not until the moment is right. First you shall have the pleasure of seeing me grow rich from the bounties Stonehaven and Franchot will pay for you."

Struan pushed Justine behind him on the seat. "Let my wife go. She has no part of this. Your argument is with me."

The man sneered. "I think not. After all, I warned you what the appropriate retribution for your crime would be." Cold eyes sought out Justine. "She's a fetching piece, despite her deformity. I'll admit, I'm titillated at the thought of having my first cripple—in front of her husband."

Justine restrained Struan with both of her hands and her entire weight.

Glory tipped back her head and laughed raucously. She leaned against a window and pulled her skirts up about her hips.

Justine averted her eyes, but not before she saw Brother John Grably slide his fingers into the black curls between Glory's thighs.

# Chapter Twenty-seven

❦

The pistol, held to Justine's temple by Grably, ensured that Struan held still while his wrists were bound behind him and a blindfold applied by a heavyset, loudly belching coachman he'd never seen before.

"Now you, m'lady," the man said, his voice heavy with cockney overtones.

"Touch my wife and you'll die," Struan told him. Thank God they had not noted his knife.

"Keep the coach here, Bottwell," Grably ordered. "We'll take them the rest of the way on foot."

" 'Ere," the coachman said in complaining tones. "I was the one what done for the other one. Don't I get to take a turn with the cripple?"

"Later," Grably promised, shoving Struan ahead of him.

"What have you done with Potts?" Justine demanded.

The cry that followed could only be hers. Pebbles rolled past his feet and he heard breath jarred from lungs.

He jerked around in the blackness. "Justine! Justine!"

"She's all right," Glory said sweetly. "Had a little fall, is all. You know how it is with the infirm. We'll just have to take her down a bit slower."

With his entire body, Struan thrashed at the air in impotent rage, only to be sent to his knees with the force of a blow to the back of his neck. Grably's pistol butt shot a shaft of white-hot pain into Struan's head.

"Get up," Grably demanded. "Try anything else and it'll be the lady's neck next time."

"Struan! What have they done to you?"

"Nothing." He stumbled to his feet. "All's well, my love."

"Free with the love talk, aren't you?" Glory said. "Told her about cold cells and hot bodies, have you? And about red wine and—"

"Enough from you," Grably snarled. "You can drop your story now. No more need for playacting. We'll get everything we want."

Slipping, tripping on sliding rock and shale, Struan staggered under the weight of Grably thumping into him. He hit a rock face and felt his sleeve tear.

"Stand there," Grably told him. "Hold the woman, Glory, while I move this away."

Grunts accompanied the sound of scratching.

A hand, roughly applied to the top of his head, bent Struan double and he was shoved forward to sprawl on the ground. Old dust and dank air assaulted his nostrils. The blindfold was yanked off in time for him to see Glory push Justine, and trip her as she overbalanced.

Struan fought with the bonds at his wrists—to no avail. Justine fell. Her head smacked a trunk evidently used as a table in the middle of a cave strewn with sheepskins and heaps of tartan.

Blood welled from a gash at Justine's hairline.

"Leave her!" Struan made his way toward her on his knees. "Do not touch her. Either of you."

"I don't have time for this," Grably said, hauling Glory back as she would have used her fists to add to Justine's misery. "I have to return to Kirkcaldy and make sure our highborn friends get the messages I intend to send."

"We'll get there soon enough," Glory said. "We've matters to deal with here, first."

Grably smiled, a smile that didn't warm his cold eyes. "Time enough for that when I return in the morning." He raised the pistol and leveled it at Justine, who lay, her eyes closed, beside the trunk. "Untie their hands."

*"Why?"*

"It will not be conventional bonds that keep these two waiting for what we have in store for them. Use the viscount's knife." He laughed. "Thought I hadn't seen it, didn't you?"

Struan shook his head in frustration.

Glory passed her tongue over her lips.

"Do as I tell you," Grably ordered her.

She reached beneath Struan's arms and coat to remove the knife, then cut between Justine's wrists with a cruel, twisting stroke. The sight of Justine, slowly moving her arms in front of her and pushing to sit up, was the best Struan ever remembered seeing.

Next Glory freed him, taking much longer over the task and using the opportunity to nibble his earlobe and feel him intimately.

Struan stared straight ahead. His body remained in complete accord with his mind. Neither was aroused.

Temper didn't suit Glory's striking features. She finished freeing his wrists and flung away.

Never taking his eyes from his prisoners, Grably had lighted torches in alcoves around the cave's walls. Then he took a glowing lantern and swung it slowly. "This is how you will die," he said softly. "The only question is when. If you're very good, it may not happen too soon. If you're bad . . ."

"Let's get on with it," Glory demanded.

"The entrance to this cave is hidden by a bale of twigs and dry straw, fashioned for the purpose. When we leave, other bales will be packed about the first. The straw is kept dry because there is a rock overhang above the cave. At the center of each bale are oil-soaked rags. One spark and the bales will ignite. You will not burn; you will choke."

Struan drew Justine against his chest and sat with her cradled in his arms.

"You are already thinking of trying to run through the bales. If you do, you *will* burn. And should you live to reach the other side, you will be shot as you emerge. Your only hope is that I will change my mind and decide to spare you."

"Let Justine go."

"To give our identities away so soon?" Grably snorted with laughter. "I think not. You might try praying, Hunsingore. You were quite good at it once. Ask God to change my heart."

"Kill us and my brother will never rest until he tracks you down."

"He will not have to track me. I shall be close at hand, commiserating, advising—and laughing. You should never have stopped the payments you sent to the monastery for Glory."

"I thought she had married."

"She was always married—to me."

"But you were the abbot of—"

"Do not be a fool. Rules are for the weak and the foolish. Men of intellect make their own boundaries. I shall leave you now. There is no need to bind you because there will be a watch outside. One move to leave this place and . . ." He smiled and swung the lantern afresh. "Well, I need not repeat myself. There is bread and wine. If the night grows too cold, avail yourselves of the skins."

"If I was to stay with you I'd make sure you were warm," Glory said, winking at Struan. "Maybe we should tie your wife up again and show her how—"

"Outside," Grably said calmly. "Glory is a woman of considerable energy. Sometimes she forgets herself in her quest to use that energy."

"Where is Ella?" Justine asked clearly. "What have you done with her?"

In his concern over present events, Struan had not thought of Ella.

"Ella?" Grably shrugged. "Why should the welfare of the viscount's plaything concern you?"

"How dare you, sir!" Justine tried to evade Struan's restraining grasp. "My husband is an honorable, generous man capable of taking the weak and needy into his care as equals. He is a man who has suffered too long because of your avarice and jealousy. He is a *saint,* sir! A *saint!"*

Struan rolled in his lips and frowned to contain himself. In other circumstances, Justine's ire—and her elevation of him—might be exceedingly amusing.

"Where is Ella?" Struan asked, as calmly as possible. "And what is your connection to Avenall? I take it you worked together in this."

"He served me well. I have nothing more to say to you on the subject."

"Ella?" Justine cried.

"Rest well," Grably said. "Until we meet again in the morning." He waved Glory from the cave and backed out after her. Immediately came the scraping of the promised bales across the entrance.

When the sounds of pyre-building ceased, Struan and Justine continued to sit, side by side, on a sheepskin.

"We should tend to that wound on your head," Struan said at last.

"It doesn't hurt," Justine retorted, her chin defiantly raised. "They could be duping us. It's perfectly possible they're not out there at all—or they won't be once they've gone."

Struan could not help but smile. "You, my dear, are indomitable."

"Not at all. Merely logical."

He pointed to the cave entrance. "What do you see?"

She frowned. "Speckles of red light."

"Lantern light through straw and sticks—and oiled rags. A reminder in case we decide to try our luck at testing their threats. We will not do so. Our only hope lies in being prepared for Grably's return."

"How?"

"I shall wait for him to appear and subdue him. Take away his pistol." He gave what he hoped was a jaunty grin. "You are in safe hands, my dear."

"I am in the best hands in the world."

He found he could not respond.

"They may light the bales without waiting, Struan."

"I do not believe they will risk drawing attention to this hiding place until they have the ransom they intend to extract."

"What do you suppose he meant about Saber?"

What harm could there be in saying what he didn't believe at this point? "Saber has Ella with him. Obviously Ella's abduction was a decoy to draw us to a place where Grably could capture us. But you said Saber is gentle, and you know him well. I believe he loves Ella and has taken her away."

Justine nodded seriously. "That is what I shall hope for. She is too young for him as yet, but I would trust him with her. He would care for her well."

"We must decide how to deal with the matter of Ella and Max once we are free." Whatever happened, he would ensure the coming hours were not filled with silence and fear for his lady. "I have certainly shown poor judgment in the matter of retaining a tutor for Max."

Justine laughed and poked his side. "If you speak of Grably, then indeed you have. If you speak of me, then you show extraordinarily *good* judgment."

He got up and prowled the walls of the cave. "There is another issue. I must find a means to ease their way—as far as their identity goes. They do not even appear to have a family name."

"That is simple."

Struan paused. "How so?"

"They will become our children. There is a legal process. We can have papers drawn up."

His throat grew tight. "You mean those words, don't you?"

"Mean them?" She smiled up at him. "What a marvel to gain a husband, and a son and daughter. I who had never thought to be other than a childless spinster."

Looking upon her lovely, joyous face turned his heart. He glanced away to the muted glow at the cave entrance. Please God let him get Justine out of this place alive.

"I do not regret tricking you into entering my body."

She startled him. "Hardly a matter to speak of aloud, my dear."

"Why?" She glanced around with exaggeratedly wide eyes. "Are we not alone?"

He smiled faintly. "Very much alone."

"And that doesn't make you happy?"

"Under the circumstances—"

"The circumstances are perfect. A man and his wife and the night ahead."

And then the morning light. Struan stood over her. "How delightful you make the situation sound."

"It is delightful. Being with you is always delightful to me."

Wonder was spread before him like a magician's sleight of hand. There and then gone. Possible and then impossible. But always desirable.

"When we last lay together you were very clever, Struan."

He raised his brows.

"You contrived to trick me. I expect you thought I should scarcely notice not feeling you within me."

His body responded instantly. "Perhaps we should try to rest. I must be ready for Grably when he returns."

"He will not return for hours. Hours we have to spend together, Struan. Alone."

He cleared his throat. "Have you . . . Have you bled again, Justine?"

Her fingers, closing on his thigh, shocked him. "Do not ask me that question again. I am not the simple woman I used to be in these matters. We may choke to death in this place. Or be killed in some other manner by the fiends who have trapped us here."

"I fail to see—"

"Of course you do not see! You are a man, you dolt! You think only in ways made of things you can see and touch and explain with wonderful male logic.

"We may die in this cave. Or you may die from a falling boulder somewhere on this estate. I may die from a fever. You may die from an accident on your horse, or beneath the wheels of a carriage.

"Or I may die from making a poor attempt at giving birth to a child. Our child."

"*No.*"

"Yes, Straun. *Yes.* We may die of any of these things. Eventually we must die. But it is the way we live that decides our worth. And unless we live to the fullest and shun fear, we are without worth."

Her passion rendered him silent.

"We are man and wife," Justine continued. "Joined together in the sight of God and our fellow men. We are to live together in that manner. I want that. And you want that."

Denying what she said was impossible. "I yearn for you, Justine. Looking at you, wanting you yet being afraid to take you, makes me half a man."

"Not half a man," she told him, rising to stand before him. "A man ready to be whole with a woman he can make whole.

If I am destined to die giving birth to our child, so be it. I will have had the ecstasy of feeling life from you within me. There is no greater gift I can receive."

He clasped her to him. "I could not live with myself if you died because of me."

"Until we die, we must live, Struan, really live. The rest is not for us to decide. And many women never become with child at all. I shall probably be one of those."

Unless she was already increasing she would almost surely be one of those.

"Don't you agree, Struan?"

"Possibly."

"Good. And you agree that life should be lived to its fullest."

He sighed. "Yes."

"Good. Just in case our time to explore that decision may be limited, I suggest we make the very best of our opportunities."

He looked down into her face. "Would you care to elaborate on that suggestion, madam?"

"Certainly. I should like to watch you take your clothes off again."

He felt color rise in his face, then felt foolish. "Surely you jest." He indicated their surroundings. "Here?"

Justine swept off her cloak and spread it atop the skins on the ground. She turned her back and said, "The tapes confound me."

He unfastened her gown, and with each contact of his fingertips with her skin, the heat in his loins grew. She turned toward him once more and slipped the blue gown from her shoulders as if they were in the safety of her chamber, or his, at the lodge.

The front of her shift closed with tiny satin bows. These she undid as far as her navel. The flimsy lawn fell open to reveal her breasts and her slender waist.

Seconds passed while he regarded her face, her body. Justine took his hands and spread them over her breasts. Rising to her toes, she settled her lips over his and stood still.

Despite himself, despite the situation, Struan smiled. His sensual nymph still had a great deal to learn before she'd be ready to complete her book. Without preamble, he thrust his tongue past her lips and set about the small seduction for which she'd already admitted a fondness.

Her nipples stiffened beneath his palms.

His rod leaped and grew heavy.

Breathing shallowly, Justine broke the kiss and stepped away, her breasts rising and falling rapidly.

He frowned. "What is it, dearest?"

"I asked you for something. I asked to see you remove your clothes."

Struan chuckled. "You are wanton."

"I know. A strumpet, I shouldn't be surprised. Definitely very badly fallen. But your welfare is my concern, and you have suffered under the weight of those trousers entirely too long."

"You really do not know what you are talking about."

"Don't I?" She arched a brow, folded her arms beneath her naked breasts, and regarded the part of him no well-bred lady was supposed to as much as glance at—ever.

Discomforted, Struan glanced down at himself.

Justine's shriek of laughter brought his eyes to hers again. "What is so humorous, madam?"

"You." She pointed at the "part." "And the horrified manner in which you look at . . . that. Don't you know how beautiful it is?"

"That is not exactly the word normally employed."

"Look again. It is exceedingly large and hard and alive and showing exactly how much it agrees with every word I have spoken."

"Justine."

"I told you to look at it."

More embarrassed than he'd considered possible, he did as she asked. Beauty aside, the rest of her description appeared accurate.

"See? And it is past time for it to taste freedom."

"Justine."

"*Justine. Justine.* What grants it the most relief is a good dose of *It.*"

Bemused, he shook his head.

"Oh, do not pretend ignorance with me, my lord. Off with your trousers, this instant. I am ready for you."

He groaned.

"I find I grow much bolder as we are together more."

"One trembles to visualize you even a month hence."

"Hah. There is something I must ask. I've been hesitant, but, for the good of my book, it is time to clear up a small mystery. Is it normal for a woman to grow wet . . . I mean, to grow wet here? She made a fluttering motion over the place where a shadow through the shift marked the juncture of her thighs. "I find I grow most awfully wet whenever I consider That. In fact, I have only to look at you—there—to become, well, like butter before a fire. As it were."

A jolt hit Struan exactly there. His knees threatened to buckle.

"Is it normal, Struan?"

"Normal in one so perfectly suited to being this fortunate man's wife."

"Oh, thank goodness." She smiled up at him. "This does seem one of those good opportunities I mentioned."


Glory had wheedled a horse out of Len and ridden to the stable yard at the lodge. Persuading Len Bottwell that he'd do whatever she asked him to do hadn't taken more than a brief tumble with him inside the carriage. Men like Len weren't used to the likes of Glory Willing. He'd mewled at her breast like a baby and all but cried when she pulled him between her legs and jounced him so hard his head thwacked the roof.

Len would sit with the cave in sight and watch until Michaelmas if that's how long it took Glory to go back to him. She smiled to herself. There was no one like Mr. Smith, but occasionally it felt good to remind herself that she could have any man she really wanted.

Mr. Smith might not always be an easy man to understand, but he needed her. And there were things he knew how to do that no other man would dream of. She held her tongue between her teeth and visualized what they would do when she surprised him in a few minutes. He'd told her he would go to the lodge to prepare the ransom note, then return to the room he'd been given at the castle and await the commotion when the demand was discovered by the duke and the marquess.

She knew where she'd find him—in Hunsingore's apartments. Mr. Smith fancied those rooms. Before he'd left her near the cave, insisting he'd be quicker on his own, he'd let on how he intended to find a way to make the duke and the marquess believe he'd been so helpful. Then they'd be grateful and "suggest" they give him a place at Kirkcaldy to use whenever he pleased. And he was going to suggest—ever so humbly—that the lodge would be out of their way and give him a place to meditate.

Glory swallowed a laugh. *Meditate.* If only all the people who thought Mr. Smith was so holy could see his idea of meditating!

She let herself into the passageway leading past the pantries and cold rooms to the kitchens. Mr. Smith might be a little cross with her at first, but she'd soon make him glad she'd come.

The sound of giggling reached her when she entered the butler's pantry with its windows on the scullery and kitchens.

And there was a voice, too, a man's deep voice. Glory tugged on the ribbons at the neck of her cloak and crept forward until she could see into the dim rooms on the other side of the glass.

Figures shifted.

Glory pressed herself against the wall beside a shiny pane and peered through. She wore deep red, and in the darkness she'd be invisible unless she made foolish moves.

Gradually her eyes adjusted to the shadowy gloom.

The giggles grew to a shriek. And the man's voice became insistent.

A flurry of paleness dashed into the scullery. A female with a mass of blond hair and dressed in something white.

Glory narrowed her eyes, then jerked farther back. The man pursued the female, a candle in hand. Light flared and Glory saw it was the Buttercup creature who leaned back against the sinks, her mouth stretched wide in a stupid grin, while Mr. Smith set his candle aside and approached.

Twisting, gripping outrage all but stopped Glory from breathing. Mr. Smith never had other women. He'd always said no woman but Glory could satisfy him.

Perhaps Buttercup had asked for too much in return for being the one to leave the letters at the castle. Mr. Smith might have decided to frighten her a bit. Very likely.

Mr. Smith delved into Buttercup's tight bodice and ripped it open. Buttercup squealed afresh. "You shouldn't," she said, all coy. She put her hands to her big breasts, not beginning to cover the abundance of naked flesh.

Glory's hands went to her own breasts. The little whore's breasts were even bigger. Mr. Smith liked big breasts.

"We're both going to remember this," he said to the girl. "I've waited for you, Butter."

"And I've waited for you," she said. "I've done exactly what you asked. And I've waited."

The rest of the dress was rendered to rags. An ample, curvaceous body was revealed and, while Glory watched, Mr.

Smith fell upon the slut like a man taking his first drink at the end of a long, hot day.

Beside the sink lay a bar of soap. Before Glory's horrified eyes, Mr. Smith ran water and splashed it over the struggling maid. She tried to fight him off, screaming aloud when he soaked her hair, then dissolving into helpless laughter as he soaped her all over.

"Stop it," Buttercup whined, batting ineffectually at him. "You stop that now. You're makin' me all wet and slippery."

"I like wet and slippery." He backed her—dripping—into the kitchen, shedding his own clothes as he went. Once naked, he propped Buttercup against the great kitchen table and rubbed against her. "Hold me," he rasped.

Glory's hands sank between her legs and she gritted her teeth. She saw Buttercup lift Mr. Smith's ballocks and squeeze. And he behaved as if he loved everything she did. He dropped to push his face into her crotch, all the while pinching and squeezing her breasts as though he'd never had the best there was to have already.

Then it was Buttercup on her knees making a feast of Mr. Smith's cock. And him wearing no cundum for a kitchen skivvy the way he did for the likes of Glory Willing, who'd served him well.

He would pay.

"How would you like to make me really happy?" Mr. Smith asked.

Buttercup nodded her idiot head and allowed him to lift her on the table. Hopping up beside her, he tied her hands to a drying rack suspended from the ceiling.

The girl pretended to cross her legs and whimper.

"Frightened, are we?" Mr. Smith said.

It was a game he was only supposed to play with Glory. She opened her mouth, then covered it to muffle her panting.

The game was to see how many times Mr. Smith could watch Glory have it before he gave her what they both wanted. Only, this time he wasn't doing it with Glory.

He suckled Buttercup's pale nipples until she pulled frantically at the ropes about her wrists, and when she begged for him, he gave her what she wanted with his tongue. Then it was fingers, and more fingers.

Glory felt for a chair and sat on the edge of its seat. She would watch it all and never forget. And afterward she'd have the strength to do what she'd have to do.

Sitting between Buttercup's splayed legs, Mr. Smith gave it to her with a pastry brush, inciting fresh moans of pleasure with every sweep of those lovely bristles. He'd never been that inventive with Glory.

The glass rolling pin made the girl scream and jerk. But nevertheless she shuddered with her release.

"Ready for me now, my *dove?*" Mr. Smith asked.

Rage sickened Glory. He used their special name on this slut, treated her as if she was better than Glory.

He released Buttercup from the rack. Stretching her out, facedown on the table, he plastered himself on top of her and they heaved and groaned like filthy animals.

When Glory finally crept away, Mr. Smith was sitting on the edge of the table with Buttercup astride his thighs.

# Chapter Twenty-eight

"Whatever they want, they shall have," Calum told Arran. "But surely we can negotiate a later delivery. I shall need to make a journey to London."

"We must meet their appointed time for the initial payment." Arran gazed at the night sky from the windows at the top of the Adam Tower. Too few hours would bring the dawn. "A sizable show of goodwill, as they put it. Before the sun rises. With the balance to be paid as ordered. What they ask for can be assembled within the hour. My father always believed in keeping what he termed 'a fund for small emergencies,' readily to hand."

"*Small* emergencies?" Calum almost managed to smile. The letter in Arran's hand scuttled the effort. "The so-called show of goodwill is a fortune. Enough to keep ten men in high style for a lifetime."

"Let them have it. Struan and Justine are worth any price we have to pay."

"Amen," Calum said softly. "But we must prepare ourselves. They may already be dead."

The obvious had been unspoken between them since Buttercup had presented them with the terrifying missive when they arrived back from their respective useless searches for Ella.

"I have a plan to unmask this devil," Arran said. "The necessary gold and jewels are already in a form easy to transport. Loading them into a cart will be a simple enough task. But, instead of you and me making the delivery, we will send two others who will be mistaken for us. We shall lie in wait. When the bounty is recovered, we'll follow."

Calum drew an uneven breath. "What if we are seen? They warned us to tell no one about the contents of the letter. We cannot risk angering them."

"Do you believe these villains will keep their word?" Arran turned his clear green eyes upon Calum. "Or do you suspect your beloved sister and my dear brother may only live until their captors are certain they do not need to produce them to press the claim?"

"The latter," Calum admitted.

Deliberate footsteps sounded on the steps from the floor below. Calum regarded Arran significantly. Arran gave a brief nod and they faced the open doorway. "I took the liberty of summoning the man I know Struan would choose."

Brother John, his thin face bearing the lines of deep concern, came into the tower room and approached the two friends. "You wished to see me?" He clasped his hands together as if in prayer. "You are desperately troubled. I see the signs in your faces."

"Forgive us for calling you from your bed at such an hour," Arran said. "We have a favor to ask of you."

"Anything. Anything at all. I take it there is no sign of the young lady? We had no good fortune by the river."

"No sign," Calum told him, turning away. "I agree with

your plan, Arran. Explain it to Brother John. I think the sky begins to lighten."

In a cart loaded with boxes and trunks of treasure, the monk—with Mr. Nudge, the butler from the lodge—left the castle within forty minutes of the interview in the tower room.

Mounted, Arran and Calum waited at the castle gates, counting off the interval they'd agreed should lapse before they followed Brother John and Mr. Nudge. Brother John had chosen Nudge as a companion over Robert Mercer because— by the monk's logic—Nudge had no family to cloud his judgment and the man was devout and trustworthy.

"Seems to me we should be on the heels of the cart," Calum said. "If we're too late, they'll make away with their haul and we may never hear from them again."

Secretly, Arran agreed, but he was reluctant to alter a plan made with Brother John when the man had so willingly accepted a potentially deathly assignment.

Uneven hoofbeats approached from behind. Calum wheeled about more quickly than Arran and let out an oath. "I don't believe it. Good God, what is *she* doing here at this hour?"

Arran crossed his arms on his horse's neck and watched his mother-in-law's ungainly progress toward them through the predawn. Swathed in great quantities of orange velvet trimmed with swansdown and with white feathers floating about the brim of her bonnet, she bore down with a determined expression upon her usually vacuous face.

"Mother-in-law," he greeted her shortly. "I didn't know you were in the habit of taking early-morning rides—very early-morning rides—and alone."

She brought her rotund chestnut to a jerky halt. "I prefer not to ride at all. And I'll thank you not to take a high-handed tone with me, young man, unless you wish me to complain to my daughter."

Arran was in no mood for foolishness, but he restrained a quick retort.

"Coming to you with this matter was not a simple decision," Blanche said, puffing at drooping feathers. "But I am a woman of conscience and conviction. When the matter of right is at stake, I have no choice but to put my own welfare aside."

"Really?" The response was irresistible.

Calum moved restlessly in his saddle. "I think you should return to the castle, Mrs. Bastible. Riding alone is not a good idea, and I fear Arran and I have important business to conduct."

"That is why I am here." She shook her head. "Such a disappointment. Brother John showed promise, I thought. At first he seemed charming. I have always had a tender place in my heart for men of the cloth. You will remember that my dear late husband was—"

"Yes," Arran interrupted. "Are you saying you have developed a *tendre* for the good brother?"

Blanche blushed appropriately. "I know monks do not marry, but I did think we might have developed a most . . . a most complementary relationship. One that would have brought us both a deal of comfort."

Arran avoided looking at Calum.

"I count myself an excellent judge of character, but in this case I admit I may have been badly mistaken."

"About Grably?" The woman never made sense.

Blanche settled herself more firmly on the chestnut. "These are not simple things to discuss, but yes. I have not been able to sleep worrying about that poor, missing child. She is a polite little thing and treats me with a respect I rarely receive from certain people." A meaningful pause elapsed before Blanche continued. "Anyway, I happened to hear you return and get some sort of communication from that dreadful Buttercup creature. Then I saw Brother John and that fearful Nudge leave the castle with you close behind. I came as quickly as I could. Viscount Hunsingore and his wife have been kidnapped, haven't they?"

Calum put a hand on Arran's arm. "We do not have time for this."

"You do not have time to ignore this, Your Grace. If my instincts are correct, you had best allow me to be your guide before it is too late."

"You eavesdropped, madam," Calum said. "And you have no idea what you're saying. No more do I."

"I'm saying that Grably and that Buttercup *know* each other. As in they *know* each other. In the biblical sense."

Arran regarded the woman with fresh interest. "How—"

"I saw them." Blanche pursed her lips. "Once I realized what manner of man he was, I decided I should keep an eye on his activities. There are things about him that do not bear repeating. He also knows that woman to whom Lady Justine gave refuge at the lodge. We are wasting time. Unfortunately I had to dress or I should have joined you sooner. Follow me, please."

She rode off.

"D'you suppose it's true?" Calum asked.

"Damned if I know. But if the man is a fake . . . Well, I suppose a little harmless rutting with a willing maid is to be excused . . ."

"Come along!" Blanche shouted. "Do you think he and Nudge—who also *knows* that young romp Buttercup—do you think they intend to deliver your precious ransom? Perhaps they do, but we should not wait to be certain."

Justine could not bear to look away from Struan for an instant. If it was intended that these were their last hours—or minutes—together, then she would go from the world with the image of his face in her head, her heart, and her soul.

"Thank you," she told him softly.

"For what, dearest?" Struan soaked a rag in wine and gave it to her. "Hold this. If I give the word, press it over your nose and mouth."

"Thank you for becoming a part of my life. Thank you for sharing yourself with me and teaching me to believe I could be whole."

"You are whole." Gently, he pushed her down on a pile of tartan he'd placed just inside the mouth of the cave. "It is almost time. If he comes as he said he would, it will be soon. He will either enter the cave and I shall attack him, or he will set fire to the bales. If he does the first, you will remain where you are until I have subdued him. If it is the fire, then I shall make a way out for us. You will hold the rag to your face and follow directly behind me. Once outside, roll on the ground to extinguish any flames on your clothes. Do you understand?"

She smiled at him and nodded. She understood that they were probably going to die together, but Struan would try until the very end to save her.

Struan leaned against the wall, his eyes narrowed. He put a finger to his lips and waved for her to be still.

The horrible scraping noises came.

Justine kept her eyes on Struan's face and prayed. At least if it were the fire, the outcome would be predictable. A fight between Grably and Struan could not be fair, since one man had a pistol and accomplices waiting outside, while the other had only his bare hands.

The first thing to enter the cave was Grably's pistol.

The rest of Grably followed rapidly.

Struan grabbed the hand holding the pistol and hauled Grably inside, tossing him in a somersault that landed the man on his back across the trunk.

Justine screamed and promptly rammed the wine-soaked rag against her lips.

Wood splintered beneath the sprawling man's weight. Instantly Struan was upon him. The two rolled, over and over, Struan grappling to gain the pistol. Grably's sinuous fingers kept their grip.

Dragging the monk—once more in his habit—to his feet, Struan dashed him against the jagged wall of the cave and slammed his hand into a knife-sharp rock. Grably's face contorted, but he did not release the weapon.

"Glory!" Grably screamed. "Bottwell!"

Struan glanced over his shoulder—and Grably smashed his knee upward between his opponent's legs. The cry that issued from Struan sent Justine's hands to her face.

While Struan slipped to the floor and doubled over, Grably made a dash for the cave entrance. Almost at once Justine heard him pulling a bale into place.

"Struan, come on!" She looked from him to the narrowed band of light stretching from the outside and rushed for the light.

With his back to her, Grably was lighting a torch near the edge of the trail. Justine could see that the cave was tucked away above a sheer drop that fell many feet to the valley floor below.

Grably had shoved his pistol into the rope at his waist. Bottwell and Glory were nowhere in sight. The taper Grably held blew out. He cursed violently and started again.

Trembling so that her teeth clattered, Justine inched closer. With bile rising in her throat, she clambered upon Grably's back and knocked the pistol from his cincture.

"Damn you to hell!" he shouted, swinging, tearing at her skirts. For an instant they teetered between the trail and the void that would surely kill them both.

Grably staggered back. "Get off me, you hellcat! I should have let Bottwell have you last night. Glory! Bottwell! Get down here. And you, Nudge! Leave Buttercup."

A jumble of scree dashed from beneath Grably's feet to clatter and dance into space.

No one came.

Justine held on, inching higher, then yanked his hair with one hand. With the other hand she reached around to gouge his eyes.

Grably screamed. With a savage heave, he threw her off and fell upon her, pummeling her face, ripping her clothes.

Again and again Justine's head pounded the rock-strewn ground. Still she kicked and fought him.

Knifing back his elbow, he drove a fist into her belly.

She retched. Blackness seeped in at the edges of her vision. She felt Grably rend her bodice apart. He squeezed her breasts cruelly and laughed. Crazed now, he shoved a hand beneath her skirts and wedged her thighs apart with one knee.

As the light began to go out, Justine saw the face that had the power to overcome any fear, any pain.

Yelling like an enraged animal, Struan fell upon Grably, knocking him off Justine.

Struan was taller and heavier. Grably was driven by some demon Justine felt and knew she had never encountered before.

The two men rained blows that thrashed bone and broke flesh. Blood ran from Struan's nose and mouth. Grably's eyes, already swollen almost shut from Justine's efforts, now oozed bright red at the corners. His habit hung in tatters over the shirt and breeches revealed beneath.

He landed a crushing clout to the jaw, and Struan slid slowly to the ground only inches from the edge of nothing.

The pistol lay a few feet from Justine. On her stomach, she inched forward, arm outstretched, fingers reaching.

Grably scrabbled to lift an evilly rough boulder from the talus. Grunting, he hauled it to his chest and staggered toward Struan.

He would smash Struan's head!

"Glory!" Grably gaped up the trail. "Damn you, you bitch! Glory!"

Justine's fingers closed on the pistol butt.

Filthy and bloodstained, Struan lay still.

*"Glory!"*

A grinding noise heralded the slow start of the carriage as it pulled away from the trail head. Nudge, the butler from the lodge, was pushing Buttercup into the coach. He jumped in behind her and slammed the door. Left behind was a cart with no horse.

Desperately trying not to distract Grably, Justine rose to her feet. Holding the pistol in both hands, she raised it until the wobbling barrel pointed at the monk's head.

"Glor—" He spun toward Justine and dropped the rock. It slithered from the trail. She heard it bounce and bounce and echo away into the deep distance.

Grably smiled at Justine, a smile that fixed his gray eyes. "You're a brave woman, my lady. I like that. Beautiful, too. We shall do very well together."

Her knees threatened to give out.

"Give me the pistol. A gentle creature like you could not commit such a vile act as to shoot an unarmed man."

"To save my husband, I could do a great many things, sir."

"Your husband is beyond saving." He stood gracefully aside. "See. He is dying even as we speak. But I am a merciful man. If it pleases you, help him by all means."

Justine's lips parted. She crept toward Struan's still figure and fell to the ground beside him. "Struan? Oh, Struan." Hesitantly, she stroked the side of his bloodied face and bent over him—and threw the gun over the cliff.

"You should have kept that," Struan murmured.

She almost jerked away.

"Stay, sweet lady. Do as I tell you. When he pulls you from me, make no fight. Rest your head upon him and cry."

"I will tear out his throat."

"Later. For now, do as I tell you."

Even as he finished speaking, Grably dragged her into his arms. "I'll need you now, my lady. Seems I've come up against a little mutiny. Time enough to deal with that later. For now we must do the best we can."

Justine pressed her lips together, leaned heavily on Grably, and contrived to sob—not that sobbing came with too much difficulty under the circumstances. He automatically embraced her.

Then, clawing at the air, he released her and sent her staggering away.

She clutched her bodice over her breasts and dared to gulp fresh air. Struan brought Grably down and fell upon him, pummeling the hateful face with both fists.

"Hit him, Struan! Stop him!" Her pounding heart kept time with the throb at her temples. Gravel embedded torn flesh on her palms, her elbows, her knees, yet the stinging pain was only a faint echo behind fear and desperation.

Grably howled and tore at Struan's hair—and heaved onto his side.

And Struan slipped over the edge . . .

He just slipped.

Justine screamed.

Then she saw Struan's clinging fingers.

Grably shoved himself upright. Staggering, laughing insanely, he stood over his victim's last hold on life. "I'll win after all, you know, Hunsingore." He gasped each word.

"What of Saber?" Justine asked, desperate to distract him. "Where is he? Will he help you now?"

"Chance," Grably said. "He was making inquiries in a certain London entertainment establishment. Fine establishment, too. One of my favorites. He wanted to know about a girl who used to be there." He raised a foot above Struan's slowly slipping fingers.

"What girl?" Justine walked toward Grably. "Ella?" She must not let Grably see her looking at Struan's hands.

"That's the one. Young Avenall was in his cups. Had someone arrange a meeting with me later. Hated your dearly departed husband's guts. Thought he was rutting with the girl while he pretended to be her father. Avenall held back nothing. Sentimental fool. Using him was useful and simple. In the end he didn't do anything, poor sop, but he'll be blamed for it all. I'll see to that. The girl's locked away at Northcliff Hall with your coachman and those idiot butlers." He laughed. "Thanks to the assistance their dratted cousin gave me, they don't know anything. Your Nudge was useful—until now. But he'll suffer. They all will."

"Good-bye, Hunsingore." The foot rose higher. "I'll take great care of your wife."

Calum peered through the bushes. "Shoot, dammit. Now. Before he kills him."

Arran held up a silencing arm. "We're too far away. I'm as likely to hit Struan or Justine." He knew too well the potential inaccuracies of firearms.

"I can't believe it," Blanche moaned. "Those poor young things. Wait till I get my hands on that rogue. Man of the cloth, indeed. Man of the devil, more likely. I followed him here twice and he was up to no good either time, I can tell you. I should have told someone then. I felt foolish, but it shouldn't have mattered."

"You've done the best you can now," Arran told Blanche. The woman had more spirit than he'd ever dreamed possible.

"Oh, my *God.*" Calum rose from his hunched position behind the bushes a hundred yards or so from the unfolding drama.

Grably's foot descended—and missed.

With Justine's arms wrapped around his standing ankle, Grably overbalanced, flailed in slow motion as he toppled sideways, and disappeared amid an endless bellow—almost endless.

"Move," Arran ground out, already in motion.

He and Calum arrived at Justine's side together. Lying flat, she clung to Struan's sleeves. Each man locked one of Struan's wrists in powerful hands and hauled him to safety.

Crying, Justine stretched beside him, stroking hair away from his swollen, bloodied face, feeling his body, leaning to look into his eyes.

Struan's grin was a pathetic sight. "Good as new, you see, my love," he said through thick lips. "Thanks to the tiger I married. I love you, you know."

Arran looked at his boots and felt Calum do likewise.

"I should think you do love me," Justine said. "I suppose I love you, too."

"You *suppose?*"

"I shall have to analyze what I feel for my book."

"You do that. Would you mind just holding me for the moment, though?"

"Not at all." Cradling his head, she rocked him against her. "Hold you. Fight fires. Fight bad men with guns. Climb mountains. This cripple can do anything, just like you said she could."

"You are not—"

"No, I'm not," she said quickly. "I'm not because you make me whole." With her face pressed to her husband's neck and his arms encircling her, Justine, Viscountess Hunsingore, became quiet.

"Look at that, dammit," Calum said suddenly. "To the right. *Listen* to it."

Bursting into view from a copse of trees several miles along a trail above, a carriage shot into the air. Even at a distance it was easy to see the vehicle had thrown a wheel.

"Poor devils," Calum whispered as bodies soared, arms flailing, then fell amid the wreckage of the disintegrating carriage to the ravine far below.

"Poor devils, indeed," Arran agreed.

Puffing to join them, Blanche murmured, "God bless them."

Trunks and boxes whirled and broke open.

Early rays of sun glittered on exploding showers of brilliant debris.

# Epilogue

## Castle Kirkcaldy, 1825

Snow drifted through naked trees. The struggling young year had yet to shrug the mantle of the old.

Trailing between the company gathered within sight of his mother's portrait in the red salon, Struan saw the beauty of the outside world with Justine's eyes—as she had taught him to see so many things in the past months.

"Sit, Struan." Grace, Marchioness of Stonehaven, looped her arms through one of his and smiled up at him, her brown eyes startling against pale-blond hair. "You will exhaust yourself with so much walking. Then what good will you be to Justine?"

He patted her hands. "How long has it been now?"

Arran stirred on his chair near the windows. "Five minutes longer than when you last asked. Do sit, Struan."

"I should have engaged a second physician."

"This man is the best," said Philipa, Duchess of Franchot, who was herself increasing for the first time. She and Calum rarely left each other's sides. At the moment, they sat together on a red brocade chaise close to the fire.

Calum nodded sagely. "The very best."

"As if *you* would know," Struan said, in no mood for empty appeasement.

"Calm down, young man." The Dowager Duchess of Franchot, with Blanche Bastible behind her chair, favored Struan with a disapproving scowl. "This is the physician who attended Grace during two confinements—and he will attend Philipa. I assure you that were he not the best, he would certainly have been eliminated from consideration for the birth of the next duke."

"Can girls be dukes?" Max asked, his green eyes innocent.

Laughter rippled around the salon, bending the tension.

The dowager almost smiled. Almost. "You are impertinent, my boy."

Ella did not smile. She hovered near the open door and darted into the passageway each time she heard a sound.

Arran looked out through the floating snow. "Come here Struan. We are not alone in our vigil."

Struan did not care to go to the windows. "They are all there, aren't they? The tenants? The villagers? Please God they will not have much longer to wait. I must go to Justine."

"Tell him he mustn't," Blanche said to the dowager.

"It isn't appropriate," the old lady said obediently.

To the amazement of all, Blanche had become the dowager duchess's companion and now made her home at Franchot Castle. The duchess had even, if disapprovingly, settled certain gambling debts that came to light when one of the late Reverend Bastible's relations tracked Blanche to Cornwall.

"Papa," Ella said clearly. "*I* think it perfectly appropriate for you to be with Mama. It has been many hours. She would wish you to be at her side."

Max, grown taller and more sturdy, joined his sister in the

doorway. "Ella is right," he said in the tones Justine had worked so hard to produce. "Please, Papa, go to her."

"Young man—"

"And ask her to *hurry,*" Max added as if he hadn't heard the dowager speak.

Struan hesitated a moment longer, then strode from the room, pausing to receive his adopted children's quick kisses as he passed.

The dowager's voice, upraised in disapproval, followed him until he was too far from the salon to hear her. The physician had chosen Kirkcaldy for the confinement, pointing out that it was better appointed than the lodge. Secretly, Struan thought the pompous little man considered himself very grand and the castle, therefore, more worthy of his presence.

Struan passed a maid carrying a covered basin and soiled cloths. He broke into a run.

Justine labored in a beautiful apartment in the tower called Revelation, once Arran's bachelor quarters. Struan heard a cry as he entered the anteroom to the bedchamber.

Justine's cry.

God, would it never be over? The door that separated him from his wife opened. Mairi hurried out to pick up a kettle of boiling water from the hob at the fireplace. She saw Struan and glanced toward the open door.

The next cry came so soon, and lasted so long.

Struan strode into the bedchamber and halted. The physician, his shirtsleeves rolled up, consulted with the nurse he had brought to Scotland with him. Gael Mercer and Mrs. Tabby, another tenant woman, busied themselves about the bed. Mrs. Tabby bathed Justine's face and stroked back her thick hair. Gael spoke steadily into her ear.

And Justine cried out again.

Struan closed his eyes an instant and struggled against a wave of faintness. She needed him.

He went to her side. "My darling?" He bent until her dark eyes focused on his face.

"My lord!" The physician noticed him for the first time. "I must ask you to leave at once."

Justine reached for Struan's hand, held it with enough strength to crack bones, and smiled.

"And I," Struan said to the physician, "must ask you to go about your business while I attend to mine. You are doing well, Justine. This will soon be over."

The nurse clucked disapprovingly and muttered something that sounded like "false hope."

"Your lordship," Gael Mercer whispered. "If ye could help her ladyship t'sit, t'would help. It's been a long time and she's a wee bit weak. Ye could be the strength for her. I can see the babbie's head."

Struan swallowed. He gazed steadily into Justine's eyes and sat beside her, drawing her up to lean against him.

Gael and Mrs. Tabby occupied themselves elsewhere. He saw Gael applying hot towels between Justine's legs. "The heat softens," she said. "Makes the tearin' less."

"We may have to consider a surgical procedure," the physician announced. "Risky, of course, but the child often does very well."

Struan gaped at the man.

"*Push*, my lady," Gael said. "Oh, do help her push, my lord. She'll not need any cutting o'her belly t'bring the wee one into the world."

"The longer we wait—"

"*Push,*" Struan said, ignoring the sawbones. "Push hard, my love. With me. I shall help." Supporting her weight, he pressed her farther forward.

"Oh, Struan! Do not risk the baby's life." Her white face gleamed, but she grunted and he felt the force of her fresh effort.

"Aye!" Mrs. Tabby said with toothy glee. "Cuttin' indeed. The wee one's comin' wi'out any cuttin'."

Justine panted. Struan let her fall back a little, then eased her forward once more and willed his strength to join with hers.

"Again," Gael said.

And again Justine cried out and bowed under Struan's pressure.

"Almost done!" Gael laughed, and swiped at her red hair with her upper arm. "We've the shoulders now. All m'lady needed was her man."

"Out of the way," the physician ordered officiously. "Very good, your ladyship. Very good, indeed."

Jigging, Gael bobbed aside. She held her fists aloft and gritted her teeth as if to will Struan and Justine's infant into the world.

Using the fresh water Mairi brought, Mrs. Tabby wrang out clean clothes to bathe Justine's face and neck.

"You've a son!" Gael all but shrieked. "There. A fine wee boy."

Justine fell against Struan and he heard her sob.

The insulted howl of new life brought a great grin to Struan's face. He glanced up from his wife to see a small, bloodied creature with a thatch of dark hair and tiny, jerking limbs.

"I want to hold him," Justine murmured.

The physician shrugged into his coat. "Nonsense, my lady. These things are not for you to concern yourself with. You have come through remarkably well. Now you must rest."

"Exactly," the nurse agreed, proceeding to swaddle the infant.

"Struan," Justine said, her voice stronger. "I want our baby."

He smiled down at her, watching faint color begin to rise into her cheeks. "They do not know my tiger, do they? We'll hold our son, doctor. Now, if you please."

Physician and nurse glanced at each other.

And Mairi promptly relieved the nurse of her little burden. "Come on, sweet wee bairn. Little miracle bairn." She carried the wriggling bundle and handed it to Struan.

So light. So small, yet so fierce. Tiny fists already ground into a seeking mouth. Struan felt the unfamiliar sting of tears.

Very gently, he unwrapped the tight blanket from the baby, settled him upon his mother's breast, and pulled a cover over them.

"Y'need t'tell your people," Gael whispered at his side. "They're all waitin'."

"You be the messenger," Struan told her. "Have them all come inside, into the warm. The castle staff can find them something to celebrate with. Tell everyone I'll talk to them later, when her ladyship's asleep.

"Mairi. Will you please ask my brother and his wife, and the duke and duchess to come up?"

The physician snapped his cuffs straight. "A job well done, I believe. No doubt you have already retained a suitable wet nurse."

Justine found Struan's hand and pulled herself up to look directly at the man. "Good day to you, doctor—nurse. We shall not require your services at the birth of our next child."

Pippa and Grace tiptoed into the bedchamber.

"Is she awake?" Grace whispered.

"Is the baby awake?" Pippa whispered.

"Yes and yes," Justine responded, still holding her son and snuggled in Struan's arms. "Come and see."

Arran and Calum were much slower to enter. They stayed close to the door and murmured appropriate noises.

"He's *lovely*," Pippa said. "And you look lovely too, Justine."

"I look like a witch, but I don't care."

"Justine," Calum said, "I finally got word to Saber. He wrote back that he looks forward to seeing us all on his return to England. And he said he regrets the poor decisions he made."

"He did no real harm," Justine said. She would not allow old, bad memories to taint this moment. "We shall start again when he comes home."

Grace looked at Pippa, who nodded emphatically.

"We have a surprise for you," Grace said. "We scarcely dared hope it would arrive in time, but it has. See?"

From behind her skirts she produced a book bound in red leather. "In fact, it has already gone on sale and is being talked about all over London and in Edinburgh."

Pippa took the volume and pointed to gold lettering on the front. "Entitled just as you requested. *Viscountess Hunsingore's Illuminations for, and Advice to the Modern Female on the Subjects of Courtship and Marriage.*"

"Oh, I think I shall burst with happiness," Justine exclaimed.

"This is my very favorite part," Grace said, flipping through pages. "I declare you are so clever, Justine. Why did I never realize . . . Well, anyway. *On Caring For One's Husband. A comfortable dressing robe for one's husband is of the utmost importance. Encourage him to undress and wear this robe as often as possible. You will discover, as I have, dear reader, that the less often a husband is constrained by heavy clothing, the better. Trousers are particularly onerous since they restrain the part of one's husband that is absolutely essential to the successful realization of marital bliss. Indeed, dear reader, this is the part which—*"

"Grace!" Arran said abruptly and loudly. He came forward to take his wife's arm. "You must not tire Justine."

"Oh, do read the dedication, Grace," Pippa insisted. "Then we shall leave you three alone."

Justine pulled herself a little higher and raised her face to receive Struan's kiss.

Pippa murmured, "Mmm."

"*This volume,*" Grace read aloud from the front of the book, "*is dedicated to my husband, Viscount Hunsingore, without whose instruction my undertaking could never have been completed.*"

"*Gad!*" Calum exploded. "I understand the thing's already flying through the hands of the *ton*. They say the printer can't keep up with demand."

"You'll be the talk of Town," Arran said, chuckling.

"Indeed," Grace said. "But listen. In addition, Justine writes: *My thanks must also go to my brother-in-law Arran, Marquess of Stonehaven, and my brother Calum, the Duke of Franchot, two men who have tirelessly dedicated themselves to the greater gratification and enlightenment of women.*"